Devon ended the kiss, opting to nibble on my chin, neck, shoulders, and my blood-warm earlobes. "Turn around." I turned to face the winking city lights once more, acutely aware of the warm breeze kissing under my skirt. Devon kneeled to draw my red silk thong down my legs. With an admiring leer, she pocketed the thong and instructed me to remove the rest of my garments. When I reached down to remove my high-heeled pumps first, she stopped me. "No. Leave the pumps. I like them."

I threw off my thin wraparound skirt. Next came the silk camisole. My pear-shaped breasts immediately fell into the embrace of Devon's waiting hands. With thumb and forefinger she began to work them, coaxing the nut-brown nipples to hardness in a matter of seconds.

I bit my lip and moaned.

"That's it baby." Devon's words were hot strokes against my ear. "Show me you like it."

Visit

Bella Books

at

BellaBooks.com

or call our toll-free number

1-800-729-4992

BACK
TO
BASICS

a butch-femme anthology

EDITED BY THERESE SZYMANSKI

Bella
BOOKS

2004

Bella Books, Inc.
P.O. Box 10543
Tallahassee, FL 32303

Printed in the United States of America on acid-free paper
First Edition

Editor: Therese Szymanski
Cover designer: Bonnie Liss (Phoenix Graphics)

ISBN 1-931513-35-X

Acknowledgments

I would like to express my extreme gratitude to Barbara Johnson, both for her service above and beyond the call in helping me edit this, and for her help in selecting the stories contained within. I would also like to thank Karin Kallmaker for all of her support and understanding, as well as Judy Eda and Anna Chinappi for their magnificent proofreading work.

I'd also like to thank all the fine butches and femmes at butch-femme.com for giving me the idea for this anthology.

Oh, and of course, to Linda Hill—for finally getting this out the door!

Therese Szymanski, November 13, 2003

Table of Contents

The Butch Across the Hall
Karin Kallmaker

I counted to ten and raised my hand a third time to knock. Yet again I couldn't do it. Beyond the door I could hear a ball game and the infrequent scrape of a spoon against a bowl. I was assuming it was soup again tonight. I'd seen the empty cans more than once in her recycling bin. Miki's diet was a lot like mine.

When I'd realized I had accidentally received her mail, I had changed my sweater and brushed my hair. I was a long way from her ex-girlfriend in the looks department, but that didn't mean I couldn't make an effort. My husband—seven years my ex—and my girl-friend—six months my ex—had both called me "cute." They had said it mostly to annoy me.

I sighed, my knuckles a long way from making contact. I was in a fresh sweater because, well, just because. Because Miki and I had both been single for a while. That's all. Because we could at least

1

watch a ball game and share a beer. It beat being alone every night. That's all. Because I couldn't look at the faint smear of makeup on her doorjamb without breaking into a sweat.

I doubt she knows it's there. Maybe she does. Maybe it's some kind of trophy. Her ex had left it last Halloween, hurriedly hiding her face when Jilly and I interrupted the two of them against the wall outside their apartment.

I'd had a bit too much to drink at the party, but I could still recall, with shivering clarity, Miki's voice. Just as we came around the corner she said, "You didn't know I was ready to go, did you?"

Her girlfriend had groaned out, "Do me, baby," and we were abruptly all looking at each other, perfectly recognizable in spite of our costumes. I forget now what Jilly and I had worn. But I remember well that Miki was dressed like James Dean, right down to a pack of cigarettes rolled into her T-shirt sleeve. Her thick black hair was slicked back, with a greaser's curl dipped across her forehead. A leather jacket was on the floor. Her girlfriend was queen of the sock hop, including the heavy artillery bra underneath her unbuttoned blouse.

After the averting of eyes on all parts, Jilly had dragged me into our apartment. I did not forget how Miki's blue jeans were loose in the back, or how her hips disappeared into the flounces of her girl-friend's red poodle skirt.

Jilly had gone to pee while I peered at them through the security peephole. Miki was grinding into her girlfriend in rhythm to gasps of encouragement and pleasure. I couldn't really see anything, but I could hear how wild it was making her girlfriend. Nothing like friction, I had thought.

Jilly caught me spying. "Are they still at it?"

"Um, yeah," I said, embarrassed.

Through the door we both heard the girlfriend say, "Fuck me . . . yes . . . just like that."

I had to look. Nothing had changed. I could see both of Miki's hands pinning her girlfriend's shoulders to the wall. The moving hips were the only clue I had before Jilly said, "I'm not surprised. Obviously, they need a man in the house. At least the strap-on kind."

My breath had suddenly burned in my throat and even now, six months later, looking at the smear of makeup on the doorjamb, I was hot and confused and hearing the echo of, "Fuck me . . . just like that."

I have to knock. I have her mail.

After assuming for twenty-five years that I was born straight and liked my sex straight, and putting five years into the unsatisfactory marriage I had thought proved my sexuality, I was pretty proud of the fact that at thirty-six I now knew who I was. When I first left my husband I knew who I wasn't. For a couple of years I wouldn't think, "I'm gay." I'd think, "I'm not straight." Jilly's one good legacy was teaching me that you can't define yourself in terms of what you aren't.

So I know I'm gay. I know I like women. I'm a lesbian. Isn't that enough to know?

Why am I afraid to knock on her door?

Jilly, when she left, accused me of regressing back to straight sex. All because I had taken the honesty page from her book and asked her to fuck me, up against the wall, to shove her fingers hard into me—okay, I was really worked up and I couldn't stop thinking about Miki. It had taken just about all the courage I had to ask Jilly to, well, "do me." I didn't know what I was asking for. It was rapidly apparent that Jilly didn't know either.

Her response had been to climb out of bed, saying she wasn't going to be a man for me.

That had really hurt. I hadn't been asking her to be something she wasn't, only to try to give me what I needed, to find a way to both be happy. Jilly, I now knew, was one of those people who vastly admired her own honesty but rarely liked it from others. We didn't talk much after that, not even while she moved out.

Even all these months later, though, I can't knock on Miki's door. Am I hot for her because—Jesus, I can feel my crotch swelling—

because I secretly want a guy? It doesn't make sense. If I wanted a guy wouldn't I still be married? It's so much easier to conform, after all. What am I doing with a rainbow flag on my bumper and in my cubicle at work? Why do I put up with the inevitable daily dose of hate and the loss of civil rights and all of that shit if I really want to be straight?

I want to give Miki her mail and I want her to fuck me the way she fucked her girlfriend that night. I want her cock inside me. Her cock—the thought of it, the reality of it makes me dizzy. What am I now? Why can't I just give her the mail and run?

I heard a knocking sound close by. Shit, it's my knuckles on her door. I've knocked. The ball game was abruptly silenced and I heard footsteps.

"Heya, Ronnie." She was wearing an often-washed polo shirt with jeans.

"I thought I had a whole crop of bills I didn't know about," I said without preamble.

She was smiling, so maybe I was, too. "Oh joy, the credit card bill." She took the envelopes out of my hand.

"What's the score?" I had no idea where that question came from.

"Three-all, bottom of the fifth. You like baseball?"

"Yeah." I shrugged. My sweater felt like it was shrink-wrapping around my breasts. "Is that Bonds?"

She stepped back and I was inside the door. We were the same height, I realized. She'd lost a little weight—all that soup, no doubt. Is she boyish? With her hair in its normal page boy I suppose so, but there's no mistaking that she's a woman. Her eyelashes are too full, her lips too red, her waist too curved above hips too round. She might not need a bra, but that was all woman under the polo shirt.

My mouth went dry.

The TV was visible from where I stood and after I cleared my throat I commented, "With one out and runners at second and third you'd think they'd just walk him."

"You'd think," Miki agreed. "Come on in," she added. "It's always more fun to watch with somebody. Can I get you something to drink?" She was halfway through a Corona.

"What you're having—that looks great."

We talked about baseball and the whole time I was feeling her hands on me and her hips thrusting against me and her teeth on my earlobes and her cock driving into me, taking me. The last time I was this wet was just before I had sex with a woman for the first time. I felt as if this was just as new and just as scary. I wanted her on top of me. I wanted her to fuck me. I wanted to be what she needed so she'd do whatever it was her girlfriend had meant when she'd said, "Do me, baby."

The game ended and we talked for a little bit about sports, then the similar layout of our apartments. She had an interesting collection of Japanese scrolls and she translated them for me. I liked "Intuition is hearing what is unsaid."

I finished my second beer and I supposed it was time to thank her and politely leave, but I couldn't bring myself to do it. I spied the empty soup bowl. "Chicken noodle?"

"Yeah, my favorite." She looked rueful. "At least it was before I had it for dinner six nights a week."

"Tomato," I admitted. Emboldened by her understanding smile, I added, "I got dumped. What's your story?"

She looked a little startled, but said without really taking much time to think about it, "Me, too."

"We'd been together three years and it stopped working in bed." Hell, I'd had too much beer even with just two. I could feel myself blushing.

"Lesbian bed death? I've heard of that."

"No, I just—she wouldn't, well, we just weren't compatible."

I wouldn't have blamed her for looking confused. But she didn't. "I know exactly what you mean." Was she blushing, too? Her olive skin made it hard to tell. "After—you know, after you guys saw us?"

I tried to look as if it was an effort to remember the event. "Oh, yeah?"

"Teena wanted it to be that way all the time. I really enjoyed it, but it was just for Halloween. She wanted me to pack all the time."

I was a little bit lost, but I wasn't going to tell her that. "And that's not what you wanted?"

"No." She seemed to relax a bit and I realized her gaze hadn't left my face for a few minutes. She spoke deliberately, as if she was trying to find out what would shock me. "I'm not just a cock, you know? I liked working up to it, her asking for it and then putting it on me. I thought that was just as hot for her." Her gaze never left me.

She'd been honest with me and I found the courage to return the compliment. All in a rush, I said, "I wanted more butch out of my girlfriend."

"But she wasn't butch to begin with . . ."

Miki hadn't stopped staring at me, and during the long, awkward silence her gaze traced a lazy path across my lips, down my throat, and then lingered for a while on the nipples I knew were showing through my bra and sweater.

Finally, I managed, "No, she wasn't. She said she wouldn't 'play the man' for me."

Miki's expression turned angry. "I've heard that crock of shit before. As if."

I just kept looking at her. My courage had run out. I hardly even knew what I was asking for, I told myself. But that was a lie. I knew what I wanted. Her cock inside me. Her pouring her desire into me.

"Do you want me to be a man for you?" Her deep brown eyes, which had been warming, turned to flint.

Chilled, I quavered, "No."

She moved slowly, giving me a chance to back away. When I didn't move, she cupped my breast with one hand. I thrust forward, offering it all. "Then what do you want?"

"I want you to be a woman for me."

The anger left her expression and her hand pulled more urgently at my breast, making it harden and ache in its confinement. "I can do that. I think I can be the kind of woman you want tonight."

I could hardly breathe. I inched across the sofa to be closer to her, so she could reach all of me.

"Take your clothes off," she said. It wasn't quite an order, but it was far more than a suggestion.

I had to stand up to do it. I didn't have the confidence to do a striptease for her. I just unceremoniously pulled my sweater over my head and undid my bra, then shoved my jeans down after kicking off my sandals. My panties were glued to my crotch and I heard her take a sharp, deep breath as I peeled them off.

Her voice was soft but firm when she said, "Sit on my lap."

We had a similar build, though my figure was more rounded than hers, and I wasn't sure I could do as she asked without it being uncomfortable for her.

"Sit down," she urged. She opened her arms.

I perched awkwardly, aware that I was leaving a smear on her pants. Jesus, I was wet. I was still blushing, too. My ears felt as hot as my clit.

"It's okay," she said, with a little laugh. "I won't break." She stroked one breast with just her fingertips. "Hasn't anyone made you feel beautiful before?"

I shook my head.

"You are, you know." Her fingers closed firmly over my nipple and I couldn't help my moan. "Especially like this."

She kissed the hollow of my throat, then my shoulders. Her fingertips were pulling more sharply on my nipple and I could feel my heart beating where my crotch was grinding into her jeans.

I heard her swallow noisily. "It's been a while," she murmured. "For you, too?"

I nodded.

"You can talk, you know." I could hear a smile in her voice as her tongue flicked my ear lobe.

"I'd have to be able to breathe to talk. I feel unreal."

"Good. I want to take you up very high, baby, and keep you there. It could take hours."

I was bereft of words again. I arched my back and offered everything.

I have no idea how long she spent teasing, biting and sucking at my breasts. I had let go of my fear for now. I felt delirious as I let go of time as well.

When her hand finally went between my legs I clutched at her shoulders, afraid I would fall.

She wrapped an arm around my waist, anchoring me to her lap. "Don't worry, I've got you. I want to taste you."

I felt two fingers slide past my clit, and they paused long enough to tease me. Butterflies danced from her fingers to the pit of my stomach. Then she slowly drew her fingers through my heat. I watched her raise her fingers to her mouth and her tongue lick up the glistening wet she'd taken from me.

She sighed and her fingers went back for more. She tasted them again, then smeared what was left on one nipple. I thought my breasts would explode. I was close to coming. I wanted to. I ground myself down on her thigh while tremors ran through my legs.

"Don't come yet," she said urgently. "Stand up."

I was so dizzy she had to help me and I nearly fell down when her mouth nuzzled at my belly. I could feel her tongue and teeth and then I remembered what had drawn me there. I wanted her cock, too. I wanted to get fucked like that.

"Let's go to bed, baby." She led me by the hand and when we were standing next to her bed, she said, "I would never hurt you."

"I know."

"Then you're not shaking because you're afraid?"

I shook my head.

"You're shaking because . . . tell me."

"Because I want you." I knew she wasn't going to let me off so easily.

"You want me how?"

"Inside me." She still had her clothes on. I felt incredibly vulnerable. I realized then that I had yet to feel her breasts, her sex. My skin chilled. No, I told myself, I wasn't here because I was going to pretend she was a man. That wasn't why I stood there, feeling wet running down my thighs, as she opened a drawer in the short table next to the bed.

Then why? She took out a leather harness that ironically made me think of a chastity belt. Wasn't she turning into a man? She fit a dildo into it that was astonishingly like my ex-husband. She looked at me intensely with the belt dangling from her hand. "Is this what you want?"

Of course the answer was yes, but yes didn't seem sufficient. "Only if you're wearing it." The air seemed to thin.

Her mouth parted and she appeared at last to be breathing hard. She pulled back the bedclothes and set the harness down near the foot. Then she took both of my breasts into her hands again, her thumbs teasing my nipples. "Undress me."

I had to find the concentration to do it while she made my nipples throb. As I expected, she wore no bra under the polo shirt and my mouth watered at the sight of her small yet firm breasts.

Her black boxer shorts surprised me. I pulled them slowly down her legs and my hand automatically went to her crotch. I found wet heat. She twisted out of my reach. "You're with a real butch now, honey. You first, always."

"I'm sorry," I said. I badly wanted to touch her, but if waiting made it better for her, I could do that.

"It's okay." Her fingers never stopped their demanding teasing of my nipples. How did she know it was what I had always craved? "There aren't any rules for myself that I won't break one time or another. But most of the time I like what I like. You like what you like, obviously. I'm hoping our likes are complementary. Or close enough not to matter."

I could only whisper back, "Please."

She circled my waist with one arm and pulled me hard against her. Her skin sizzled against mine. My aching, reddened nipples went from hot to burning as she kissed me, as her tongue deliberately and firmly explored my mouth. She had not kissed me before this and I realized, with a shudder, that this kiss was not foreplay. It was the first penetration and I surrendered to it. She bent me in her arms, cupping the back of my head with one hand. Her fingers wound into my hair and I moaned into her mouth.

"Get on your hands and knees," she told me, when she finally finished that incredible kiss. She pushed me toward the bed. "I want to make this as good as it can be."

I was breathing so fast and hard my arms were shaking. I heard the faint click of buckles. The sound sent a hard charge down my spine, as if I'd been struck by lightning. The bed rocked as she joined me on it.

Her hands on the backs of my thighs made me jump. "Don't be scared," she said.

"I'm not." I was, but I didn't care. I found the words, finally. I just said it, flatly, as I gasped for air. "Fuck me with your cock."

She pulled on my hips. Her voice flowed over my ears like molten silk. "Put me inside you."

I had to reach for it, between my legs, to take hold of her cock. What could she think of me? We didn't know each other except to nod hello in the hallway. I brought her the mail I got by mistake and now I was sliding her cock into me as I dripped onto her bed.

"Take me inside, just the way you want it."

The head of her cock slipped in—God, I was soaked. I groaned all the way through the long slide of it going into me as I slowly went back on my haunches to rest on her thighs. Her hands were on my hips. I leaned forward slightly to feel it sliding back out, then she pulled me down again. Up, down, oh shit, why did I love it so? It was more than I could stand and a contraction hit me hard.

Her hands were on the back of my neck. "Don't come yet." It would have been a coldly issued order if I hadn't heard the faintest edge of a plea in it. I had a choice. "Give yourself a good fuck first, baby. Make it last."

I chose to please her though I wanted to come so much. I was fucking her cock. She was letting me take it at my own pace, letting me rise slowly and drop down hard, then I was going faster. I tried to stay there, in the sensual plateau of almost coming. I had no sense of time. "I'm going to." I was barely coherent. "I have—I'm there."

She pulled out of me. Her hands like iron, she flipped me over. I was as high as she had promised.

She was on top of me, pushing my legs apart. "Now I'm going to do the fucking."

Her cock was inside me again, and she pushed it deeper than I had been taking it. It seemed to split something in me open and I felt a gush of wetness and a clench of muscles like nothing I'd ever experienced before.

She fucked me through my orgasm, thrusting against a seemingly endless stream of contractions. I got very, very tight and she knew to stay inside me, rocking so I could not possibly forget she was there.

Why did I want it like this? Her firm, small breasts were against mine—she wasn't a man. I didn't want her to be a man. But I wanted her cock.

The answer was so simple. It was so much easier to think now. I wanted *her* cock.

With a jolt in the pit of my stomach, I got wet again. I should have been satisfied—I had never come like that in my life. But instead I wanted more, all because of her cock and the way she fucked me with it. She felt me move under her and she lifted her head to gaze into my eyes.

"Like this?" She moved slowly, very slowly.

"Yes," I said. I cupped her face, then stroked her shoulders. "You've taken me someplace I've never gone before."

"The first time is—nothing will ever be like it again." She was flushed. "This will be even better." Her voice cracked. "I promise."

I arched my back as one hand massaged me from shoulder to thigh. How could she be moving with such deliberate care, as if learning every muscle that would grab at her? Her skin was damp from her exertion. Her body rose and fell on me so slowly I couldn't stand it.

"Fuck me . . . oh, please don't tease me. Just fuck me, give it to me." God, I had never begged anyone for it like this. I pulled my knees to my chest and wanted to turn inside out if that would make her cock harder, bigger, deeper, hitting the places I could finally feel were hungry.

She moved faster, but only after I had begged, over and over, to be fucked, to get fucked, all night like this if that's what it took for her. My ankles were on her shoulders and I closed my eyes to a cascade of lightning through my senses. Over my own gasps and moans I could hear the sharp creak of the bed, testimony for how hard she was taking me. I cupped my breasts, cried out. I wanted her to fuck me until she was done with me.

"Please," she gasped. "Don't come yet. Please. Wait—" She groaned hard and pinned my arms against the bed so I couldn't move. "Baby, please."

I stuttered out that I was trying. I needed to come now, she had done that to me again. All my energy was in my sex, taking it deep and steady, and all of it. It took a massive effort to open my eyes. When I focused I saw her face in a spasm of arousal that matched my own. She slammed down on me one last time and groaned long through clenched teeth. I was coming, too, coming as she ground her cock into me. Her entire body shook and I could feel her pleasure deep, deep inside me.

The kiss she gave me was lazy and thorough, a thank you and a promise. "What do you want that you haven't had?"

I sighed with fulfillment. If there was some sort of official definition of "do me," I didn't care. As far as I was concerned, I had been done. "Give me a minute to think."

But for my racing mind, I would have gone to sleep. I had been afraid to knock on her door, then afraid to show her I wanted her. My honesty had been rewarded—yes, indeed. I was afraid again, but I thought I would see what more honesty would get me. I didn't know if I was breaking all the rules. "I haven't had you."

She smiled in a way that told me I was being a bit forward, but she liked it so far. "How do you want me?"

I twisted to look at the curves of her face as the light from the hallway spilled over it. "I want you telling me what you need. Just tell me. Let me try."

She kissed me, her mouth tender yet urgent. I gave myself over to it and quivered when her teasing fingers slipped between my legs. "Be what you are," she murmured. "After what we've already done, that will be more than enough for me."

"It hardly seems fair—God!" After the fullness of her cock I couldn't believe how her fingers aroused me. I felt as if I was swelling again, greedy and hungry when only moments before I had been nearly asleep.

"Just take what you need, baby."

"Promise me," I gasped. "Say that you'll let me try to please you." It was important to me.

"I promise. But right now you need this."

I spread my legs. I spread them wide. "I just want to be this, open for you. Yes, oh yes."

Yes was so easy. She wanted me to say yes and I loved saying it, showing it. I loved her cock and her fingers and her mouth. Her eyes. Her voice. Her voice urged me now to relax, to let it feel good—there was no hurry. No hurry while she pleasured the still hungry depths of me. My hips wouldn't stay on the bed. I was trying to fly.

She captured my waist with her other arm and yanked me down against her. She was flushed, her olive cheeks tinged red. She gazed into my eyes while she fucked me with her fingers, listening to me moan, holding me in one place as I tried to fuck back frantically. She didn't make it look easy. Her face was fierce with effort. She was so strong and I was testing her.

I felt like an Amazon.

I felt beautiful.

When I came again she was the one who cried out, "Yes!"

❧

She kissed me, later, and reclaimed the sheets and blankets from the floor. She had taken off the harness while in the bathroom and I gazed hungrily at the black hair that would lead me to her desire.

"Tomorrow is another day," she whispered as she joined me under the sheets. Her hand found my breast and she stroked it gently. If I'd been a cat I would have purred. As it was I wound myself around her. "Shall we take it one day at a time? One fantasy at a time?"

"This wasn't a fantasy," I said seriously. "Nothing I did was pretend. I don't want you to pretend either."

"I didn't mean to imply that I was. I just think you had wondered what this would be like—"

"Just a little," I hedged. She kissed the side of my mouth. "Just a little every night for the last six months or so."

She laughed. "How did it compare to your fantasies?"

"There's no comparison." I shuddered, remembering how I had put her cock inside me. When had I learned to know what I wanted and more importantly, how to reach for it? What was it about her that made me braver than I knew I could be? My fantasies had not included such revelations.

"Good, beautiful one." I heard tiredness in her voice.

"Do you want me to go?" I would have and not felt slighted. After all, she had hardly planned to spend the night with me. She hadn't known when she'd invited me in for a beer that she would be in bed with me hours later. The bedside clock told me it was long after midnight.

"No." She pulled me closer. "Stay." Her breath warmed my ear. "You might wake up and need to be fucked." She must have felt me quiver. Her tongue flicked my ear lobe. "You'd like that wouldn't you?"

"Yes." It was so easy to admit the truth.

Then again, perspective is what it is. Need is a doubled-sided coin.

"Or," I said softly, "you might wake up and need to fuck me."

Her breath caught. This time it was her turn to shiver. "That's a distinct possibility."

On the Road Again

Barbara Johnson

As the gust of artificial wind shook her police cruiser, Trooper Taylor Donovan estimated that the 18-wheeler barreling down Interstate 95 was doing at least 90. She didn't have radar set up, so she pulled out onto the highway, intending to pace the truck. Traveling behind it, she noticed that one brake light was burnt out. She could pull the truck over and issue a citation on that violation alone, but she decided the jerk behind the wheel certainly deserved a speeding ticket. Taylor accelerated—65, 75, 85, 95. She followed the truck for at least three miles, and her speed didn't drop below 95. She flipped on her lights and siren.

It was at least two more miles before the trucker noticed the police car in pursuit and signaled to pull off the road. The shoulder was barely wide enough. Taylor cursed silently. She would be standing awfully close to the road. Her lights continued flashing blue and red as she came to a stop behind the truck and got out of the car.

She walked purposefully toward the driver's side of the truck, but before she got there, the driver climbed down from the cab. That always made Taylor nervous. As she hesitated, she automatically clicked the holster release and placed her right hand on the butt of her gun. The truck driver walked toward her, his arms dangling at his sides and hands empty.

He was a lot smaller than Taylor expected, not more than five-feet-five. He wore faded blue jeans, a red- and blue-checked flannel shirt, black cowboy boots, and a Buffalo Bills baseball cap. His walk had more of a sway than a swagger. As the driver came closer and stopped, Taylor did a double take. It was not a man who stood smiling before her, but a woman. A woman with caramel-colored skin, laughing dark brown eyes, and a full, rosy mouth that begged to be kissed. Wisps of dark hair peeked from beneath the baseball cap.

Slightly nonplussed, Taylor said nothing at first. The truck driver's smile got wider. Her eyes boldly flicked over Taylor from head to foot. Finally, Taylor asked, "Do you know how fast you were driving out there, ma'am?"

"I'm sure you'll tell me." She had just the trace of an accent.

Smart-ass, Taylor thought as she said, "Let me see your license and registration, ma'am. I'd also like to see your bill of lading."

The woman returned to the truck and then came back and handed Taylor the items she'd asked for. Taylor noticed the hands, small-boned and delicate with buffed nails extending just past the fingertips. For the briefest of moments she allowed herself to imagine those nails tracing a path along her bare skin. "Let's go back to my car, Ms. Sanchez," Taylor said, after glancing at the Arizona license. She motioned the woman to walk to the inside of the shoulder. Taylor was careful to stay on her outside as she escorted her to the police cruiser.

"Do we get to sit in the backseat?" the woman asked, a suggestive purr to her voice.

"You do, Ms. Sanchez," Taylor replied as she opened the passenger-side rear door. As much as she might have liked having her in the front seat, it was potentially dangerous for her to allow it, and against regulations besides.

"Call me Rose, please," the woman said as she climbed in.

It had been a while since Taylor had encountered a woman so bold, so obvious. A lot of women that she pulled over assumed that she was a dyke, and rightly so. A lot of men did too, but they were usually more hostile. The women, straight or gay, frequently flirted. Their little games seldom prevented a ticket, but on rare occasions could result in just a warning if the violation wasn't serious.

Taylor climbed into the front passenger seat. "Now, Ms. Sanchez, I clocked you doing ninety-five miles. In the state of Maryland, doing thirty or more over the speed limit is considered reckless driving. Why the big hurry?" As she spoke, she keyed Rosita Sanchez's license number into a computer and then typed in the truck registration. Within minutes she would get a report disclosing if the woman had other traffic violations or any outstanding warrants.

"I get a bonus if I deliver my cargo early," Rose said. "I wasn't really paying attention to how fast I was going."

Taylor glanced into the rear-view mirror. She had heard that one before. It was as if people were proud of the fact that they didn't pay attention on the road. She glanced over the bill of lading. Rosita Sanchez was delivering pine furniture from a factory in Maine, her destination a warehouse in southeast D.C. The trucker was only about an hour's drive away. Even with this delay, she'd make her delivery at least three hours early.

"I'm staying in the city tonight," Rosita said above the crackle of paper as Taylor's report printed out. Taylor ignored her and scanned over the paper. No prior arrests, no outstanding warrants, no other citations. Lucky girl. Taylor decided to forget about the reckless driving and issue just a speeding ticket.

She glanced in the mirror again. Rosita Sanchez appeared to be unconcerned, but Taylor knew she had to be thinking that a speeding violation could result in immediate suspension of her commercial drivers license. In those few minutes when Rosita obviously thought she wasn't being observed, she let her guard down and Taylor saw a vulnerability she didn't expect. In that instant, she decided to let her off with just a verbal warning, something she'd never done before for excessive speed.

"Ms. Sanchez, I'm giving you a break this time on the speeding ticket. Please don't make me regret that. Stay within posted speed limits. However, I am charging you with an equipment violation for your burnt-out brake light." Taylor handed her ticket pad to Rosita. "Please sign at the bottom." She watched as Rosita signed the ticket. "The fine is fifty dollars. All clear?"

With a big smile, Rosita handed the ticket book back. "*Sí*. Indeed it is, Trooper Donovan. And thank you. I appreciate your consideration." Her voice again held that suggestive purr.

Taylor ripped off Rosita's copies of the ticket and handed them over. Rosita's fingers brushed hers and the sensation was like fire. She shivered involuntarily. Rosita got out of the car and walked up the shoulder of the road to her truck. The sway of her hips in the tight denim was enticing. Taylor watched, mesmerized. When Rosita took off her baseball cap and let waves of jet-black hair tumble down over her shoulders and back, Taylor gasped. This time the image that came to her mind was of herself lying naked while that hair brushed across her breasts. Maybe she should have accepted Rosita's unspoken invitation. Instead, she sighed deeply and waited for Rosita to pull safely into traffic. She turned off the flashing lights as she followed.

Rose watched in disappointment as the Maryland State police cruiser merged into traffic behind her. She was so sure the cop was family, but she hadn't responded to any of Rose's suggestions. Well, at least the handsome Taylor Donovan with the deep green eyes had given her a break on the speeding ticket. She'd only had her commercial license for about a year now, and a speeding violation, plus reckless driving on top of that, would result in suspension of that license, plus a hearing in front of an administrative board. Not to mention the teasing she'd get from her brother, Manuel, who thought women did not belong behind the wheel of a truck.

She looked at her watch. She could still get her bonus. She continued south on I-95 toward the Capital Beltway, careful to keep her speed right at 65. She watched a bit nervously while Taylor stayed behind her, breathing a sigh of relief only when the officer pulled off at the next exit.

She found the warehouse without any trouble, surprising because she'd never delivered to the District of Columbia before. She left the truck to be unloaded and flagged down a taxi to take her to a reasonably priced Dupont Circle hotel recommended by her friend, Antonia, who traveled a lot on business. After a long hot bath, she made a quick call home to tell them she'd arrived safely.

"*¡Hola, mamá!*" she said. "*He llegado a Washington.*"

"*Que alegría me da que has llegado bien. Te echamos de menos. La fiesta no será lo mismo sin ti.*"

Yes, back in Arizona her family would be celebrating *El Grito de Delores*, Mexican independence from Spain. Times like these brought home how much she missed her family. "*Te echo de menos también. Tomaré una Tecate esta noche pensando en todos ustedes. Un abrazo.*"

"*Un abrazo de mi también, y mucho cuidado allí.*"

Rose smiled. Her mother was always concerned about her safety. "*Claro que si y adiós mamá.*"

She hung up and then took out her lesbian travel guide and found the number of the local bookstore. She preferred to ask the locals where the best bars were rather than rely on the listings in the travel guide, which sometimes could be inaccurate. As they gave her directions to the store, she was already pulling out her D.C. map. She was in luck; Lambda Rising was only five blocks away. It was Friday night, and she was ready for a good time. She'd go to the bookstore and find out where the lesbian bars were.

She put on a new pair of jeans. The snug fit molded them to her hips and butt. She pulled on a white lace camisole top and then put on a sheer white blouse that she left unbuttoned. She liked the way white contrasted with her brown skin, something other women had told her they liked as well. Deciding to forgo her usual boots, she put on a pair of barely there white sandals. She swept her long hair away from her face and clasped it at the back of her head with a Taxco barrette made of nickel silver and abalone shell, which had been a gift from her *abuela*. A pair of teardrop-shaped earrings in the same silver and abalone and a silver watch were her only jewelry. With a quick glance in the mirror, she left the room and went outside into the mild September evening.

As she walked up the street, she began to notice that a lot of the people around seemed to be family. Yes, several same-sex couples walked hand-in-hand. Her friend had told her she'd really enjoy the hotel and surrounding area, and now Rose could see what Antonia had meant. Smiling, Rose walked a bit more briskly.

She spied a tall butch across the street and felt her heart jump. Could it be? She looked again. No, it wasn't Trooper Taylor Donovan. Just thinking the name made her feel tingly all over. She licked her lips as she recalled the attractive state trooper. She'd been about five-feet-eight and filled out the tan uniform in broad-shouldered perfection. The green eyes and wide, generous mouth had attracted Rose immediately. Hidden under the regulation hat was hair that Rose guessed was probably blonde. And Rose had no trouble imagining what Taylor's strong hands could do to her.

In no time, Rose found herself at Lambda Rising right on Connecticut Avenue. Several men and about five other women browsed among the racks of books. Not one to find much time for reading, she walked directly to the counter. A slight woman with glasses and short hair dyed purple smiled a greeting.

"Can I help you?"

"I'm new in town and wondering if you can tell me where the lesbians hang out. Besides here, of course," Rose said, flashing a smile.

The woman seemed to be appraising her. After a few moments she said, "I think you might like The Phase. The other popular bar caters mostly to the college crowd."

"Great. Is it walking distance?"

"Not from here, but you can either hop the Metro or catch a cab."

Rose wrote down the address and then took a quick walk around the store. The shelves of brightly jacketed books always intrigued her, but she quite literally had no time to read. Her job kept her on the road constantly, and when she did stop she was either sleeping or partying. Like tonight. Why stay in the hotel with a book when she could be out dancing and meeting someone new? Still, she felt a little guilty coming to the store and not buying anything, so she found a CD of music she liked and bought that.

After a quick bite to eat, she caught a taxi. The cab ride was short. Rose paid the driver and stepped outside. It was still relatively early. She paid a cover charge and walked straight ahead to the bar that stood on the left side of the long rectangular interior. She slid onto a stool and surveyed the room.

Across from the bar and to her back was a tiny dance floor, above which a mirrored ball reflected prisms of colored light. A few small, round tables surrounded the dance floor. In the front of the room stood the DJ's booth. At the back the inevitable pool table shared space with a couple of video games, followed by a short hallway to the bathrooms. The pool table occupied the attention of the only other women in the place other than the bartender and bouncer who'd taken her money. The DJ was playing an old slow-dance tune by Janis Ian. Rose smiled. This was just the kind of place she liked. Small. Dark. Smoky. And sure to be frequented by lots of butches.

The big, blonde bartender came over and gave her an easy grin. Rose ordered a Tecate.

"Haven't seen you in here before," the bartender said as she placed Rose's beer in front of her.

Rose raised her glass in a silent toast and then took a sip. Perfect. "Got into town a couple of hours ago. Just here for the night actually."

"Oh?"

"I drive a truck for a living."

The bartender seemed surprised. She wiped an imaginary spot off the top of the bar. "Must be quite an adventure."

Rose smiled broadly, thinking of some of the women she'd encountered in her travels. "It sure can be."

When the bartender turned away to help another customer, Rose twirled on her stool so she could watch the women as they came in from outside. Singles and couples seemed to arrive first, then groups. Soon all the tables and the rest of the stools at the bar were filled. The DJ played a little of everything, seeming to go from era to era as she played first old rock-and-roll hits through disco and on to hip hop. The dance floor filled and stayed that way through all the musical changes. The sluggish ceiling fans did little to clear the smoke-filled air or cool things down, but Rose didn't mind.

She'd sat at the bar for a little over two hours. Several women had approached her, but she had talked with them a bit and then politely turned down their offers of drinks and dancing. She was puzzled. Usually, she clicked with someone early in the evening and would spend a pleasant few hours with her, just dancing and talking. Sometimes they would end up back at her hotel. Rose sighed inwardly. Not tonight though.

She checked out the room once more. There were lots of cute dark-haired butches around, the kind she was usually attracted to, but none of them really caught her eye. In truth, there was only one woman she was interested in, and she was probably giving some other hapless trucker a ticket right now. With a sigh, Rose turned to the bartender. One more drink, then *adiós*. She took a sip of her beer and glanced in the mirror behind the bar. Then she glanced up again and swung her stool around so quickly she almost fell off.

There, on the dance floor. In the back. Yes, Rose was sure it was Taylor Donovan. How had she missed her coming in? Taylor's dance partner was a woman with shoulder-length curly blonde hair. Rose watched them, hoping for a sign that they were friends and not lovers. She was incorrect in her guess that Taylor had blonde hair.

As Taylor moved to the music, the light caught the brilliant fire of deep auburn. She had looked marvelous in her trooper uniform, but in tight black jeans and a short-sleeved, white button-down shirt she looked even better.

At the end of the dance, Taylor kissed her partner on the cheek and headed toward the bar. The woman joined another at a table and greeted her with a passionate kiss before sitting in her lap. *¡Muy bien!* She and Taylor were just friends. Rose quickly relinquished her stool and stood where Taylor was sure to see her.

Taylor left the dance floor and decided she needed something cold to drink. It had been months since she'd been to a bar, but she'd had a rough day and thought a night out would help her unwind. In any case, she'd run into some old friends she hadn't seen in a while so that was good. As she approached the bar, the gleam of jet-black hair caught her eye. She looked again. Where had she seen hair like that before? Then it hit her. Just hours earlier as she'd watched a cocky young woman walk back to her 18-wheeler. She looked more closely. It was indeed Rosita Sanchez. And as Taylor approached the bar, it became obvious that Rosita was waiting for her.

"Why, Trooper Donovan, fancy meeting you here," she said, flashing a seductive smile as her eyes again gave Taylor a once-over. She had to be the boldest femme Taylor had ever met.

"Ms. Sanchez."

"Call me Rose." She put her hand on Taylor's bare arm. Her touch made Taylor's scalp tingle. "Would you like to buy me a beer? A Tecate."

Taylor caught the bartender's eye. "I'd love to. And you can call me Taylor."

They got their beers and managed to find an empty table. It was hard to talk above the music. Taylor gave up and gestured toward the dance floor. Rose nodded and took her hand as they stood.

They'd only just met, but her attitude was one of possession, which Taylor found strangely exciting.

Rose moved well to the fast, popular tune. Her body was naturally sensuous, and Taylor enjoyed watching her, especially liking the way she would toss her long hair back behind her shoulder. And as one dance merged into another and then another, all Taylor could think about was how she wanted to take this woman to bed. How she wanted to touch that smooth body and, in turn, feel Rose's hands on her. Finally, she signaled time out and the two headed back to their table. She took a long drink of her rather warm beer and then did something she'd never done before.

"Want to come home with me?"

Rose smiled. "I'd love to, but how about we go to my hotel instead?"

Taylor hesitated. It was bad enough that she was actually contemplating a one-night stand, but going to a hotel made it seem so sleazy. Rose leaned over and kissed her neck. The sensation made Taylor tingle all the way to her toes. Her inhibitions flew out the window. She was ready to do whatever this aggressive, sensual femme wanted.

"I make it a point never to go to anyone's house," Rose said as she continued to kiss Taylor's neck.

Taylor pulled back in surprise. "But I'm a cop."

"And an extraordinarily attractive one at that." She ran her nails along Taylor's arm, just like in Taylor's brief fantasy earlier that day. "But a girl can never can be too careful."

Taylor thought quickly. She was not prepared for sex tonight, especially not somewhere other than her place. She prided herself on being able to give a woman just about anything she desired. Rose smiled again and took Taylor's hand, leading her out of the bar. The cool night air chilled her. She must have sweated more than she thought.

And then it seemed as if Rose had read her thoughts. "I probably have everything you need."

Taylor could feel the blush spread across her cheeks and down her neck. She suddenly felt awkward and out of control. But then she remembered something she always carried with her, something she would bet even Rose did not possess. Feeling confident once again, she led Rose to her Mustang convertible and drove quickly to the hotel.

Once parked in the hotel garage, she hurried to open Rose's door for her and offered a hand in her most gentlemanly manner.

"Why thank you," Rose said as she got out and tucked Taylor's hand into the back pocket of her jeans.

They were only a few feet from the car when Taylor said, "Oh wait, I forgot something. Wait right here." Hiding her grin, Taylor slipped handcuffs from the glove compartment. Something in Rose's brown eyes had seemed to challenge her, and Taylor was always up for a challenge.

She followed Rose into the hotel and across the lobby, admiring all the while the swell of her hips in those tight jeans. Her long hair swayed with each step, begging to be touched. Rose gave a backward glance and smiled in a way that took Taylor's breath away. She quickened her step.

Rose paused to let Taylor catch up with her at the elevator. It seemed to her as if Taylor's attitude was somehow different, as if she had more confidence. Not that the handsome state trooper hadn't had it before, but she seemed more sure of herself and very much in charge. Rose liked that.

In the elevator, she took matters into her own hands and grabbed Taylor for a deep kiss. Taylor kissed her back, hard. It sent shivers through Rose's whole body; she could feel the wetness begin to flow between her legs. And as Taylor pushed her against the elevator wall while thrusting her hand under Rose's camisole, Rose felt her legs turn to water. If Taylor hadn't been holding her, she was sure she would have fallen.

Rose was stunned when Taylor pushed her away, then realized an older couple had entered. The man leered at them while his female companion glared, her disapproval obvious. Rose smiled wickedly and turned to Taylor.

"I can't wait to feel your big cock inside me," she said as she ran one hand along her zipper and then between her legs

The woman gasped in outrage as Taylor choked back a laugh. The man's leer changed to a look of distinct discomfort. The elevator stopped at Rose's floor. Taylor grabbed Rose's ass as they exited.

"I've got eight inches waiting for you, baby." She turned and winked at the gaping man.

"Can you believe the look on their faces?" Rose laughed as she opened her hotel room and flipped on the light, illuminating the king-sized bed.

"I can't believe you were so bold."

"Bold is my middle name." She had quickly stripped off her sheer blouse and was already unbuttoning Taylor's shirt.

"Hold on there, sweetheart. I think we should get to know each other a bit first, don't you?" She rebuttoned her shirt.

Rose couldn't believe Taylor had said that. She was kidding, right? But Taylor looked perfectly serious. With a somewhat disdainful flip of her long hair, Rose turned away from Taylor. She'd had such hopes after their elevator ride. Didn't Taylor want her? What had she misunderstood? She took a deep breath and turned to face Taylor again. The woman was now standing beside the bed, and the look on her face was no longer serious, but determined and calculating.

"You mentioned earlier that you have everything I need. Care to elaborate?"

Rose suddenly felt a trifle nervous. After all, cop or no, she didn't know this woman. It wasn't as if she'd never had a one-night stand before, but she'd always felt like she was the one really in control, even though she let the butch think otherwise. And here tonight, that was changing. Taylor was unlike any woman she'd ever picked up before. She gestured toward a small bag beside the bed, but wondered if she should put a stop to the evening. Just as she began to open her mouth, Taylor looked up and smiled. In that instant, when her eyes met Taylor's green ones, Rose's fears melted away.

Taylor sensed Rose's nervousness. It wasn't what she'd intended. She looked quickly through Rose's bag of toys and then smiled at her reassuringly.

"That's quite a collection you have there, but I think I might only need these." She held up latex gloves and a bottle of Astro Glide.

Surprisingly, Rose blushed bright red. Taylor strode quickly over to Rose to take her into her arms. After a quick, hard kiss, she grabbed Rose's waist and pushed her backward to the bed. The headboard was made of individual wooden slats, perfect for what she intended. She lightly played with Rose's silky hair while she kissed her throat, softly at first and then with more urgency. Rose moaned, a sound that made Taylor's knees weak. She pushed Rose down on the bed, expertly stripping her of her camisole and leaving her naked from the waist up. As Rose sank into the pillows, Taylor nuzzled her neck and stroked her smooth body. She quelled the urge to strip her and take her right then and there.

When Rose had completely relaxed and her body responded with sensuous abandon to Taylor's caresses, Taylor gently raised both of Rose's hands above her head and quickly looped the handcuffs around a slat before snapping them shut on her wrists. Rose gasped, her eyes wide with surprise and a touch of fear. "I don't know if I want this."

"Don't worry, lover." Taylor soothed as she stroked Rose's arms and breasts. She could feel the tension ease from Rose's body. She kissed and licked her way down Rose's neck to her breasts and took a hardened nipple into her mouth. Rose groaned and squirmed against the handcuffs. Her legs seemed to open of their own accord. Taylor sucked one nipple and then the other, all the while running her hands over Rose's luscious body that curved in all the right places.

"Taylor, my God, you're driving me crazy," Rose murmured. Her struggles against the handcuffs had the delightful effect of raising her hips toward Taylor's mouth.

Taylor slowly unzipped Rose's jeans and pulled them off. Her legs were long and lean. Taylor chuckled when she saw that Rose wore a thong. She might as well have not been wearing anything at all, Taylor thought as she easily removed the wisp of material. The hair underneath was as dark as the hair on Rose's head.

Rose was breathing heavily as Taylor stood and looked down at her naked body. Stretched out the way she was made her appear taller. Her fingers curved, the white tips of her nails brushing her palms. Her legs were spread invitingly open, knees slightly raised. Her eyes, so much like dark chocolate, pleaded with Taylor's.

Taylor leaned down and kissed her again. Rose moaned softly, her body arching upward. Taylor stroked the velvety skin and whispered, "Tell me what you want, sweet Rose." She let her fingers find Rose's center. She was oh, so wet. "Tell me," she whispered again.

"Taylor," Rose breathed. "I want . . . I want you inside me." She looked at Taylor, her lips red and swollen from their kisses, her brown eyes begging. Her face glowed in the lamplight, shiny with sweat. In fact, her whole body glowed. Her fabulous black hair spread out like a cloak beneath her.

Taylor snapped on a glove, letting Rose watch and anticipate. This kind of intimacy was rare for her on a first encounter, but Rose's complete trust in her had Taylor's heart pounding. She lightly bit Rose's neck as she thrust two fingers inside, then another, and another. She wondered briefly if she was moving too fast, but when Rose moaned loudly, arching her body to meet Taylor's fingers and take them deeper inside, she knew Rose was completely ready for her. She still fought against the handcuffs, groaning in seeming frustration at times. Taylor played with her and then suddenly withdrew her fingers, making Rose whimper. She put a pillow under Rose's ass and then caught Rose's attention. She purposefully poured lube all over her right hand and wrist.

Rose's eyes widened; she licked her lips.

"You like that?"

Rose nodded and licked her lips again.

Taylor leaned down and whispered, "I'm going to fuck you like you've never been fucked before." She was dizzy with the anticipation of knowing every clasping response of Rose's body.

"Oh dear God . . ."

Taylor silenced her with a kiss before tracing a languid path from Rose's mouth to the object of her desire. She knelt between Rose's legs, forcing them farther apart as she teased her with her fingers before she thrust them deep inside her. Rose moaned and moved her hips, her body matching the penetrating motion of Taylor's hand.

As Taylor added more fingers, her fingers curled until they formed a fist and went deeper. Rose's eyes widened as she gasped, her vaginal walls tightening around Taylor's fist. Taylor paused just long enough for Rose to relax and then plunged her hand in and out, Rose's body moving with every thrust. Rose cried out, a sound of pure primal desire.

The sound made Taylor moan herself. She continued fucking Rose, listening to her ever-increasing moans, until she could wait no longer. She pulled her hand out and put her mouth to Rose's wet center. Rose's breathing quickened as she gasped for air. Her legs squeezed Taylor's shoulders as Taylor alternately licked and sucked, drinking in the taste and scent of her.

Rose suddenly stiffened. "Taylor," she cried out. "Oh yes!"

Taylor held firm as Rose's body writhed beneath her and then relaxed. Rose whimpered softly. Taylor couldn't get enough of her. As she continued to lightly suck, Rose's breath quickened again as she moved against Taylor's mouth until she stiffened and another orgasm rocked her. Taylor heard the jingle of the handcuffs as Rose struggled against them.

"Taylor. Taylor, *por favor*. Please release me."

She quickly unlocked the cuffs and kissed her wrists gently before she took Rose into her arms. She could feel Rose's rapid heartbeat. Her breath was warm and a little erratic against Taylor's shoulder. The heat of Rose's body penetrated through Taylor's clothes. She stroked the soft hair and lightly kissed her forehead. Taylor could hear the murmur of someone else's TV. She thought Rose had fallen asleep, but then she stirred and her beautiful eyes looked up at Taylor.

"When will you be back in town, sweet Rose?" Taylor asked, kissing her again.

"Next weekend." She ran her fingernails gently along Taylor's bare arm. The sensation made goosebumps rise on Taylor's skin.

"Could I take you to dinner?"

"*Sí*, I'd like that very much," Rose said as she sat up and pushed Taylor into the pillows. "But now, I have other things on my mind."

Taylor's breath quickened as a tremor coursed through her body. Rose deftly unbuttoned Taylor's shirt and unzipped her jeans. Each time Rose's fingers touched her body, Taylor felt as if flames licked her. When she was naked, Rose's mouth blazed a trail of kisses down her body, all the way to her feet and back to her mouth. Her breath was warm, like a tropical breeze against Taylor's skin. The fine silk of her long hair brushed over Taylor's body.

Taylor couldn't help but moan from the different sensations. She wrapped her arms around Rose, holding her tight, but Rose wriggled free and grasped both of her wrists and held them against the bed. Taylor knew she could break Rose's hold, but she allowed herself to enjoy the feeling of being restrained.

And then it seemed as if Rose's hands were everywhere on her body, driving her crazy with desire. Taylor moaned again, willing Rose to lower her mouth. As if reading her mind, Rose moved between her legs. Her warm mouth connected with Taylor's clit as her fingers thrust deep inside her. Taylor didn't know how many. Was it two? Three? Even four?

Taylor's mind went completely blank, her body responding to an overload of physical sensations. Fingers thrusting and fluttering inside her. Lips and tongue licking and sucking. Shoulders against her thighs, pushing them apart. And then a hand upon her breast, squeezing one nipple and then the other. The tickle of hair against her legs.

"Rose!" she called out as her orgasm shook her body. She grabbed the headboard as her body arched into Rose's mouth. Her whole body tensed before the shudder of release, and she felt her breath flee. No femme had ever taken care of her like this, so sure and so thoroughly.

"Rose . . . Stop . . . Please . . . I can't . . ."

Rose pulled her fingers free and slid her way up Taylor's slick body. She smiled, her lips red and swollen and her brown eyes darkened with passion. Tangled black hair glistened wet in the lamplight. Taylor pulled her close and kissed her deeply. She could feel their hearts beating in unison, rapidly at first and then more slowly.

She felt herself dozing off, when Rose pulled away and sat up, looking down at her, her expression serious. Taylor felt a twinge of anxiety, and then Rose smiled. "Trooper Donovan?"

"Yes, Ms. Sanchez?"

"Next week . . . When you're on the road again . . ."

"Mmmm?"

"There's a trucker out there with a burnt-out brake light. Drives like a maniac. For the good of the citizenry, you should keep an eye out for her. I think she might be traveling your way again."

With a big grin, Taylor reached over and grabbed her handcuffs. "I'll catch her next time she's in town. You can bet on that."

The Fan

Therese Szymanski

". . . she turned and looked into the most amazing deep blue eyes she had ever seen. 'Haven't we met somewhere before?' he asked, a hint of a smirk touching his finely chiseled features. 'I . . . I'm not sure,' she said, feeling faint. She really wasn't sure if she knew him or not," I finished reading in my most seductive, teasing voice.

The only sound was the background noise of the bookstore, but even that was faint. None of the fifty or so women sitting in the area was making a single sound.

"Fallon McGuire, ladies! Isn't she wonderful?" Cynthia said, coming to the front of the audience. Her words made my audience break into applause. Cynthia was one of those older ladies who was perpetually cheerful. A bookstore employee, she obviously lived for the moments when she could see the likes of Fallon McGuire, internationally known romance novelist, weave her spell over a group of women whose only romance was in the pages of whatever stories beautiful, young, feminine women could give them. "Does anyone have any questions for Miss McGuire?" Cynthia asked when the applause quieted down.

"Oh, yes," one middle-aged woman at the front said, meekly half-raising her hand. "How do you create such vivid romance?"

I shyly looked up from under my eyelashes in a carefully practiced look. "Well, now, you should know a real lady never reveals her secrets." I shaded the words with just a hint of the Southern accent my agent had carefully trained me in.

It would probably blow their minds if they knew what this particular beautiful, young, feminine woman really thought about when she was writing such stories.

Which was about the same thing I thought about when I wrote my sleazy lesbian romance novels.

I wrote mainstream romance for the money, I did the lesbian stuff for fun.

"Miss McGuire," another voice chirruped, this time from an older woman in a wheelchair. "However did you start writing?"

I almost didn't hear her question because I was entranced with the woman standing just behind her, obviously a relative who had brought her to the reading, because she certainly wasn't the sort to read my Fallon McGuire books and probably wouldn't even read my lesbian romances. But she was the sort of woman I thought about when creating both.

I was on autopilot while I finished answering questions. I'm sure I smiled demurely, and kept my legs crossed at the ankle under my light sundress with its long skirt. I knew all the questions and answers, and every movement was scripted, as was every word. Fallon McGuire was the perfect twenty-first-century Southern Belle, Georgia accent and all.

It was a good thing I knew the part so well, because although I'm a femme who plays demure at times, I am not exactly the lady they think I am. In fact, the lady I am was quite distracted by the slender, dark-haired butch who guided the old woman's wheelchair into line when I began signing books.

After all, it was women like her who lit the fire under my romance and gave my sex scenes all of their heat and passion.

"God, it's a gorgeous day," Sandra said, her strong hands lightly caressing the steering wheel of the Bronco as we drove across country, "but all this sameness is gettin' to me." She looked over at me with her deep blue eyes. "Think you can come up with somethin' to keep me awake?"

"Coffee?" I asked, sitting up to grab the thermos.

"Nah, that'll just make me hafta pee again."

"Well, I've got this book of trivia . . ."

"Aw, don't make me think too hard. It's too nice of a day."

"Um," I said, searching my mind for games to play on a road trip. "How about we keep track of how many different state license plates we see?"

"Oh, c'mon, when was the last time you saw another car?" She looked at me over the top of her dark sunglasses. "Though I was thinking of something kind of visual . . ." A slow grin began to spread across her features.

A faint chill enveloped me. "What're you thinkin'?"

She just grinned back.

"What do you want?"

"Something to keep me awake." She reached over, ran a finger lightly across my chin and down my neck, pausing at the dip in my shirt.

"And just what are you thinking?" I asked, grabbing her hand and sucking her forefinger into my mouth, running my teeth lightly over it as I sucked in and out.

"I want to watch."

"Huh? Watch what?"

"I want to watch you touch yourself—y'know, play with yourself."

A thrill ran down my spine. "But it's broad daylight!" It was so bad, it was exciting. I knew I wanted to do it, but she had to convince me.

"When's the last time you saw another car—or saw anything at all? C'mon, babe . . . Y'know you want to do it." She looked at me hard. She

pulled her hand out of mine and her nimble fingers began quickly unbuttoning my shirt.

I let her do it. "Sandra . . . I . . . can't," I said, pulling back away from her, playing hard to get.

"You want to, you know you do. C'mon, babe, show yourself off. You've got an incredible body, and since I can't do you right now . . ."

"Sandra . . ." I was so wet, I could feel it trickling down my thighs. The very thought of getting naked for this hot butch, showing myself off for her, touching myself, was almost enough to make me come. It took all my will power to stay put, to not squirm, to not show her how hot just the thought was making me.

"I could pull over if you weren't so hell-bent on making Boise tonight . . ."

"What's so great about Boise?"

"You're the one who wants to spend the night there." She again glanced over at me.

I knew what I wanted. I wanted to strip for her. I wanted to fuck myself for her. But I had to keep her, us, in the car, on the road for that. That would be my only excuse.

"You're pantin' baby, you know you want this as much as I do."

She could read my mind too well. "Do you want me completely naked?" My hands were at the buttons of my shirt.

"Yes. Take it all off."

It was so bad, it was good. I was wet even as I pulled off my shirt and undid my bra. I leaned against the door and looked at her, running my fingers over my breasts, my nipples, and then squeezed them. Hard.

Her gaze was like a touch. I felt naughty, bad, like I was doing something I shouldn't be, which I was. It was broad daylight, and I was stripping in a moving vehicle—I mean, what if we got pulled over? What if a trucker came by? He could see right down into the car!

I was already barefoot, so I just had to unzip my jeans and pull them and my underwear off. Totally naked, I opened my legs wide, stretching one through the space in the seats and into the backseat while I put the other on the floor.

If I was going to do this, I'd do it all the way, and leave nothing to the imagination. I'd show her everything.

"*Keep your eyes on the road,*" *I ordered, tugging at my nipples. I was so turned on, I was practically dripping onto the seat.*

"*I am,*" *she said while her eyes ping-ponged between the road and me.*

I smiled at her, and dipped my fingers down between my legs, where they slid across my swollen lips. I traced them up and down, quickly finding the hardened nub . . .

I wanted to hold off, but I was so ready, I needed it and couldn't help myself. My fingers began beating across my clit, while my other hand teased and squeezed my nipples.

"*Oh God, oh God,*" *I moaned, my pelvis rising and falling, my body acting of its own accord. Her gaze was hot upon me as I spread my legs even farther, opening myself up to her smoldering gaze, wanting her hands on me, but still knowing what I was doing, and feeling so bad about it because it was so damned hot.*

"*That was pretty fuckin' hot,*" *Sandra said when I was done.*

I reached down for my clothes.

"*Don't. Stay like that. After all, you might just get the urge to do it again.*"

I spent most of the Midwest naked after that, stripping as soon as we got into the car in the morning, and only putting my clothes on for food and restroom breaks, and when we were driving through cities.

I was shy about my body, but I loved showing it off to her—it felt so naughty, and so very, very good . . .

"My mother was so upset she couldn't be here today, but she's getting on in years and doesn't get around as well as she used to, but she always makes me pick up your latest novels and read them to her as soon as they come out," a woman was saying to me. Her book was open in front of me.

I looked up at her. She looked to be at least seventy-five, so it was beyond my comprehension that she could read my books to her mother, but . . . "And you wanted me to make this out to . . . ?"

"Her name's Virginia, but all her friends call her Ginny."

I looked down at the title page and quickly wrote, " 'Ginny, a woman to model heroines after. Thank you for the chat! Love, your friend, Fallon McGuire.' "

Ginny's daughter read the inscription and said, "Oh, thank you so much! She will just love this—and it'll make all her friends so jealous!"

I smiled at her and lifted my hand for the next book. The butch and her elderly companion were still a few minutes away. The old woman was chatting companionably with those around her, and the butch was being most gallant, shaking hands and smiling amicably—when she wasn't looking at me.

There has always been something so spectacularly hot about public, or near-public, sex that just gets to me. Perhaps it's that it's so easy to be discovered that there's a level of danger to it, maybe it's that it's something you're not supposed to do, and those sorts of things always get me wet, or maybe it's simply that it's different, and I have always enjoyed trying new things.

Sandra was always my go-to-it gal, always knowing what I wanted, what I fantasized. And she always made those deepest thoughts and desires come true.

When Sandra and I got to California, we started to fall apart, and decided that we should try non-monogamy. In fact, it was through her that I met Kathleen.

Kathleen was petite compared with Sandra's rugged midwestern build, even though Kathleen was an inch or two taller than Sandra. The two were almost a study in opposites—pale to tanned, brunette to blonde, blue-eyed to brown-eyed.

But they were both very, very butch, and it turned out that not only could Kathleen help get Sandra into advertising, but they also had a common fantasy.

"Hey, babe," Sandra said one day. "A friend of mine introduced me to this restaurant I know you'll love. Why don't we do dinner there tonight?

You can get all dolled up and we'll enjoy a nice dinner out—just like old times."

"Can we afford it?"

"C'mon babe, it's my treat."

I should've known then that something was up. But still, I let her decide my attire, down to the short skirt, and garter belt and stockings, with no underwear.

We got to the restaurant and had to wait about a half-hour before being seated, but as soon as we were at a booth with a bleached-white tablecloth, I felt Sandra's hand high up on my thigh.

I batted it away. "Behave."

"C'mon babe," she whispered under her breath, her eyes on the menu, "can't I have a little fun?"

Her hand played its way up my thigh, under my skirt, teasing me. I put my hand over hers.

"You know you want it, babe."

We placed our drink order, and her hand remained on my thigh.

"Are you wet yet?" she asked under her breath.

"Behave!" I whispered, longing for her touch.

"I think you are." Her fingers inched higher, regardless of my restraining hand.

"Sandra!"

I looked up to see a woman with short blonde hair, clad in a beautiful silk men's suit, with matching tie and shirt, leaning on the table. I know I blushed, thinking about what Sandra and I were almost caught doing.

"Kathleen! Imagine seeing you here!" Sandra said, standing quickly to shake Kathleen's hand. "We were just about to order."

"Oh really? I'm waiting for a table myself."

"Why don't you sit down and join us for a drink?" Sandra asked, waving toward our waiter. "Fallon, this is Kathleen Lindstrom, the woman I interviewed with yesterday."

"Pleased to meet you," I said, half-standing to shake her hand as she sat on the opposite side of me from Sandra.

"The pleasure's all mine," she replied, taking my hand, kissing it and looking deep into my eyes.

I looked over at Sandra, who merely gave me a brief nod.

The waiter brought Sandra' and my drinks, took Kathleen's drink order, and returned with her bourbon on the rocks before we had much of a chance to make small talk.

And that was when I felt her hand on my thigh. I looked nervously at the menu. "Do you like calamari?" I asked her, trying to pull away.

"I love it," she said. "Do you two mind if I join you for dinner?"

"Not at all," Sandra replied before I could say anything. "In fact, I was hoping you might join us."

"Good," Kathleen said, looking at me, with her hand on my thigh, before she looked at Sandra.

By the time the waiter took our order, I was feeling extremely uncomfortable. Sandra was ignoring any hints I was trying to give her, verbal or physical, and I now had one of each of their hands on my opposite thighs, slowly pulling me open. "Excuse me," I finally said to Sandra, starting to stand up, "but I need to use the ladies' room."

"No, you don't," she said, pushing me gently back into my seat.

"Tell me," Kathleen whispered, "have you ever had two women inside of you at the same time?" She looked at me and winked.

Then she looked at Sandra and grinned. And Sandra returned her grin.

I gulped. Sandra did have a way of making all my fantasies come to life.

I sat back in my seat and looked at the two women. I took a deep breath. Then I put my hands on theirs, slowly leading them even higher up my thighs. "Just do me one favor. Don't make me come before dessert."

They needed no further encouragement. Their fingers quickly found my wetness, and began caressing me slowly and gently.

The waiter delivered our appetizers, and the two women kept chatting about advertising, all the while fingering me under the table, their movements hidden by the tablecloth.

We were past the appetizers and salad, and into dinner, when Kathleen lifted the tablecloth up over my lap and pulled my skirt up. "Look down," she ordered.

I looked down to see the tops of my stockings, with the garter belt tracing its way up to my waist. And then I looked between my open thighs, and saw how each of my legs was draped over one of theirs, giving them full and total access.

And then I realized they were both inside of me, slowly bringing their fingers as one in and out of me.

"What?" I said, realizing that I hadn't heard a word.

"I said, don't I know you from somewhere?" It was the butch. She was standing in front of the table, her older companion eagerly looking at me. I looked down to realize I had written the same note for Gertie that I had for Ginny.

"Here you go," I said, handing Gertie the book. I looked up at the butch and fluttered my eyelashes. I had to work to bring out my Georgia accent. "I'm not sure where we might've met."

"Do you write under any other names?" butch asked.

"Oh, I wouldn't even dream of such a thing!" I said.

She shrugged. "Well, maybe we might run into each other again."

I stood up and took Gertie's hand. "It was a pleasure to meet you."

"Oh thank you," Gertie said. "I'm just so excited to finally meet you! I've heard so much about you!"

"You better get right to bed," Angie, my agent, said to me as soon as we left the restaurant where we had dinner. "After all, you have a plane to catch tomorrow, and I don't want my star to give less than a stellar performance in Detroit on Thursday." A native Chicagoan, she had no problems hailing a cab.

"Oh, no thank you," I said. "My hotel's just a few blocks, and I need some air."

"Fallon, you need to sleep. Detroit's a short plane trip away, but

. . . the airports both here and there can be a pain. This is your biggest tour yet, and you'll be having long days till it's over."

"I know all about the plane trip from Chicago to Detroit—and that's exactly why I need to get some air."

"Lady, you goin' or not?" the driver asked.

"Yes, I am, dammit!" She turned to me. "Be careful, Chicago ain't no Cincinnati. Love ya, take care, break a leg and all that shit," she said, then got into the cab and left. Finally.

I looked up at the darkening sky and took a deep breath. Would Angie ever remember I grew up in Columbus, Ohio, not Cincinnati? Would I ever make it through the next month? I was bored with eating by myself or with strangers, tired of flying or driving, and really exhausted with playing my role and being hit on by disgusting men in hotel lobbies and bars.

I just wanted to take off my shoes and run through full, deep, soft grass.

I looked up the street and started walking, hoping I was heading in the right direction. I let my long legs take control, my handbag at my side, the brisk air providing a welcome relief from the heat and staleness of restaurants and bookstores.

Sandra was a fantasy butch to this femme. She always knew what I wanted.

"I love this bed," she said when we moved into our new apartment in Los Angeles. "But you wanna know the best thing about this bed?"

"What?" I asked, carrying an armful of clothes from the living room to the bedroom. It was much smaller than we were accustomed to, but I was glad we had saved up to buy some things for this new place.

"This," she said, grabbing me and throwing me down on the bed.

"It is a nice bed," I said, squirming under her. I still didn't know how we'd fit all our kitchen stuff in the tiny space.

"Not the new bed," Sandra said. "I'm talkin' 'bout the new headboard."

She grabbed me and wrestled me nearer to the headboard, holding out my right wrist until she slipped something over it. I pulled my right hand toward me and realized she had tied me down.

She grabbed my left wrist and tied it down as well. "Sandra! We need to unpack!"

"That's what I'm doin', babe," she said, ripping my blouse open and pulling my shorts and underwear off before tying down my legs.

I wiggled against the ropes, but could only move an inch or so in any direction.

She stood up and looked down at her handiwork. It was only then that I realized how open I was. I was fully restrained and spread out for her enjoyment.

"Sandra . . ." I moaned, pulling against the ropes.

She stood at the end of the bed, looking down at me. Then her hand dropped to her zipper. "By the way, babe, I bought us another housewarming gift." And with that she pulled it out.

I looked at it and couldn't believe she would . . . It couldn't fit . . . Not possibly . . . But still, I wanted it inside of me . . .

I suddenly became aware of another set of footsteps behind mine. They were solid footsteps, the sound of someone powerful and self-assured walking just behind me.

I quickened my pace.

The footsteps quickened, staying just behind me.

I looked around, noticing for the first time how dark it had become. The street was devoid of people. The streetlights gave some light, but still, the night air that had given me such solace suddenly felt eerie. My blood was pumping fast in my veins and arteries, and I could feel my heart beating.

I had no idea who was behind me, but my mind was already running through my options, wondering just what I should do and what I could do. I glanced back and saw a figure in a black leather jacket and heavy boots quickly approaching me.

I saw it, then I heard it—my stalker was suddenly upon me, a strong hand over my mouth, an arm around my waist pulling me into an alley. I tried to scream, but I couldn't even gasp for air.

I felt the cold brick of a wall behind me, and the only pale light came from the street, which might've been miles away. I bit the hand covering my mouth.

"Goddammit!" she yelled, yanking her hand from me. She raised her hand automatically as if to strike me, but held it back at the last moment. "Make another sound and you're really gonna get it." She lowered her hand and looked at me. It was the butch from the bookstore earlier in the day.

The blood rushed through me. I was scared. "Please don't hurt me."

"I'm not gonna hurt you. Don't worry about that." She ran one strong hand over my face and down through my hair. "There won't be any problems, so long as you don't make them."

Her thigh was wedged between my legs, hard against me, forcing my legs apart.

"What do you want?" I whispered.

"You know what I want." She dropped her backpack to the ground and ripped the bodice of my dress open with one hand. "And you know you want to give it to me."

I was being assaulted, but it was by a strong, butch woman. "No, no . . ." I cried, but I involuntarily arched against her, wanting this, wanting her.

"Just say no again if you really want me to stop."

I couldn't say it. I could only stare at her, wanting her touch, wanting to feel her against me.

One strong hand at the back of my head brought my lips to hers. Her tongue quickly parted them and she began tongue-fucking my mouth, making me comply to her wants.

"Oooh, baby, you're so hot," she said as she quickly ripped the waist of my pantyhose and dove under my panties with her hand.

"Oh, God," I moaned, wanting her inside of me.

"That's it baby, that's it, give it to me." She ripped off my underwear so that I stood in the alley with my dress shredded, revealing everything to her.

I lost any will to fight.

She dropped to her knees and tasted me, her tongue teasing me while two of her fingers thrust inside of me. I knew that this was the time to do something, but I was melting under her touch. "Oh, God," I said, my hands in her hair, urging her to go deeper, faster, harder. "Give it to me, baby, give it to me!"

"Oh, fuck me you little slut, you want it, you got it," she replied, pulling herself from me just long enough to take a small bottle of lube from her pocket. She quickly poured some over her hand and wrist and I quivered, knowing exactly what was coming.

There were two fingers inside of me, then three, then four, and then . . .

"Oh God fuck me!" I screamed.

"That's it, baby, take it all," she growled, riding me hard with her fist, ramming it in and out of me.

"Oh God, oh God!"

"Argh!" And then her mouth was on me, licking and sucking my cunt while she took me.

My knees buckled and she caught me with her left arm, easing me down to the cold hard ground while she fucked and sucked me.

"Oh, fuck, Sandra!" I screamed.

Where do I get everything from?

Well, you see, there's this butch who's bold, brave and talented enough to make all my fantasies come true . . .

I'm just glad her grandma never knew what she was enabling.

Found in an Antique Trunk
Julia Watts

November 3, 1894

Dear Elsie,

I am nervous as a cat writing this. You go to that fancy girls' school up in Lexington where they teach you pretty English and handwriting. Me, when I turned sixteen back in April, Pa said it would be foolish for me to keep going to school. He said I was more use helping out on the farm than sitting in a schoolroom, and besides, what was the point in educating a woman when all she was going to do was cook and look after younguns?

Of course, Pa said this knowing that I am hopeless at cooking and other woman's work and that Ma always runs me out of the kitchen because I spill the flour or burn the biscuits. What Pa really wanted me home for was farm work—plowing, baling hay, looking after the cows and chickens. And all that I am happy to do, as you know. There's nothing like working outside, smelling the sweet hay and feeling the sun on my face.

So just like I'm no good at housework, I am no good at letter writing. As you read this, instead of seeing my bad handwriting and poor words, I hope you will see me as I am at my best, out in God's nature, brown from the sun, the legs of my brother's old britches rolled up, wading in the creek.

That was fun, wasn't it, when we went wading last summer? Especially when you stepped out too far and got mired up in mud to your knees and got your dress and petticoats wet. When your pa decided you should spend the summers with your aunt and uncle in the country, the picture he had in his mind was probably not you running off with the daughter of your aunt and uncle's much poorer neighbor and wallowing in the mud like a hog. But that is the way it's been the past three summers, you and me running wild in the woods, laughing and yelling, with me free of my farm chores for a few hours and you free of having to act like a lady.

In this letter I was going to tell you about my life since we saw each other, but there is nothing to tell. On the farm one day's chores fade into the next until the days are a blur of feeding and egg gathering and milking. The only time my life is worth writing about is when you are here, and so I live from summer to summer when we can be together again.

Your devoted friend,

Betsy

✍

December 18, 1894

Dear Elsie,

My heart is breaking because you won't be visiting this summer. I know your pa says that when summer comes you will be finished with your schooling, so you should start spending time with the young man he has decided is suitable for you, but Elsie, is this what you want? If you married Mr. Tadlock, I know that you would live in a fine house never wanting for anything. But what about the Elsie that loves running in the woods and climbing trees and laughing out loud? What would happen to her when you had to spend all your time in a parlor, doing needlework, which you hate, and pouring tea for company?

I know the day will come when my pa starts asking me about fellows, too, starts saying I should get married. But Elsie, I won't do it. I'll run away before I'll do it. But maybe you and me are different that way. Do you love this gentleman? If you say you do, even though I know it is wrong of me, I will feel very sad.

Oh, Elsie, without you, I'm afraid the summer will never come! The flowers won't bloom, the trees will stay bare, and it will be winter forever.

Your sad but devoted,

Betsy

❧

January 20, 1895

Dear Elsie,

I have been thinking crazy thoughts since I got your last letter, thoughts that a good girl might not ought to think. I have been thinking about the future. Usually a girl doesn't have to think too much about the future because it's already planned out for her, but when I have been alone lately, milking the cows or feeding the chickens, I have found myself wondering, does life have to be this way?

If I lived the future my Pa planned for me, I would help out around the farm until I found some old boy who'd marry me even though I am plain and gangly, and then I would help out on his farm the same as I do for Pa and have a passel of younguns. And you would marry Mr. Tadlock and do needlepoint and wear whalebone corsets and have his younguns. But if you don't love Mr. Tadlock, as you say, then why should you marry him? And why should I live my whole life as an unpaid farm hand, first for my Pa and then for a husband?

Elsie, do you remember last summer when we were up in the hayloft, throwing hay at each other and cutting up and acting foolish? We were sort of wrestling and tickling each other and laughing, and then there was this moment when you ended up underneath me, your yellow hair all spread out on the hay. Your arms were around my waist, and your blue eyes stared into mine. We both stopped laughing. Elsie, I don't know what it was, but something passed between us at that moment, something that can change everything, if we let it.

If you don't think I am crazy yet, what I'm about to say will convince you of it. My idea is, why don't you marry me instead of Mr. Tadlock? You are probably laughing right now, but I am serious. In my brother's britches, I could pass as a boy easy if I cut my hair short. We could go across the state line to where nobody knows us and find a country preacher who wouldn't ask us any questions. And then we could go wherever we wanted to. I am a good worker and could get a paying job as long as everybody thought I was a boy. And you've been to school long enough that you could be a schoolteacher if you chose to.

Elsie, I know I would make a terrible wife, but I think I would make a very good husband. Mr. Tadlock could never love you the way I do. He would try to tame you, to put you on a leash and make you his pet, but I love you for the wild girl that you are. And when I think of our summers together and of your eyes meeting mine that hot day in the hayloft, I think that you might love me, too.

I beg you to give this matter serious thought. If you say yes, pick a date to take the night train to Morgan, and I will meet you there. If we get caught, the worst that can happen is we'll be sent home and whipped, and then our lives will go on like our fathers planned. If we do get away, then I will be the happiest girl in the world, and I will work every day to make you just as happy as me. Until I hear from you, I will think of nothing else.

Your devoted,

Betsy

&c&

February 1, 1895

My dearest Elsie,

Your words to me are always pretty, but there is no prettier word in the English language than "yes." I will meet you at the train station at half past eleven the night of February 24. Remember when you see me to call me Billy, not Betsy. Burn this letter.

Your devoted,

Betsy

A Femme in the Hand

Lesléa Newman

The first time I saw her, I got weak in the knees, I swear to God. She was a beauty all right, but beautiful doesn't begin to describe her. Try strong. Powerful. Built. I stared at her until my eyeballs ached, and something else ached, too—that sweet place between my legs that butches like me don't talk about very much. But that's where I wanted her, and frankly, the sooner the better. In other words, ladies and gentledykes, in case I'm not making myself perfectly clear, I had it bad.

I guess I've been out of circulation longer than I thought, because for a good twenty minutes, I felt like I had no bones in my legs. They just wouldn't budge even though I kept telling them to move. I mean, as much as I wanted to, I couldn't just stand there all day staring at the vision of loveliness before me; I had to take action. So even though I was scared shitless, I strutted right over to the man standing next to her like I knew what I was doing, cleared my throat, prayed my voice wouldn't crack and asked, How much? The price was fair, so I whipped out my checkbook, scrawled the amount, and in a flick of my Bic, she was mine.

Now, let me tell you something. I know I'm nothing special. Just an average butch. Average height, average weight, average smarts, average looks. But with this baby between my legs, I'd be way above average. I'd be brave. I'd be bold. I'd be bulletproof. You know what they say, right, clothes make the man? Well, let me tell you what I say: the bike makes the butch.

I swung my leg over my prize and dropped my weight onto the seat. A deep sigh of pure pleasure escaped my lips, and my bones settled inside my skin in a different way than they ever had before. Have you ever felt that all was right with the world, even though you know that babies are crying all over the planet, and we've made a total mess of the environment, and somewhere right that very second some asshole of a man is making a woman do something she doesn't want to do and you've got job troubles and girlfriend troubles and family troubles, but still, you're amazed at the miracle of your own heart beating inside your chest and your breath coming in and out of your nostrils without any noticeable effort, and your muscles move a certain way just because you want them to, and hey, you're alive, and the sky is blue and absolutely nothing else matters? That's how I felt the first time I started up that bike.

My hands were shaking as I inserted the key, but she turned right over, my baby, my darling, my Harley. I still couldn't believe she was mine as I walked her back a few steps to turn her around and point her in the right direction. Then I gave her some gas and picked up my feet, and before you could say Moving Violations we were out of that tired old parking lot and out on the street.

Now in case you've never been on a bike—and if you haven't, I feel mighty sorry for you—let me explain why it's so different from riding in a car. It's like the first time I ever got glasses. I didn't even know the world was blurry as an out-of-focus movie until my mother hauled me in to see old Doctor Norton, who took one look at me and pronounced me blind as a little bat. Not to worry though, my vision was nothing lenses thick as Coke bottles couldn't fix. My mother and I started fighting immediately right in the office over my frames; she wanted me to wear these light-blue, glittery cat's eyes monstrosities, and I, being a baby butch even then, had already picked out a cool pair of square black frames that made me look like a miniature Clark Kent. Of course, my mother won in the end— after all, she was the one with the checkbook—and I was so pissed I vowed never to let those spectacles within a foot of my face. But when the doctor hooked my new glasses around my eight-year-old ears, the world was so sharp, so bright, so crystal-clear, I pushed my butch ego aside and put up with looking like a girly-girl (and an ugly one at that) because I just couldn't believe my eyes. It was like I had just been transported to another planet. And that's just what riding a bike is like. If you're not Nancy Nearsighted like I am, the only other way I can describe it is through *The Wizard of Oz*. Remember when Dorothy lands in Munchkinland, and all of a sudden the world isn't a drab, dull, black-and-white affair, the world's an amazing, sparkling, dazzling show of Technicolor? That's what life is like on a bike. Everything's in ultra mega-focus. That's because there's nothing between you and the world. You're a part of it, and it's a part of you.

See, when you're out on the road, the air unzips to let you by as you and your bike slice through it, and once in a while, a warm pocket of air surprises you, just like when you're swimming in a lake and you hit a warm spot of water (which hopefully isn't pee). Smells come and go: the sweet smell of burning leaves in autumn, the even sweeter smell of lilacs and honeysuckle in the spring. If it rains, you get wet; if the sun's out, you get burned. But you don't complain. You're like a kid again. Ever hear a kid complain about the weather? Me neither. If it's snowing, a kid makes snow angels. If it's raining, a kid goes stomping in puddles. If it's 90 degrees, a kid heads for the nearest swimming hole. Kids are very Zen; they're right there in the moment, which is how I am when I'm on my bike. Whatever comes my way is what I deal with. If there's a fallen tree in the middle of the road, I figure out how to get around it. If there's a scumbag trying to pass me on the right, I figure out how to lose him. If there's a babe on my backseat, I figure out how to give her the best ride of her life. And speaking of babes, I was definitely in the mood to pick one up. It was just about Miller time, so I headed for my favorite hangout, a beer dive called Where the Girls Are. And truer words were never spoken. Especially on a Friday night.

I zoomed into the parking lot and took a space right out front. Separation anxiety hit as soon as I was about two feet away from my bike, but I made myself not look back. *She'll be all right*, I told myself. *And besides, this is my moment, the moment I'd been waiting for my whole life—to walk into a bar with my hair all flattened out on one side and my helmet dangling from its strap off my arm, feeling like the coolest dude in the world.* I swaggered past the dance floor and the pool table and swung my leg over a bar stool the same way I had swung it over my bike a few hours ago, just knowing I was God's gift to women. But that illusion was shattered two seconds later when I ordered a club soda. I mean, how dorky can you get? The bartender, a pretty gal named Fuzzy, raised one perfectly tweezed eyebrow at me, as if to say, *Oh Jamie, don't tell me you've gone AA on me, too?*, especially since I usually down a glass of whatever's on tap pretty quickly and immediately snap my fingers for another. But I wasn't taking any chances tonight, not when there was nothing between me and the hard, cold concrete but my reflexes and a four-pound helmet. Pretty funny when you think about it. Many a woman's tried to straighten me out, so to speak, but it took a bike to keep me sober. At least for tonight.

I leaned against the bar and chugged my club like a dyke who had it made. *If that bike isn't a babe magnet*, I told myself, *I'll eat my jockey shorts.* I was sure that by the time I finished my soda and sauntered back outside, there'd be a beautiful broad standing by my Harley, tapping her foot with her hands on her hips, all ready to be my one and only biker chick. Or maybe there'd be a crowd of girls, each one of them sure they deserved the first ride. Maybe there'd even be some pushing and shoving. A cat fight. Wouldn't that be something? Just the thought of it raised me off my barstool and propelled me back out to the parking lot. And believe it or not, there was a crowd of girls standing around my bike, much to my amazement and delight. Better yet, as soon as I got near them, they were all over me. "Hey man, nice bike. Where'd you get it?" "How much did it set you back?" "What's it cost to fill?" "How big's the engine?"

Christ, was I disappointed. Why, you ask? Because these are not femme questions now, are they? No, they are not. My rehearsed, *Ladies, ladies, one at a time, please, everyone will get a ride*, stuck in my throat because the mass of females swarming around my bike wasn't exactly a hen party. It was just a bunch of jealous butches, one admiring the chrome, one stroking the leather seat, one fitting her greasy paws around the handlebars . . .

"Outta my way," I said, and with a wave of my hand, I parted the crowd like the Red Sea, claimed what was mine, and left them all in the dust. Though the truth is, they left me in the dust by a mile, because I knew most of those girls, and I knew they had femmes to go home to. Terry had Susie, Sal had Rita, Ronnie had Clara, Riki had Buffy. All I had was me, myself, and I. And even though none of those femmes were exactly my type, and I loved riding solo, I knew after a while I'd get tired of feeling the wind at my back. What I wanted to feel was a girl at my back, with her arms around my waist, and her legs snuggled up to my thighs, her helmet clinking against mine every once in a while as she leaned up close to whisper something in my ear. The girl had to be out there, but the question was, where?

The problem with this town, though, is it's smaller than most people's high schools, and I'd already gone through most of the femmes in this county and the next one over. And even so, I had yet to find what I was looking for. I wanted a girl with style. A girl all powdered and puffed who wore lipstick and lace. High heels even.

A girl who was no stranger to hair spray. A girl who smelled like my mama. I know those kind of girls live in big cities mostly, but I had moved here to escape the rat race, and if I had done it, wasn't there a chance that my femme counterpart had done so, too? You know what they say, right, anything's possible, so I wasn't giving up hope. A friend suggested I put a personal ad in a lesbo paper with a wide circulation, which I thought was a fine suggestion. Until I sat down to write it. I never sweated so much over ten little words in my life. Finally I came up with something I thought sounded clever: "Well-equipped butch with bike looking for high femme to ride." That says it pretty well, don't you think? I thought so, too, until the calls starting coming in. One woman actually said, "Do I bring my own pot?" What, is she planning on moving in already? As I've already told you, I'm not the quickest horse in the race, so I'm thinking, *pot . . . pot . . . what can she possibly be talking about here, chicken soup, beef stew?*

"See," she went on, "I didn't know if you wanted me to get stoned first, or wait until you picked me up . . ."

Oh, high femme. I get it. See what I mean about the dykes around here? "Never mind," I told her. "The bike's in the shop. Maybe some other time."

And that was just the first call. The others aren't even worth mentioning. Except, for what it's worth, let me give you gals out there a few pointers, okay? There are certain things you do not say to a butch about her bike. Number one: "It's nice, but it's not as big as my boyfriend's in college." Number two: "Does it have to be so noisy?" Number three: "Can I drive?" I met some lulus, let me tell you, but they say you have to kiss a lot of frogs before you find your princess. I tell you, I was getting so desperate, even a frog was beginning to look good to me, but you know, it's always darkest before the light, or calmest before the storm or something like that, because just when I was going to bring my extra helmet back to see if I could get a refund (hey, those babies aren't cheap), I got a phone call, and I knew as soon as I heard her voice that this one was different. You've heard of love at first sight, right? This was love at first sound.

"So you're the butch with the bike?" she said, like she was issuing me a challenge.

"Yep, that's me," I said, in what I hoped was a deep, mature, Marlon Brando kind of voice.

"What color is it?"

"Black with white hub caps and a dash of red. Why?"

"Because," her tone was impatient, like she already thought I was a fool, "I don't want it to clash with my outfit."

"Great," I said, hoping she couldn't hear that I was grinning like an idiot. "I'll see you on Saturday."

Saturday didn't come a moment too soon, let me tell you. I spent a good part of the morning fussing with my hair (all two inches of it) even though I knew by the time I got to Valerie's house, it would be a total, helmet-shaped wreck. I put on my best riding outfit: black leather pants, black leather jacket, black leather boots, black leather gloves. Thank God it was one of those glorious autumn days with just a few wispy clouds in a blue-as-the-sea sky, the air as crisp as the first bite of a perfectly ripened Macintosh apple. Otherwise I'd have sweated to death. Though even if it was 98 degrees outside, I still would have dressed in black leather from head to toe. I could tell from her voice that Valerie expected it. And I could also tell this was not a woman you wanted to disappoint.

I picked her up at high noon, and I have to say, she looked gorgeous. I'd gotten up extra early to shine up my bike, and boy did she shine. You know the way the sun glints off the ocean so it looks like there are hundreds of little diamonds shimmering up and down with the waves? That's just how sparkly my bike looked, from chrome to shining chrome. And Valerie wasn't exactly hard on the eyes either. When I roared into her driveway, she was standing there wearing jeans so tight, I wondered how the hell she was going to get her leg up over the seat of my bike, but hey, that wasn't my problem. Her T-shirt was even tighter than her Levi's, and she looked so fine I almost broke my own rule and let her ride without a jacket, but I wouldn't be able to live with myself if anything happened to those pretty little arms. She was all in black like me, except for these sweet little red boots that damn near broke my heart. Femmes, I swear to God, I'm like putty in their hands. Make that Silly Putty, because if you want to know the truth, I was already half in love with Valerie and totally in lust with her, and she hadn't even opened her mouth or set foot on the bike yet. But I played it cool. I said hi, and she said hi, and then the fog I was in lifted slightly, and I noticed that instead of carrying a pocketbook, she was clutching an enormous yellow balloon that I hoped to hell she wasn't going to ask me to tie onto the back of the bike.

"What's with the overgrown lemon?" I asked, handing her a helmet.

"Oh, P.J. has this rule," she said, rolling her eyes.

"P.J." I stopped dead in my tracks. "Who's P.J.?"

"Oh, did I forget to mention P.J.?" she asked, all innocence.

"Yeah, I guess you did," I answered, already removing my helmet. A girl like this was bound to have a butch who would turn me into chopped liver if I came within two inches of her chick's aura. But who was I more afraid of, P.J., who was nowhere in sight, or Valerie, who was standing there with this are-you-a-butch-or-a-mouse look in her eye that said *listen, sister, you promised me a ride, and you damn well better give me one?*

I sighed. "What's P.J.'s rule?" I asked, already tucking my head back inside my helmet.

"P.J. said it was all right for me to go riding with you as long as we keep this between us." She bonked me lightly on the arm with the balloon.

"And how do you figure we're going to manage that?"

Valerie shook her head like she was saying, *You poor butch, you have no imagination*, and unzipped her jacket. She reached down under her T-shirt where the sun don't shine and came back up with a safety pin. "Will you do the honor?" she asked, holding out the balloon and the pin. I popped that sucker while Valerie covered her ears.

"Oh, it broke, isn't that too bad?" Valerie curled her bottom lip into an adorable pout, looking sad as a little kid at a country fair whose ice cream cone had just dropped to the ground. For a second, anyway. Then she put the safety pin back from whence it came and dangled the bit of deflated rubber in front of me. "Problem solved, sugar. So, are we going to spend the whole afternoon standing in the driveway or what?"

"Let's go." I put my helmet back on and started up the bike. I knew Valerie was danger with a capital D, but I figured what the hell. I also knew from bike riding that danger and excitement go hand in hand and I was excited all right. So excited, I could have wrung out my BVDs like a sponge. I practically gushed a geyser when Valerie hopped on behind me and leaned up against my back to put that dead-as-a-doorknob balloon between us and keep it there. Then she said the three words I've been waiting forever and a day to hear, "Where should I hold on?"

I sighed like a butch in paradise and gave her my well-practiced reply, "Anywhere you'd like."

We took off, and let me tell you, P.J. is one hell of a lucky woman because Valerie knew exactly how to ride. She stayed with me the whole time, through every curve, turn, and bump of the road, not letting an inch of air come between her chest and the back of my jacket. You know what it's like riding with a gorgeous chick on the back of your bike? It's like the first time I got contact lenses. I already told you how my world changed 360 degrees when I got my glasses, right? Well I didn't know things could get any better, until the doc handed me my contacts. I popped those pieces of plastic onto my eyeballs and the world, which I thought looked fine as could be, grew so sharp, it was absolutely breathtaking. I felt like Rip Van Winkle—isn't he the one who fell asleep for a hundred years? That's how I felt with Valerie on the bike; something inside me that had been dead to the world had just woken up, and boy was it great to say good morning.

We rode for a good hour before my butt began to ache, which of course I couldn't admit, so I asked Valerie if she was ready to take a rest.

"Hell, no," she yelled over the roar of the bike.

"Aren't your legs tired?" I yelled back.

"No," she answered. "I'm used to keeping them spread like this."

Christ almighty, this girl was really something else. I mean, who was taking who for a ride here? I picked up the speed, and off we went, across highways and byways, over hill, over dale, winding our way around beautiful country roads with nothing but that bit of busted balloon between us and not a cloud in the sky. It took every ounce of strength I had not to reach down and squeeze one of Valerie's pretty little hands or reach behind me to stroke one of her sleek, denim-covered thighs. I was in butch heaven and butch hell at the same time, let me tell you, with such a knockout of a lady a hair's breadth behind me, her hands holding fast to my love handles, her legs pressed up against my quivering thighs. This was more action than I'd had in longer than I'd care to admit, and I was getting mighty worked up, but hey, I'm no home wrecker. There was no way I was going to do anything naughty. Unless of course Valerie made the first move. And what the hell, maybe Valerie and P.J. were nonmonogamous. It was pretty weird that P.J. would let her chick ride off into the sunset with a butch she'd never even met before. What the hell was wrong with her? And even if she didn't give a damn about what I looked like, any butch worth her weight in chainsaws would have at least come out to check out the bike.

Well, it looked like I wasn't going to ask, and Valerie wasn't going to tell. It was hard to talk on the bike anyway, and even though I have an intercom system, I don't like to use it. I'm not that much of a talker, especially when I'm on a bike. It's too distracting. I like to just feel when I'm riding, and right then I was feeling pretty fine. So fine, in fact, it didn't even matter what happened between me and Valerie once I took her home, and we got off the bike. Just seeing her drop-dead gorgeous face grinning in my rearview mirror was enough for me. Well, almost, anyway. Someday I'd have a femme of my own to ride with, a femme who'd throw her arms around my neck and press her breasts against my back as we ride off into the sunset to live happily ever after, at least for a week or two.

Well, you know what they say, right, all good things must come to an end. The day was fading fast, so I started heading back toward Valerie's place. We'd put in a good couple of hours, and I hoped she'd gotten what she came for. When we pulled up into her driveway, I killed the engine and thanked her for the ride.

"Thank *you*," she said, shaking her head like a horse tossing its mane as she handed me back my helmet. "Why don't you come up for something tasty?" she asked, in a voice that wasn't about to take no for an answer.

"Uh . . . okay," I said, hanging both helmets onto the bike. I followed her inside and then halfway up the steps, I couldn't help myself. "Um, where's P.J.?" I asked.

"Who knows?" Valerie lifted her hands and shrugged her shoulders. "She could be anywhere."

Anywhere? Like in the bedroom with a shotgun? Even though warning bells loud as sirens were going off in my ears, I kept following Valerie, whose jean-clad ass was pulling me along like a magnet.

She sat me down at her kitchen table and disappeared into the bathroom. I counted silently—one, two, three—and then right on cue, Valerie shrieked like I knew she would, "Oh my God, my hair!" She came out freshly fluffed a few minutes later and tossed her jacket over the back of a kitchen chair. I tried not to stare at her breasts, but I was a deer caught in the headlights of an approaching car. And Valerie came closer, and closer, until she swung her leg over my lap and plopped herself down, her face only an inch from mine.

"Wanna take me for another ride sometime?" she asked in a husky voice.

"Uh, sure," I stammered, "how about next Saturday?"

"How about right now?" Valerie leaned even closer and whispered in my ear.

"Um, I think I'm out of gas," I said weakly.

"We don't have to go very far." Valerie punctuated her sentence with a flick of her tongue against the side of my neck. "The bedroom's right in there."

I knew I would be a fool to say yes, but even a bigger fool to say no. I knew I should think with my head here, not my crotch, but they were having one hell of an argument. My head was saying, *Now Jamie, don't do anything foolish. You'll have a femme of your own someday.* And my crotch was saying, *The hell with someday. You know what they say, Jamie, a femme in the hand is worth two in the* . . . and as soon as the word "bush" entered my mind, I knew I was a goner. And so I was, for I didn't even attempt to protest as Valerie interlaced her fingers with mine and led me toward her bedroom over the threshold into Paradise.

Valerie plumped up some pillows and lay back on the bed like she had all the time in the world. She smiled at me, and my heart just turned over because nothing does it to me like a femme fatale all ripe for the taking. *The hell with P.J.*, I thought, as I knelt before Valerie and removed her sweet little boots. I took off her socks too, and kissed each red-painted toe. Somehow, tight as they were, Valerie's jeans came off pretty damn quick, as did her T-shirt, black lace bra, and matching bikini underpants. I was practically on fire as I kissed her everywhere—her neck, her breasts, her belly, her thighs, the palms of her hands, the soles of her feet.

I inched my way back up the bed until her head was right next to mine. "I've got a surprise for you," I whispered into her velvety ear.

"I *love* surprises," Valerie whispered back. "Lay it on me, sugar."

Without a word, I took her hand and guided it down between us until it landed on my crotch. "Feel that?" I asked as I unzipped my zipper.

Valerie's eyes widened. "I should have known, you naughty girl," she said, her lips spreading into a grin as her legs spread wide as well. "Well-equipped indeed."

"Hey, no one can accuse me of false advertising," I said as I rolled on top of her and slid the dildo inside. Valerie gasped a short, sweet intake of breath, which to me is the most beautiful sound in the world.

We moved slowly at first, getting used to each other and finding our rhythm, and we were just getting into a groove with our lips and hips locked together and Valerie's fingernails digging ditches down my back when all of a sudden, I felt her stiffen.

"I'm coming," Valerie yelled, turning her head to the side.

"Come on baby," I said, raising myself up on my elbows to move faster inside her. But Valerie pushed me away.

"I'm coming," she yelled again, clamoring out of bed. "Just a minute, P.J."

"P.J.!" I sat up and tried to get my tool back into my pants, which was easier said than done, because my hands were more than shaking, let me tell you. Even all zipped up, I was in a heap of trouble, as the air was thick with the smell of sex, the bed looked like a hurricane had hit it, and Valerie, for some reason, had gone to the back door in nothing but her birthday suit. I didn't know if I should head for the closet, jump out the window, or dive under the bed, but before I could move a muscle, I heard Valerie's voice, and her words froze me to the spot.

"P.J., where have you been all day? I missed you. C'mon, baby, there's someone in the bedroom I want you to meet."

Oh my God, was Valerie psycho? Was this a lesbian remake of *Fatal Attraction?* And what the hell was I supposed to say to P.J.? *Pleased to meet you? How do you do?* Before I could decide, Valerie came back into the bedroom and the sight of her, naked as the day she was born, undid me all over again.

"P.J.'s here," she announced all smiles, like now her day was really complete. "C'mon in, P.J., don't be shy," Valerie coaxed. She took my hand, and we stood there waiting, Valerie's bare skin rippling in the breeze and me sweating like hell inside my leather jacket, my heart pounding so hard, I was sure my chest would be covered with black and blue marks in the morning. It felt like we stood there for hours, but I'm sure it wasn't more than a minute before P.J. gathered up her courage and strode into the room.

"Isn't she amazing?" Valerie bent down to scoop up the biggest, hairiest, fluffiest black and white cat I had ever seen. I didn't know whether to kiss Valerie or kill her, I was so relieved. "This is P.J." Valerie extended one of P.J.'s paws for me to shake. P.J. started to purr, and Valerie lowered her head until her ear was next to P.J.'s neck.

"What'd you say, P.J.? Oh yes, we kept the balloon between us the whole time, didn't we, Jamie?"

"We sure did," I said, relaxing a little and petting P.J.'s head. "So, this is the famous P.J., huh?"

"This is my girl." Valerie scratched the cat under the chin.

"And she's the one who makes the rules around here?"

Valerie looked a little sheepish. "Well, I had to bring the balloon with me, Jamie. I mean, what if you turned out to be a dog?"

"And did I?"

Valerie grinned. "I'd say, sugar, you're more of a wolf."

That made me grin in my boots, let me tell you. We were both standing there rubbing P.J.'s fur, and each time our fingertips touched, my snatch shuddered, and I could tell from her breathing that Valerie's did too.

"So, what does P.J. stand for, anyway?" I asked her.

"Pussy Junior."

I laughed. "Is there a Pussy Senior?"

Valerie gave me a look that was already becoming dear to me and batted her big, brown eyes. "Does a femme wear mascara?"

I took that to mean yes. "So when do I get to meet her?"

"You already have." Valerie reached for my hand again and led me back to the bed. "And I think it's high time you two got better acquainted."

"Sounds good to me," I said, but before I could lay Valerie down, P.J. leapt onto the bed, turned around in a circle three times and plopped down right in the center of the sheets. "I wasn't talking about you," Valerie said, picking up her pet. "Why don't you go into the kitchen for a while?" She shooed the cat out, and before she shut the bedroom door, I had already unzipped my zipper. We hit the bed flying and resumed right where we had left off, and believe me, it wasn't long before all three of us, Valerie, P.J., and I, were yowling to beat the band.

The Trick

Amie M. Evans

It is seven o'clock on a Saturday night. I look at my reflection in the full-length mirror: six-inch come-fuck-me pumps with ankle straps, silky black stockings attached to a black lace garter belt peeking out from under the hem of a too-tight micro-mini, a plunging red lace sleeveless shirt exposing all of the cleavage the black push-up bra has created, and a wide silver belt around my hips. I put on Fire Engine Red lipstick, then throw the tube into my purse along with my keys, $40, a few condoms, ID (in case I turn up dead), cell phone, and Mace. I look like a hooker and I cannot believe I am doing this.

The headline in Monday's paper will read "Professional Lesbian Found Dead in Chinatown." The story will describe how I worked at an Ivy League College and grew up in rural Pennsylvania. The reporter will probably interview people who barely knew me and quote them in the article. The story will go on to describe my non-traditional parents and siblings, maybe mention my roommate who is my ex-lover, and then describe the clothing I was wearing when my body was found. A really good reporter will uncover the fact that I was a stripper while an undergraduate at a Junior Ivy League College and that I now write pornography for a living. But I doubt my obituary will be written by a good reporter.

If I am lucky, in the weeks following my untimely death a series of letters to the editor on the op-ed pages will be devoted to the issues of (1) lesbians as prostitutes, (2) legalizing prostitution to make it safer for hookers, and (3) the implications of what the victim was wearing when she was killed as a valid topic in an article about a murder.

The murder will go unsolved because the police will never think to look for a female suspect, and I've told no one about this girl. Lesbians don't frequent hookers and they don't have anonymous sexual encounters like gay men in the popular consciousness of America. There will be a momentary pulling together of the not-so-diverse but distant communities of lesbians and sex workers, some public actions, campaigns for reform, and a candlelight march. Then the two groups will fight about whose needs are more important, participation will slow to a trickle, and the uneasy coalition will be history.

I cannot believe I am doing this. I thought I was smart enough not to let my hormones get the best of me. It has been one week since I picked up that hot James Dean butch for a one-night anonymous sexual encounter at that lesbian bar. Her name is Karen, but I didn't know that until after I had sex with her. I look at the scrap of paper on which I wrote the information. It reads: "5th and Washington, Chinatown; Karen, 8:00 PM, Saturday; red '56 Chevy; push-up bra."

She was so cocky announcing where and when to meet her, no less what she wanted me to wear, before roaring out of the parking lot on her bike before I could say, "Fuck you."

Damn, she made me so hot. I've been masturbating to fantasies containing her image all week.

All I wanted was anonymous sex—which I got. Then I spilled my fantasy about being paid for sex and well, now I'm meeting this woman I barely know in a bad part of town to have her pay me for sex. I'm crazy. I haven't told anyone about last Saturday night's encounter or tonight's rendezvous. My roommate would freak out if she knew. She is a much more sensible lesbian than I am. She never has one-night stands, except with men whom she already knows when she's in between serial lesbian monogamous relationships. She never goes to "bad" parts of town except in groups during the daytime. She believes sex between women should be about love, and I agree with her—in theory. But sex is sometimes just about sex. And sometimes, when you are really, really lucky, sex is about fantasy.

I decide public transportation is a bad idea and take a taxi one block from where I am to meet the John, or Jane, as it were, and I walk the difference. When I get to the corner it is five minutes to eight and no one is there. No "other" hookers, no red Chevy, just a grandmotherly Asian woman who looks at me and frowns disapproval while muttering something in what I think is Mandarin. I walk the three corner slabs of concrete from the intersection up Fifth Avenue and back to Washington. I let my hips swing as I walk, exposing my legs with long, slow runway steps. A car of frat boys honks and one of them yells something about how big his dick is. I ignore them and hope my Jane shows up before the frat boys return, the cops come, or worse yet, a pimp or real hooker arrives to demand I get off of their territory.

I feel cheap and that excites me. She really is going to pay me for sex. Since that's the fantasy, and I don't know her, I won't have to give her back the money. I may have it framed and hang it over my bed.

I lean up against the building, sticking my left hip out and allowing the tight skirt to pull across my ass. I see a red '50's Chevy coming down Fifth Avenue. It slows to a crawl, then makes the corner onto Washington. My heart is racing as I slowly walk over. When I get to the car, I lean into the open passenger's window, bending at the waist so my butt sticks out and she gets a great view of my cleavage. "Hi. You looking for a party?" I look into her piercing blue eyes as I speak.

She looks back at me as if she's never seen me before. "Yeah, I'm looking for a party." Her lean body, in tight blue jeans and a white T-shirt, is pinned to the driver's seat by a lap belt. I can see the bulge of a big dildo.

"You a cop?"

"No, I'm not a cop." Her hands grip the steering wheel and the well-developed muscles in her forearms flex. I notice how her white T-shirt clings to her tiny breasts. And how her rolled-up sleeves expose her firm biceps. "How much for a party?"

"Depends on what you want."

"I want to fuck you and taste your pussy. How much?"

Her words send a jolt through me and I can feel myself getting wet. I have no idea how much to charge or what this James Dean dyke would be willing to pay. "Seventy-five bucks," I say, considering what dinner would have cost her and adding in she wouldn't be getting fucked if she'd taken me to dinner.

"Get in," she says as she pulls her wallet from her back pocket.

I open the door and slide into the seat next to her. She hands me three twenties, a ten, and a five, replaces her wallet, and pulls away from the curb. I clip my seat belt and wonder if I should have planned for a place to go to have sex.

"So what's your name, sugar?" I ask, stroking her bare arm.

"Jane," she answers, completely deadpan.

I almost laugh, then say, "And what's my name?"

"Trixy." She smiles, cocking an eyebrow at me.

"You're a mind reader, baby." I wink at her, then run my tongue along the curve of her biceps. She smells lightly of spicy musk and leather.

By now she's made a number of turns and I have no idea where we are. Factories and warehouses, some of which look long abandoned, line small streets badly in need of repair. She pulls into an alley between two large buildings covered with urban gang graffiti between smashed windows. The road's about ten car-lengths long and spills into a square paved lot surrounded on all sides by similar abandoned factory buildings. There's an open loading bay with the doors missing on the far left-hand side of the back building. She drives the car into it, turns off the lights, cuts the ignition, and leaves the radio playing. I undo my seat belt.

I know from the movies that it is my responsibility as the hooker to get this party going. I reach over and undo her seat belt. I lean into her and kiss her neck, running my tongue up to her ear. I reach between her legs and stroke the fake cock between her legs, pushing hard to make sure there's pressure against her clit. "Oh, you're so hard—feels like you're ready to fuck."

She grabs the back of my head and pulls me toward her, burying her face in my cleavage. Her tongue plunges between my breasts and she licks up to my right nipple. Her teeth lightly bite into my flesh.

"Yeah, I'm ready," she says as she releases the hold that she has on my hair. "Bend over the middle of the seat," she orders as she slides the bench seat as far back as it will go.

I get up on my knees so I'm facing the rear window and bend over the back of the front seat. She positions herself behind me. Her hands pull my tight skirt up over my hips, exposing my bare cunt and the straps of my garter belt. She pushes my legs apart and kneels between them.

"You got a condom?" I ask.

"Yeah," she says as her finger plunges into my wet cunt.

I groan as she adds another finger. "Wet already. Umm." She withdraws her fingers. I hear her putting on the condom and the sound of lube squirting from a bottle, and then she positions her cock against my cunt. Her left hand grabs my hips as she slides into me with one long stroke. I moan. Her cock is huge.

"You feel so good inside me, baby." I try to say things I think a hooker would say to a trick.

She starts to fuck me, sliding in and out with an easy, slow rhythm, using both of her hands to hold my hips in place. I can't help but moan as she increases the speed and force of her thrusts. "Oh yeah, fuck me, baby." I groan as she slams into me. I am holding on to the back of the seat, my arms thrust along the top edge, my fingers gripping the cloth. "Give it to me. Yeah. Like that. You are so good." I feel like I am in a bad '70s film, but she really is a good fuck. Her strokes are steady and smooth, sending chills of pleasure through me. This is exactly what I wanted.

I hear the snap of a latex glove and then her finger pokes at my asshole and slides inside. I groan and push back hard, surprised and delighted by this unexpected addition to the game, unable to control my deep sigh of pleasure.

"You like that?" She adds another finger as she speaks. "Yeah. You like it."

The cock slides completely out of my cunt. There is a pause, then the shock of cold slippery lube on my butt. My rapid heartbeat is matched by my rapid breathing. She spreads the lube over and into my asshole with her gloved hand, then positions her cock-head against my opening. She pushes the tip in and I squeal at the sensation. "Hey, you'll have to pay me extra . . ." Before the words come out of my mouth, she's effortlessly buried her cock in my slippery lubed asshole. The twinge of pain is intense, then eases as she slides in and out. She works her cock in a circular motion, then in and out. I groan and meet her thrusts with my hips. The shaft is thick and my asshole feels full.

"Talk to me, Trixy."

I can barely think, but I manage to moan, "Oh, baby, your cock feels so good buried in my ass." She rams into me harder. I gasp, spitting each word out as if it was a sentence to itself, "I've never had anyone fuck me this good."

She groans and without losing the rhythm of the fuck, snaps off the glove and places her fingers onto my clit. She starts to work it—

rubbing gently in a circle while her cock fucks me in a steady rhythm.

"Yeah, like that." I groan as I completely slide into the fuck.

Her other hand grasps my hair, pulling my head up and back. She grunts and groans as she continues to slam into me. Her fingers firmly rotate on my clit. She leans forward so her breasts are on my back and her face is near my neck. In a steady voice she says, "Give it to me. Come for me, Trixy."

I don't want to come, and I momentarily make the myriad collection of sensations she is giving me stop, but her words push me over the edge and I come, thrusting my hips back at her as she slides her fingers deep into my cunt. She releases the death grip on my hair and wraps her arm around my waist, clutching my bucking body against hers. I am clinging to the seat for dear life, my face against the rough material. I can feel it burn against my skin.

The orgasm shakes my body but more importantly it rejuvenates my soul, filling me with energy, light, and power. For a moment that feels like slow motion, we are joined by our animal passions in a deep primitive act of pure pleasure. I am screaming with sheer ecstasy. Then it is gone, over, done. I am a little shaken as the last spasm of my orgasm passes, and she removes her fingers and cock.

"Get in the back. I want to eat your cunt," she says, and her matter-of-fact tone helps me shake off the last traces of ecstasy left by my recent orgasm.

A thrill shoots through me. My cunt begins to throb anew. "You spent your seventy-five bucks, baby. That little anal action was a bonus. You want to taste my pussy, you'll have to lick your fingers or give me twenty more." Her eyes flash with amusement as she pulls out her wallet and hands me a twenty. I tuck it into my cleavage.

"Now I'll get in the back."

I crawl over the seat, letting her get a good long view of my ass and pussy, and lie down with my back against the door. She joins me—half kneeling on the floor, half on the seat between my legs. She lowers her face, resting her cheek on my thigh.

"You're so wet," she says. She takes a deep breath. "You smell like sex."

She slides her face up my thigh and the tip of her tongue ever so lightly searches the folds of my outer labia, grazing over my clit hood, then finally plunging into my wet pussy. I moan as her tongue enters me and pushes against the opening of my vaginal walls. I try to spread my legs farther apart—to give her better access to my cunt—but the car seats prevent me. She pauses only long enough to throw my right leg over her shoulder; I rest my foot on the back of the seat.

She licks straight up from my opening to my clit. "Umm, you taste like sex, too." She places her mouth on my mound, centering her tongue on my clit and working it in a tight circular pattern.

I groan and start to move my hips, countering her tongue strokes. She slips two fingers inside me. I shift to a back-and-forth pumping motion and her free hand grasps my left hip. Her fingers dig into the flesh, forcing me to remain still—intensifying the sensation by restraining my movement.

She slips a third finger inside me and concentrates the friction of her strokes against my top wall. She increases the force of her tongue work. I smell my pussy, her sweat, and the faint scent of spicy musk and leather. I close my eyes, grabbing her short dark hair, and allowing the waves of orgasm to flood through me. My hips jump forward as I come and she captures the flesh of my labia between her teeth. I am suspended in time. My heart races, but I feel as if I am outside of space, moving between the lines that make up reality. The muscles inside my vagina contract and spasm as my mind explodes with pure pleasure. Then it is gone, over, done.

We are both breathing hard. The scent of sweat and sex permeates the air. It is only when my neck begins to ache from my awkward position against the door that we finally put ourselves back together, giggling as we climb into the front seat. I smooth my skirt down over my hips and buckle in. She hands me a bottle of water before she backs out of the warehouse into the open space and turns the car around. At the street entrance she waits as she watches me apply fresh lipstick. She reaches across the seat to stroke my hair, then my cheek, and leans over to kiss me softly on the lips. She tastes like me. She returns both hands to the wheel and speeds out onto the empty road.

She drops me off at the same corner that she picked me up on. We look at each other for a second before I open the door and get out.

"Hey, Trixy." I look back at her. She holds out a manila envelope. I reach into the car and take it. "See ya," she says as she pulls the car away from the curb and disappears into the night.

The envelope isn't thick and it is only sealed by the metal clasp. I open it and find a letter addressed to me along with a sealed, addressed, stamped envelope. The address on the envelope is a P.O. box with the name Nikki Canter. The letter reads:

I've enjoyed our exploration of your fantasies so far. I have fantasies also that I wish to explore. I want our next encounter to be about my fantasy. I hope you are interested in continuing our game. You can assume if you are reading this that I enjoyed myself during our last encounter.

You seem to understand the nature of desire and the way fantasies are constructed out of the material that is so distant from our reality or so close to our reality that it can be eroticized. Few people understand the depth of fantasy as I, and now, I believe, you do. I trust you because of this. That may be a misplaced trust, but I'm willing to take that gamble.

I want to know what it feels like to be a bottom, something I've never done. I want to be topped by butches like myself. Not that I doubt your ability to top me, or, for that matter, any other femmes' ability to top, but I would rather maintain our sexual relationship as it is—with your body under my hands. And I find the idea of being topped by butches rather exotic because I have only dated femmes.

If you are interested in continuing our game, open the enclosed envelope. It contains all of the information you will need. If not, drop it into the mail and I'll know we are done.

Karen

I grin and shove everything back into the manila envelope. "Taxi!" I yell to a passing cab. The cab comes to a halt and I jump in. "Jamaica Plain," I say as I settle into the seat.

Interesting, very interesting. James Dean has a fantasy of being topped by a bunch of butches. I force myself not to open the envelope again until I get home. The wheels in my mind are already turning, planning out our next encounter.

nine inches

krysia lycette villón

The last time Lydia had come to this club, her ex, Lu, had broken her zipper, finger-fucking her in the back by the main bar and the ATM machine. She was only here for Chancla's birthday. They all called the birthday girl that because the back of her head was flat, like her mother had hit her too many times on the back of the head with her chancla, or house shoe. Her inability to sit still was beginning to bring attention to the fact that she was less than entertained by the idea of this planned event. Lydia watched as Chancla, leading her New-Butch-of-the-Week to the dance floor, wobbled on her stacked heel boots. Too much sangria at dinner, apparently.

Lydia sat at one of the tall round tables by the window overlooking the street. She was perched on top of her leather coat, feet swinging awkwardly back and forth, searching for the metal ring that went around the base of the table for short people like her. She automatically looked for her cigarettes, only to remember smoking was no longer allowed inside and that she didn't smoke anymore anyway. Her hand went deeper and deeper into the depths of her purse only to pull out a lighter. "Shit. Where the hell are they?" She glanced toward the bar and watched Rene, another one of her exes, juggle several beers and a Coke while checking out the prima donna girls coming up the stairs from street level.

"What is it with you and girls who look like they do speed, Rene? Could they look any more anorexic?"

"You know what, Lydia. Leave it alone, huh? I can't help it that I got good taste. They're some fine lookin' young ladies," Rene said, biting her lower lip and nodding in their direction. They smiled back.

"Eww, how did we ever get together when all you . . ." Lydia's hand swung up in triumph, producing her tea tree toothpicks. "Aha, here they are!"

"Quit smoking again?" Rene put the beers down, holding on to her Coke.

"Three days, now. This is the hardest time yet."

"Well, good for you. It made you smell bad."

"You know what, Rene? Here. Take this money for the damn drinks and go sit over there."

"This is why things didn't work out between us. You're such a bitch." Rene gave her a smile, a wink, and sauntered over to the blond waif with the flat chest and hard nipples.

"And because you're such a pig . . ." Lydia waved the toothpick back and forth with each word, flashed her best Barbie doll smile, and shoved the toothpick between her pearly whites. EsterandRaquel came back from the bathroom holding hands, shoulder to shoulder, as usual.

"Did Laura and Dez leave already?" EsterandRaquel asked in unison.

"No, they just went to get cigarettes."

They separated, as they were known to do, and sat on either side of Lydia. "We'll protect you. You can do it. Just resist!" Ester leaned over and kissed Lydia's right cheek. "And don't go outside with them when they smoke."

"You must want to go home." Lydia sat up straight so Ester could lean her head lightly against her shoulder. Ester and Lydia had been friends since college and had founded a support group for lesbians of color together. It had been an incestuous group for the most part, only the two of them made sure to keep their love interests outside of it, always admitting their mutual attraction for the other when one of them was newly involved or broken up. The timing always seemed off. And then Lydia realized she was more attracted to Ester being attracted to her than wanting to actually be with her. Ester was a sweet woman. A good friend. A lesbian. Lydia was realizing she wasn't. Not the common updated definition of one, anyway. She was slowly realizing that she wasn't into this whole woman-loving-woman thing. She liked her women . . . well . . . manly, for lack of a better term. Strong. Masculine. Aggressive.

Ester raised her head from Lydia's shoulder and leaned over to get the beer Rene had left for her and Raquel to share. They shared everything.

"No, I'm okay," Ester said. "I mean, it's been a whole month already. I don't really miss her. At least this place doesn't really remind me of her too much." Lydia fixed her ponytail while her eyes strained far to the left to look at the area in which she last stood, Lu pressing her up against the back wall, teeth on her neck. "We only came here once together. You know, just that one time." Ester laughed loudly enough for other patrons to hear her over the music and smile with her. She had a contagious laugh. Raquel was laughing, too. They high-fived each other in front of Lydia's face.

"Quite literally!" Raquel squealed and made a gesture toward her crotch of her zipper being stuck while smacking the table with her other hand. Their laughter had started to sound the same. They both had the same perfume on. Wore the same hairspray. Did each other's nails. Probably had on matching bras. Lydia smiled painfully and excused herself to the bathroom.

"I'll be right back." She heard Ester say she would give her a ride home if she wanted, but she knew she had to stay. Chancla would never forgive her.

She walked past pool table number one, up the stairs, and past pool table number two. She glanced just long enough to see who was writing their name up on the chalkboard. It was that sweet Papi she'd seen at Good Vibrations buying a Mr. Softie. Lydia slowed her pace to wait for the woman to turn around, just to make sure. And when she did, Lydia almost walked right into the snack machine. Shit, she wasn't packing her softie. Lydia could see the shaft of a nine-inch dick running down the inside of her thigh even though she was wearing baggy jeans. She suddenly got hot around the neck and wondered if her face had turned red. There was a short wait to get into the stall, so she stood still for as long as she could. She looked at everyone around the pool table except this butch. She noticed that everyone, butches and others alike, had all caught a glimpse of what Papi was packing. Papi carried herself like she was her dick. Though Lydia wasn't much into arrogant butches, for some reason, this one seemed like the flavor of the month.

To keep from the temptation to look, she began fixing herself up. She took out her compact and lipstick and touched up. She wouldn't have done this in the bathroom anyway because there were too many men coming in and out to use the urinal. As she put her makeup back in her purse, she lazily glanced down at her shimmering cinnamon legs. She knew her legs looked great in this skirt, the kind that hit just below the knee. It accentuated her small waist and wide hips. She had covered herself with lavender body oil, so her shoulders would have a nice sheen to them. Feeling flushed, she decided to take the sweater off. As the sweater slid off her shoulders to reveal a matching tube top, the material grazed her nipples just enough to make her shiver, hardening and tightening the tips. She closed her eyes for a minute, listening to the music. The short Latin house run they usually did, followed by dance versions of popular R&B songs, was just beginning. When she opened her eyes she realized this butch was standing behind her, looking at her.

"Um, the bathroom's free," Papi said. She was bigger than Lydia realized. Taller, maybe five feet nine or ten. She had a big chest and the sports bra wasn't doing much to hide it. Her arms were covered with tattoos of Chicano art, half-naked Aztec women on both upper arms, and a tribal-looking band around the thickness of her right forearm.

"Oh, thanks. Does that one go all the way up to your shoulder?" Lydia traced her fingernail up the butch's right arm to her shoulder.

"Yeah, it does." She pulled up the sleeve of her faded United Farm Worker T-shirt.

"The sun is magnificent. And this one . . ." With her left hand Lydia grabbed Papi's right wrist, then wrapped her right hand around the muscle of the forearm. She stroked her arm up and down. "Now this one, this is nice. You designed it yourself?"

"Yeah, actually I did. Designed it in about an hour. Got it done a year, maybe a year and a half ago, now." Papi stood there, almost expressionless except for the heat in her eyes.

"Mmm. Nice. Thanks for showing them to me." As Lydia released her grip on her arm, she began to back up first into the doorway of the bathroom and then into the stall. Papi began to walk forward with her. "Are you finished with your game?" Lydia whispered, the music almost drowning her out.

"What?" Papi wrinkled her brow and then smiled. "Oh, yeah. The game. Yeah. Finished."

"You lost?"

"I guess." Papi smirked.

They closed the stall door behind them. Lydia locked it, draping her sweater over her purse and hanging her purse on the coat hook. Every time they took a step anywhere, toilet paper could be heard and felt dragging across the floor. They avoided the toilet itself and leaned back against the left wall of the stall. The place smelled like urine no matter where you turned your face except . . .

"Here. Oh, you smell so good." Papi buried her face in Lydia's neck. Licking, kissing, sucking, biting. Lydia pressed her small frame into her so she could feel her through all the layers of clothing between them. She, too, buried her face into this butch's neck. Sucking, sucking. Papi bent her knees a bit so they could be face to face, hot wet lips moistening her own almost immediately. Lydia pulled her skirt up, throwing her right leg over the left hip of her lover. Papi caught it and quickly ran her hand up the length of Lydia's thigh. "Aaaaah. You're not wearing any fuckin' underwear. Mmm. Nice." She went to reach in to touch Lydia, but Lydia caught her hand.

"No, not your hand, baby. Unless you got a glove in your back pocket." She let her finger circle the round shape outlined in Papi's right front pocket, then let her hand caress the length of her hard cock. Papi grinned, dropped Lydia's leg, and spun her around to face the wall. She listened to Papi undoing her belt, unbuttoning, unzipping, taking out, ripping open, rolling on. Lydia peeked around just in time to see her squirting on some lube and stroking her own shaft. She turned her face back toward the wall, leaned forward just a bit, and braced herself. Papi placed the head of her cock at Lydia's opening and slid it in just an inch or so, pulled it out and let the shaft run all the way down over her cunt, hitting her clit and drawing back slowly to her gaping hole. She slid it forward, letting the head pop in and out, groaning each time it popped back in. The bass of the music and Papi groaning was all that Lydia could hear. Papi held on to her hips and plunged her cock inside her, deep inside and almost all the way out. She began to move a bit faster, then a bit harder.

Lydia's ass cheeks rippled with each drive, her breath coming shorter with each grind. Papi began thrusting into her so hard Lydia thought she might be able to come just from the sound of the pounding alone. Lydia reached for her clit and rubbed it voraciously. Above all the other sounds, she focused on the slapping sound of Papi beating on her pussy. As she began to climax, her legs started to tremble and finally almost collapsed, cum dripping down her inner thighs. Papi held on to her hips tighter and pumped her even harder. Lydia opened her mouth, but no sound came out, it felt too good. She could tell that her Papi came when she finally stood still, then started grinding slowly again inside her and let out a loud sigh. She pulled out slowly. With her back still to this butch, Lydia pulled her skirt down, smiling, and waited. Lydia could feel Papi's eyes on her back. Then she heard the sound of rubber slapping, retucking, rezipping, rebuttoning, and the stall door opening. She heard the water running in the sink and footsteps walking away. Lydia relocked the door and cleaned herself up as best she could; she really didn't want to wash away any of the sweet smells wafting from her skin. When she opened the door, she saw Rene leaning against the sink counter, a sly grin on her face.

"You know why else we didn't work out, Lydia?"

Lydia turned on the water, washed her hands, shook them off, and looked around for some paper towels. She walked over to Rene, grabbed her T-shirt, and wiped her hands off on it.

"Why's that, Rene? Because I'm a slut and you're a bad lay?" She kissed Rene's cheek and patted her ass on the way out the door. She looked to her left out onto the balcony and saw Laura and Dez laughing and smoking their cigarettes, then looked to her right beyond pool table number two to the outside patio and saw the butch tugging on a stick of her own. Papi turned toward Lydia as she was exhaling and shyly smiled. She held a cigarette up in offering.

Lydia laughed and nodded, walking toward her. "What the fuck."

Coming Out of Left Field

M. Christian

Gerry:

Daddy used to call me his Little Princess. Yeah, I know, everyone's daddy calls his little pigtailed daughter "princess." But I always felt that Daddy really meant it with me. I'd lie down on the dull yellow sofa in the living room, my feet in his big lap, and he'd rub them for hours as he watched wrestling, baseball, or something manly and tough like that. Birthdays were candy and jewelry, dresses and fancy hairdos (I was the first girl in Miss Graves's fifth grade class to sport a small aircraft-endangering bouffant). Christmas was nasty, sugary perfume (but, oh, I loved it), fancy new shoes as shiny as a new penny, and books with pretty girls, castles, and unicorns on them. I'd lie in bed and just stare at those girls for hours, imagining all their servants, their wonderful gowns, and the princes that sooner or later would come knockin'). In third grade, when other girls said they wanted to be mommies, I said I wanted to be a Lady. And when Miss Graves asked us to write down our future careers, and other students wrote things like "mommy," "doctor," "a teacher, like Miss Graves" (the little suck-up), I put down in lovely flowing letters: "Her Right Honorable Princess of All the Land, Lady Geraldine Kowalski the First." The others got A's and I got a C; but I didn't care, because when I got home there was Daddy. "How'd school go today for the most lovely princess in all the land? Many princes fall at your feet? Unicorns follow you home? Dragons spell your name across the sky?"

In the seventh grade, when the other girls were discovering boys, I spent all of October putting together my royal attire for the Halloween dance: conical hat, scarves, and a beautiful gown of gold and red. I even had a fucking train, if you can believe it, and Shirley Baston to carry it for me. I took first prize, and even got my first kiss from Shirley Baston in the cloakroom—my royal reward for such a job well done.

But then college hit me, like a speeding copy of *Our Bodies, Ourselves*, right between the eyes. I went in with tight sweaters, bright pink nails, perfectly polished Mary Janes, and hair just so, all panting and eager to meet the Prince of my budding young dreams . . . except that in all my fantasies the prince had boobs just a tad smaller than mine (about Shirley Baston's size, or so), nice tight muscles, and down between those strong legs nothing at all like a penis. I didn't really have a word for what I was, but then I hadn't needed anything but "princess" before, so there didn't seem to be any reason to change.

Like I said, I went in a Prom Princess and came out the tightly wrapped radical. No nail polish for me, bare (i.e., ugly) nails were the way to go. I razored my lovely long hair into choppy spikes. No pretty loafers, Mary Janes, or heels. Instead I marched around the campus with the rest of them in sensible (and ugly) brown work boots. I joined in protests, roasting Barbie and chanting "Real

Women Aren't Plastic," or something that rhymed better, at any rate. It was a good (if ugly) time: all us women together, defeating the patriarchy, reclaiming our natural (if ugly) womanhood.

As Barbie melted, her hair stinking something awful (somewhere deep inside me a little voice whispered "she'd look better in a white tennis outfit; that pink cocktail dress just doesn't work"), I met Barbara. It was love, a love based on mutual respect; an equal, completely logical parity between two young lesbians. That's what we agreed on then, and we still do today. I nodded along during the hours on hours on damned hours of discussion about what we are and what we were doing and where we were going (fairly, always fairly) because, well, I was really horny and I needed to get laid.

Not that I don't love Barb; I really do. It's just that I'm not just a woman. Deep down inside me, there's a dark shameful secret that I've kept from her for the seven years we've been together. I'll get there, don't worry; just be a little patient, okay? It's my story and I can keep you waiting if I want to.

Like I said, I love Barb, no question about that. I love her from her mousy brown dull-as-dishwater hair, right down to her (sigh) boring, sensible brown shoes. Hell, she even wears gym socks!

The relationship was okay for those first years. I was a girl and she was a girl; we had sexual relations based on mutual respect; and I was getting laid pretty regularly. We'd get undressed, crawl into bed, and spend five minutes or so kissing. Barb would kiss and fondle my breasts, then it would be my turn to kiss and fondle her breasts. Then she'd spend four or so minutes manually stimulating my genitalia (that's what she called it, firmly believing that any other word was a creation of the oppressive patriarchy), then I'd spend about five minutes stimulating hers. She could orgasm, and then it would be my turn. They were nice, those first young woman orgasms under scratchy blankets in our first damnably cold flat near the Commons. But now . . .

We don't have sex, we negotiate mutual pleasure exchanges. At Christmas, we decided that we would both give each other exactly

$50 in gifts. (A helluva lot of thick books, sensible clothing, and scented candles. Our place started to smell like a French whorehouse even if it looked like some monk's cell.) Our bills are split right down the middle, and if there's any discrepancy we alternate who picks it up. Our chores are based on equality of time and effort, though I think Barb gets the short end of the stick on that because she's the one who spends hours over a calculator figuring it all out.

We're fair, we're equal, we're mutual, and we're respectful. It's good, but . . .

It started in little ways at first. Just experiments that felt wonderful at the time but, man, did I feel the guilts after. I started to window shop, wondering how that gorgeous frock or that magnificent dress would look on me. I started to look at shoes, sometimes even putting them on and walking around the store, practicing a sultry walk in heels, a frilly prance in flats. I snuck into Victoria's Secret just to stare at the satin, silk, and lace, but when they asked me to sign up for their catalog I put down a fake address. Barbara wouldn't understand.

Then, a few days ago, while Barbara was away at a Womyn's Retreat (Or was it Wimmin's? They spelled it in some kind of weird way that I never could get straight), I really sinned. Lesbians don't have hell, but if they did I'd be roasting there with demons tearing at my new hairdo, picking at my painted nails, tearing up my bright pink skirt. I had it all figured out, the perfect way to cover up my pink and satin sins: before she got back, I'd wash the spray out of my hair, hide the new clothes under the bed, and carefully peel off my new fake nails.

Then something happened. Walking down the street in my new frock and frills, my done-just-so-hair bobbling along with me, heels doing a sweet click-clack-click on the pavement, someone whistled. Wheee-whoo—you know, a wolf whistle. A truck driver kind of thing, a form of patriarchal auditory oppression. I swung on my heels, ready to dispense female-empowered outrage on this form of behavior (nearly sexual assault, when you think about it), when I saw the whistler. First I saw a little battered-up roadster stopped at a light, all dents and scratched paint. Behind the wheel was a lesbian . . . no, a dyke, right down to flannel shirt, buzz-cut hair, and big hands. She smiled and winked. Then I did something I hadn't done for years, not since those days on Daddy's knee. I blushed. I giggled.

Well, right there something had changed. I couldn't hide in the closet anymore.

On the way home, the feeling boiled up. No way in hell could I cram it all back down into my fair and equal life. Fuck that, I didn't want fair and equal; I was a Princess, dammit! I was the most lovely Princess in all the fucking land. I didn't do fucking dishes, I was a Princess, for chrissake, and I had them done for me. I wanted someone to open the car door for me, to call me "Ma'am." I wanted to dance, to feel strong arms around me. I wanted a night on the town with my handsome stranger, someone who'd take care of me, treat me right, bring me chocolates and flowers and dance the night away. I wanted to be pretty and witty and wild. I had enough of fucking Maria, and I wanted out of the convent.

I wanted to get thrown on the bed and just plain, hard as anything, fucked. I didn't want to worry about someone else for a change, whether they were getting as much as they were giving. Princesses don't do, they get done, and I wanted to get fucked good and hard. I wanted to get tossed onto the bed, my skirt lifted up, my white lace panties ripped off (my handsome beau would always buy me more) and totally, mind alteringly done. I wanted to look down and see a mean-as-nails butch between my thighs, face buried in my pussy. No "genitals," but the wet, pink thing I have between my legs. I wanted to strip for my lover: dress, shoes, bra, hose, panties, bare as the day I was born, watching her tough face soften with lust, watching her hand dip down between her own strong-as-corded-steel thighs to stroke herself. I wanted to be a Princess again, on Daddy's knee. I wanted to be a frilly, femmy slut for my own, private, mean-ass dyke. I wanted to be a girl, on my knees before my dyke, sucking her black plastic cock because she liked to watch those other pretty pink lips at work. I wanted to get wet from a kiss. I wanted to be called "darling," and "slut," and yeah, deep down, I wanted to be called "Bitch" every once in a while, while my dyke grabbed my hair and pushed me down to her own cunt.

Washing the spray out of my hair, I felt suddenly angry. Sure, I was angry at Barbara and her "fair," "equal," and boring life. But I was also angry at myself for not having the pussy to stand up and scream at the top of my girlie lungs: "I'm a femme! I like to wear dresses, makeup, and have my nails done. I love to dance in fancy shoes, and get wonderfully, powerfully fucked by someone strong, dark, and handsome."

I looked around our little efficiency apartment, at the books, the posters, the row of sensible shoes, the browns and grays hanging in the closet, that ugly goddess figure on the mantelpiece. A nice enough place, but not the castle of a Princess.

It was too damned appropriate, even though it was a little mean. But I was a pissed-off Princess, forced to wear dowdy dresses and comfortable but hideous shoes for way too long. One thing about all that sensible stuff, it sure made packing real easy. There was jack-shit I wanted to take.

Lipstick was just too right, you know what I mean? Besides, it was in my hand and a mirror just seemed like the perfect place to write my goodbye note. I hoped Barbara would understand, but a part of me didn't care; I was just too happy to have finally admitted who I really was down deep. LOVE YOU, SORRY, BUT I NEED TO GET IN TOUCH WITH MY INNER FEMME.

I locked the door, put the keys through the mail slot, and walked away. Outside, it was cool—a typical Northeast fall late afternoon—but I didn't feel the cold. I was the happiest little girl in all the world. The cold just meant I'd have to get myself a nice new coat, maybe something with a fake fur collar? Oh, and shoes, got to get some new shoes . . . and a new dress. No, LOTS of new dresses, and accessories, lots of accessories. Got to dress the part, right?

Paula:

"Do you know who these boots belong to?" Sarah, the collective's part-time accountant, part-time stock person said, holding my freshly polished Doc Martens. The ones I'd finally started to break in. I felt flushed, hot.

"N-no. I don't know. Sorry." I hated the stammer, but it came out anyway.

"Gabby found them next to the lockers. I thought you might know who they belong to." Did she look at me a bit too long?

"Sorry. Maybe one of the Soko guys left them behind." The Soko brothers did a majority of the collective's shipping. They were notorious, if anything because they were the only men we had regular dealings with—aside from customers, that is.

"That's probably it, thanks," Sarah said, smiling woodenly and stepping out, leaving the office door open.

I waited a good ten minutes, just staring at my monitor, looking at but not seeing the Excel spreadsheet I'd been working on, before I got up and closed the door. Depression filled my shoulders with lead, made me feel sleepy. I wanted to go home, just crawl into bed. I loved those boots. It had taken me so much courage to order them, pick them up, and spend endless late-night hours breaking them in. Even if the Soko brothers didn't take them I couldn't claim them unless someone left them out where I could get to them. Not that there was much chance of that. Ever since I'd stupidly left my copy of *Doc and Fluff* out in the break room, Sarah had been looking at everyone—especially me—with a half-suspicious eye. Just waiting for someone to step forward and take the blame. It was dumb to bring them, but I was tired of having them but not being able to enjoy them—even if it was just taking them with me off to lunch, or after work, to stroll the dark streets away from the collective.

The rest of the day crawled by. I toyed with the idea of logging on and ordering another pair but didn't, remembering how expensive they were, how much skimping and scraping it took me to afford them—let alone how long it took me to break them in, the blisters and trying to explain my sudden limping.

Better to lie low for a while. Play it safe.

Finally it was five and I left, timing it just right to slip past the rest of the collective members on my way out. I can't really explain it, but I felt ashamed as well as stupid, as if they'd already caught me. God, I could already imagine the processing. How could I let them and their ideals down, how could I support the wearing of such dominance symbols, such patriarchal, oppressive sexual devices in a place dedicated to the safety and support of women—let alone that mean-ass black boots were such an obvious lesbian cliché—and all the rest of it.

I took a long walk. I love Boston in the fall: the chilly air, refreshing without the headache of snow. After an hour or so I was getting a little hungry, so I stopped in to a little all-night sub place. I smiled a bit as I went in, lucky that the members of the collective never, or very rarely, ventured this far south and so wouldn't see me commit another PC crime: the consumption of animal flesh.. "What can I do you for, bud?" the kid behind the counter said, lifting his head for just a second from the motorcycle magazine he was reading.

"Ur . . ." I said, suddenly frozen in place, his confusion making me feel strange inside. "I'm still thinking about it."

"Sure, pal, take your time. Hey, who do you like in Sunday's game?"

Three thoughts running together, I was almost dizzy. What was he seeing?

I had on my long down coat, more than padded enough to hide my tits, my hair was cut really close (just had it done the other day), and stress had deepened my voice. The second thought: I like it. Not being mistaken for a man, but the illusion of masculinity. I liked being called "pal" and "bud"; I just wished I could get him to call me "sir."

The third thought was: What game? Who was playing?

I leaned on the counter, tried to lower my voice even more. "You gotta root for the home team, right?"

He laughed and I expected him to slap me on the shoulder or something. "You got that right, man. You make your mind up yet?"

I ordered a gyro, Coke, and onion rings. The Coke might be a problem if anyone spotted me, but I doubted that. The place was much too heavy on the testosterone scale to make any of the collective women comfortable. I sipped, ate, and tried to pull myself out of my depression. I could go home, but since I was living with Judith WaterWoman, I doubted I could relax. Judith was okay, but she wasn't someone I could talk to about my . . . feelings. I had started to feel really bad lately, like the business with the boots and *Doc and Fluff*. There was something about it all that just . . . excited me. It was like the reaction of the kid in the sub shop. I should have been pissed that he took me for a man, but down deep it felt good. Not that I wanted to be a guy, mind you. I wasn't that far gone. It was more like a recognition of strength. I liked that. Strength.

I sipped my Coke and fell back into my favorite fantasy: leather jacket, leather pants, Harley Davidson between my legs, a beautiful girl behind me, arms wrapped tight around my chest. I imagined her lovely face turned just enough so she could rest her cheek on my leather-clad back. We never went anywhere in these fantasies, just down the road.

Sometimes I'd imagine stopping at a motel somewhere, roaring up to the check-in on my bike, knocking the kickstand down, leaning the heavy machine over. I'd get off, leather creaking, and then help my treasure off the back, making sure she didn't get dirty.

Fast forward. In a room. Man, she's pretty: lovely eyes, full mouth, blond—hey, it's my fantasy, okay?—nice little body, too. Pure Playmate, pure Miss October, and all mine.

I'd take my gloves off slowly, listening to the sounds the leather makes. She'd look at me, eyes widening over my toughness, and lick her lips.

The other glove. Make her wait: I put both on the night stand slowly, carefully. Then, and only then, would I turn to her. Reach down, finger under her chin, lift her head, look into her face, and see there some love, some affection, but a lot of lust. Without needing to check, I knew she'd be wet. Very, very wet.

I'd kiss her hard and thoroughly, and she'd purr like a happy kitten. Then I'd grab her hair, pull her head back, and kiss her again—even harder—and she'd purr like a happy tiger.

It was getting uncomfortable in that sub shop. Normally, I'd go further with the fantasy if I had a place to plug in a buzz. But there was something about that night, the shame of the boots, the kid's guy talk. I sipped my drink and absently played with a loose strand of onion.

I'd grab a chair, sit straddling it, and tell her to strip. This is where the fantasy changes, depending on my love of the moment: the clerk who works at Victoria's Secret, Miss December 1986 (who got me through a lot of my puberty), that blond girl on Ally McBeal (hate the show, love her—well, want her, at any rate), the girl in the red convertible stopped at the light.

The woman doesn't matter, the strip does. Slowly, carefully, showing herself off to me, revealing herself to her Butch: shoes, bra, stockings, panties, then bare as the day she was born. Oh, man, she's gorgeous.

But I'm stone, I'm tough. Hell, I'm "Doc." I'd stand up, tell my pretty little femme to "come over here, slut," then I'd unbutton my leather pants and pull out my tool. I found the perfect one the other day on some deep dark website. Big, but not too big, not too anatomically correct, and black as night. "Suck it," I'd tell her, and she would, because she's mine.

"Later, dude," the kid said, past me, heading toward the door—end of his shift I guess—"I hope they really kick ass on Sunday."

"You and me both, kid," I said, grinning ear to ear as he went out into the night.

It was getting late. I stepped out, welcoming the cold wind. I didn't want to go home. I sure didn't want to work in the morning, at least not the way I'd been feeling: scared, not able to be the person I was inside.

I stood on that corner for what seemed like ages, feeling the wind, feeling the walls closing in, feeling my fantasy would always be just that.

I wondered what my fantasy self would say. I imagined her standing next to me, real as life, butcher than anything.

The words came surprisingly easy. "Fuck it!" I screamed. "FUCK IT!" It came in a blast and I felt like hysterically laughing. Today I am a butch.

And I knew, hard-core and certain, what my new butchness wanted to do—a fantasy as powerful and appealing as that woman in that room: roar up to the collective on a thundering bike, black leather from head to toe, wicked grin on my stone-hard face. Up to the front doors, throwing them open and bellowing that I was gone, never to return, and that they all, every last one of them, could KISS MY BLACK LEATHER DOMINANCE SYMBOLS!

Later—maybe later—but for now I was a newborn butch in need of certain symbols, and so I headed off, wondering where I could buy some new Doc Martens this late at night.

Gerry and Paula:

The realtor was downstairs, setting up a folding plywood sign. There were only two people in the apartment itself: a beautiful woman in a very pretty red dress, lips painted vivid rose, hair spectacular, and a strong, stocky woman in tight jeans, a white T-shirt, a black leather vest, and a pair of stern, handsome black boots.

They arrived separately, meeting in the kitchen. They didn't say anything at first, just looking at each other for a long, slow minute. Finally, the beautiful woman in the red dress said, "Seems like a great place, don't you think?" smiling brightly. "Lots of light, hardwood floors, and nice closets. Never can have too many closets, right?" She was definitely a vision, polished, perfumed, and—most of all—drop dead gorgeous: a perfect femme.

"Yeah, it's quite a place," the woman in the black boots said, shy smile on her face. "Big bedroom, too. Lots of space." She was definitely striking, dark, leathered and—most of all—tough: a perfect butch.

"Big enough for two," the pretty woman said, imagining this perfect butch's strong hands around her wrists, holding them above her head as she brought her lips and, most of all, teeth to her neck—to bite.

"More than enough," the butch woman said, imagining this perfect femme in her arms, melted, covered in a shine of salty sweat.

"Hey, you want to get some coffee?" the femme said.

"Sure. Never can turn down a cup of joe," the butch replied.

"Great. My name's Gerry."

"Paula. You can call me Paula."

Leather and Laces

L. Elise Bland

My butch boy Wen loves to see me in boots, any kind of boots—cowboy boots, ropers, disco boots, fringed hippie boots, go-go boots, but most of all, high-heeled boots. During a trip to San Francisco, I bought a daring new pair that would make her little baby butch tongue flutter: cruel six-inch stiletto heels and black leather that reached up my legs to the gates of my pussy. Good old-fashioned nasty naughty boots. "Wen will be on her knees in no time at the sight of these babies," I thought.

The shoe salesman fumbled around with the leather and black laces draped loosely around my leg. He seemed more nervous than the usual clerk. I, as a Femme Domme, recognized his type—he, too, was a submissive.

"You're just like my boy back in Texas," I told him with a coy pivot of my stiletto that set the toe into a half-moon motion. His eyes followed appropriately. "She loves boots, too. They drive her mad."

My girlfriend Wen keeps up a stoic butch front, but teasing her with femme boots turns her into a yipping little chihuahua ready to lap up the leather and all the smooth skin above and beneath it. I love to feel her thick dark hair grazing down my leg as her lips massage my calves and ankles, her cock stiffening under the sole of my shoe.

The clerk worked nervously on the other leg, starting at the arch. He tugged on the laces and created out of my small, pale foot the most elegant talon in San Francisco. Then he proceeded to edge up my calf, all the while adjusting the corsetry to my frivolous specifications: "Tighter around the ankle. Yes, that's good. No, a bit looser at the knee, and straighter seams in front. I want it all to be exact."

When he had finished covering both my legs with the kidskin, I knew I had found the perfect boots—powerful and commanding sheaths for lethal femme swords. In traditional Texas gear, my shapely legs were sometimes too stubby in the two-steppin' cow-patty kickers, but now they had been galvanized into black leather icons for all to adore, especially my Wen. In the big boots, I stood six full inches taller than before, towering over the groveling man at my feet. Super Femme was ready for the annual San Francisco Drag King Ball.

"Come in Butch or High Femme drag," the flyer read. Perfect. I arrived as my own High Femme self, black leather bustier and fancy new boots underneath a long lace skirt. "Five dollar discount for those in costume," the flyer continued. I received no discount, for I was not in costume—just not flamboyant enough compared to the fluorescent wigs and groovy blue sunglasses of the other Femmes.

My concealed boots wandered through the crowd of exaggerated gender roles and personas. I felt quite invisible and lost in the foreign lesbian culture of Bay Area camp, but before long I heard a deep, even voice behind me, "You are a very beautiful woman." It was a butch, of course. She was attractive, rugged, a good decade older than me, and dressed in a white button-down shirt, dark tie, and black jeans.

Beautiful? How did she even notice me in that eclectic crowd? Could she see my hidden boots? Or maybe it was the way the heels made my ass stick out? The new boots were my little secret, or so I thought.

"Thank you." I nodded her way and took two hesitant steps back. My leather legs rubbed together under my skirt and the friction nearly started a campfire in my crotch. I was hot. When she offered me a cold beer, my burning pussy screamed out, "Sure, why not?" I warned her that I wasn't there to be picked up, just to watch the show and maybe hit a party later. Nothing serious. I had somebody back home.

"No problem, just come hang out with me," she said. "I'm here alone, from Tahoe." I followed her back to her much-coveted table in the balcony. I leaned on the railing and she sat down and made a place for our beers.

"You can take my seat," she offered gallantly and stood back up. "A lady like you should not have to stand, especially in high heels." She eyed the daggers that protruded from my hemline.

"No, that's okay," I declined. I had a better idea. I pushed her back into the chair playfully. "I'll just sit on you instead." I was such a tease. Before she knew it, I had nestled my ass deep into her lap where I felt an unmistakable stiffness; she was packing.

"You say you're from Texas." She shifted under me. "Can you ride sidesaddle?"

"Sure thing." Clever trick of hers, but I fell for it willingly. I turned to one side so that my right breast was pressed firmly against her left suspender, cushioned by her own large, but modest, chest. Her dildo struggled against my ass, opening my cheeks across her lap, polite and firm. I felt a rush of wetness through my lips and hoped I wasn't making a mess.

"So, did you dress up tonight?" I fondled the buckles on her suspenders, trying to ignore the cock that was practically penetrating me through my lace skirt. She was very butch indeed, but hardly a drag king. The strutting kings were much glitzier. My new friend was serene and settled in her masculinity, and had no use for a drawn-on mustache or furry cowboy hat.

"Nope. I'm always like this. I've been wearing this kind of stuff for as long as I can remember." Just what I wanted to hear. As much as I enjoyed over-the-top drag kings on stage, I loved a subtle, strong butch in private who knew good manners. This butch was a total gentleman. Hands to herself. She wasn't touching me at all, but when she reached over to get her beer, her denim bulge wedged itself even deeper between my lips. I felt like I was back in Texas being fucked sidesaddle doggy style. She had to know what she was doing, and she was certainly no bottom. I wasn't either, but we could work something out. Or maybe not.

To distract myself from her hard-on, I began to ask strings of questions: "So what do you do in Tahoe? How far is it from San Francisco? How's the scene out there? How's the weather? Do you want to see what I bought for my girlfriend? My new boots?"

Dangerous final question.

"Yes, please do show me," she said quietly.

What was I doing? I try to stay out of trouble, but it's just so hard. And it's always the hard stuff that gets femmes in so much trouble.

I glanced down at the floor. Tough steel-toed boots sat patiently alongside my stilettos. I guided her calloused hand across the top of my thigh just where the top of the leather boots met my skin. She played along, letting the lace skirt snag lightly on the hooks. The fabric slid outside and inside my legs, sometimes even brushing against my panties and pubic hair. Unmistakable wetness seeped through my lace onto the denim that concealed her cock. She would have been such a great fuck, I could just tell. I wanted her to bend me over that tiny cocktail table in my tall leather boots, her cock strapped securely in her button-fly jeans, edging its way into my pussy until I felt the metal buttons rubbing against my ass, the rough denim against my skin and leather, her firm grip on my shoulder that would send rivers of cum running down my new heels.

Yet nothing of the sort happened. Her hand moved slowly and surely in the designated areas. We didn't even look at each other. On stage, a king pranced around in a tiger-print shirt and feather headband, lip-syncing to a Loverboy song from the 1980s. Garage mechanics and Mafioso types hooted and hollered in the distance.

"There are a lot of masculine women out there," she said calmly, her hand still resting on my thigh. We watched the spectacle going on below, knowing that we didn't quite fit in. As a femme, I was not campy enough. Nor was she, as a butch. We were all too real, maybe even too real to get into the games. Or perhaps we weren't real at all. Who's to say?

I wore my boots on the plane back to Texas underneath the same long lace skirt I had moistened the night before. The boots were hardly comfortable; the leather made me sweat, the zippers on the inner thighs pricked my flesh occasionally, and whenever I tried to cross my legs in the cramped space, the laces came undone so that I had to sneak off to the even more cramped bathroom to re-tie them.

As inconvenient as it all was, I knew that I would get the proper rise out of my butch boy Wen once I got to the airport. She had been instructed to wear a starched white shirt, 501's, black cowboy boots, a hat, a bolo tie, and my favorite cock in her pants. Not her cushy packing cock, but the hard, ribbed one that could keep me going for hours. Most likely, Wen was also experiencing some discomfort with that stiff, oversized toy wedged into her crotch. I smiled at the very thought of our butch/femme dilemmas and stretched out my long boots under the seat in front of me to take a nap.

The plane landed right after dark. My hometown butch was waiting for me at the baggage claim area, her hands deep in her pockets to conceal her huge hard-on. I slinked over toward her in my pointed little hooves. She didn't even notice the footwear at first. She hugged me and pressed her oversized dick into my abdomen.

"I missed you. And I wore what you told me."

"I missed you, too, baby," I said as I tightened the bolo around her neck. "And I brought you back something from the big city. I'll give it to you once we get outside."

"Ok, I can't wait." She bowed her head humbly and shuffled her cowboy boots. "I've been so worked up all weekend."

"You aren't the only one." What a weekend. I thought about my boy at home alone. I thought about the drag kings and the butch. Then I thought about shopping for shoes.

Wen loves surprises. Her step quickened even more when she realized I was wearing heels, heels that maybe even blossomed into boots. With excited ease, she hauled my eighty pounds of luggage out to her pickup truck in the short-term parking and hoisted it up into the bed. She was such an attentive boy, and butch grace is always rewarded.

"No, Wen," I said. "Put those up in the cab for now. I want you to come help me with something first."

"But I want my present!" She fumbled with the bags longingly. Maybe she thought I had bought her some new leather suspenders or something.

I grabbed her by the belt and guided her to the back of the pickup. I unlatched the tailgate and scooted my ass up onto the shelf it created. Wen stood before me, impatiently shifting back and forth, her dark short hair splitting this way and that in the wind. In spite of the occasional conservative passers-by we began to kiss. The floodlights were shining down on us, but as long as nobody looked too closely, they would assume we were a straight couple.

I sat on the edge of the truck and spread my legs under the skirt. As always, my boy ran her hands up my calves to get up into my skirt, but this time, she didn't meet bare flesh at my knees. It was all leather. She continued up several inches, but the kidskin didn't stop there either. Intrigued, she yanked me closer to discreetly explore the bizarre new boots.

"This is your present, boy. Do you like it?"

I clasped my legs around her hips. Wen's hand had discovered a wet pussy that had fidgeted in leather boots for three full days with no release. Her cock grazed my thigh and landed on the outside of my lips. I shuddered.

"You'd better watch out, Wen, because I've been waiting all weekend for this. You know how worked up I get when I show off my boots. I drove all those west coast butches wild with them."

"I'm sure you did, baby. Just make sure you always come back home to me."

Wen was so sweet and unassuming. I scooted my legs higher and clasped her ass with my thighs. Her cock sidled in another three inches. As tough as I felt in my boots, I slumped into my butch's chest and moaned. I was finally at home and free.

"I want more," I told her. I recalled the Tahoe butch who had packed her lap so well. My boy's was even better because it was all mine.

Wen wanted more, too, but she apparently had other ideas. She pulled her cock out before even starting to thrust, knelt on the ground before the tailgate, and took my stiletto foot in her hand. "I want my present first. Then you can have yours," she told me.

"Hey, no fair to start fucking me and then stop!" I was shocked, not to mention frustrated. Although I loved foot games, I needed to come, and soon. How dare she stop in mid-fuck? "No fair!" I squealed again and tried to kick her.

"No fair to tease poor innocent butches with leather boots, either," she replied, dodging my sharp, pointed toe.

She took the back of my ankle in her mouth, turned me sideways in the truck bed and ran her hand up the back of my leg, resting it just above my knee. Her tongue and lips followed. Wen's favorite part of my leg is that back of my knee—my "kneepit," as she calls it—and even through leather, she can make it feel like she's eating me out. She licks deep and soft, fast, slow, and then presses her lips as hard as she can against the skin, her tongue inside the crevice that feels so much like a pussy under her touch. In fact, Wen can make any part of a woman's body feel like a sex organ.

Tonight my kneepit was wrapped in leather. While my boy's mouth worked its magic, her hand crept up between my ass cheeks and entered my cunt. I needed her back inside me. I started thrashing against the cold metal of her truck.

"Stop! I'll rip my skirt up on these boot hooks."

"Too late. I can't stop till I get you calmed down," she snarled and smiled. I had never seen this side of her before. She must have spent a long hard weekend alone.

Finally, Wen sat me back up, moved the delicate skirt away, and pressed her hips between my legs. This second time around, her cock didn't hold back. No more teasing. She let loose, all the way inside me, in one fast blow. I was so worked up that as soon as I felt the dildo hit my G-spot and the tough folds of her fly on my clit, I came. Not only did I come, but I squirted—for the first time in my life. I shot pussy juice down one long leather boot, soiling Wen's jeans along the way.

I was embarrassed, but also proud. My boy had done something to me that no one had ever been able to make me do before. And there's nothing like a "first time" to bond a couple for life.

I leaned back and sank against the metal of my butch's hard steel pickup truck, but much to my dismay, the big ribbed dick had abandoned me. Then, under the floodlights, I caught a glimpse of Wen easing back down my boots on her hands and knees, her still-wet cock dangling between her legs. She was on a new mission—to clean the shiny white cum from my fancy high-heeled boots. I propped myself up and watched her handsome bowed head swirl around my feet.

"Thank you, ma'am," she mumbled into the leather and laces.

Scoring

Jean Stewart

A lofted pass came rocketing across the mouth of the goal. Lee jumped up, reaching for the spinning black-and-white ball. For a moment, the soccer ball seemed to just hang there, inches from her outstretched hands. Then, the leather orb ricocheted off her fingers and sailed up over the crossbar. Seconds later, a body slammed into her. Hard.

Lee fell, entangled with the other woman in a sweaty, muddy jumble of arms and legs and hair. It was her own hair, she discovered, once she'd stopped rolling. She ended up sitting on her ass, stunned. Her ponytail scrunchie was somewhere, but no longer on the back of her head, and her long hair was blowing in the brisk October wind like a banshee's mane. Looking down, Lee found the other team's center lying in her lap.

Referee whistles were shrieking in the distance, and someone was yelling for Lee to get up and get ready for the corner kick. The center draped across Lee's legs lay there, breathing hard and staring up at her.

"Jeez," Lee commented in a sharp exhalation of breath.

She spent what seemed like a long suspended moment gazing into the deep, dark blue eyes of the enemy.

"You the wall I ran into?" the center asked, then reached up and caught a wavy length of the hair swirling around Lee's head.

Lee nodded. The movement made her dizzy, and she closed her eyes.

"Ought to have noticed you sooner," the center remarked.

Opening her eyes, Lee had a brief moment of disorientation. *Is she flirting with me?*

Lee frowned, studying the woman. Shining, straight dark hair fell over her eyebrows and ears, and beneath a spattering of mud was a ruddy, flawless complexion. Those features, combined with the mischievous blue eyes and black lashes, caused Lee to conclude that there were more than a few Celts in that family tree. Simply put, the woman was amazingly attractive, but by her brazen regard, Lee sensed that the center was also certifiably butch.

Reminding herself to be practical, Lee dismissed any thought of possibilities with this one. Turning her head, she abruptly tugged loose the strand of red hair the woman was admiring. Puzzled, the woman watched her, dark brows slightly furrowed, obviously not used to resistance.

In the back of her mind, Lee thought, *Get a clue.*

After all, she knew her own rangy frame and quiet toughness declared the nature of her own inclinations. She looked better with her hair long; she had heard it from enough women to accept what worked for her. For some reason, among women of her own sort, there never seemed to be any confusion about just what kind of lover she'd be. And strangely enough, she always attracted one type: what she privately called "barracuda femmes." Aggressive, high-maintenance, mini-skirted females who wanted Lee to dominate things in bed while they dominated Lee everywhere else.

Like Sherry, Lee thought ruefully. *Our last fight erupted when I told her to stop calling me "Geek." Okay, I make my living developing computer programs—and from my coworkers Geek is an affectionate nick-name. But that was never the way Sherry said it. She said it like I was some . . . soulless nerd.* Lee gave a deep sigh. *Over a year since then . . .*

"You okay?" the center was asking. "I think I fell on your head."

Unable to reply, Lee watched the tall, lean woman put a hand on her ribs, grimacing as she pushed herself to her feet and stood. Nearby, Lee could hear someone calling, "Hey, Jo! You giving her your number, or what? We're waiting for you guys!"

Unaccountably, though, Jo didn't move. She continued to just stand there, and dazed, Lee inspected the long, muscled legs before her. Lee noticed the painful-looking bruise on one knee, then became completely distracted by the sleek set of quadriceps that disappeared into a pair of baggy soccer shorts. Suddenly, she realized the woman had been speaking to her again, and was waiting for a response.

"What?" Lee asked faintly, trying to gather her wits.

"I said, 'Want a hand?'"

Lee glanced up and saw the open palm the woman was extending to her. *God, she's making me look like a wimp!*

Annoyed with herself, Lee declined, muttering, "Thanks. I can manage."

Quickly, she scrambled to her feet.

The earth seemed to tilt sideways and a cloud of black dots descended like a curtain across her vision. She felt herself swaying, then an arm encircled her waist. As Lee's face heated up, her head rapidly cleared. She glanced up, thinking, *Damn, taller than me*, then firmly, she pushed Jo away from her.

"Looks like I rang your bell, huh?" Jo said, giving a solicitous smile. "Maybe you ought to get a sub, and sit the rest of this one out."

Lee gave her an incredulous look. "Hell, no." *We don't have anyone else here who can play goalie, but, I'm not about to tell you that!*

With a rueful laugh, Jo said, "Well, you won't be able to stop me next time if you can barely stand up."

Leveling a hard stare at the woman, Lee managed, "Oh, yeah?" She touched her temple, too overwhelmed by the way her head ached to come up with any truly creative trash talk. She found herself reduced to, "Fuck you."

"Heh." Jo's eyes flashed. "I dare ya."

Chuckling, Jo turned and walked back toward the row of blue shirts milling restlessly farther out on the field. Without intending to, Lee watched her go, watched the slight, athletic swagger as she moved. The short, dark hair lifted as Jo glanced back over her shoulder and caught Lee's eyes on her.

"Lee!" a teammate called. "C'mon! It's a corner kick!"

Grumbling to herself about soccer dykes who thought they were the Goddess's gift to women, Lee strode over to the goal. She snapped, "I'm fine," to one fullback's concerned questions, and took her place at the white chalk goal line among the ranks of red shirts. Someone handed her the lost hair tie. Aggravated, she snagged her unruly locks, securing them in a ponytail again. Several players clapped her on the shoulders, congratulating her for breaking up the last goal rush, but Lee's head was still spinning. It was all she could do to keep her attention on the enemy.

The sun came out from behind the clouds. A gust of wind rustled through the yellow alders that flanked the end of the soccer field. Lee squinted at the row of blue shirts before her. Separated by twenty-five yards of green grass, the center returned her stare, grinning.

Off to the left side, the wing booted the ball, and Lee moved out into the rush of players jockeying for position. The ball was over everyone's head and zooming closer. From the corner of her eye, Lee saw Jo rising for a header. Lee timed her leap, then snagged the ball, curling it into her arm and body. This time, Lee spun in mid-air, angling her shoulders enough to fall away from Jo and miss the collision. She landed on her side, her limbs neatly tucked around the ball.

As she came to her feet and looked for an outlet pass, she saw several of her own forwards wide open at midfield. Knowing a good attack opportunity when she saw one, she quickly kicked the ball out to them.

"You're crazy, you know that?" someone announced. "Crazy . . . and I hafta tell ya . . . pretty damn cute."

Cute?! Feeling lashed, Lee turned and saw Jo getting up off the ground. *So what the heck does she think I am—Gabrielle to her Xena?!* Struggling to mask her temper, Lee said, "*All* goalies are crazy. Goes with the territory."

Jo gave an answering laugh.

As Jo moved by her, obviously intent on getting downfield, Lee added, "And in case you didn't quite pick up on it, I'm not your type."

Jo stopped and pivoted. Denim eyes raked over Lee. "Like you know what my type is."

Lee felt her cheeks heat under the suggestive gaze. "Take my word for it, it's not me."

The woman took a step closer, as if ready to debate the point, then glanced over her shoulder to check on the action downfield. Giving a sudden, soft curse, she broke into a run, calling out, "Later."

Lee put her hands on her hips and watched the center hustling to get in position for the next play.

Disgusted that she was allowing herself to be baited into cheap mind games, Lee bent her head and kicked dirt. She was behaving as if she were still in high school, for God's sake. This was only a Seattle recreation league, but she was three years out of college now, and some of the most talented post-NCAA players in the Pacific Northwest played within this league's ranks. Lee knew she needed to get a grip and compete like the veteran she was. Letting a good-looking center get under her skin was not part of her game plan.

The afternoon wore on, but there were only a few more goal skirmishes at her end. By the time the game ended, she'd preserved the shutout, even though her head ached terribly and she was feeling increasingly nauseous. Her red-shirted teammates were cheering and exchanging high-fives as they came off the field because a goal scored early in the first half had given them the win. Lee joined them, trying to enter into the camaraderie, but soon found it was impossible. She ended up sitting by herself on the bench, her face in her hands.

Someone smoothed a hand over the top of her head and handed her a water bottle.

"Thanks," Lee mumbled, accepting the plastic container.

It was only after she'd taken a long drink that Lee glanced up at the woman standing beside her. Surprised, she gazed into a pair of serious, dark blue eyes, not knowing what to say.

Jo seemed to read her weary confusion. "You probably ought to see a doctor."

"Probably," Lee agreed, keeping her voice noncommital.

"But you won't, will you?" Jo stated more than asked. "Too tough for that . . ."

Shrugging, Lee said, "I'm okay. Just a bump."

Decisively, Jo slipped the sport bag she carried off of her shoulder. "How about letting me be the judge of that?" Again, she wasn't asking a question.

Jo sat down on the bench beside her and reached for Lee's head with both hands.

"What the—?" Lee demanded, leaning away from her.

"I'm a resident at Harborview Hospital," Jo offered.

"You're a doctor?"

"Yep, now, hold still." Her fingers made contact with Lee's cheeks and gently, but firmly, she turned Lee to face her. "Hold still," she repeated, as Lee halfheartedly tried to pull free. Leaning forward, Jo looked deep into her eyes.

Lee felt stunned by the blue gaze.

Breaking eye contact, Jo murmured, "Pupils seem okay."

Her touch was professional and expert as she released Lee's thick hair from its ponytail and pushed her fingers through it, searching across the scalp. Just above Lee's right ear, she hit a sensitive spot, making Lee flinch.

"Ow!"

"Sorry," Jo said, then fingered the tender area with greater care. She leaned around Lee, smoothing aside strands of hair and peering intently at the side of Lee's head. "Don't suppose you'd agree to go in for a CAT scan?"

"It's just . . . a . . . ." Unaccountably breathless, Lee lost the end of the sentence.

Jo's hand slipped from the lump to Lee's cheek, then dropped. "It's a head injury," she corrected. Her eyes narrowed in annoyance. "And by your attitude, I doubt if it's the first time you've had one."

Her face felt hot, and Lee knew her guilty blush had confirmed Jo's guess. Anxious to escape all this disconcerting attention, Lee reached under the bench and grabbed her backpack. "I'll go home and put an ice bag on it," she assured Jo. "And I won't go to sleep. I know the drill." Standing up, she extended her hand, and Jo took it. They shook hands like cordial political opponents, all display with no sincerity. "Thanks for the free checkup, Doctor . . . ?"

"Morrighan," Jo finished. Lee tried to get her hand back, but Jo held on to her, looking directly into her eyes. "And you are Lee . . . ?"

"Lee Jackson."

There was another long moment of eye contact before Jo released Lee's hand. "Well, take care of yourself, Lee." With a nod of farewell, Jo pulled her sports bag back onto her shoulder, and began walking toward the parking lot.

On her way to her own car, Lee's eyes followed the confident stride of the woman in front of her. When Jo paused beside a blue Beetle, unlocking the driver's door, she turned and gazed back at Lee, obviously aware of Lee's steady regard. Bemused by her reaction to this woman, Lee gave a quick wave. A devilish grin spread across Jo's face before she waved back.

❧

Three months later, Lee allowed her coworkers to talk her into going out for drinks after a particularly hard workday. They'd just completed a grueling programming job, and the company that had contracted them was so pleased with the results they were setting up another project. As a reward, Lee's supervisor had given the entire programming team a generous bonus. Spirits ran high as the programmers hustled from their office building into the fine mist of January rain falling outside. They marched down First Street, kidding each other and laughing. By the time they had traveled the four blocks to the Flying Fish restaurant, all of them were wet and crowing about their good fortune.

Inside the Flying Fish, Lee immediately began snapping her fingers to the fifties jazz that was a mellow background to the crowd noise. A wealth of tantalizing aromas assaulted Lee's nose. Hungry, she tried to read a menu board posted by the door, but the younger, wilder members of the group grabbed Lee and pulled her with them, all the way up to the shining chrome and mahogany bar that graced one side of the restaurant.

"Martinis for everyone!" her friend Tom yelled, and the rest of the programmers took up the call.

Lee hunched lower. It was the dinner hour on a Thursday night, and the Flying Fish was filling up with patrons. To Lee's mortification, it seemed a host of curious faces were turning to see what all the noise was.

"I'll have a Red Hook if you have it on tap," Lee called when the bartender came their way.

Tom insisted, "Lee, you have to be hip, just this once, and have a martini."

"Yeah, c'mon, Jackson," Sally, one of the older women, said. "Let us get your square ass drunk."

The group roared with laughter.

"Ick. I don't like martinis," Lee protested, even as a big, stylish glass was pressed into her hand. "They taste awful!"

The group started making toasts, insisting Lee participate. They toasted the Seattle Mariners, then Lou Pinella. One by one, all the members of the programming team were hailed. By the fifth raucous, long-winded salute, many of the participants were reordering. Lee, however, was taking tiny sips, and had half a glass left. In her opinion, it was still too much martini. When Sally turned away to gossip with Tom, Lee leaned over and poured the remainder of her drink into the woman's glass.

By now, she was starving. Decisively, Lee parked her empty glass on the bar. She eased her way from the middle of the group and went back to examine the menu by the door. She was peering at a description of grilled salmon that made her mouth water, when someone walked over and stood beside her. Lee glanced up and froze.

"I've got a table over in the corner," Jo said, that same I-dare-you expression in her dark blue eyes. "Care to join me?"

Lee was speechless. Against her will, her gaze swept over the woman. In the three months since Lee had last seen her, Jo's short dark hair had grown longer. It curled over her collar in a stylish cut, gleaming even in the subdued lighting of the restaurant. Her lean figure was set off by a loose off-white sweater and a pair of very faded blue jeans. Between the waist-cropped sweater and the slouch-cut denim, there was a glimpse of a shadowed navel and tight abdominals. Feeling like a voyeur, Lee raised her eyes to Jo's face; she found the corner of Jo's mouth quirking up.

Embarrassed, Lee ventured, "Uhh . . . what was that again?"

Jo edged closer, invading her space. "How's the head?" The grin was gone, and her eyes were intense.

"Okay," Lee managed.

"Good." She reached for Lee's hand. "Come, help me finish my dinner."

Lee felt the slight tug, and then she was being led back into the restaurant. She glanced toward the bar, saw Tom watching them, and shrugged at him. Tom laughed and called, "I'll make your excuses," then motioned to her to be on her way.

Jo had slowed, her eyes flicking between Tom and Lee, watching this interplay. When Lee turned back to her, Jo gave a small smile, then drew Lee deeper into the restaurant, toward a table in the rear. Hesitating by the white linen tablecloth, Jo gave Lee's hand a slight squeeze before releasing it. They both slid into their seats, and Lee idly wondered what on earth she was doing.

Maybe that half a martini on an empty stomach is catching up with me . . .

"Here, help me with this," Jo was saying, pushing a plate closer to her. Most of the grilled salmon was untouched. "I filled up on bread and salad, waiting for someone."

Too hungry to refuse, Lee took the spare fork Jo placed in her hand. Wordless, she began eating, turning that last phrase, "waiting for someone," over in her head. Not sure what to think, she looked across the table at Jo and found she was being watched.

"Your face is full of questions," Jo told her. "I was waiting for a blind date. I think she stood me up."

Swallowing a mouthful of salmon, Lee blurted, "She must be nuts!"

Hearing the vehemence in her own voice, Lee quickly ducked her head. *I can't believe what comes out of my mouth when I'm around her!*

Lee spent the next few minutes absorbed in the food, while Jo casually explained how she had placed a personal ad in the Seattle Gay News. Curiosity and disbelief finally got the better of Lee, and she met Jo's eyes.

"How is it that someone like you needs to run a personal ad to get a date?"

"I only moved here in September, and doing my residency doesn't leave me with a whole lot of free time." Jo leaned back in her chair, watching Lee.

Disconcerted by the direct gaze, Lee returned her attention to her meal.

"And I'm particular."

The way she said it made Lee look at her again. The tone had been softer, almost inviting. And sure enough, there was a glint in

Jo's eyes that was unmistakable. Despite her initial alarm, Lee felt an answering rush of body heat that took her by surprise. All the same, she decided it was time to clear things up.

"Jo," Lee began, "you seem to have gotten the wrong idea about me."

"Really?"

"Yes," Lee stated. "Just because I wear my hair long doesn't mean I'm femme."

A throaty laugh burst from Jo. She leaned across the table and grabbed Lee's hand. "Oh, I know . . . *I know* . . ."

Lee was subtly aware of the pressure of Jo's warm fingers as they moved against her open palm. She tried to withdraw her hand and found Jo tightening her grip.

Jo smiled disarmingly, cocking her head as she looked at Lee. "And don't you think that's one of the greatest things about being queer? I mean, who's butch, who's femme . . . who's both? Talk about the mystery of the ages!"

Confused, Lee gave a brief nod. *What's she talking about— mystery of the ages?*

As if reading Lee's expression, Jo's laughter began again, lower and more intimate. "Hard to come up with a game plan, sometimes, huh?"

Not really clear if Jo expected an answer, Lee instead searched her eyes. Then she fumed at herself for how tongue-tied she was.

"Have you had enough to eat?" Jo asked.

Lee looked down at the empty plate before her and gave a brief nod.

"Okay. C'mon. As they say, the night is young," Jo stated, standing up and throwing some money on the table. She pulled a sleek black leather jacket from the back of the chair. As she thrust an arm in, she looked over at Lee impatiently when Lee didn't move. "Where's your coat?"

"Up in front, on a bar stool, I think." Lee blew out a breath. "I don't think—"

"We're all leaving, toots." As if he had been summoned, Tom came along an aisle between the tables, carrying Lee's forest green anorak. "Do you need an escort to your bus stop?" he asked Lee, then cast an arch look at Jo.

"I've got my car. I can give you a lift," Jo quickly volunteered.

Lee stood and Tom handed over her coat. "Thanks," she told him. "This is Jo Morrighan, soccer nemesis." As Tom and Jo both smiled, she informed Jo, "This is Tom Campbell, gay guy friend and coworker."

Tom gave Jo a mocking once-over. "I've been trying to hook her up with someone for months, but no wonder I've been wasting my time."

"Tom," Lee warned quietly. Irritated, she pulled her anorak over a shoulder.

"She's been avoiding me," Jo replied to Tom, her eyes on Lee.

"I have not," Lee said, keeping her gaze on the coat zipper as she maneuvered the ends together.

"You had my phone number. I gave it to your team captain and she told me she gave it to you months ago," Jo replied, not as an accusation but rather as a statement of fact. "*And* you skipped the soccer league banquet."

"I was busy," Lee countered, a little more defensively than she intended.

"She was," Tom interjected, as if making excuses for her. "We get these contracts and have to develop programs by one insane deadline after another. There are times when we don't have a life."

"Sounds like you need to run a personal ad yourself," Jo commented, her eyes moving over Lee like a warm, slow hand.

Instead of the flip reply she'd intended to make, Lee merely looked down and swallowed. *I'm out of my depth here. God knows why she wants me, but this isn't what I want. Not some butch-on-butch head trip that will only end up breaking my pride or my heart . . .* Abruptly, Lee began moving.

While Lee walked through the restaurant, hands jammed in her pockets, Jo and Tom fell in step behind her. She could hear Tom whispering questions and Jo answering back, *sotto voce*, but she swore for the life of her she was not going to turn around and betray any interest. *Better to just keep going, get outside, say goodnight and get away from her. Before she decides to do more than just look at me . . .* Lee couldn't help the shiver of response that moved through her.

Once Lee pushed through the glass door, exiting the restaurant, she turned toward the two behind her, ready with a little parting speech. However, before she could open her mouth, Tom pulled her into a bear hug, proclaiming, "G'night, toots," and then moved out into the rainy mist. He gave a small wave and a kidding grin as he looked back at her, then swung around and kept walking. Lee watched him go, astonished by his hasty retreat.

She turned to find Jo waiting patiently. "So, are you at least going to walk me to my car?"

Lee frowned and looked away. "Why are you doing this?"

"Doing what?"

"Acting like . . . like . . ." Words failed Lee, and she stood there helplessly. She felt frustrated and bewildered and not at all sure, anymore, that she wanted to resist whatever Jo had in mind.

"Acting like . . . I like you?" Jo asked, her voice very gentle.

The force of Jo's gaze finally made Lee face her. For a long moment they stood in the fine rain, their eyes locked onto one another's. A few other patrons came out of the restaurant, pushing by them and forcing them closer together in the process. Jo reached out and took Lee's elbow, at first merely guiding Lee out of the way. Then her step grew purposeful and she steered Lee into the dark entrance of the narrow alleyway that ran between the Flying Fish and the old brick building beside it. Before Lee quite knew what was happening, they had moved completely into the darkness of the alley. Lee leaned back and tried halfheartedly to resist as Jo tugged her away from the lights and action of the busy street.

Lee realized they were both breathing quickly, gazing into the dim features of each other's face. "What are we doing here?" Lee asked, knowing, and yet overcome with a sudden, inane need to make casual conversation.

"I want to show you something," Jo whispered, her hand slipping up to caress the back of Lee's neck.

A prickling, electric wave of anticipation flashed over Lee's whole body. Jo edged closer, her head bending lower. Warm lips made contact with Lee's cheek, traveling along the curve of flesh until they found Lee's mouth. Sweetly, those lips brushed across Lee's mouth, barely touching, gradually drawing Lee out until she was unconsciously following Jo's lead. Then the hand at the nape of Lee's neck began doing enchanting things, and Jo's mouth eased in harder, claiming her, driving every thought from Lee's head.

Flustered and lightheaded Lee broke the kiss and stepped back. *She's seducing me!*

"Easy," Jo whispered, her arms reaching slowly around Lee, gathering her in again. "I just want to hold you."

The embrace felt wonderful. Against her will, Lee gradually relaxed. She was aware that Jo carried an odd scent, a mix of some subtle, expensive perfume and medicinal antiseptic. Probably the hospital, Lee told herself. She found herself leaning into the firm strength, while Jo's hands moved comfortingly over the back of her coat.

Then, in a move of feline swiftness, Jo used her body to move Lee backward. Lee stumbled into the hard, rough support of a brick wall.

Jo's voice came, low and quiet. "So . . . is this so bad?"

Before Lee could even think of replying, Jo kissed her. A leg slipped between Lee's thighs, pressing into her. Delirious sensation flared, and the desire Lee had been battling all evening erupted. For a moment, she lost herself, lost where she was, who she was, lost everything. She found herself tightening her arms around Jo, kissing her back, feeling a dizzying sense of abandon. When Jo finally stopped, gasping for breath, Lee sagged against her, damning herself and wanting more.

"Oh, girl," Jo muttered. "I knew you'd be like this." Her hands were unzipping Lee's coat and reaching inside. Within a few moments, those hands were coasting over Lee's breasts, then searching beneath her shirt, mercilessly teasing.

Helpless, caught in a spiraling web of passion, Lee could only gasp and arch into the exquisitely torturous attention.

"Look at you," Jo crooned. "You love this. Been a long time, huh?"

One hand pulled her shirt from her pants, then searching fingers were making lazy figure eights across Lee's belly, firing every synapse in Lee's body. Aware of how ragged her breathing sounded, Lee willed herself to stop this before it went any further. *You're in an alley for Christ sake!* She was fighting being reduced to whimpering aloud when the hand began a slow, heart-stopping descent.

"Wait," Lee pleaded, trying to grab Jo's wrist. "Not here."

"Then come home with me," Jo whispered, her tongue beginning a light caress of Lee's ear. "You want to . . . don't you want to?"

"Yes," Lee nodded, gasping, "yes," even as the rational part of her mind quailed at her complete and utter surrender.

She was trembling as Jo took her hand and led her from the alley.

For Lee, the ride in Jo's Beetle was a blur. Maybe because Jo kept one hand on Lee's khaki-covered thigh, caressing slowly, keeping Lee tensed with a hard desire. They parked in a lot next to an older, graceful building, and when Jo got out, Lee followed blindly in Jo's purposeful steps. They climbed a flight of stairs. Jo unlocked and opened a door and strode quickly inside a black apartment. She switched on a lamp on a chest-high bookshelf by the door. As Lee stepped in, Jo closed the door behind her. Lee had time to take one glance around, noticing with interest a conservatively tasteful decor, before Jo was on her.

Literally, on her. In one smooth, practiced move, Jo pulled Lee in close.

"Now we solve the mystery, huh, little butch?"

There was a brief, teasing kiss, and when Lee leaned forward, chasing the retreating lips, Jo began stripping her. Lee's open anorak was pushed from her shoulders, onto the hardwood floor. Briefly, Lee wondered if she should assert herself, take back some control of events. Then Jo looked down into her eyes, smiling as if she registered the conflicting emotions warring in Lee. Jo's hands went to the buttons of Lee's yellow oxford shirt, and Lee felt almost paralyzed with excitement. The buttons steadily opened, giving way, and those hands slipped past fabric and found skin.

Lee swayed, awash in sensation. Her brassiere and the shirt were eased away, and the warm, compelling hands began roaming, blazing across her flesh. Thoroughly overcome, Lee's eyes closed. She felt her head drop back, exposing her neck. Jo's mouth answered the invitation. When Jo's palms began moving in circles over her nipples, she nearly passed out. Small, needy cries were escaping with each breath.

"God, you're so ready," Jo told her, then grasped her by the arm. "Come on," she said urgently, pulling Lee into the shadowed hallway off the left.

There was a momentary pause to light a few candles on the night stand by a queen-sized bed. Lee glanced around, examining the room. There were more bookshelves, loaded with an array of texts and paperbacks; a framed, artsy photo of Mount Rainier took up most of the wall above the bed. Stacked on a rocking chair was a pile of folded surgical scrubs.

When Jo saw where she was looking, she said, "Didn't put the laundry away," and smiled. "I'm not neat, and I can't cook either."

Lee shrugged, her eyes still moving. The closet door was open, and in the dim recesses Lee thought she saw a variety of silky looking blouses and short skirts suspended from wooden hangers.

Skirts? Her mind suddenly felt like it was engaged in a back flip.

Then, in a few deliberate, sinuous strides, Jo came back to stand beside her.

"You're kinda shy, huh?" Jo said, another soft remark that was more a statement than a question.

Wide-eyed, Lee just stared at her. *She plays a fierce game of soccer, but she's got skirts in that closet* . . . She swallowed nervously. *Is there a girlfriend* . . . ?

117

Undaunted, Jo's fingers were gliding up her arms. Lee found herself trembling beneath warm hands again, being completely undressed. When Lee was finally naked, Jo maneuvered her onto the sheets. Tenderly, she pulled up the plush quilt, keeping Lee from the chill of the room. Efficiently, Jo pulled off her shoes and skimmed off her own clothes.

And as Jo was progressively revealed in the golden glow of candlelight, Lee caught her breath. The strange, delightful passivity that had rendered her powerless all evening began to fall away. Desire to touch Jo, to sexually rule Jo, rose up in Lee like a fire on well-seasoned kindling.

"I've so wanted this," Jo said, her voice low as she climbed into bed beside Lee.

Lee whispered back, "Wow," her eyes taking in the splendid body that moved against her side.

Wonderingly, Lee ran her hands through Jo's dark hair, then over Jo's back and full breasts. Intrigued by the suede-soft skin that cloaked solid, defined muscle, Lee's fingers swept indolently over the woman above her. Subtly, the direction of the seduction began to shift. Jo's attempt to continue her sensual exploration of Lee was faltering, becoming a stop-and-start reaction to how close Lee was coming to Jo's flinching pubis.

Looking distracted, Jo pinned Lee with a glare. "Hey! Let me give you what you're so hot for, tough guy," she panted.

In answer, Lee caught her mouth in a fierce kiss. It was a combative kiss—first Lee's, then Jo's—then Lee's again. It finally ended when a long, quavering moan came from deep in Jo's throat.

Recognition slammed through Lee's body. *Barracuda femme*, she thought, almost laughing aloud at herself for taking so long to pick up on the cues.

"What . . . what're you doing?" Jo asked, almost rhetorically, as Lee's fingers slid between her legs.

Looking stunned, Jo squirmed, almost lifting away from Lee's coaxing stroke. She closed her eyes, whispering, "Oh my God," as she responded to Lee's fingers with a thrust of her hips.

Gently, subtly unfurling her own bed skill, Lee suckled the breasts Jo offered her with each arch of pleasure. The delirium of erotic greed slid in, overtaking Jo, making her more and more help-less against Lee's hands and mouth, and Lee reveled in it. She teased Jo into submission, answering each small surrender of posture and position with clitoral caresses that made Jo whimper and follow her fingers.

"Do you like this?" Lee demanded, her low voice burring by Jo's ear.

When Jo didn't answer, Lee teased her with a little less of what she so obviously craved.

Jo gasped, "Yes." Within seconds, her face betrayed how turned on she was by being made to acknowledge her acquiescence.

"I'm going to do what I want, now," Lee informed her in a quiet voice. "That okay?"

She waited, her fingers pressing lightly, repeatedly.

"God, yes, do what you want!" Jo hissed.

Quickly, Lee rolled Jo, flipping her onto her back and then descending between her legs. She worshiped Jo's body, licking and priming and filling it, until Jo was writhing, clutching the bedsheets and crying out in almost primal sounds. The first time, Jo came hard against her hand, and Lee felt an elation no soccer victory had ever brought. She let the tall woman rest in her arms for a few minutes, then began a leisurely, slow stroke, taking Jo into another ascension. Her half-lidded, dark blue eyes stayed on Lee, betraying a blazingly helpless mixture of awe and joy. The expression reached right into Lee and enveloped her heart. Soon Jo went into a series of quieter, but still utterly fiery orgasms. Lee felt as if she had a comet by the tail.

They were both drenched in sweat when Lee finally let her rest. She pulled the rumpled sheets free of Jo's limp body and covered them. As Lee eased herself down, she couldn't help running her hands possessively over Jo, delighting in Jo's long deep sigh.

One of the two candles guttered and then flickered out.

In the muted golden light, Jo said, "Are you always this competitive?"

Lee huffed a laugh. "No." After a brief silence, she smoothed a hand along Jo's neck. "But you were right in the restaurant. I've been avoiding you."

"Why?"

"You . . . scare me." Lee took a steadying breath. "I'm not really sure of anything when I'm around you. I think I knew that if you touched me . . ." Frowning, Lee wasn't sure she wanted to reveal any more. "And I had no idea you were femme."

"Why?" Jo asked. "Because I play soccer better than you?" She smiled archly.

"No way," Lee laughed back, enjoying the banter. "But I don't get you."

"I'm a feminist, babe," Jo announced. "I do what I want. I go after what I like. And I love to compete."

"Well, every time I've seen you, the way you were dressed . . ."

Languidly, Jo turned onto her side, studying Lee. "I think every time you've seen me it was either at a soccer game or I was on my way to or from the hospital." Jo reached over and lifted a lock of Lee's disheveled red hair. "It's more practical to dress down for work. I'm in the E.R. and between the blood and the barf—well, I refuse to keep ruining my wardrobe like that. Plus, I'm on my feet all day, so I'm doomed to the obligatory comfortable shoes. I mean, no wonder I have trouble meeting women!"

Lee nodded. *Makes sense.*

"So . . . why do I scare you?"

"I . . . I don't know," Lee admitted, meeting those cool blue eyes.

"Meaning you have this thing about losing control . . ." Jo stated, her voice soft, but oddly challenging.

Alarms went off in Lee's mind. She tried to rid her face of the vulnerability she felt, worried that she had confessed too much. "That's not what I meant."

Jo's laughter was soft with exhaustion. "Okay," she said, as if she were letting Lee dodge the topic. "Well, you certainly did take up the slack once I got things started, didn't you?"

Lee smiled, feeling inordinately pleased with herself.

Then Jo moved, enfolding her.

"So, little butch girl," Jo asked, her mouth nearly touching Lee's ear. The whisper was edged with something that made Lee quiver. "Now it's my turn . . . right?"

In answer, Lee's breathing quickened.

Slowly, Jo smoothed a hand across Lee's breasts, lingering delicately on her nipples until Lee's back went into a reflexive arch.

"I'll take that as your answer," the voice above her chuckled.

Jo's hands swirled lower, playing across her stomach and along the inner length of her thighs. "You know, femme doesn't mean submissive . . ."

Lee had a moment's anxiety over that, before she lost the thought completely in the steadily rising carnal intrigue. The tease went on and on, and Lee moved with the caresses, a live wire snaking in a flow of current. Cries began tearing from her throat, her head began twisting from side to side.

Jo bent over her. "Do you really want to be in control all the time?"

Lee fought to clear her head, trying to make sense of what Jo was saying. She was fully engulfed in mind-numbing lust and her one focus was the spectacular ache between her legs. Then at last, at last, she felt the hand going where she desperately wanted it to go. With one expert move Jo made Lee's hips buck.

"I think I'm in love," Jo whispered.

Lee couldn't answer. She was making sounds she had never dreamed she could make. She was craving every authoritative play of Jo's hand, until Jo was her only awareness, her one link to consciousness.

At some point, deep in the darkest part of the night, with whispered demands and tantalizing strokes, Jo proceeded to initiate her in things Lee had only done to other women. But, by then, it was all white-hot sensation and absolute surrender. By then, Lee's voice was hoarse with incoherent cries, and she was thoroughly addicted to the wash of salacious emotion and insatiable bliss pouring through her.

Somewhere between midnight and dawn, Jo took her to a place that Lee had not known existed, where Lee found herself calling out the name of this woman she still half feared.

By the end, Lee was left feeling dazed and exhausted and incredibly blessed. Jo snuggled up behind her, embracing her. "There's more than one way to score," Jo whispered in her ear, gathering Lee's limp body closer. "Huh, little butch?"

Lee could only nod faintly, before she slid into a dreamless sleep.

Butch Between the Sheets
Jesi O'Connell

There was a buzz of excitement in the bookstore. Kylie lifted her head from the magazine article on safe fisting practices she was reading and looked around, feeling a thrill of anticipation spark along her nerves.

"Excuse me, hello, everyone." A friendly-looking woman dressed in a shirt with the bookstore's logo, standing at the podium set up in back, was talking into the microphone. "We're getting ready to begin. If you'd like to take your seat." She gestured expansively at the thirty or so chairs squeezed into the small reading space at the back of the store.

There was a general movement and a stately rush toward the seats. No one wanted to appear enthusiastic; that would be juvenile. Kylie didn't particularly care. Hurriedly placing the magazine back on the shelf, keeping a few books held firmly under her arm, she shoved her way past a solid woman wearing the dreaded dyke-a-do and mumbled "pardon me" as she was glared down at. Well, she was short; she always had to either scramble or smile sweetly if she wanted to get something. This time, her score was a chair in the front row, practically right under the mike. The bookstore woman awarded her a slightly amused look before turning and heading into the private offices at the back. Did she look that desperate?

Kylie tapped her feet against the floor, enjoying the sound of her brand-new butterscotch suede Ferragamo heels against the tile. Unfortunately, dyke-a-do and her friend had managed to snag the seats right next to Kylie. After receiving another pointed glare, Kylie meekly kept her heels primly together. She couldn't help but be excited by her new shoes and the new swirly skirt and clingy silk blouse that draped over her frame. She'd never paid such a fortune for clothes before in her life; she'd nearly passed out when the snobby store clerk at the Century City mall shop had given her the total with a smug little smile. But, as her best friend Mara had said, "This is your chance, girl. Splurge on yourself. You'll knock the socks off that luscious butch!"

She studied the books on her lap. *The Life and Loves of a Butch in the City* and *Butch Between the Sheets: Everything You Wanted to Know and Aren't Afraid to Ask*. Kylie flipped them over and felt herself melt at the photos of the author on the back covers. Syl Salsberg was a fine-looking butch if Kylie had ever seen one, and she'd seen lots. Short dark hair slicked back, small studs winking from the neat lobes of her ears, a devilish little grin that seemed to say, "Catch me if you can." In one photo Syl was leaning casually against a tree, arms crossed over her chest, looking quite the professional in a crisp white button-down shirt under a snappy blazer—was it Armani? Gucci? Kylie couldn't quite tell. The other photo showed her in a studio, strong legs straddling a backward-facing wooden chair, arms draped over the other side as she cocked her head at the camera, grin still jauntily in place. The light bounced off the buckle of the belt around her jeans.

Kylie sighed. Syl Salsberg, please goddess, had to be as hot in person as she was in her words and in those pictures. Apparently several other women had had the same thought. Looking around, Kylie noticed a multitude of fully decked-out femmes either twitching with impatience or quietly waiting in the hard chairs. *Like a pack of bitches in heat*, she thought uncharitably, conveniently forgetting her own new clothes and freshly pampered, shaved, and plucked body.

There was a rustle from the door in the back; everyone in the packed audience straightened up and craned their necks to see, and suddenly there she was. Syl Salsberg, in the flesh. And what powerful-looking flesh it was. Especially in that white T-shirt and just barely, very hip, raggedy jeans, and those black Doc Martens made for stomping all over. Kylie felt her lower lip drop a bit and she squirmed in her chair.

"She's to die for!" someone behind Kylie whispered, and a few titters escaped the imprudent mouths seated around her.

"On behalf of The Flying Rainbow Bookstore, I am proud to introduce Syl Salsberg, acclaimed author, lecturer, and butch around town," the bookstore woman said into the mike, and everyone hooted and clapped. A few of the more daring women blew kisses at Syl, who expertly caught them with an outstretched hand and sent kisses right back. A few even more daring women pretended to swoon, but Syl laughingly waggled her fingers at them, as if to say, *Now, don't think I'm going to come out there to pick you up from the floor!*

"Syl was able to squeeze the time into her busy schedule to come be with us tonight, so let's give her our full attention, ladies. Syl Salsberg!"

Syl came forward amidst a roar of applause and whistles and sauntered to the mike. She spent a moment adjusting it, waiting for the noise to die down. Then she looked out at her audience and displayed that Cheshire cat grin. Kylie just about slid off her chair. Was Syl grinning directly at her?

"I can't tell you all how exciting this is for me," said Syl Salsberg. Her voice sounded like Billie Holiday's, all husky and sweet, wrapping around a girl's body like velvet. Kylie thought she heard someone next to her moan just the littlest bit. "An audience all to myself, to influence with my nefarious, radical, outrageously subversive ideas! All right!"

The audience cheered again as Syl stood there, arms pumped in the air above her like a boxer. The bookstore woman, seated behind Syl, seemed a bit awed.

"Now, to settle down to business, I'd like to start by reading a section from my latest book, *Butch Between the Sheets: Everything You Wanted to Know and Aren't Afraid to Ask.* Any objections?" She flashed that saucy grin again, raised her eyebrows at the eager women before her, and said, "No? Let's jump right in, then, and start with the section on—pleasing your lady with your tongue. Hmm, interesting—I don't see nearly as many butches out there as I do femmes."

Several women giggled, including, to her mortification, Kylie. This time Syl Salsberg definitely did look right at her, giving her a playful wink before turning her attention to the opened book on the podium.

"That's all right, really, ladies. I know you'll be running home to daddy tonight to demand the immediate implementation of the fun little techniques I'll be telling you about here. Won't you?"

A woman at the back of the room said loudly enough for all to hear, "And she'd better listen!"

Kylie giggled again, her eyes glued on Syl Salsberg's neatly manicured fingers holding open the pages of the books. If those hands could hold *her* open . . . A delicious tingle rushed down her spine and straight between her legs, and damn if she didn't start breathing faster.

"First off," Syl read from the pages of her bestseller, "you have to understand that this is a lady to honor, cherish, and pleasure. If you're in this just to please yourself, forget it. This is a two-person tango." She paused to look out at the listeners again and added, "Unless it's a three-person or more tango, of course!" which shot Kylie's eyebrows practically to the ceiling. "A-hem, where was I? Oh, yes . . . This is a two-person tango, and you'd better be willing to dance your partner off her feet and into a blissful state."

Oh, yes, please, Kylie thought, looking up at Syl with wide eyes and a longing that was virtually panting. Syl looked down at her, crooked up the corner of her mouth again, and continued in that molasses-rich voice.

"The human tongue is an amazing instrument. So strong, but extremely soft and sensitive, it can bring unbearable pleasure with just a few strokes."

Kylie felt a familiar wetness dampen her Victoria's Secret French-cut silk panties. As she shifted her weight just slightly to the left, a tingle zipped through her clit and made her clench her vaginal muscles. A gentle throb began between her legs. Very subtly, she began to clench and unclench, clench and unclench. Mm.

"Exploring the labia is the first priority. The labia can be very pleasurably stimulated by long strokes or short, hard licks."

Kylie heard another distinct moan behind her. She felt like letting one out herself. Syl glanced up for a split second, locking pleased dark eyes with Kylie, then went on reading with that grin still naughtily tugging at her lips.

"I myself experiment with all sorts of sensations to discover what my partner is most interested in at the moment. Some women enjoy the feeling of a large wet tongue lapping them like a cat washing its fur."

Kylie suspended her breathing and all movement for a split second. She heard a faint gasp from somewhere in the room before she began her motion again: clench and unclench, clench and unclench. It was becoming more and more pleasurable.

"Other women prefer the jabs of a tongue fluttering as hard as it can against her clit as long as the tongue can hold out. Sometimes, of course, this sensation is too much for the recipient, and she has to push her lover's head away so she can collect herself for a moment. Ladies?"

Kylie stared up at Syl Salsberg and her sleek head. Syl wore a curious expression on her face as she went on, "Just interested. How many of you out there like both sensations in a single session of whoopee?"

The audience giggled, squirmed, looked at one another surreptitiously to see who would be the first bold one to raise her hand. To Kylie's amazement, dyke-a-do and her girlfriend shot their hands into the air.

"We've read your books cover to cover, Syl. We like to practice what you preach!"

The crowd roared with the laughter of those needing relief, and Kylie took the opportunity to readjust herself on the chair so she was on the edge, with the firm corner of her seat tugging her underwear tight so it pressed against her clitoris. Ah, now that was relief.

"Just checking," said Syl Salsberg with a beaming smile. "So. Let's see. Oh, yes. When your femme is ready, she'll usually indicate this by pulling your head back to where it can do the most good: right between those lovely shaved, perfumed, trembling legs of hers. Mm, is there anything that smells better than a woman who wants you?"

Oh, my, Kylie thought, and she increased the tempo of her hips and the clenching, unclenching. She could smell a hot, pungent scent, similar to ripe herbs growing in rich garden soil on a lazy summer's afternoon, drifting in the still room. Her own smell? Someone else's? She didn't know and didn't care. She heard a rustle behind her and the sighs of chairs as the weight in them was shifted. Dreamily, she wondered if anyone else was enjoying the reading as much as she was.

" . . . the silky inner folds of the labia must be handled gently, with respect and care. They are extremely sensitive to even the tiniest pressure of tongue or lips or fingers, particularly when engorged with desire. Most women enjoy having every inch of the labia stroked in some form when they are rushing toward orgasm, but remember not to get caught up in the excitement of it all and become too rough. This can check the orgasm and bitterly disappoint your femme, who may label you as a rough bully. Then again, some women really like being handled more forcefully, which may smack of politics, so I will simply caution you to know your lover's needs well . . ."

As she rocked back and forth, feeling her eyes half-close, Syl's husky voice tickled at Kylie, demanded her attention, showered it on her, in fact. She could almost feel those strong lips traversing her skin, kissing up and down her thighs, traveling over the satiny straps of her pink garters, pausing at the damp patch of curls above her puffed-up labia, delving deep into the folds with a touch that was alternately tender and aggressive, responding instinctively to her cries and gyrations. *Oh, yeah, that's right.*

"When you can tell she is approaching climax, you've got to make sure she explodes and sees stars, particularly if this is your first time together. If you can see her face, you can tell by how unaware she is that you can see her making all kinds of grimaces."

Giggles, but mostly a breathless anticipation. A slow flush was starting in Kylie's chest, she could feel it, the way it always did when she was aroused. It usually spread to her entire body as she tipped closer and closer to orgasm, finally leaving her tinted rosy and breathless. The glow of passion, Mara liked to tease her after she told her friend about this embarrassing trait. A dead giveaway as to whether she really came or not. Well, it was lucky that no one in this room knew her quite that well. Shutting her eyes, she let her cunt get wetter and looser as she let that velvet voice carry her.

"You should also notice if her muscles are tensing up—her legs, her stomach, even her toes."

Kylie felt her toes tensing in their expensive, rather tight pumps. She slid her feet out of them and inhaled. The slightest whisper of noise left her mouth as she exhaled, and her eyes flew open. Syl Salsberg was looking right at her again, and that little devilish streak was lifting the corners of her mouth. *She looks like a cat about to pounce on the hapless canary*, thought Kylie. She could not stop the rocking motion of her hips, even though she thought it might now be obvious. That white-hot current had seized control of her body, and she was being taken along on a ride she had no control over. Kylie kept her eyes locked on Syl's until the dark head bent down to read more. Something hot and wet was seeping out of her, making her naked thighs stick together as they rubbed against one another.

"The next part is tricky. Some women gyrate wildly until the very moment they are seized by orgasm, the pulsing, liquid feeling in their cunt heating up the rest of their body and making it sizzle and jump without conscious control."

Did she really say that out loud? The hush in the store was so loud Kylie's ears rang with it. She could sense the women on either side of her on the edge of their seats, lips moist and slightly parted, watching Syl Salsberg read with a hungry delight. Her own lower lips were so thick with longing they pushed against her thighs. She knew she would leave a big wet stain when she finally rose from this seat. Her head was beginning to thrum, and she could feel the flush spreading down to her belly, out along her arms, creeping up her neck.

"Some women, however, hold their entire body so still in that instant before orgasm that you think they've lost it, or fallen asleep, or are bored. Don't be fooled. This woman is waiting, tense and still and open, just waiting and willing that final rush to overcome her, to shoot over her like a freight train, a butterfly, a thousand tongues licking and probing and lapping over every shaking inch of her flesh."

Kylie's own flesh jumped, leaped, trembled. *Oh goddess, oh goddess*, she thought, shutting her eyes again, tensing her body, holding herself very still. A hot pit was building in her center, spreading out over her extremities, along the skin encased in silk and satin and pricey linen, perfumed and shaved and damp with impatient expectation. "Oh . . ." she murmured. She couldn't help it, and she opened her eyes to see Syl's eyes move quickly from the page to her face, still reading, smiling, then looking to the book again. Kylie bent her head back just the littlest bit and imagined white teeth nibbling from her ear down to her collarbone.

"And when she does come, finally, lets the floodgates loose, sometimes you have no trouble identifying it; she screams, yells, moans, calls out your name, someone's name, her hands grab your head or her nails scratch your back, her legs thump against the bed or the couch or the floor or your back, and your can feel the blood pulsing under your tongue or lips or fingers and she comes, and comes, and comes."

Dear goddess—don't let me yell, don't let me make a sound, please, just let it happen. Her head was spiraling around, her spine was shooting off sparks, her cunt was throbbing and dripping, and she could definitely smell the sex rising off her in damp, spicy waves.

"Then there is the quiet one, the one who just sort of—mmm—just like that, the littlest sigh—"

Oh, yes, here she went—

"—and her legs might just stiffen a little—"

Uh-huh, yes, they were, silk stocking-covered toes curling on the hard linoleum beneath them—

"—and you might not be able to tell at all, but she is indeed coming all over the place, that beautifully applied makeup shiny with perspiration—"

—yes, she could feel drips of sweat on her forehead, so what, glorious white hot lightning strike, rumbling earthquake deep inside—

"—that mouth making a perfect 'O' of pleasure and almost surprise—"

Oh, goddess, was she? Fire leaping upward, coursing down, all over, shaking like leaves in a wind, *bitch in heat and loving it.* Quiet, though, yes, thank you, no noise. Coming all over the place and not moving a muscle, not making a single sound, just sitting rigid with pleasure on her damp seat at the sound of Syl Salsberg's voice. Wet, even dripping, a sharp scent in her nostrils, slick, throbbing, screaming orgasm between her legs but not from her mouth, perfect secret, yes! Kylie felt half-drunk.

"And, with some women I know, they flush everywhere, turning a bright rosy color over every inch of skin, so you can always tell when they're coming. They just can't hide it."

Kylie shot her eyes open, feeling like a skyful of stars was raining down on her head, and looked at Syl Salsberg standing there in front of her reading from her book, and Syl was looking right at her, grinning, the tip of her tongue just touching the corner of her mouth. Kylie knew she was flushed all over, every inch of skin, she could hide nothing, and the waves pounding in her body drowned out every other sound, except Syl's voice.

"That's it for this evening, wow, thanks for being such a fabulous audience. Really. Any questions?"

Kylie sat there, feeling it all blissfully ebb away, and relaxed in her seat. She smoothed her hair, tucked her feet back into their shoes, and took a deep, unobtrusive breath. No one else had noticed. Her face was cooling down. Her clit was still ticking, just a bit. The new panties were soaked. Her thighs felt slick when she imperceptibly moved them apart.

Syl Salsberg grinned down at her and waggled her eyebrows, then winked again, before answering someone's question.

Kylie couldn't wait to tell Mara about the reading.

Three to Tango
A Chain Gang Chronicle

by Peggy J. Herring, Laura DeHart Young,
and Therese Szymanski

The sudden turbulence sent her drink flying one way and her laptop another. "Damn," she said, grabbing the Diet Coke at the last possible second. The computer was a different story. It landed on the empty seat next to her and then bounced onto the floor. "Shit!"

Seat belt be damned, Selina Garcia thought, as she unhooked her seat belt and lunged for the expensive laptop. The guy in the aisle seat made no move to help her. He was too busy clutching the armrests with his white-knuckled hands, eyes closed tightly as the plane continued to bounce in the rough air. She finally snatched the computer by its lid and carefully lifted it to her lap as she settled back into her seat and buckled up. Holding on to the machine for dear life, she rode the turbulent air like a bucking bronco. Ten minutes later, calm was restored to the cabin and she was typing away again, the laptop purring along unharmed.

In the last two years, her work had become her life. She had started her own consulting business specializing in market research for consumer products. Recently, she had landed two big clients after months of legwork. Mostly, she worked out of her home in the suburbs of St. Louis. Now the fun had really started, as she began making frequent trips to Chicago for client conferences and consumer focus groups. This trip to Chicago would also include pleasure, however. She was visiting an old college friend whom she hadn't seen in years. There was going to be a big party and she was in the mood to celebrate. Her business was going better than expected, and she stood to make a substantial amount of money in the months ahead. Selina smiled to herself. She had fought all the bourgeois prejudices corporate America had thrown her way. But the Mexican-American, with the fiery temper and iron will inherited from her grandmother and mother, had finally won. From a small dirt-poor southern Texas village to the St. Louis suburbs and now the skyline of Chicago, she had fought and scraped her way to success.

Building the business had not come without sacrifices, the first of which had been her social life, which was next to nothing. Eighteen months ago, she had broken up with her lover of four years. Dana had complained that she had become a "workaholic." Selina didn't totally disagree. For many months, Selina had been torn between her long days at work and her passion for Dana. She was, in fact, still in love with Dana. But at that time she was also committed to her job and the groundwork that needed to be established so she could start her own business. Thoughts of Dana were still vibrant and alive. Not a day passed that Selina didn't think about her.

Dana nibbled playfully at Selina's ear while two hands caressed her backside. "I've been thinking about this all day," Dana whispered.

"You're making me crazy."

"That's the idea." Dana slipped the straps of the black lace nightgown from Selina's shoulders. "My boss came in my office at lunch and started talking about this new data center project. I listened and nodded and grunted for twenty minutes. But the whole time, inside my head, I was fucking your brains out."

"Ohhh, you're bad."

"Yeah, but you're so good." Dana cupped Selina's breasts with her hands and kissed her deeply. "I want to make you beg me."

Selina watched as first one nipple and then the other disappeared into Dana's mouth. She ran her hands through Dana's short curls, the blond hair thick and soft between her fingers. Biting her lower lip, she moaned and felt the pleasant desire between her thighs that only Dana seemed to excite.

Suddenly, Dana went down and teased with her tongue until Selina thought she might explode. But at the last moment Dana stopped and moved back up to kiss her, her fingertips sliding gently over her nipples, Dana's knee pressing into her thighs. "How badly do you want me, my Chicana princess?"

"Yes, you always want a piece of this ass—as much as I want you to have it."

"Always."

Selina wrapped her thighs around Dana's knee and pressed into her as hard as she could. "I'm so hot for you, darling."

Dana broke down first, as always, slipping her hand between Selina's thighs. Her fingers found the moist brunette hair and then that beautiful wetness. She began to fuck Selina slowly, looking up into Selina's dark eyes. "I couldn't stand it any longer. I had to be inside you."

"You always want me to beg, but it's you who gives in first." Dana started pumping harder and Selina responded, her hips moving upward. Selina grabbed Dana's muscled shoulders. She was riding the edge of a beautiful orgasm when she whispered, "Harder, Dana. Fuck me harder." Dana responded and Selina came, her deep moans filling the room.

"Ma'am, can you put your seatback upright, please? We'll be landing soon."

Selina emerged from her daydream slightly disoriented. She nodded, giving the flight attendant a half wave of her arm. She fixed the seat and shut down the computer. Remembering Dana in bed was always a delight. Missing her every day was not.

Her parents named her Lucretia Maria Teresa Siciliano, but everybody called her Luca. Except for all the women who called her darling, honey, or lover. Well, of course her Mama and Nana called her Lucretia, usually with their characteristic wildly expressive hands, occasionally with a thrown loaf of bread. And then there was the spaghetti incident, but Luca tried to forget about that. A perfectly good pot of her Mama's best marinara sauce lost all over the walls of the kitchen.

"Yeah, and when I was growing up, I wanted to be a priest because nuns never got to do anything fun," Luca said, pulling on her white T-shirt and jeans. Luca took the naked woman into her arms, caressing the silky olive skin while wedging her thigh against the patch of dark curls between the woman's long legs.

"Oh baby, you go starting that and I'll never make it back to work this afternoon," Elena purred, opening herself up to Luca's teasing hands and playful tongue.

Luca knelt and ran her cheek over the unruly patch of curls that were still damp from their last time around, dipping her tongue between still swollen lips to taste the intoxicating nectar found there. Elena groaned, opening her legs wider and pushing herself against Luca's mouth. Luca loved it when women opened themselves like this to her, when they gave themselves to her. Opened their arms and legs to her, took their clothes off for her, let her have her way with them, let her be inside of them and taste them.

She especially loved women like Elena. Elena was a true femme, the way the goddess had wanted femmes to be. Her long black tresses fell like wavy strands of silk around her face, her smooth unblemished skin was rich and creamy, and her dark eyes spoke of secrets and mystery. Luca loved such hot-blooded Spanish girls. You could keep all the blondes in the world as far as she was concerned—she found blondes to be passionless creatures focused only on themselves. Spaniards on the other hand were passionate women who could fight like cats in heat and when they got it on, they were even better.

Elena pulled at Luca's hair and ground herself against Luca's mouth, moaning and groaning loudly enough to wake Luca's great-grandpapa, who lay in his grave in Italy, God rest his soul.

Luca moaned loudly enough with her own pleasure to wake Elena's great-grandpapa in Spain. It didn't matter how long you were in this country, there was still some of the old land in your blood and in your loins.

"Fuck me, Luca!"

Of course Luca, being the good butch she was, did as she was told. Her entire fist slid easily and deeply into Elena.

"Oh, God! Oh my fucking God!" Elena cried, thrashing wildly about the bed while Luca's fist plunged in and out of her, her tongue flicking back and forth over Elena's clit the entire time.

"Luca!" Elena cried when she came, tightening on Luca's fist like a vise and spurting her incredible juices into Luca's mouth.

When she lay back onto the bed, spent, Luca gently extracted her hand from Elena, wiped her mouth on her arm, and crawled up to pull the gorgeous, sexy woman into her arms.

"You know, I could fall in love with you," Elena said huskily, laying Luca's head on her soft breast and running her fingers through her hair.

"Aw, now you don't want to go doing that too quickly. There's no telling where I've been," Luca said, pulling her head up to give Elena a devilish grin.

"Oh, lover, I know that, but you can fuck me anytime you want. And you know that."

Luca smiled at her and got up to go to work, leaving Elena to close up the house.

❧

As Jane Osborne sat at the bar in the hotel lounge, she gave the little straw in her gin and tonic another twirl and tried to imagine herself actually going into the ballroom that lurked ominously across the lobby. There was a Valentine's dance already in progress, and a friend had made Jane promise that she would attend and stay at least an hour. Jane was glad right then that she hadn't specified which particular hour it would be—the first or the last. Giving the straw in her drink another spin, she shook her head. So far she wasn't having much luck at convincing herself that this was a good idea.

"And we've got a nice big table reserved just for singles!" Kim had said on the phone the day before. "You'll have dance partners all night long!"

Great, Jane remembered thinking, *a table full of losers.*

She glanced at her watch again and felt uneasy at the time that was slipping away. She couldn't stay out here all night. Just then someone opened the door to the ballroom, sending music spilling out into the lobby and into the lounge. Jane turned in that direction to make sure Kim wasn't on the prowl looking for her. Getting caught on a bar stool wouldn't be a good thing. *You really need to get in there and get this over with*, she thought. *And make sure Kim sees you there and maybe find someone harmless to dance with a few times so she'll think you're having fun.*

While Jane had been getting dressed earlier that evening she tried to remember how many years it had been since she had gone to a dance. Fresh from a lengthy bubble bath, she was perched on the edge of her neatly made bed and tried recalling the last Valentine's Day she had spent without a date. Slowly squeezing lotion into the palm of her hand, she started at an ankle and began rubbing it up her smooth legs. She could honestly say that she had never been to a dance alone before. Even in junior high, she and her friends had attended dances in groups of three or more, with everyone standing in a corner of the gym waiting for shy, pimply boys to come over and talk to them. Even then boys didn't interest her, but Jane had liked being around all those giggling, silly girls.

With a grin, she slipped into black lace panties and strategically dabbed perfume in a few interesting areas. *Alone*, she thought while studying herself in the mirror. *Alone is such a lonely word*, she mused with a chuckle. It was finally getting to the point where she was less resentful about being single again. It had been five months since Gloria had packed up and left for Seattle, taking Jane's dog and rabbit with her. They were still arguing long distance about when the pets were to return, but as always Gloria was quick to offer nothing but empty promises.

Checking her watch again, Jane noticed that another three minutes had gone by and she was still sitting there on the same bar stool nursing the same watery drink. *Get it over with*, she thought. *Get your butt in there and do it. Just think. An hour from now you could be home doing something really exciting . . . like reading a book or re-arranging your sock drawer again.*

The room was already filled with people. Selina stood in the doorway, staring at the Valentine decorations and smiling. For a few hours, she could forget about work, talk with an old friend, and meet some new people. The women looked good and she thought she looked good too, as a quick check in the restroom mirror off the main lobby confirmed. She had been saving the black silk, sleeveless blouse and leather pants outfit for this very occasion. She had also saved the black sequined pumps; they had been Dana's favorites. Dana had referred to them as Selina's "come-fuck-me pumps." Selina couldn't count how many times Dana had fucked her while she was wearing them. Tonight, she hoped that maybe someone else would get the same idea. It had been far too long. But first she needed a drink to steady her nerves.

≈≈≈

With the powerful bike rumbling between her legs, Luca was happy to be going on a somewhat longer ride than usual. There was an exhilaration in straddling the powerful engine with the wind hitting her face. She loved speeding along without a care in the world. Except perhaps of becoming road kill, but we all die some-day, so what did it matter? Luca would rather die instantly in a motorcycle crash than excruciatingly slowly from cancer or AIDS or . . . life itself. She wanted to die young and in a blaze.

She deserved to have fun tonight. After all, she'd be spending a lot of time this weekend at several of the adult establishments around Chicago, seeing if she could talk some of the best dancers into coming to Detroit to dance for a bit at the adult theaters she managed.

Once checked into her hotel, Luca donned black leather pants, a white Pierre Cardin shirt, a thin black leather tie, and her boots and went to meet Isabel.

Luca had never been much into all this online crap, but she had finally gotten online to research some new sources of revenue. She had already done real sex and phone sex, so it was interesting to investigate cyber-sex. And that was how she had met Isabel, a true Spanish princess. Luca could only wet her lips in anticipation of meeting her. If a woman could be so passionate in cyber-sex, Luca could only itch about how hot she'd be in real life with flesh against flesh. Naked skin meeting. No clothes.

A few moments later she was striding across the lobby when she noticed an elderly woman on the street selling roses. On impulse, she went outside to buy a fiery red one, then continued on to the hotel restaurant.

She glanced across the room and found the woman with the lavender carnation in her hair. She had gained at least a hundred pounds and had dyed her hair blonde.

Luca backed out of the restaurant and glanced around. Dammit, she had been looking forward to some fun and games tonight. Hesitating in the hall, she first heard music coming from the direc-tion of the ballroom. She paused just long enough to watch several amazingly attractive women walk by her, alone, and then headed off in that direction herself.

There might be hope for the night yet.

As she passed the hotel gift shop on her way to the ballroom, Jane caught her reflection in the window and slowed her pace a bit. She liked the way she looked in her long, mint-green dress. Someone once told her that green was her color and that it complemented her red hair. With a confident smile and a new glide in her stride, she entered the ballroom.

"There you are!" Kim said over the blaring music. "Let me get you started."

They were whirling around the dance floor to a bouncy polka before Jane could even take in her surroundings, colliding with other couples like bumper cars at a carnival. After that particular dance was over, Kim got them each a glass of wine and then escorted Jane to the singles table where only one other woman sat. Jane waved at the people she knew at tables close by on that side of the room and immediately began looking for the exit.

"I'd like to keep you all to myself," Kim said, "but my date would probably never speak to me again."

"They don't come any more harmless than me, honey."

"That dress tells me otherwise," Kim said with a wink. "I hate to just leave you here, but I've got door duty and ticket-taking responsibilities right now."

Giving the singles table another once-over, Jane realized how pathetic she would look sitting there. That table, with its lone occupant, definitely had the word "loser" written all over it.

"Can you use some help with that door duty thing?" Jane asked. "I'm great with doors, actually. I've got several of my own at my home, and no one gets in without my knowledge or approval."

Kim laughed. "No, no! You stay here and have some fun! The other women sitting at this table are dancing right now. They'll be back when they get tired and need a rest."

Jane finally noticed all the drinks and empty glasses sitting on the table. *So some of these single women have already paired up for the evening*, she thought, *while you were out there being indecisive on a bar stool.*

"Just a few minutes of door duty?" Jane asked, trying not to sound too whiny and desperate.

"Well, come on then. I could use the company."

The bar station was crowded with women, but Selina was undeterred. Her stiletto heels served to make her even taller than she already was, and she used that advantage to catch the attention of the tuxedo-clad bartender over the heads of the women three-deep in front of her.

"I'm in a hurry. Can you help me?" she asked with a flirtatious wink.

"What would you like?"

Several women glared at her. Selina smiled and yelled over the music, "A glass of Chardonnay and a hot date."

The bartender laughed. "The Chardonnay I can help you with. Getting the hot date is up to you, but I doubt it'll be a problem."

Selina sipped the wine as her eyes swept the large room. Unfortunately, she hadn't run into Kim yet, but there would be plenty of time later to reminisce with friends. She still could hardly believe she was here. She should be in her hotel suite working on the research proposal for her newest client, not in this grandiose ballroom with its red and pink streamers and heart-shaped Mylar balloons. This kind of thing could only lead to trouble. She'd only end up missing Dana more.

Some chairs and tables had been set up for guests on the other side of the ballroom. Selina's "come-fuck-me pumps" were killing her so she headed for a chair and a chance to scrutinize the crowd more closely.

Navigating the dance floor was like tiptoeing through a minefield. Selina began to sound like a broken record. "Excuse me.

Excuse me, please. Pardon me." Just as the crowd of couples began to part like the Red Sea, a woman bumped her hard from behind. So much for the glass of Chardonnay, which sailed from her hand onto the floor. The glass broke and the wine splattered all over her feet. She had worked hard to get that drink!

Angrily, Selina swung around to face the offender, but the eyes of the woman, dark and turbulent, left her speechless. She just stood there with her mouth open, hands on hips.

Luca was about to quickly mumble an apology, but the woman had taken a stance that Luca couldn't help but grin at. So while she was at it, she quickly assessed the woman in front of her. She was every bit the hot Chicana princess Luca had been hoping to meet tonight. Her fingers could already feel the warmth of the woman's skin under the sensual blouse, and those tight black leather pants brought out every curve of her luscious body. She seemed extraordinarily tall, but a quick glance down revealed shoes that could only be described as come-fuck-me pumps. They probably added at least four inches to her height. Any question Luca had was answered. This woman had come here tonight to get fucked, and Luca was just the woman to do it right. Luca prided herself on being a hunter, one able to smell the need on a woman.

She again met the woman's now somewhat flustered gaze; she obviously had been aware of Luca's assessment. "Sorry about your . . ." Luca paused, bent, picked up the broken wineglass, sniffed it, and stood. "Chardonnay? But no need to cry over spilled Chardonnay. I'll get you another." She quickly took the woman by the elbow and guided her to the edge of the dance floor, not believing her luck at finding one of the bar stations practically empty. She ordered a Chardonnay for the lady and a Glenlivet on the rocks for herself.

"Luca, Luca Siciliano," she said, meeting the stranger's dark, tempestuous eyes.

"Selina Garcia," Selina said, putting out a hand, like the businesswoman she probably was. Even better. Luca loved peeling through the business layers of a femme to unleash the wild woman within. Those who were best behaved out of bed were usually the least behaved in bed.

Luca bowed ever so slightly as she took the offered hand and lifted it to her lips, to gently touch the graceful, long-fingered hand and steal her first taste of Selina's soft skin.

As she released Selina's hand and straightened, she felt another set of eyes on her. She turned and met the longing gaze of the gorgeous redhead at the door with whom she had flirted briefly. Her parting words to the woman had been, "Come find me when you get off duty."

And so there she was, at the intersection of two sets of gazes. Luca was unaccustomed to having to make such choices—a luscious hot-blooded brunette or a hot-to-trot redhead, both of whom looked like they needed to get fucked.

Luca had had a Spaniard for lunch. Now, what shall dinner be? Would it be another olive-skinned beauty, or a fiery redhead in a slinky dress that outlined all her lovely curves?

Jane saw them together and felt silly for having believed that the handsome butch who had flirted with her at the door had really wanted to dance with her later. She'd obviously come to meet someone else. Jane held the rose that the woman had given her and inhaled its fine, delicate scent. She smiled wistfully at the couple and then turned to make her way back to the loser's table. She had to dance with someone other than Kim before she could leave. Otherwise, Kim would accuse her of not even attempting to have any fun.

Jane found an empty seat and nodded at the other women, smiling as she observed several of them rubbing their feet from having had them stuffed in uncomfortable shoes all evening. She heard the music change to something exotic with a strong Latin flavor and then applause coming from the dance floor. Two other women hastily returned to the table to claim their drinks, and one of them announced over her shoulder as she was leaving again, "There's the cutest couple out there doing the tango!"

Within seconds Jane had the table all to herself. *The tango,* she thought with a chuckle. *I wonder how much of it I remember?* Her older brother was a marvelous dancer and used to practice the tango with her so he could impress his girlfriend. Jane loved dancing with him, and at his wedding he chose her as his tango partner instead of his new bride, which caused quite an uproar.

"There you are!" she heard Kim say behind her. "Come here. You've gotta see this!"

Jane grabbed the rose, thinking that she would never see it again if she didn't. She had no choice but to follow because Kim had her by the hand and was yanking her along like a reluctant child. They worked their way to the edge of the dance floor and were finally able to see the dancers in action. And it didn't surprise Jane at all to find the cute butch dipping her partner—the gorgeous woman in the stunning outfit—as though they had been dancing together forever. Their movements were precise mirror images that must have taken hours of practice. And the teasing, sensual way their bodies seemed to want to touch but didn't had more than one onlooker beginning to squirm.

Jane smiled and put the stem of the rose between her teeth. Her feet began to move all on their own as she watched the dancers prance around and tease the crowd. Caught up in the swell of the music and the hot, twirling bodies on the dance floor, Jane tossed her head back and struck a dramatic pose for her own amusement. The cheers and synchronized clapping had everyone in the ballroom on their feet enjoying the show. The dancers seemed to both notice her at the same time and used several dance steps to urge Jane out on the dance floor with them. Jane clenched down on the rose stem as she let the two women in black leather pants dance around her. Jane struck her pose again to the delight of the crowd, but the only thought that entered her mind at that particular moment was, *How the hell can anyone dance that way in those come-fuck-me pumps?*

Their dancing was more than just dancing, Selina thought. It was eerily sensuous the way three total strangers moved like one seamless thread across the dance floor. She wasn't the only one who noticed. The women watching them knew it, too. She could read it in their expressions—the look of awe in their eyes. Selina knew in an instant that she was part of something almost ethereal. A thrill moved up and down her spine, and the hair at the back of her neck stood on end—sensations caused by the highly charged dance chemistry.

"Luca," she whispered as Luca's face leaned up against hers. "Let's get some air and invite our redheaded friend along."

Luca smiled and bowed. There was loud applause as Luca grabbed each woman by the hand and escorted them from the dance floor. Selina could well imagine Luca grabbing them both by the hair and dragging them from the ballroom like two prized trophies. But she was playing the gallant butch tonight—the very kind of woman that started Selina's pulse racing.

As they stood outside under the ballroom canopy, the redhead introduced herself as Jane. *But she's no "plain Jane,"* Selina thought, *with her white porcelain skin, beautiful smile, and curves in all the right places. Damn, if I have to make a choice between them, I'm not sure I can.*

"And I'm Luca Siciliano," Luca said, taking Jane's hand and kissing it. She wrapped an arm around Selina and said, "and this tempestuous Chicana is Selina Garcia."

Luca's warmth penetrated Selina's skin through the fine fabric of her shirt, and her musky cologne invaded her senses. Selina took Jane's soft, warm hand in her own. "Pleased to meet you." Their hands touched a moment too long as Selina lost herself in Jane's deep green eyes.

Selina shivered in the chilly Chicago air, and Luca brought her even closer.

"I don't want my girls getting cold," Luca said, reaching for Jane's hand to bring her near. Obviously, Jane was not wearing a bra, because her hardened nipples easily pushed up and through the silky fabric of her dress.

Selina couldn't take the chilly Chicago night air any longer. She couldn't stand making a choice either. The swaggering, self-assured, amazingly-in-control butch with the beguiling dark eyes? Or the quiet and shy femme with the easy humor and luscious body? Seeking warmth and not wanting to lose the company of either woman made her unusually brazen. "I'm staying in a suite here in the hotel. Anyone interested in a nightcap?"

Luca leaned back against the balcony railing for just a moment, assessing these two gorgeous women and not believing her incredible luck. She had been wondering if there was any chance for a *ménage à trois* tonight, and now Selina was apparently suggesting just that. Her mouth watered in anticipation. If their tango had been any indication, she was in for a wild ride.

Luca wasted no further time. She grinned at the two needed-to-get-fucked femmes, then laid a hand at the small of each woman's back, getting a thrill out of the feeling of her hand on Jane's bare skin, and leading them quickly into the ballroom and to the hotel lobby.

Luca turned to Selina. "What did you say your suite number was?"

"Three thirty-three."

Luca grinned. "How apropos. Will you excuse me just one moment?" With that she went to the front desk, leaving Selina smirking at her pun while Jane blushed wildly and looked at the floor.

"Are you ready, *mi amor*?" Selina asked when Luca returned a moment later.

Luca smiled at being referred to with so intimate a phrase. "For you two, I am always ready." She then led them into the elevator and pressed the button for the third floor.

"So, have you two known each other long?" Jane asked, apparently uneasy with the situation as well as Selina's and Luca's ease with each other. Luca was willing to bet she had never done anything like this before, although she wasn't so sure about the hot-blooded Chicana.

"We just met tonight," Selina said, as she entwined her fingers in the hair at the back of Luca's head. She then reached for Jane, running her hand up her bare arm and urging her closer.

Far too quickly the elevator arrived at the third floor. Luca again led the women, taking the key from Selina to open the room for them.

"This is certainly a lot nicer than a regular room," Luca said when Selina turned on the lights in the spacious suite, noting the thick carpeting, the oak furniture and complete entertainment center.

"I'll be having some meetings here this weekend," Selina explained, as if apologizing for the grandeur, while she turned on some low music. Luca dropped to one knee in front of Jane and put her hand through the long slit in Jane's long dress to run her hand up her shapely, stocking-clad leg.

A few seconds later there was a knock on the door. "I'll get that," Luca said, quickly jumping to her feet.

A waiter followed Luca into the room, pushing a cart laden with a chilled bottle of Dom Perignon, three glasses, and silver bowl full of strawberries. Selina was sitting next to Jane on the couch. Luca felt a flare of desire rush through her body. She wanted to see these two women intimately touching. She quickly paid the waiter and sent him on his way.

"Champagne?" Jane asked, standing.

"I thought we needed something to celebrate our meeting." Luca carefully opened the bottle, handed each woman a glass, and poured.

"A toast, then," Selina said, giving first Luca and then Jane a deep, sultry gaze, "to our meeting."

And then again, as when the three of them had danced, they thought and acted as one, drinking simultaneously from their glasses with arms linked—while somehow, amazingly, not spilling a drop—their eyes meeting, dancing, flirting the entire time.

Luca put down her empty glass and ran her fingers gently across Selina's cheek. She then tenderly touched her lips to Selina's full ones, experiencing their softness for just a moment before turning to Jane. She didn't want to leave the silkiness of Selina, but she knew Jane still didn't believe she and Selina had only just met. Jane was obviously ill at ease, something Luca meant to change.

Leaving one arm loosely wrapped around Selina's waist, Luca reached up and ran her hand lightly over Jane's soft yet aristocratic features, and back down through her incredibly silky hair, until she laid a hand gently against the back of Jane's head and tenderly directed her lips toward her own. The soft kiss heightened to passion, a passion evidenced by Jane's soft moan.

Luca's hands clasped each woman's waist while she kissed Jane, and then she pushed them slowly toward each other. Selina wrapped her arm around Jane's waist, completing the circle. Luca pulled a bit from Jane, toward Selina, and Jane followed. Luca ran her lips for a brief moment over Selina's, then turned toward Jane, who still leaned forward.

She directed them and, overcome with their need, they succumbed. They fell through the ice that Luca had broken, their eyes first meeting for less than a millisecond before their lips were on each other's.

Luca thrilled at the sight of these two luscious femmes kissing while she touched them both. One of her hands slowly unzipped the back of Selina's tight black leather pants while the other pulled down the zipper at the back of Jane's form-fitting dress.

Her mouth watered for the taste of these two women.

✧

At first Jane wasn't sure she had consumed enough alcohol to do this. At least, that was what she had been thinking in the lobby and then again during the short trip to the third floor. But the moment Selina touched her arm in the elevator—that sensual way she had included Jane in their intimacy—helped her decide that this was where she wanted to be. These two seemed very confident about what they were doing, and Jane was willing to take directions and follow someone else's lead. If she didn't like where things were headed, she knew she could always decline the offer and go home. But the one thing that surprised her the most about all of this was how much she wanted to be with them. *Both* of them!

Luca's tender kiss was a very pleasant surprise, because Jane was still convinced that these two were lovers, and that maybe the purpose for her being there was to play in some voyeuristic way. But Luca's kiss had been hot . . . inviting . . . and turned passionate very quickly. It was at that point, when Luca gently encouraged Selina's participation, that Jane was glad she hadn't drunk too much. She was relieved that none of her senses had been dulled when Selina kissed her. And that kiss was everything Jane had imagined it would be. During the tango, Selina had looked at Jane as if undressing her with her eyes. And to keep from getting too caught up in that smoldering lust, Jane had lightened the mood a bit by taking the rose from her teeth and tossing it over her shoulder, to the delight of the crowd.

They pulled her in closer as Selina's lips found Luca's again. Jane watched them and then felt the thrill of anticipation as Selina touched one of Jane's breasts while Luca touched the other. Jane was certain that these two women could hear her heart pounding in her chest, or could somehow sense that her knees were weak from wanting more.

"I have a bed built for three in the other room," Selina whispered.

"Then let's tango in that direction," Luca suggested without further ado.

Jane gulped the last of her champagne for a burst of courage and became the center of a conga line on the way to the bedroom. *If these women make love the way they dance*, Jane thought, *then I'm in for the night of my life!*

Reluctantly, Selina left the two women in the bedroom, excusing herself to visit the adjacent powder room. It was nerves, rather than need. As she closed the bathroom door, she could hear Jane and Luca laughing, and probably refilling their glasses with champagne. *What am I doing? It's nice to finally meet some new women, but this? This is something I've never experienced before.*

Selina sat at the edge of the spa tub. She thought of Dana—of Dana's hands working their incredible magic all over her, loving her like she had never been loved before. Selina studied the closed door, trying to imagine what might happen on the other side. Maybe a new memory could replace the old, finally putting the past to rest. Dana with the sky blue eyes. Dana with a passion and touch that made her ache with desire.

She undressed quickly and put on a robe. Selina put her hand on the doorknob and hesitated. For a few moments she thought again about the two women on the other side of that door. How much they had made her laugh that evening. How much they had already made her forget about her lonely, work-filled life. They were both charming, intelligent, and deliciously wicked. Luca with the dark, turbulent eyes and perfect butch swagger. Jane with the angelic face, coy smile, and sharp wit. What did she really have to fear but her own inhibitions?

When Selina opened the door she found Jane lying practically naked across the bed, laughing as Luca swirled her silky mint dress in the air above her head. The dress landed on the loveseat across the room, draping the cushions as sexily as Jane draped the pillows on the bed.

"Ah, she returns," Luca said with a smile, cocking her head in Selina's direction. "We've missed you."

"Selina, Luca is being disrespectful to my wardrobe."

"I can't imagine Luca being disrespectful with anything," Selina answered, nervously running her fingers through her hair. "She's been nothing but gallant so far."

Luca laughed and shook her head. "I'll show you gallant." She waved Selina over to the bed. Soon, she was in Luca's arms, Luca's hands slipping beneath her robe at the same time Luca kissed her. Selina felt Luca's hands moving slowly from her breasts to her thighs. The hands were strong, yet gentle. Selina fought the memories of the past and looked into Luca's eyes, dark like storm clouds. There was something behind those eyes that made her want to surrender—something that took the nervousness and fear away.

In the next instant, Luca picked her up and laid her next to Jane. Her robe fell open, her darker skin a pleasant contrast to Jane's lustrous ivory. Luca smiled and leaned over both of them. Tugging playfully at Luca's black leather tie, Jane deftly untied the knot with one hand and slowly pulled it from Luca's shirt. Selina grabbed the tie and slid it across her bare breasts and then smiled and sat up. She took one end of the leather tie and playfully tightened it around her right wrist. Before she could say anything, Jane kissed her neck softly from behind. At the same time, Jane pulled the tie gently around Selina's back and secured it to Selina's left wrist. Selina lay back down on the bed, her arms tied beneath her. Moistening her lips with her tongue, she said, "Well, Luca. Looks like the next move is yours."

Jane leaned over Selina's lush body and pushed the deep red satin robe completely open, then slid her hand down Selina's right leg, which was crossed over the left in a cute attempt at modesty.

"Why should Luca get to have all the fun?" Jane asked, nudging Selina's leg aside, opening her up.

Feeling a bit overheated, Luca undid the top buttons of her shirt before kneeling on the bed on the other side of Selina from Jane.

"You should've taken the robe off her before you tied her up," she said to Jane, sliding the robe down Selina's arms, stripping her as much as she could without cutting the robe off of her.

Jane just glanced up at Luca before returning her attention to the smoothness of Selina's thighs.

Selina took a deep breath, her breasts rising with their hardened nipples, as she looked nervously from Luca to Jane.

"Oh, there's no reason for you to get all nervous, baby," Luca said, letting her hand wander freely over Selina's body. "I'll make it even-steven." She stood and walked around the bed to Jane. "We need to take care of these first." She caressed Jane's stomach and hips lightly with her fingers, then hooked her thumbs into the lacy black panties. "I could take them off with my teeth or . . ." She suddenly pulled, ripping Jane's panties right at the hips, then quickly threw them to join the silky green dress on the loveseat, leaving Jane wearing only her black thigh-highs and heels.

"I guess you won't be wearing those again," Luca said, grinning. She leaned over Jane, running her fingers lightly over Jane's breasts, taking a bit longer with each nipple, then put her hand palm down on her stomach, and lower, "but this way, over breakfast tomorrow I can think about this . . ." and she gently cupped the triangle of pale red hair between Jane's legs.

Luca lay down next to Jane, reached over, took Jane's hand, laid it on Selina's stomach, and slowly moved it upward to caress Selina's breast, slowly pushing Selina down to a lying position. She smiled over at Jane, who looked down at the softly moaning Selina.

Luca leaned over Jane and softly brushed her lips against Selina's full ones, their tongues briefly touching and doing their own tango. She looked at Jane, who was nibbling at Selina's ear while fondling her breast.

When Jane began lusciously kissing Selina, Luca stood and quickly pulled off her boots and shirt, leaving her clad in a white tank and her tight black leather pants.

The Latin music from the next room pulsed through the bedroom, pulsing through their veins.

This time Luca slid behind Jane, pressing up tightly against her. While Jane's hands roamed and caressed Selina's body, Luca kissed and nibbled at Jane's neck, ear, and between her shoulder blades. Her hands slid easily up and down Jane's shapely curves, relishing the soft, smooth skin, reveling in the way Jane lightly moaned and opened herself further for Luca's enjoyment.

Jane's legs opened, welcoming, when Luca ran her hand down over her tummy and to her thigh, where she brushed lightly against the patch of red hair nestled hidden there. "Oh, not yet baby," Jane whispered.

Luca reached over and took Jane's hand from Selina's breast in her own, gently running it down Selina's body to rest high on her thigh, so she could feel the thick, black hair of Selina's pussy brush her hand.

She looked at Selina over Jane's shoulder. "Have you ever had two women inside of you at the same time?"

Selina's eyes grew wide and her mouth opened, and Jane lifted her head briefly, but then Luca guided Jane's hand into the incredible wetness between Selina's legs so they could share that amazing first feel. And this time, all three of them moaned as one.

Luca and Jane ran their fingers through the damp curls, and then Luca guided Jane's fingers with hers up and into Selina, who gasped and spread her legs wider still.

"Don't worry, Jane," Luca whispered into her ear, "you're next. Have you ever had two women between your legs at the same time? Eating you? Inside of you?" Luca knew that simple words could get a woman incredibly turned on, and she couldn't wait to feel just how turned on Jane really was.

"*Madre de Dios*," Selina whispered as the two women continued fucking her.

"What'd she say?" Jane asked.

Luca responded by pushing Jane's fingers deeper into Selina along with her own. "I translate it to mean, 'Fuck me harder.'"

The combined thrusts of the two women touched every nerve in Selina's body. This sensation of desire started in her groin and shot to the top of her head, flushing her cheeks and numbing the tip of her nose. Jane ran her hand through Selina's hair and leaned over to kiss her deeply. Selina closed her eyes and felt a rush of emotion. It wasn't the kind of emotion she had expected. She felt a deep eroticism unknown to her before this night. Two beautiful women were fucking her and it was all for pleasure. It meant nothing more than what it was—and at that moment it was all for her.

Selina arched her back and moaned into Jane's mouth. With Jane still inside her, Selina felt Luca tugging at her robe, which tightened the hold on Selina's arms. As Luca's strong fingers slid across her nipples, it was enough to make her come for the first time. As she rocked to the intensity of the orgasm, Selina's wrists throbbed against the restraints. *Yes, they can do whatever they want to me and I can't get away. I'm their love slave*, Selina fantasized. *Oh, yes, yes, yes!*

Luca seemed to agree, whispering into her ear as she withdrew her fingers, "All tied up and nowhere to go. The fun's just begun, my femme princess." While Jane nibbled hungrily at her breasts, Selina felt the bed move as Luca stood. She then heard the sound of a zipper coming down.

"I have a present for you," Luca whispered. "Never travel unprepared. That's my motto."

Jane twirled her tongue around a swollen nipple and then looked up. Her long, golden-red hair flowed across her body. "Wow," she said to Luca. "You do travel with the right equipment. Let me help you with that." Jane kissed Selina lightly on the lips. "Darlin'," Jane said, glancing down. "You'll probably want to see this."

Selina turned her head and watched in awe as Jane took the bottle of lube from Luca's hand and began caressing the sizable dildo between Luca's legs with it. The black leather harness that wrapped around the back of Luca's slim waist perfectly matched her undone leather pants.

Jane giggled and rubbed up against Luca's new appendage. "Nice and erect," she murmured, glancing between Luca's legs. "Is that a dildo you've got there, or are you just glad to see us?"

"All of the above," Luca said, with a devilish grin.

Luca wasted no time as she pushed Selina's legs apart and straddled her. She fondled the moist hair between Selina's legs. Selina squirmed beneath her.

"Still beautifully wet, but we don't want to take any chances on hurting you," Luca said as she and Jane rubbed lube all over the dildo.

Selina gasped as Jane directed Luca deep inside her, and then feasted once again on her hard nipples. Biting her lower lip, Selina managed to gurgle hoarsely, "Yes, ladies. Suck me and fuck me at the same time."

Luca rammed the dildo to the rhythm of Selina's thrashing hips. Selina came again with a throaty scream, her fingers clutching the sheets as her hands fought against the tie that bound her.

Jane had never heard anyone come like Selina, and she liked being part of the reason why it had been so good for her. Selina's exhausted "I've just been fucked" look made Jane smile. One of her favorite things in the world to do was to hold a lover once she had achieved that look. "Can I hold you?" Jane asked Selina, and got Selina's sleepy grin and slight nod in reply.

"Don't forget, lovely Jane," Luca whispered, standing up with the dildo between her legs bobbing in all its glory, "you're next, my sweet."

Jane untied Selina and stretched out next to her. She then took Selina in her arms and they cuddled.

"There's room for you, too," Jane said. She motioned to Luca to join them on the other side.

"You're next," Selina said sleepily. She kissed Jane on the cheek and then found her lips. The kiss was deep, her tongue probing. Her hands slid down Jane's body, her fingers finding wetness. *She sure as hell isn't acting like she's sleepy*, Jane thought. Then in one smooth movement, Selina rolled on top of her and began to grind against her. Selina kissed her deeply before rolling off again and lying beside her, her fingers trailing down into the wetness between Jane's legs, teasing the swollen flesh until a burst of heat flamed up from Jane's center and up into her stomach.

Luca was caressing Jane's legs through the silky stockings, pushing her legs further and further apart, opening Jane up for Selina's inquiring hands and fingers.

"You should be in the middle now," Selina said.

"Oh, my goodness," Jane murmured.

"Tell us what you like," Selina whispered. "Or would you prefer that we discover that on our own?"

Luca's mouth and tongue were now doing some very interesting things to Jane's breast, making it hard for her to think. Her hand between her legs, next to Selina's, made it almost impossible for Jane to think . . .

"I'm somewhat partial to sucking and licking, as opposed to sucking and fucking." Jane smiled shyly. "I'm so vanilla they named a wafer after me."

Luca's breath tickled as she continued teasing Jane with flicks of her tongue.

Selina reached over and ran her fingers through Luca's hair. "So," she said, tilting Luca's chin up. "Should we flip a coin to see who gets to lick and who gets to suck?" Selina's hand moved to the side of Jane's face and caressed her so tenderly that it took Jane's breath away.

Luca's unbelievably soft fingers caressed her soft wetness, fondled her swollen flesh, making flames leap throughout Jane's body.

"The winner of the coin toss, *mi amor*," Selina whispered, "will get the pleasure of licking."

And then, as if realizing there were no coins in the bed, Luca went back to worshipping Jane's oh-so-sensitive breasts while Selina slid down between her parting legs.

❦

Luca loved having both the girls, and the hardness of the dildo between her legs reminding her that there was something—someone—left undone. Her attention was all on Jane now.

Damned good thing it's a king-size bed, Luca thought, thinking back to Jane's desire to cuddle. She could well imagine sleeping between two naked femmes—two naked, fully satisfied femmes. Shit, she was really earning her butch credentials tonight.

But who said they even had to sleep?

She started by gently licking one of Jane's already erect nipples while fondling the other breast, her fingers moving across Jane's breast to tweak and tease the other nipple. Jane was moaning from deep inside herself and writhing under Luca's and Selina's expert touches. Now Luca began nibbling lightly on one of Jane's beautiful, deep red nipples while squeezing the other, then she graduated to biting a nipple, which made Jane jerk and moan louder . . .

. . . or maybe it was from what Selina was doing between Jane's shapely legs—what she was doing to Jane's hot, wet pussy.

Luca looked down at Selina's dark head, bobbing between those legs, and knew she wanted some, too. She wanted to taste Jane, to be inside of her. But the sight of that long-haired Chicana head between Jane's luscious thighs was enough to almost make her come herself.

She ran her free hand lightly over Jane's smooth stomach, then across her hip, and then wound her fingers into Selina's thick, dark hair and pulled lightly.

Selina looked up at Luca with a sly, meaningful smile and slowly licked her lips. Luca smiled back, turned, looked into Jane's eyes, then gave each of Jane's incredibly hard nipples a quick bite before she started moving slowly down her body.

Suddenly, there was a loud banging on the door.

Luca looked up at the door, then back at first Jane, then Selina, who was also looking up expectantly. Ignoring the knocking, Luca ran her fingers over Jane, into the hair nestled between her legs, and then into her.

Selina grinned and Jane gasped.

"Selina! Selina! Are you there?" Kim's voice carried over the moans.

Selina looked at Jane and Luca, and the thought that Kim must sound so frantic for a reason was like a tangible object in the room with them.

"Selina! I know you're in there!"

Selina jumped from the bed, frantically grabbing the blanket, forcing Jane and Luca to roll off of it as she pulled. Luca hurriedly pulled the sheet over Jane, whose flushed face and heavy breathing showed her intense disappointment at being so rudely interrupted.

"So, you *are* here!" Kim cried as soon as Selina opened the door, wearing only the blanket. "Omigod," she continued, seeing Selina's disarray, "did I interrupt something?" She tried to step into the suite to peer around Selina and into the bedroom. Selina, however, kept blocking the doorway to keep Kim out.

Kim finally pushed past her, into the suite and into the bedroom before Selina caught her. But she still caught enough of a glimpse to give her ideas. "Jane? Is it Jane? You weren't kidding when you said you were picking up Jane and that cute butch?"

Luca, fully aware that the dildo still hung out from her shorts and pants, swaggered out of the bedroom, strolled over to the shocked Kim, and asked, "Do you wanna make somethin' of it, or do you just wanna join us?"

And she deftly caught the swooning Kim in her strong arms.

In 1999, Peggy J. Herring, Laura DeHart Young, and Therese Szymanski began writing **The Chain Gang Chronicles** *for WomanSpace, a San Antonio, Texas, lesbian publication.*

One author begins a story, passes it along to the next, who does her part, then hands it off to the last to finish. The stories can also be found at www.BellaBooks.com (under Online Stories). This is their first full-length short story written together.

The Curve of Her

Karin Kallmaker

I am watching her at the top of the sliding ladder, her weight all on one foot while she uses the other as a counterbalance to the arm that stretches for a book almost out of reach. She is a curve of hip, a sweep of hair, then a flash of humor as she hands the volume down to the waiting customer.

"That do it for you today, Belle?" I take the Hemingway anthology to put in a bag.

"Thanks, Louisa." Belle pats her pockets in search of her credit cards. "I don't know why Jean likes Hemingway, but it's her birthday tomorrow and she doesn't have this collection yet."

"Girlfriends," I joke. "Can't live with 'em, can't live without 'em."

"Hey," Rayann protests from the top of the ladder, where she is spreading books out on the shelf to hide the large gap where the anthology had been. I watch her fingers on the spines of the volumes, savoring the texture in the same way that I do. I think, then, of her fingers on my skin.

I'm intensely aware of Rayann shimmying down the ladder. The fog of the past week has finally given way to summer heat, at least here in our part of Oakland, and forced her into a simple top and shorts, with the skimpiest of sandals passing for footwear. Her figure seems more ripe and alluring at thirty-two than it was at twenty-nine. She complains about the effects of gravity but I always tell her she hasn't seen anything yet. When she's my age—just shy of fifty-nine—gravity will be an old friend.

She disappears into the recesses of the store. During our vacation, an enthusiastic volunteer made a mess of shelving the new paperbacks, and Rayann has been steadily fixing the mess. I wave goodbye to Belle and go in search of Rayann. I need to gaze at her today; I want more than that.

She is frowning and muttering to herself as she kneels in front of the lower shelves, but the frown dissolves when she looks up at me. "Maybe when we go away we should just tell them not to . . ."

My silence is heavy with desire, then after a moment, her response twines into that silent wanting and I see her arms prickle with gooseflesh.

The silence is broken by her whispered, "Lou," and then she lifts her face. Standing over her I cup my hands in her hair, loving the curving line from her chin to her throat to her breasts. I kiss her then because her eyes ask me to.

When our mouths part she murmurs, "After last night—"

"Because of last night," I answer, after I have kissed her again.

She pulls me down to her and I am—perpetually—in awe of her love for me. I never thought I would have this mystery again. I loved Chris as much and as deeply. When she died in an automobile accident I thought that was all the love there was for me, and it had been enough. Years later, Rayann burst into my life, then into my bed. There is never any danger of mistaking Rayann for Chris—Chris would never have pulled my hands to her breasts, not in the daylight, nor with the lights on, not in the back of the store, no matter how much she wanted me.

Rayann and I were wild together last night and this passion is all the more surprising because of that. She is shivering at the threshold of surrender. Only the time and place holds her back. The bell at the door could ring at any moment, but when she wants me this way, when I want her this way, it will be impossible to stop once I have touched her.

She is unzipping her shorts, inviting my hand inside. Chris—the only other lover I have ever had—would never have done that. There were so many things Chris and I never did, even in our most private moments, things Rayann takes for granted. She grew up in a different world, never having been closeted. Chris and I lived in two closets, the first to hide who we were from employers and my son's teachers, and the second for the benefit of friends we could not and did not want to survive without.

Rayann still does not understand. I've told her how many times my best friend Danny was arrested for not having enough items of women's clothing on her, and how anyone who suspected I was a lesbian could make a call to social welfare to send someone prying into my suitability as a mother. But part of her can't understand and in a way I'm glad of that. Her innocence gives her the freedom to want me like this, to be panting in my arms, to surrender so readily, without worrying if society or friends would approve of who does what, of who goes first, of who comes and how.

I was a mother, and mothers weren't butches. Danny impressed that rule upon me forty years ago. In the world I navigated then, it made sense. Never mind that the labels Danny and our other friends insisted on were backward for me and Chris. Friendship and staunch loyalty meant more to me—and to Chris as well—than any concession I might make over a simple label. We needed our friends and never questioned that we had to hide a part of ourselves to keep them. We were living together, and happy. Back then it was nearly an impossible dream. But it is also true that it was only when we were truly alone, in the dark, that we were free to be who we really were.

Chris would shiver the same way Rayann does, but at this moment, in the dark, Chris would have whispered, "Please make love to me."

In broad daylight, a product of a different world, Rayann pushes my hand down her hip and moans urgently, "Fuck me."

It makes me dizzy that she has forgotten where we are. For a moment I think the ringing in my ears is faintness, but it's the door. A customer. She is too shattered to move, so I get up, kissing the blushing angles of her face one last time.

The afternoon drags on and I catch Rayann watching me as I am watching her, aware of what we want, knowing we will wait, and feeling every tick of the clock as a pulse of building desire. Fifteen minutes before closing she announces that she's going upstairs to our apartment. She'll make a light dinner. I tell her I'll close up.

Only ten minutes have elapsed when the door opens and Danny comes in, her swagger, leather jacket, and thick denims a familiar and loved sight. But tonight I'm hoping she's just stopped in to pick up a book for Marilyn. No such luck—she pours herself the last cup of coffee and settles in for a chat.

I go through the motions of closing up, and like every other time she has dropped by near closing time, she follows me into the stairwell and locks the door behind us, then tromps right behind me up to the door to the apartment. I open the door and can only say, "Uh . . ."

Danny gasps, then grins. She hits me on the shoulder. "I'm in the way, aren't I?" She steps delicately over the trail of clothing Rayann has left, pointing the way to our bedroom.

Rayann, clad only in a very short silk robe that I bought her as an anniversary gift, says, "Oh my God," and disappears from the bedroom doorway.

"I'll just let myself out," Danny says, heading for the apartment's back door, not one whit embarrassed. "You have a nice evening, now. Come to think of it, I have a femme at home who might need taking care of, too."

The door slams and Rayann peeks out the bedroom door. "I'm sorry," she begins.

I am across the room in moments, seizing her by the shoulders, kissing her hard, then pulling her breathlessly to the nearby kitchen table. I am dying for her and she cries out when I take her, her hand circling my wrist as my fingers dive into her heat.

She clings to me with another cry, her legs circling my hips. She makes my head spin. I can't believe she can yield so quickly, and with such strength. She gives and takes in a moment like this, and doing both—letting me know with her body, her voice—only makes me want to please her even more. My own trembling begins. She opens new doors in me, doors that Chris never knew existed. Doors I have deliberately ignored.

Her head is on my shoulder. The first storm has passed. I am listening to her gasp and loving the sound of it when I hear a voice.

"You might want to close the windows," Danny calls smugly from the street in front of the house.

"Oh my God," Rayann says again. She is blushing as she hides her face in my hair. She can't see that I am blushing, too.

My stomach is flipflopping as I close the windows while she goes into the bedroom to do the same there. She is sitting in the shadows of the tapestry over our bed when I join her, her mouth looking swollen. I abruptly understand why I'm thinking about Chris and Danny and labels. I had thought my mind was over it. My body seems to be. Tonight, with her looking at me like that, I am wanting her touch. If I was over these labels, my stomach wouldn't be churning.

I want to give myself to her. Nearly six decades and still I can see myself anew.

I draw the curtains against the evening sun, wanting the dim light because I am on unfamiliar ground.

She undresses me eagerly, her mouth on my throat, my breasts. Until tonight I have thought of this as indulging her need for foreplay; she knows I am usually satisfied when she is.

I am cresting on a river of fluid self-perception, too old not to understand that anything, anyone can change, and still young enough to revel in new experience. With Chris, always in the dark, she wanted me inside her. I loved to inhale her female scent, to taste it until her hands were in my hair, holding me there. I found my own climax—when I needed it—on top of her, straddling her thigh as she touched me. Rayann knows this and has never asked me to be different for her. But tonight, deep in the well of her forthright desire, I am changing anyway. Chris would never have wanted what Rayann needs at this moment, and for the first time in my life I need it, too.

She looks up at me, her eyes full of hunger, her lips curved in thirst. I love filling my mouth with her, knowing her in the most intimate way. She wants to feel that powerful intimacy and I don't want to withhold it from her just because of a label.

I'm not indulging her. Finally, I am aware that I can give and take at the same moment. I want her mouth on me, now. I want it so badly my legs won't support me. She is on top of me and I cannot believe the sensation of her skin on mine. I have seen burning fires in her eyes when she calls my name, but I am the one in flames tonight. My temples are pounding and I make a sound—a plea, an order, something in between.

Her mouth engulfs me. I am washed over with a wave of pleasure that leaves every muscle taut, anticipating. I feel the tensing of her shoulders under my thighs. I have loved giving her what she wants and this is no different. She wants me to come. I never have, like this, but I can't help it, I don't want to help it. My satisfaction is hers, taking now. The battle between past and present is academic. I am opening, offering, clenching, shaking. Her muted cry answers my release. I give her what she wants and finally see that it only makes me stronger.

❧

I manage to raise myself onto my elbows, so I can look at her as she pants for breath after her mouth leaves me. My God, but I love her. I stretch to stroke her cheek and her eyes flutter open. The desire in them is even brighter than before. Partly because I love her so, but mostly because I want it, I cup the back of her head and draw her to me again. Her moan sends a shiver through my hips. Words finally escape me. "Ray, I didn't know."

I don't know if she hears me. It doesn't matter. I think of Chris, who let me be this to her. I remember the first time I was with Rayann, who let me be this to her. She devotes herself to my pleasure with her tongue, her teeth, then one slender finger is inside me and I go with the new wave of ecstasy, spreading from her hands and mouth and into parts of me that have never ached before.

I am impossibly drained. For the first time in my life I consider dozing off before my partner does.

Rayann murmurs, "Thank you," as I often do when I have exhausted her. I hear the pleasure in her voice.

"I'm not done with you," I tell her, though my eyes are closed. "I'm just savoring how wonderful that was."

"Have a nap," she whispers.

"Tempting, but I want you too much to sleep."

She says something, almost shyly, but it's lost in my hair as she turns her head away.

"What did you say?" My fingers at her chin, I turn her face toward me.

She sends a jolt through my spine with, "Prove it."

Touching Stone

Joy Parks

I make the mistake of tickling you.

Your body responds. It rebels against your mind, against what you think should be. What you should be. Your nipples harden under the tight ribbed undershirt you wear to obscure the considerable rise of the breasts you loathe. The softness you conceal under the stiff cotton men's shirt. Hidden under. Always hidden.

I notice. But I don't think it through, don't think at all. The knowledge that I have touched you in such a way, that I might have inspired this loss of control, moves me in places that don't think, cannot think, only feel. I have excited you. But it is a feminine excitement, stirring you in a place that for you should not exist—does not exist. I have been laughing with you, playing; I had forgotten to guard my touch. Let my hand slide slow up from your belly, drift outside the boundaries, allowed my fingers to stop at the firmness beneath your shirt. Unthinking, I touch, gather your breast in my hand, full of excitement, enclosed within my unthinking fingers.

You stop moving, you stop laughing. You stop me. Your fingers are strong; this I know from other nights. I know it now when I feel them circle my wrist, force my hand to release. You pull my hand away, shove me away, push my arm above my head, as far away as you can without hurting me. Without causing me physical pain. You slip away, you shut the door.

It's days before we actually talk, more than a week before you are willing to risk touching me again.

This, I think, is yearning. This is what it is to want and never have. Me, doubled over in the dark, shivering to myself, every night, wave after wave of want washing over me. Never enough. My desire for you, lying beside me, sleeping. Your face turned to the shadows, your thigh warm against me. It would be so easy, I think, to carelessly slide my open palm along your skin. So easy to part your legs, to touch you in your sleep. Would you stop me then? In sleep, are you still on guard, still closed to my touch? Do you sleep with one eye open against the world? Or is the promise of my hands, the curiosity of my mouth, is this enough to bend your resolve? Would you surrender, relinquish this control, submit to me? Could you pretend it's just a dream? That in sleep, you are not responsible, not accountable. Would you allow that?

I wonder. But I never have the courage to try. Or if it were to happen, if I was to succeed . . . I never have the courage to wake with you in the morning, for what that morning would bring.

One day, you decide to legally use your second name, because it is more neutral. It is more masculine. One day, the woman I fell in love with ceases to exist.

I want to know what you feel. What you refuse yourself. I want to know what you mean when you say that making love to me is enough. To see what you see when you watch me rise, strain against your fingers, unveil myself to your mouth. Do you envy me my lack of resistance? The way I melt open under your touch, allow myself to come undone? Do you ever wish for a release like mine, the way I hand over control like a gift? Envy how generous I am with my own need, how I come screaming, shaking, crying, trembling in your arms, every time? Or do you ever resent the way I flood with submission, beg you closer, deeper, harder? Does this disgust you? Or do you secretly wish for my hunger? How my words alone, my raw and open need, must bring you close to the edge, make you wet, stinging, cramped with need. Is it really enough? Does the pleasure lie in your denial, or, on some level of truth you refuse to accept, do you long to fall on your back, pull my hands to you, allow me to give you this, this that you give to me, those things you cannot, will not, allow yourself to want? I want to know.

I wonder. From the way you grind into me after, the sometimes roughness, the almost punishing blows of your angry body crashing into me. I know what you are wishing for, what you wish was between you and me.

Which means what lies between you and me is a lie.

I cry a lot after we make love. I want you to want me. Sometimes I think that you don't want me because you don't believe I can make you happy. That I won't satisfy you. That this will not be enough. And it's true, I'm not sure I know how. Not having the chance to learn. I realize that I don't even know how to give you what you don't want. That scares me most of all.

You tell me you love me. That loving me is enough. *Enough for whom?* I want to ask.

You tell me "it's not that I don't want you. It's that I don't want what wanting you means." All I hear is don't. *Don't want. Don't want you.* You don't want me to want you this way. Not as a woman wants a woman. And I cannot want you any other way. I realize that the way I love you is a violation.

There are nights when the need is almost too much for you to bear. Nights when you nearly break, when I feel your legs open, your hand on mine, considering. Your fingers laced through mine, measuring the need, calculating the cost. It's always too high. I long to find a way to stir you further, take away your options, take you beyond where you care. I want to remove the decision, knowing full well that for you to want me out of desperation, physical need gone out of control, is to not want me at all.

And having to live with you after, knowing how you will pull away from me as you pull away from your body betraying you with the kind of desire you do not want. As much as I long to touch you, I think of the days that would follow, the depth of your humiliation, the damage done to your pride. I cannot be responsible for that.

I'm becoming obsessed, you say. Too much for you to handle, I ask questions that don't have answers. But all I want to know is what this feels like. What it feels like to hold such closeness in my hand, to taste love, the intimacy of such a revelation, to ride wave after wave of desire with my tongue. But no. Some nights after, when I hear you finally drop to sleep, I put my hand between my own legs, feel myself still swollen, drenched with my need of you. Silent, barely breathing, I run my finger down through the soft rings of wetness, stroke the slip and fall of me. Shudder quietly. I pretend that this is no longer my body; I block out the feel of my own touch. Open myself only how it feels to touch. Nothing more.

I pretend that this is me touching you. I think about bringing my fingers to my lips. Taste what you taste. But I never do.

We used to go dancing in straight clubs. You passing successfully for male, more gentlemanly than any man in the room, better at this than anyone would think possible. The easy way you lit my cigarette, ordered my drinks, how practiced. How frightening. Your expensively cut suits, your breasts bound beneath, so tightly even I feel not even the faintest swell beneath my own breasts when we dance close. And we do. But I can never relax, never settle into this rhythm, dance this dance in which you always lead. I feel like a fraud. My teeth on edge, my heart on edge, sitting at the edge of my chair waiting for someone to notice your lack of beard, your sweet-toned voice strained against the noise.

Just one stray gesture, that's all it would take. But it never happens; we are never found out, each night out is a triumph. And you, later, strutting to the car victorious, hang on to me like I am something you have won.

In this city where no one knows you, you humor me. You laugh at my fear of being revealed in a straight bar and consent to come with me to lesbian clubs where women who look like women dance with other women who look like them. Mirrors dancing in the darkly lit room. I have no mirror. You are not a reflection of me, you would hate the idea of that. It makes me lonely in a way I have never been before.

I cannot take my eyes off the women dancing, slow, their faces soft in the candles that glow on each small tabletop, the cheap

Christmas lights that adorn the ceiling. I stare at the pairings of round hips, see breasts relaxed one into the other like a range of hills, a landscape from a country for which I'm just so homesick. I watch couples snuggle, kiss, touch each other's faces and necks and shoulders, their fingers lightly grazing breasts when they think no one will see. This is what I want. No one policing where a hand might go, where lips are brushed; no rules on what can be said or by whom.

I long for this. And you know. You can see it in my eyes, in how my lips are parted in the dark. The way I breathe, low, watching, how excited I become, how I have to press against you on the dance floor just to still myself. You know it. You pull my hands from around your waist, place them on your shoulders, firm, like a warning. Your mouth is set hard, your eyes are uneasy, the stiffness in your shoulders tells me, "I'm not one of them; you are not one of them. You can't be one of them and be one with me."

After a while, we stop going dancing altogether.

I read about our history. No. My history. You are not one of us. Passing women. Stone butch. No. Not you. A butch is a lesbian. A lesbian is a woman.

You would never admit to this.

"I want to marry you," you whisper. You have been talking about the operation. That makes you feel romantic.

No. Can I say that? Can I say no to marriage, no to what you want to become and still love you? I don't want to be your wife. I don't to be anyone's wife. This is why I chose you. This is why I chose this. This was what I thought choosing you, choosing this, would mean.

I want to be your lover. This is not what you want at all.

I watch lesbian couples now all the time, whenever I can. I seek them out, go places I know they will gather, try harder than ever to convince you to come with me. And sometimes you do and I am surprised, pleased until I see you sitting there, among us, sitting silent, superior.

Us. I am starting to say this too, *us*, not to mean you and me. Meaning them and myself. But you are above all this. You are beyond this kind of need. And each day, you grow a little more beyond me.

Sometimes I sneak out alone, go to places where you will no longer go. I watch women make advances to other women, I go to bars where this is done. I wonder what this feels like, to know a woman wants you, that she wants you to want her because she is woman. That this want in you is what she finds irresistible. That we would both want the same thing. This is what I want.

I find lesbian friends, fill the house with lesbian books, and put lesbian art on the walls. I stop shopping, stop cleaning the house so much, develop politics, casually begin to use words like "patriarchy" and "oppressor." You recede, remove, refuse to comment. I grow closer to all this as I grow further from you. We stop going out of the house together, stop being a couple in public. I want to be in places where women are together, I want to be with them. I know this is not what I have with you. I watch and long for you and me to be like this, to be easy. It seems so natural, so loving. This is what I want; I want loving you to be this easy. That is how I imagine loving a woman to be.

But it isn't all that easy. My hair isn't right, my clothes aren't right, my smile is too ready. There is nothing right about me. Sometimes I forget to fully wipe the smear of lipstick from my lips. The times aren't right for this now. Not lesbian enough for them, too much so for you, not enough of one thing or another for either. I cut my hair, I buy new clothes, I dismantle everything you know about me. Eventually, you stop touching me at all.

I find myself wondering what happens after you.

Later, there will others like you—but not like you at all. There will be women I am afraid to touch at first, my fingers tentative in the dark until I hear the right tone of sigh, till I hear them call for my touch, words unintelligible, the low gurgle of need in their throat. I will not touch them until I know their need is real.

In spite of myself, I will continue to want women who are strong against the world, tough in their Levi's and leather, their boots pronouncing their arrival, their sneers and their silences, their undeniable presence and their quiet unshakable anger. But unlike you, they will open themselves to me. I will know these women by their skin, by how they will undress for me, peel away their guard with each piece of clothing. Lie backward, let me touch them shaking, undone with need, let me hear their want whispered low. Just for me. And I will understand all that this means, how much it takes.

For years, for me, it will take a hand on mine, pressing gently, guiding me. I will need to be led, coaxed down their bodies, need to feel the soft, firm pressure on the back of my neck, my cue to taste them. Through this, through them, I will learn my own strength. I will know what it is like to feel the flutter inside, the grip of yearning for my touch, how desire tastes, how far it can take me. I will learn so much about them. And about me.

Each of these women will be more than precious to me. Because I will know what it means to touch a woman who walks through the world untouchable. And I will be so careful, so gentle, so grateful. I will know how far to go, when to yield, when to hold my ground. I will know when to pull a woman back on top of me, let her regain her strength, when to give and when to give up. I will learn how to take without taking over. How to calm them, make them lose inhibitions without losing their power, without losing themselves. I will know how to make a women feel as butch on her back as she does in her boots. I will learn that it is my gentleness, not my weakness, that can make another woman feel strong. And I will touch them with everything I could never give to you.

You are pacing the apartment; your boots click the wood floor like a clock, measuring what time is left to us. Your jacket flying, your smooth creamy skin and hard, set jaw. Do you have any idea how beautiful you are? No, of course you don't. You are raging, angry at the world and at what you cannot be within it. That there is no home for you, not in this world, not in this apartment, not in me, not even within your own body. There is no way I can make you feel at home any longer. You rage at me, your anger turned inside, rage on about how I should find a real man, not you, what you can never be.

I grow brave, I grow wings; I fly above your fury with the truth, something you will have no part of. We argue over what I want, what I want to be. You talk me down from my desire, like a jumper from the rooftop.

Then you grow calm. Now I'm the one who won't be consoled. You tell me, for a final time, "You're not like that, not one of them. If you were, you wouldn't be attracted to me."

You hate what I have become, hate me for what it says about you. You dismiss my feelings like you dismiss me from your body. I tell you that a man is the last thing I want, the last thing I want you to be. That what I want, all I want, is standing right in front of me.

You walk away.

I think about how I want to touch you, try one last time to touch you beneath your clothes, how easy it would be to walk the few steps across the floor to you, slip my hand inside your shirt, unzip your fly, reach inside. How it might change everything.

How easy. How utterly unthinkable.

More tender, later, exploring, slow. This is all I want, just your fingers, stroking the soft cries from beneath my skin, this is all it will take. Just to feel your tender strength stir gently inside me. But no, it's not enough for you. Later, you on top of me, riding me, our fight earlier takes hold of you, I feel you rise, free yourself from your shorts. I pause, feel the tug inside, the agony of waiting for you to press against me, skin nestled inside skin. I feel you slippery with need, the wet of you, the heat. You whisper, "I want to come inside of you." I raise my hips, wrap my legs around you. As you dream of being inside me, I dream, too. I shudder as my wetness finds yours, soft as a mouth, the soft slip a kiss, the thrill and pull and wonder of your finally bare skin touching mine. I strain against you, close enough I hope, to make you feel what I feel, close enough that you will know how much I long for this, how I long to pull the kiss inside.

How can I tell you that this is not just enough? That it is every-thing?

Much later, I dream. I am sitting at the edge of the lake, my legs in the water, my thin gown grown wet and transparent. My curves revealed, my breasts exposed to the warm sun, my legs moving gently with the rhythm of the waves. I begin to slide into the water, rock deeper into the wetness. The surface of the water licks at my lips, my tongue darts out to taste. Salt. I long to dive beneath, drink my face wet. Below, my fingers graze a mossy crevice in the rock, lake-bottom slippery, so smooth. I grow wet, aroused, my breasts pushing forward, demanding to be touched, stroked, sucked. My fingers search, explore the creamy wetness of rock, feel the firmness beneath. The sun beats down on me now, my whole body awash with heat and sun and light, my fingers moving over each wet smooth curve and round of rock. Seeking out, touching the space between. Such smoothness, such softness, such exquisite heat. Waking to realize . . .

. . . I am touching stone.

Pandora's Box

D. L. White

Even as rain drizzled softly around me, I paused to watch my reflection ripple in the puddle at my feet. The purple and acid pink of the club's neon sign traced my watery image like electric patchwork. I checked my watch and then checked myself, mentally preparing for what was to come. How long had it been since we had last done something like this? Two years? Yeah, two, how could I forget? That vacation to Mexico and the anonymous butch surgeon who seduced me in the hotel bar with only tequila and words. Two years, three months, five days and . . . A truck rumbled by in the night, causing tiny quakes to disturb the puddle on the corner on which I suddenly felt apprehensive standing.

A pack of lesbians high on the after gleam of sex—or the hope of it—were cramming the entrance of the club when I stepped under the blinking lights flashing *Pandora's Box* in bold letters. My reflection in the window showed that the light turned my auburn tresses to purple sheen, and the female bouncer with the crooked smile waved me past the throng of waiting women. Her eyes spared a second glance at my bare legs and the short skirt that displayed them. I whisked past the large woman, before allowing the deep recesses of the club to swallow me up.

Music vibrated under my feet inside the club's dark, cavernous surroundings. The loud music was a living entity, sliding between the women smoking, laughing, and dancing. I moved through the sea of pulsating bodies on the dance floor. Cologne, smoke, and heat swept over me, but I managed to reach the bar successfully.

I sat down and watched as a constant onslaught of orders from the crowd kept the three bartenders busy. Tension slithered under my skin. I yearned for a cigarette but cheated myself by pulling out a pack of gum instead. Two chews of spearmint and I couldn't take it anymore; my anxiety hit its peak. I dipped into my handbag and pulled out the infamous pack. Tapping a cigarette out I realized all too late that I didn't have a lighter.

There was a short rasp, then a lambent flame danced silently in front of me. Hesitating briefly I leaned forward, kissing my cigarette to the flame. I sat back and inhaled slowly. The hand that held the lighter moved away and I stared up into eyes the color of dark chocolate. The warm scent of cologne and cloves teased my nostrils. The barwoman regarded me silently. "Thank you," I uttered softly.

Her eyes took me in, cradled me momentarily, and then flicked down to my cigarette. "Hate to see a woman in distress." The liquid cadence of her voice belied her hard appearance.

I nonchalantly shook my head. "I'm trying to quit."

"I see."

I blinked, not knowing how to interpret the slight grin tracing the bartender's full mouth. I eyed her: loose jeans, black-ribbed tank top, spiked dog collar around the strong oak-brown neck, and a shrewd crew cut that was left devilishly long in the front. *Different, so different.* The type of dyke that would ride me on her Harley and then let me ride her mouth afterward.

"Free drink for your name."

"Jayda." I tapped the cigarette against the ashtray that sat in front of me. "Gimme my drink."

"Jayda," she repeated. "Beautiful."

Moments later she put a tall glass of translucent liquid in front of me. With a wink she dropped in a couple of plump cherries. I eyed the concoction suspiciously. "Try it," she encouraged.

I stubbed my cigarette out and took a few tentative sips. It was strong and sweet with a flicker of heat going down. I nodded approval and unconsciously allowed myself to smile. "Nice."

Her grin was slow. "Glad you like it, Jayda."

"It's delicious, thank you."

"Haven't seen you here before. What brings you to Pandora's Box tonight?" She leaned on the bar, muscles flexing underneath the tribal tattoos covering her arms.

"Slow down. Tell me your name first."

She licked her bottom lip deliberately; causing the silver stud adorning her chin to dart up. "Devon."

"Well, Devon, don't you have some work to do?" My eyes flickered over the bar full of people.

"They can wait." Devon's gaze wandered over me—I swear they were ripping my clothes off and touching the heat and flesh they exposed. "What can I say? You got my attention. Here with friends?"

I shook my head, stirring my drink with the straw.

"Waiting on your lady, then?"

"Hardly."

Realization dawned in her features. "I see. So, how long have you and she been apart?"

"Brilliant deduction, Watson."

"Are you over her yet?"

"And just what do you hope to gain by my answer?"

"Free rein to seduce you, my dear." Devon gave a smile that was part perplexing and part intense.

The heat of her gaze sent a delicious frisson through me. I swallowed slowly, sliding my focus back to my drink. In my mind I immediately invented a falsity my heart wouldn't dare believe. No more butches, I declared, to keep the rhythm of the evening flowing. Not even suave, dangerously handsome ones like Devon. For good measure and to help me meekly battle the other woman's seductiveness, I gave myself an afterthought about being wronged by one too many a butch. I played to win, and I wouldn't allow Devon to score unless I was good and ready.

We danced in conversation, skirting the edges of the mutual attraction that swung like a pendulum between us. Her voice held me to the moment; captured, I swam in its timbre.

She touched me as she spoke—a gentle stroke of her fingers tracing my wrist, nostrils flaring gently, inhaling my scent like an animal on the hunt. I flushed with a desire I could not claim. Devon's words claimed it for me. "Do you know how damn sexy you are?"

I tried my best to hide my blush.

"Do you?" she asked again.

"No." I took more of the fiery drink into my mouth.

She held my hand and traced a pattern into my palm with the tip of a finger. "Can I show you?" Her voice was a silent storm, falling dark and deep. "Show you how sexy you are?" Her finger ran circular patterns into my flesh, jolting me to every nerve ending.

"Damn . . ." I breathed. I looked down at the lips now pressed against my palm. A soft lash of hot, wet tongue and Devon straightened, unwilling to release my hand.

The kiss seeped through my skin, invisibly marking me, staking claim. Arousal swam through my body, flooding my senses and playing against the smooth heat from the exotic drink and the heat caused by the tall woman in front of me. I watched Devon's lips lift slightly, begging to be licked and deliciously tortured by my own mouth. If she licked her lips one more time I would have to jump her ass right behind the bar and do her until security separated us. The mere thought of taking this butch and having her take me in return made my nipples hard.

"I like you," she said simply.

Lust stirred in my belly. "What should I do about that?"

"Jayda!" I heard Carmen's familiar voice shout from the crowd, but the alcohol and Devon's eyes had me drunk and immobile.

"Trust your instincts." And then she swung toward the other end of the bar to attend to the busy crowd.

I closed my eyes and savored the last traces of the drink in my glass. When Carmen drew close with her innocent flirtations and curious hands, I allowed her to lead me onto the dance floor. Tonight it wasn't her awkward seduction that had her thinking she had scored, but the lust Devon had previously planted within me. Carmen and I moved together on the dance floor, two femmes to one groove. The thumping, hypnotic music was reminiscent of a loft party where clothes cling and sweaty bodies melt into one another. Carmen was sweet, innocent, and safe. She curbed my insistent craving for the raw intricacy of a butch, but one like Devon could easily sway my decision.

She pushed against me until something or someone else was pushing back. My ass touched hardness and a wall of heat. A hand adorned heavily with glinting silver rings swung around my waist, pulling me close. I was dizzy and supple. Devon's voice spoke my name behind me while she molded my back to her front. Through eyes slit by desire and intoxication I watched Carmen dance in front of me. Lengthening my arousal with a long kiss, Carmen wrapped herself in my arms and the three of us were moving like a single wave.

Devon's hands were strong and sure, guiding my hips and pressing my ass against the definite bulge in her pants. I moaned and continued to do so while her mouth sank into the curve of my neck. Boxed in between two heated, touching bodies I was steam—weightless and hot. Through the haze Carmen kissed me, her lips cool against mine, before she smiled knowingly and melted away into the crowd. Devon spoke without speaking, continuing to grind her thoughts against my ass and allowing my desire to read her mind like telepathy. The humidity between my legs was overwhelming as was her scent, her embrace, and the kiss she turned me around to taste.

"God, you're fucking sexy." Her words were a slow growl against my lips as her tongue swirled into my moist mouth.

I knew at that moment that I'd let this handsome woman take me right here on the dance floor if she so chose. My tongue darted to meet hers until I was treading the edge of a pounding orgasm. The want was in place; we needed only to fulfill it now. Devon reluctantly pushed our bodies apart. "My shift is over in a half hour." She tilted my chin up with a single fingertip. "Meet me out front."

I nodded weakly, unable to deny her anything at this point. She gathered me for one more lingering, wet-sliding assault on my mouth. "Half hour." Then she was gone, her cologne a potent afterthought in which I breathed.

Two more drinks and five songs later I lit a clove cigarette on the balcony of the two-story home. As I exhaled, I suddenly felt the hairs on the back of my neck prickle. A soft quake went all the way down my body.

I didn't need to turn around to know Devon stood behind me. In confirmation, a long, leather-sheathed arm reached over my shoulder to deftly pluck the cigarette from my mouth. I turned around and Devon's gaze slid over me.

She took a drag on the cigarette, letting the smoke escape her nostrils. I admired the dangerous look of her leather jacket.

"Can I get you anything?" Devon took another pull on the cigarette and then flicked it over the balcony. "Coffee, beer, my bed?" She grinned, animalistic lust glinting in her dark eyes.

I smiled. "Nice pad for a bartender's salary."

Devon pulled off her jacket and slung the leather on a patio chair. "I have a roommate and stock interests."

"Oh, stock interests. Why didn't I guess?"

"Come here." It was not a statement, but a request.

I made the necessary steps to close the distance between us. She swept me into her arms and devoured my mouth in a deep kiss that shook me to my knees.

Her tongue plunged into my willing mouth. Callused hands raked over my body, smoothing me to creamed warmth. When her hands reached under my skirt to cup my bottom, I felt a flare of heat scorch through me and settle between my legs. I don't even know how it was possible, but I screamed softly.

Devon ended the kiss, opting to nibble on my chin, neck, shoulders, and my blood-warm earlobes. "Turn around." I turned to face the winking city lights once more, acutely aware of the warm breeze kissing under my skirt. Devon kneeled to draw my red, silk thong down my legs. With an admiring leer, she pocketed the thong and instructed me to remove the rest of my garments. When I reached down to remove my high-heeled pumps first, she stopped me. "No. Leave the pumps. I like them."

I threw off my thin wraparound skirt. Next came the silk camisole. My pear-shaped breasts immediately fell into the embrace of Devon's waiting hands. With thumb and forefinger she began to work them, coaxing the nut-brown nipples to hardness in a matter of seconds.

I bit my lip and moaned.

"That's it baby." Devon's words were hot strokes against my ear. "Show me you like it."

She then slid her hands down the front of my nude body while her lips burned their way down my back. I grasped the balcony rail, its solidness anchoring me to the moment. She squeezed my cheek and whispered, "Spread your legs, little one."

For a moment I was apprehensive, thinking Devon rather arrogant to believe that she could have me any which way she pleased, but the soft smack on my vulnerable ass quickly shut up my silent debate and I parted my legs as I was told.

Humid air teased between my parted thighs. The current slipped across my exposed center, stirring the moisture that was already gathering there.

Then came the softest, sweetest pleasure that ripped yet another groan from my throat. Devon's tongue was there, teasing and light as an eyelash fluttering against a warm cheek. She coaxed me wonderfully with the tip of her tongue, barely giving me a chance to exalt in the supreme gratification of pressure.

Her tongue flicked around and dipped briefly into slick folds, carefully covering every inch of drenched flesh. She pressed up hard until the delicious tip of her tongue caught the cleft at the top. Then her flat, thick tongue swept everywhere at once, conjuring cream from me like a well-versed magician. Devon drank from my well greedily, smoothing her tongue to me in a rhythm that had my breath coming out in staccato beats.

Damn, I thought, this stud in all her urban finest was turning my body out, and I responded to her attentions as if I were already captured and claimed. When her full lips enveloped the tender bundle of nerves between my legs, I felt my mind go right along with my body. I felt my clit hungrily extended beyond my plump, swollen lips, and Devon took advantage of it, stroking and massaging the hardened nub between her wet lips until I shook all over.

Her tongue stiffened and began to lap long and hard in between my lips, feeding my heat deeper and deeper. My moist insides gripped and contracted along the smooth length of her tongue like life itself depended on it. Bent over with head thrown back, I rode on the delicate muscle pumping into me, my hips thrusting backward to get a firm grasp on the pleasure that Devon was pounding into me.

Heat, fluid and mind-blowing, swung through me, as an intense orgasm began to ripple and expand within my body. Tears stung behind my closed eyelids as her wet tongue thrust deeper into me, producing tiny vibrations that shook me internally. I cried out and shamelessly didn't stop until the last tremor rocked my body.

Devon gently stroked the back of my trembling legs as she made the trek back up my body. She softly bit my neck, heightening my arousal even more.

"That was nice, but I need more."

She indicated the apparent hardness encased in the crotch of her jeans. My mouth watered at the implications. Devon slowly unzipped her jeans, exposing her black dildo. She crooked her finger, beckoning me forward. "Your mouth. Here. Now."

I gracefully kneeled to the task, feeling dirty and desirable all in one instant. I was overwhelmed and high on the thought of having a butch, deep and hard, in my mouth once again. To surrender and to pleasure was so powerful a combination that my body trembled uncontrollably with the implications. Devon grabbed my head to guide her cock between my lips. The large tip split my lips wide and I felt my mind go along with my mouth. When she had bottomed out, when the extent of her reached depths in me I never imagined feeling again, I held tight and kissed the very essence of this butch with my throat. My reward was a hungry groan, low and deep. She needed me and I wanted to be needed by her.

I allowed my softness to envelop her and boldly, in slow degrees, she let me swallow her whole. I worked her desperately, feeling the responding heat between my own legs while she guided my head forward and back. Then there was a deliberate and firm ascension to the tip, only to plunge me all the way forward onto her again. Her hard breathing pierced through the pockets of suckling noises coming from my mouth. I had come undone. I held her in my hands, stroking up more fire while I tasted her hard length against the contrasting softness of my tongue. I sucked and swirled my tongue on her, dying to feel and see her unravel like me. Teasing the tip with the wet flicker of my tongue and sliding back down to the base caused her to shove into me, physically demanding more.

I wanted her to come, to release herself in the warmth of my mouth. I tightened my lips, challenging her resolve; she grunted and held back. Her stamina amazed me and I tirelessly let her fuck my mouth as I reached between my legs to stroke myself. My mouth became the tangible tie that held us together. The rhythm was caught and we moved as one, my head dipped and bobbed to take more of her in and she thrust forward to bury herself in me. I cradled her with my lips and lashed at her mercilessly with my tongue. Her powerful body began to shake all over and I held on tight, sucking her with the clamping breadth of my mouth, the hardness of her prick sawing back and forth between my lips until she began to groan in a tortured cry. Deep circles now, she held my head close, preferring to prolong the moment by now teasing me with her cock. She plunged in, letting it slide down my throat, and I moaned to let her know how good it felt, and then she slowly withdrew until the bulbous end lay at the tip of my tongue. Hard ebony and moist pink never looked so good together. Or felt good for that matter, I thought, as she swept the dildo back and forth on my tongue and along the shiny wet of my lips. My eyes caught hers, and I could actually feel her internal moan as I suddenly ducked low and captured all of her back into the heat of my mouth in one sliding movement. I held her captive with the tight suck of my mouth and the stroke of my hand. In slow motion, I watched her eyes glaze over with desire and a second orgasm. The sight of her made my insides clamp hungrily over and over again, desperate to be filled and satisfied. I needed her now. Her orgasm made her grunt and buckle uncontrollably and I held on for the last strains of her panting sonata.

Devon sensed my need and was surprisingly ready for me again. In a blur of motion, she pulled me up and pushed me against the balcony railing. I immediately gripped the brick overlay with my hands. This time we shot straight to the point without pretense. Devon was slick and hard all at once, torching me internally. My breasts jiggled with her grinding motions and she couldn't resist clamping her hand around one soft, bobbing tit. She groaned hard, closing her eyes as she pumped mercilessly into my slick sheath.

Noises crashed all around me and I finally realized they were coming from my own mouth. I shouted, I screamed, I whimpered and begged to the strong woman who panted out her verbal lusts against my ear while her hips ground hard and close.

"That's it, Jayda, let me fuck you."

Her words sent a bolt through me, my body responding to her voice like a physical stroke. I thrust my hips firmly into the white-hot heat that stroked into my clinging depths. Her elongated thickness was a welcomed assault inside of me, and I felt like crying because it felt so good. She was talented, knowing how deep to go and what places to stroke. I was split open and wet by her, taking her hard into me and panting out for more of the hard sensation that would eventually throw me over the edge. Bodies joined in mutual need, we melded together, moving as one entity—grinding, undulating, and caressing until we exploded into particles of burning light.

Our breaths came out ragged and fast and Devon held me until we both were able to descend into calmness. She slid out slowly, tucking herself back into her jeans with a long sigh. I melted into her large arms and she gave me a kiss to remember and a slap on the ass to go with it.

I stood on the same corner again, a new night sky stretched overhead. I needn't bother checking my watch pretending I was apprehensive. This night was mine. I crossed the street and swept through the doors of Pandora's Box directly through a group of paying dykes. Again the large bouncer gave me an appreciative glance, but said nothing.

The crowd was pulsing, the drinks flowing. I drifted through the throng, searching for the face that had filled my fantasies all day. She was not at the bar. I scanned the mass of sweaty bodies, trying to spot her waiting on tables, but her tall form was nowhere in sight. Without a second thought I made my way over to the stairs that led the way to the private second floor.

I took the steps two at a time, passing through hallways paneled with cherry wood and soft lighting. Excitement fueled anticipation; anticipation fueled my lust as I followed the curve of the hall that broke off into several doors. I stopped in front of the first door, licked my lips, and smoothed my hands over my strapless, form-fitting black dress. I tentatively knocked and stepped inside at the muffled response.

The head bartender and my friend Carmen, who was one of the club's DJs, were talking at once, standing in front of the large desk. The clamor died when I stepped in looking as if I belonged there.

"Carmen, Lee, we'll finish up later," the voice behind the desk confirmed. "I need you on the floor yesterday."

Lee and Carmen nodded. Carmen came over and kissed my cheek, and I turned as if to follow her but closed the door behind them instead.

Behind the desk sat the club's owner dressed in tailored black slacks, crisp long-sleeved shirt, gray vest, and sharp burgundy tie. As she perused online stock reports on the laptop centered on the desk, the light caught the flash of her wide-faced Swiss watch.

She looked up from the screen and grinned at me. "Hey, love of my life."

I pouted playfully. "You said no more late nights."

She held up a hand in defense. "I know, and I promise it will be the last, but I had some unfinished business to take care of." She dug into her pants pocket and pulled out my red silk thong, twirling it around her finger as she eyed me with sudden anger. "A little gift you left with one of my bartenders, baby?"

I gasped, knowing I was caught, fumbling for words as my wife's hard, penetrating gaze finally transformed into a lustful grin. "We shouldn't wait so long to do this again, love." Devon winked. "So, what will the role be for tomorrow night?"

I crossed over to my lover and straddled her lap. I immediately became victim to Devon's lips as she kissed me full and long, drenching my mouth with need.

Pulling away in a daze, I wrapped my arms around her strong neck as Devon Pandora slid my dress over my hips and began to massage my bare bottom.

"How about I tie you up tomorrow night?" I suggested with a wicked smile.

"Jay-da," Devon drawled deeply.

"Okay, scratch that idea. Well, I've always had this fantasy of being ravished by a woman in uniform . . ."

Escapade

Carol Rosenfeld

Louisa Crette lived alone in a small house by the river on the outskirts of our small town. I could tell Mama didn't approve of her. When she saw Mrs. Crette in church on Sundays, Mama would just nod her head and say, "Louisa." She wouldn't ask Mrs. Crette about her roses or vegetable garden, or comment on the weather, the way she would with other women.

I tried to figure out what Mama's objection might be. Mrs. Crette was divorced, but so was our neighbor Irene Watkins, and Mama had her over to our house for coffee at least once a week.

So I asked Mama what she had against Mrs. Crette. She said, "Louisa Crette left her husband."

"Irene Watkins is divorced, too. What's the difference?"

"Mrs. Watkins' husband left her for someone else."

"Was Mrs. Crette the one who left? Did she leave her husband for someone else?"

"I've heard some talk," Mama said.

"Well?"

"You know I don't pass on rumors. I'm not going to tell you something unless I know for a fact that it's true. Now go do your homework and put some practical information into that head of yours."

I wondered if Mama was jealous. Mrs. Crette had a way of making other women look a little faded. Her lipsticks were brighter, and her hair seemed to have more shine to it. Looking at her, you were aware of her body. Where Mama would leave only one or two buttons of her blouse undone, Mrs. Crette would leave three.

I didn't tell Mama that sometimes when I was walking along the river path, Mrs. Crette's dog Sandy would bark to let her know there was someone around. Mrs. Crette would look up from her gardening or step outside the back door onto the porch and wave me off the river path and up to her house. The house was wood, painted a grayish-blue that made me think of water.

Mrs. Crette always seemed to have some little chore she needed help with, like taking down the curtains so she could wash them, or putting some canned goods on the top shelf in the little pantry. Wasn't Mama always saying I should help our neighbors?

Afterward, we'd sit out on the porch, drinking iced tea. Mrs. Crette liked to sit in the wicker rocking chair, while I preferred the chair with the ottoman. We'd talk about what I was reading, and sometimes I told her about being teased for being the tallest girl in my class. Then Mrs. Crette would say she had reason to be glad of my extra inches, and I'd feel proud instead of awkward.

Mama's friends were always pestering her about me and boys. One night I was in my room, supposedly doing my algebra homework, but I was really listening as Mama served Mrs. Watkins and Mrs. Harvey coffee and pie in the kitchen.

"Grace, did Ameza get a date for the prom yet?" Mrs. Watkins asked.

"She could go with the Jackson boy; he's almost her height, 'long as she doesn't wear high heels," Mrs. Harvey said.

"Ameza isn't going to wear high heels," Mama said. "And the only dancing she's likely to do is on the basketball court."

"I've seen the way that Crette woman looks at your sweet little lamb," Mrs. Harvey said. "Mark my words, the fox is getting ready to pounce."

"Ameza is sweet," Mama replied. "But I wouldn't exactly call her a lamb. She's more like a wild colt—all legs and always running."

"You mean a filly, don't you Grace?" Mrs. Harvey asked.

"Yes Doris, you're right. A filly."

I didn't understand what Mrs. Harvey meant about the way Mrs. Crette looked at me. I wished Mrs. Harvey would mind her own business. But she didn't.

"Ameza, Doris Harvey told me she saw you walking with Louisa Crette, carrying two bags of groceries."

"Mrs. Crette asked me if I would carry them for her, Mama."

"And where was Andy Noonan? He's the delivery boy."

"Andy wasn't around, and I was."

"Did you go into her house?"

"Well, I had to put the bags down on the kitchen table, didn't I? I couldn't leave them out on the porch."

Mama's hands were on her hips and her lips were pressed together. "Did she touch you?"

"Why would you think to ask such a thing, Mama?"

"Never mind about that. Just answer me, Ameza. Did that woman put her hands on you?"

"She asked if she could feel my bicep," I said.

"Your what?"

I bent my arm and clenched my fist. "Mrs. Crette said she thought it was a good thing for women to be strong. She asked me to flex my bicep. Then she asked if she could feel it. She said she likes to see women have some muscles."

"I'm sure she does," Mama said. "Stay away from Louisa Crette, Ameza."

But I hadn't told Mama everything. I hadn't told her that while Mrs. Crette was running her fingertips over my bicep, I asked her if she was wearing perfume.

"Yes, I am. Do you like it?"

"You smell nice," I said.

"It's real French perfume. Very expensive, so I only use a little bit." She went on, demonstrating as she talked. "I put it behind my knees, on my wrists, inside my elbows, behind my ears. Here"—she touched the hollow at the base of her throat—"and here." She slid her finger underneath her dress, into the cleavage I couldn't see. And because I couldn't see it, her action made me more aware of her breasts than I would have been if the neckline of her dress had been lower. She was wearing a short-sleeved, long-skirted dress in pale blue patterned with small, dark blue flowers. The dress buttoned all the way down. That night I dreamed I unbuttoned every single one of those buttons. The dress fell open, and Mrs. Crette was naked. I put my hands on her waist and kissed her. I woke up hot and twitchy, and ran double my usual laps around the track before class.

"I won't do it," I said.

"Please, Ameza. Every other girl in your class will be wearing a dress."

"I don't care."

"It's one day out of your life," Mama said.

"No!" I ran out of the house, grabbed my bike, and headed for the river. I found a shady spot and lay down under a willow tree. I put my hands behind my head and looked up at the sky. My breathing slowed and the fury that had fueled my flight cooled to frustration.

"Ameza, is that you?"

I sat up and twisted my body to one side. "Oh hi, Mrs. Crette."

"May I join you?"

"Sure."

She sat down next to me, leaning back against the trunk of the tree, spreading the skirt of her dress over the ground.

I lay back down and put my hands behind my head again.

"I love this river," Mrs. Crette said. "It makes me feel so peaceful. At night I lie in my bed and fall asleep to the lullaby of the water."

"I know what you mean," I said. "I come here when I need to get away from things that are bothering me."

"Would you like to tell me what's bothering you today?" Mrs. Crette asked.

"Mama wants me to wear a dress to graduation."

"Of course she does," Mrs. Crette said. "She's your mama. It's a special occasion for her, too—her only child graduating from high school."

"I hate dresses," I said, sitting up again and turning to face her.

"Well, not on you. Dresses suit you."

Mrs. Crette wore dresses a lot. Most of them had flowers on them. The dress she had on that day was pale green and strewn with large pink roses. I looked at her face and realized her lips were rose-colored too.

"Thank you, Ameza," Mrs. Crette said. "Y'know, when you go away to college, you'll be able to wear whatever you want to." She stretched out her arm and slowly ran her hand over my head, letting her thumb trace a path behind my ear. Her fingertips brushed the nape of my neck, and I shivered.

I looked at her. "Do you know why my mama acts so funny around you?"

Mrs. Crette smiled. "It's just part of her worrying about you, honey," she said.

She'd never called me honey before. The way she said it, I could almost taste the word—liquid sunshine, warm and sweet.

❧

The following Sunday, Mama and I went over to Greenvale for Cousin Ruth's seventieth birthday party.

Cousin Ruth was Mama's oldest living relative. I hadn't seen her for several years. When I went up to her to pay my respects, she squinted and stared at me.

"You have the look of her."

"Who, Cousin Ruth?"

"Mathilde. My youngest sister."

I was confused. I'd never heard of Mathilde. I thought Ruth's youngest sister was Florence. "Will she be here today?"

"Who?"

"Mathilde.

"She disgraced our family," Cousin Ruth said. "Moved up north; calls herself Mattie. She sends me Christmas cards, but I don't open 'em."

I realized that Mama was standing next to me. "Go help Cousin Flo put the food out on the table," she said.

On the ride home I asked Mama if she knew what Mathilde had done.

"Whatever it was, she did it a long time ago."

"Do I really look like her?"

"I've never seen any pictures of her," Mama said. "But from what I've heard, Mathilde didn't like wearing dresses either."

I looked over at her. She was focused on the road ahead. "I love you, Mama," I said.

"I love you, too."

On the day of the senior prom, Mama went into town for groceries. When she came back, she told me she saw Vera Harvey and Julie Wilcox in Rosalie's beauty parlor, and Taylor Jackson walking out of the flower shop with a corsage in a clear plastic box. I left the house, needing to get away from Mama's sadness.

It was the hottest day yet in a summer that promised to be one of the hottest I could remember. I was walking by the river, hoping for a breeze. Sandy couldn't manage the exertion of her usual greeting, and hailed me with a yip and a whine. Mrs. Crette called to me from her bedroom window, "Ameza? Can you come here a minute? I got a lightbulb that needs to be changed."

The back door was open. I could hear Emmylou Harris singing about her sister coming home as I walked through the little dining room and living room and up the stairs. When I entered Mrs. Crette's bedroom I saw she was only wearing a slip—a full-length, plain white cotton slip.

"It's so hot," she said. "I've just been layin' on the bed in my slip, listening to records. You don't mind, do you, honey?"

" 'Course not," I said, though I knew Mama would have plenty to say about it if she ever found out.

"The lightbulb in my closet burned out," Mrs. Crette said. "There's a package of new bulbs in the pantry."

I went back down to the kitchen and brought the bulbs and the stepladder up to the bedroom. I opened the stepladder inside the closet. Mrs. Crette followed me in, carrying a fresh bulb.

I turned my head and looked down, my left hand holding the burnt-out lightbulb. Mrs. Crette exchanged it for the new one. I saw the shadowed hollow between her breasts and I felt dizzy, even though I was only standing on the first rung of the stepladder.

Emmylou Harris was singing and Mrs. Crette was humming along, sashaying around in her white cotton slip. My mouth was dry but I didn't want any iced tea because I couldn't swallow. Everything was stilled by the heat; everything but the ceiling fan, the record revolving on the turntable, and Mrs. Crette's hips.

I put in the new lightbulb and stepped down onto the floor. Mrs. Crette shimmied over to me, singing along with Emmylou Harris, "Save the last dance for me."

"C'mon, Ameza, dance with me."

"I'm not much for dancing," I said. It came out in a parched whisper.

"You just haven't been dancing with the right people, honey. It's easy."

She slipped her arms around me and molded her body to mine. My heart was pounding so hard I worried it might bruise my skin. My hands settled on Mrs. Crette's hips, fingertips tingling as though coated with some kind of charged residue from the burnt-out bulb.

The record finished playing, but the dance continued as the fan softly purred.

Mrs. Crette put her arms around my neck, tilted her head, and stretched up to bring her lips closer to mine. Her kiss was light, and quick. Stumbling, I pushed her back and onto the bed. She took my head in her hands and pulled it down. The next kiss was harder and longer; our lips parted as though ordained to do so.

I cupped one cottoned breast with my hand, the nipple brushing the center of my palm, then bent my head to touch my lips to it through the thin fabric. The slip had traces of its time on the clothesline—the smell of the breeze coming off the river through the willows mingled with the smell of sweat and something else, something tangy.

I slid the slender straps off her shoulders. She sat up and slipped her arms out and the fabric dropped. I held her naked breasts as though weighing them while her hand stretched forward, unsnapped and unzipped my cut-offs.

"Take these off," she said.

I stood up, tugged them down, stepped out of them and sat back down on the bed.

I felt like I should say something.

"Mrs. . . ." I stopped.

She smiled. "I think you can call me Louisa."

I looked at her face, then her breasts; gently pressed her right nipple with the tip of my index finger. The nipple was hard and the skin surrounding it was puckered.

197

"You're very beautiful, Louisa."

The power Louisa was giving to me both frightened and excited me. I lay down next to her, and covered one breast with my mouth.

Everything about her body seemed plush, the physical equivalent of her generosity, offering herself to me.

I was working my way down Louisa's body. As I pushed the bottom of her slip up and over her stomach, Louisa opened her legs so I could lie between them. I rested my head on her left thigh.

I'd never really seen a woman's sex before. As I lay between Louisa's legs, I took a good look.

Damp, wiry hair. A hood, wrinkled folds and furls, pink smudged brown at the edges, framing the opening.

Louisa moaned when I dabbed my finger in the silky liquid flowing out of her and painted her whole outside with it. I felt something hard under the hood and ran my finger around it.

I wanted to watch her come.

I'd been listening to the girls at school. They all agreed on what happens for boys, but women—that was more mysterious. Vera said she screamed so loud and high she expected the neighbor's dogs to start barking, but she didn't say anything about what went on lower down. And besides, Vera was always the first to see escaped convicts, UFOs, and angels. When I asked Julie, one of the girls I shared stuff with, if she knew what it was like to come, she blushed and said I shouldn't be asking her about that.

"Will you show me how to make you come?" I asked Louisa.

She sat up, leaning back on her elbows. "I'll show you how to do it for me today. But it's not always the same every time for every woman, Ameza. Sometimes it's not even the same for the same woman."

She put her hand over mine, guided my index and middle fingers into her, and put my thumb on the right side of the hood. "This is what I need you to do," she said. As I moved my fingers in and out and rubbed up and down and circled around with my thumb, Louisa pushed against my hand and whimpered simple words—yes and please and so good. She gave a little wail and I felt the walls open and close on my fingers.

"Come up here and kiss me, Ameza," Louisa said.

I slipped on top of her body, one leg between hers and one of hers between mine. She put her hands underneath my T-shirt, stroking my back from my shoulders to my waist, then down to my hips, and finally my ass. There was a slick patch where my thigh was pressed up against her and I could feel that my underpants were soaked through. My body kept giving me one surprise after another. It felt good, rubbing against Louisa. It felt so good that it scared me. I pushed up with my arms, holding myself over her, and pressed down with my crotch. My hips seemed to be on some kind of autopilot. Louisa moved her hands around to my front, gently caressing my breasts and circling my nipples with her thumbs, and that exquisite touch took me over the edge. I felt a flutter, then a clenching as my breath rushed out of me.

It was a bird that brought me back, made me realize there was a world beyond Louisa's body and the bed. I heard the dusky warble, and realized the light through the curtains had dimmed. I sat up.

Louisa sat up too, slid the straps of the slip back up onto her shoulders. "You'll still come to see me, won't you, Ameza? We don't have to do this again, if you don't want to. But I hope you'll stop by and chat once in a while."

She seemed to be drawing into herself, and I thought, *Maybe that's what adults do; they have sex, leave, and never come back.*

I kissed her. I kissed her gently and slowly because none of the words whirling around in my brain were making it into speech.

When I came in the door, Mama was sitting at the kitchen table, reading the newspaper.

"I'm sorry I'm late," I said. "I was down by the river, and I fell asleep."

"There's a plate for you in the refrigerator," Mama said. "Chicken, potato salad, some tomatoes and cucumbers."

I carried the plate to the table, took a glass from the cupboard, and filled it with iced tea.

We sat at the table in silence, as we had on other occasions. I'd almost finished eating my dinner when I heard the soft splat of something dropping onto Mama's newspaper. I looked up and saw that she was crying.

"Mama?"

She pushed back her chair and went to the sink, pressed the dish towel to her eyes. I went over to her, put my arms around her waist, pressed my cheek against hers, and asked, "Mama, what is it?"

She turned and hugged me tightly. I knew that all of this had something to do with Mrs. Crette and the change that Mama sensed in me. But where I feared her anger, I was panicked by her grief.

She stepped away from me, and sighed. "Oh, Ameza. You just have to make things hard for yourself, don't you?" She went on talking, more to herself than to me. "The Lord made you, and I have to believe He knew what He was doing." Then Mama took my face in her hands, and looked at me. And she was my Mama, fierce and proud. "You remember that, Ameza. Anyone ever calls you some hurtful name, you remember that the Lord made you, and He knew exactly what He was doing."

The first time someone whispered "bulldagger," just loud enough for me to hear, Mama's words came back to me as clearly as if she were standing right beside me. "The Lord made you, and He knew exactly what He was doing."

That was the day I knew just how much my Mama loved me. Her love was stronger than her fear of something she didn't understand and couldn't approve of; something she wished she could change and recognized she wouldn't. Mrs. Crette was Mama's first defeat.

Double Take

Sabrina Wilcox

It only said sixty-eight dollars. It didn't matter what transaction she attempted, the cash register would only ring up sixty-eight dollars. Sarah had already had five customers that day, and she had to do the math by hand each time. She was pretty frustrated by the time she called the company from which she'd leased the register.

She stood behind her counter, waiting on the damn maintenance tech. The company said they would send someone to fix the register about an hour after she called, and it had already been two. She cursed them, and figured they had no idea what it was like to run the town's only lesbian retail shop. She held her breath and looked to the door as the bells above it chimed.

A woman walked in, and Sarah forgot about the register. This woman, in her khaki pants, polo shirt, and men's shoes, had Sarah's undivided attention. As the woman walked closer, Sarah saw that the polo shirt was embroidered with the register company's logo.

"Are you the manager?" the woman asked.

"Yes. Well, actually I'm the owner, and the manager." Sarah hoped the woman didn't notice the nervousness in her voice. She tried to smile. "I'm also the only employee."

"Then you're the person I need. I'm here to fix your equipment."

"It's right here. You can come around the counter." Sarah watched the woman walk around the counter and stand next to her. She loved the way the tan polo shirt complemented the woman's olive skin. "I'm Sarah."

The women shook hands. "Ronnie Fernandez. I'm taking over this account, so I'll be your new maintenance and repair technician."

"What happened to that other guy? He was supposed to fix my safe too. The damn thing won't lock."

"He's been moved to another account. I don't do safes, but I can get someone else over here next week. Now, what's your machine doing?"

"It'll only ring up sixty-eight dollars. It doesn't matter what I'm ringing up, or how much it is."

"Hmm." Ronnie pressed some buttons on the register. "You know what that means, don't you?"

"What?"

"Sixty-eight. You do me and I owe you one."

Sarah let out a laugh. She was glad Ronnie kept her eyes on the register, because Sarah was sure she was blushing. She hopped up onto the counter, crossed her legs, and began to play nervously with her hair.

It was convenient that the machine had stuck on sixty-eight dollars. Ronnie could finally use that cheap line she'd been saving. And it worked. Sarah was so flustered that she didn't care what Ronnie was doing to the machine. Ronnie only started sweating when Sarah sat on the counter.

She could see the woman's legs through the practically sheer skirt, well-formed legs that were crossed and swaying lightly. Ronnie imagined those bare legs wrapped around her, her fingers working between them. She watched Sarah play with her hair and wanted to run her fingers through it.

She knew a little bit about Sarah from the guys at work. If they'd had a picture of her, it would have been up in the lunchroom.

They didn't describe her that well, Ronnie told herself as she coolly glanced at the woman. Her mind filled with questions that had nothing to do with the register. *Are her eyes blue or gray? How far down do those faint freckles go? Is her skin as soft as it looks?*

For just an instant, Ronnie imagined exploring the soft skin with the tips of her fingers. *Flirt, damn it, but don't feel anything*, she thought as she attempted to keep her attention on the register. *Desire will only get you confused about the real job, and it'll screw you later in the game.*

The game was important to Ronnie. Like a huntress seducing the prey to come closer, she embraced the thrill of the game. The key was to remember the goal, or else the attack would be impossible.

Unlike Ronnie, Sarah indulged herself in her desires. She discreetly admired Ronnie's muscular arms as she casually watched her. Ronnie's back swayed as her arms worked. Her movements were rhythmic, led by the clicking of the clock. Like ancient tribal drumming, the strangely sensual rhythm nearly coaxed Sarah into a trance. She rocked to the rhythm as she imagined Ronnie's hands working on her instead of the machine.

"I think that'll do it." Ronnie's voice whipped Sarah out of her fantasy. "One of the wires inside came loose. The last transaction must have been for sixty-eight dollars, and that's why it was stuck there. It's all fixed."

"Thank you." Sarah hopped down from the counter and hoped there wasn't a wet spot on her skirt. She followed Ronnie around the counter, her eyes fixed on the woman's shapely rear. "Can you recommend a good alarm company? The alarm is busted, too. The back door opened right up without even a beep from the damn thing, and the idiots I'm using now can't seem to fix it."

"I can't think of one offhand. Let me ask around." Ronnie smiled as she walked out.

As Ronnie left, Sarah put the "closed" sign on the door. She rarely closed for lunch but today wanted a little time to herself. She locked the door and went to the back office.

Rather than sitting at her desk, Sarah lay down on the small sofa in the corner of the room. She stared at the wall and thought about Ronnie's arms. They were lean and muscular. Her hands were big and her fingers looked strong. Sarah thought about those fingers as she slid her long skirt up to her waist. With one leg stretched out and the other resting on the back of the sofa, Sarah slid her own fingers under her panties. She grinned as she felt the warm wetness.

It wasn't unusual for her to want sex in the middle of the day. It seemed it was her favorite time for it. She was a very sexual woman who believed there were few finer things in life. Coupled with her intense sex drive was a yearning for excitement. Together, they made her a little wild at times.

She closed her eyes and the reality around her faded away. She was in a large tub, warm water surrounding her. Candles flickered across the room, and the shadows on the wall announced the presence of another person. Ronnie walked toward the tub, dressed in nothing but the bath towel around her waist. With a slight tug, the towel dropped to the floor and Ronnie was bare.

Sarah's hand dripped warm water along Ronnie's leg as she stepped into the tub. As Ronnie slid her muscular body into the water, she pulled Sarah closer to her. In a breath, Sarah was on top of her. She straddled Ronnie's legs and ran her fingers through her hair.

As they kissed, Ronnie caressed her. Her fingertips touched every part of Sarah, and Sarah loved every burning sensation. When she thought she could take no more, Ronnie's fingertips stroked her past ecstasy.

❦

Ronnie was still thinking about Sarah's legs when she drove back to her office. *I wasn't prepared for this. She's enchanting, like a priestess who can summon fire by raising her arms. Hell, she made me burn just by raising her eyes.*

She and her coworker Matt had hoped Ronnie could seduce Sarah. Ronnie often bragged about her ability to seduce any woman. Now, she had the chance to prove herself.

Matt was the service technician for Sarah's shop, but they knew Ronnie would be able to get closer to the owner. Matt had seen Sarah flirt with women in the store, and the women usually met Ronnie's general description: tall, muscular, and butch. Matt would be upset if he knew how close Ronnie wanted to get. *Close enough to taste, that's how close I'd like to get.*

Matt and Ronnie had been working on their plans for a couple of months, and Ronnie would hate to ruin things by being too attracted to the owner. *But, that incredible body makes it difficult. How far can I take this without either of them finding out what I'm really up to?*

The following afternoon, Sarah stood behind the counter and stared at the cash register. It was working fine, but she wasn't. Her thoughts kept turning to Ronnie. *She's hotter than I thought she would be. It'll make working with her so much more fun. Maybe it's time to pick things up a little.*

Sarah glanced around the room, to be sure no one was watching as she casually picked up her iced tea and poured a bit into the register keyboard.

"Now you've done it," she said aloud before calling the register company.

It was an hour later when Ronnie arrived. Sarah was helping customers, frantically pushing the numbers on her calculator to get the people out of the store as fast as possible. Anticipation pulsed through her as she watched Ronnie walk through the door.

"Thanks for getting here so quickly."

"No problem. Can I go back there and get to work?"

"Certainly." Sarah was eager to feel Ronnie standing near her.

Ronnie brushed against Sarah as she walked through the small space between her and the wall. The excitement of Ronnie's touch consumed Sarah like a raging fire. She wanted to turn and grab the woman, to kiss and touch her. Instead, she stood still and tried to catch her breath.

"You know, you don't have to spill tea in your register just to get me out here."

"It was an accident. Really." Sarah tried to sound innocent, but she'd been caught. Ronnie knew Sarah had just wanted to see her again. She was glad when Ronnie changed the subject and made small talk about the shop.

"How's business been lately?"

"It's really been picking up. The film festival brings in a lot of money."

The film festival is tomorrow. What will you think of me afterward? Ronnie shook off the thought. *No time to worry about that now.* Ronnie looked up at Sarah and decided it was time to move in for the kill. "So, are you single?"

"Kind of."

"What does that mean?"

"Well, I broke up with my girlfriend a month ago, I just haven't moved out of her house yet." Sarah was afraid she'd just blown it. *Why would a woman want to date someone who's still living with their ex?*

"Hmm." Ronnie didn't look up. "I suppose that's good enough."

"Good enough for what?"

"The register is clean enough. I think I've removed all the tea." Ronnie turned to face Sarah. "I think you'd like me to do more than clean your register."

"And what do you think I'd like you to do?" Sarah knew what she wanted, but it was much more fun to play. Flirting was always a little exciting, but this time it seemed more adventurous. *It's a game of cat and mouse,* Sarah thought, *but, who's really the cat, and who's the mouse?* Her mouth watered with temptation.

Ronnie reached out and touched Sarah's arm, then slowly leaned closer. Sarah's heart raced with the anticipation of the kiss that was sure to come. With all her femme sexuality, she let her smile invite Ronnie closer. She stared into Ronnie's eyes as she felt Ronnie's breath on her skin, and Ronnie's tongue running along her lips.

Ronnie's mouth was warm and inviting, her tongue soft as it met Sarah's. Sarah put her hand on Ronnie's shoulder and returned the kiss. She felt Ronnie's free hand slide to her hip, and the electricity sent desire to her center. As the kiss deepened, Ronnie tilted her body and pressed her hip against Sarah's dampening crotch.

Sarah's body moved with Ronnie's hip; her hands splayed across Ronnie's muscular back. The women kissed as they found their rhythm together.

"I have an office." Sarah's voice was nearly a whisper.

Ronnie forgot all else as she kissed the woman. Sarah's soft lips parted for her tongue, and Ronnie could taste all of her. Her hand felt Sarah's breast under the thin blouse, and Ronnie's groin ached with anticipation. She rubbed against Sarah's body, fantasizing about taking the woman all the way to rapture. If she hadn't been on the clock, she would have screwed Sarah right then and there.

She loved screwing femmes; in fact, she only dated femmes. She loved their softness, the long hair, painted nails. Something about a woman in a skirt really got her going. The sultry smile of a femme could send her to her knees and make her work while she was down there.

"I don't think I have time for that." Ronnie slowed her grinding movements. "We'll have to continue this later."

Sarah sighed as Ronnie pulled away. Her lips formed into a playful pout as Ronnie gave her a final kiss. "I'm not going to be able to wait until later."

The women were just inches apart when the bells above the door chimed. Both tried to contain their heavy breathing as a customer browsed through books.

"I'd better go. Maybe I'll see you tomorrow at the festival." Ronnie's hand was still on Sarah's hip; she wasn't ready to let go.

"Okay." Sarah didn't know what else to say. As Ronnie left, Sarah tried to figure out how she would accidentally bump into Ronnie at the film festival. Her plotting stopped when she remembered who was accompanying her.

Sarah sat in the third row at the festival. She'd seen two movies already, and was set for a third, but still hadn't seen Ronnie. She glanced at her ex-girlfriend sitting next to her and wondered why she agreed to go with this woman even after she'd broken it off. She toyed with the hem of her short skirt and suddenly wondered if it was too short. She didn't want to send any wrong signals to the woman next to her. They made it clear that it wasn't a date, but since they had already bought tickets for neighboring seats, they might as well go with each other. Sarah knew Pat would do anything to get her back. That was why Sarah was able to move into the spare bedroom when she ended the relationship. She paid rent, and the two lived as roommates, but Pat still wanted more.

Suddenly feeling uncomfortable, Sarah glanced down at her blouse. She was too dressed up. Her white silk blouse buttoned up to a deep v-neck that showed off her pretty cleavage. Her royal blue skirt matched her shoes, which were perfectly feminine with four-inch heels. Her outfit complimented her body and coloring wonderfully, which is why she wore it even though it was a little chilly that evening. She wished she were in jeans and a baggy shirt. She didn't want Pat to be attracted to her.

"Hi." Ronnie's voice grabbed Sarah away from her thoughts.

"Ronnie." The excitement was audible in Sarah's voice. Sarah stood up, and as she did, Pat followed.

Ronnie put her hand out as she introduced herself to Pat. "I'm Ronnie. I service Sarah's cash register."

Sarah was horrified as Pat and Ronnie shook hands. Before she knew it, her fears played out in front of her.

"Do you just do registers, or do you service other things as well?" Pat was going to be a bitch.

"Just registers."

"Oh. Must be a little boring." Pat stood perfectly erect and stared at Ronnie. They were matched in height, inch for inch. "I'm Pat, Sarah's girlfriend."

"I see. I just wanted to tell you hello. I'll see you later." Ronnie could hardly control herself as she walked away. Her mind was whirling with problems. This ruined everything. She was supposed to make sure Sarah didn't go back to the store that evening. She was hoping to do that by getting the woman in bed. Ronnie felt like everything had just crashed in front of her.

Sarah grabbed her purse and smacked Pat in the arm.

"How could you say that? You most certainly are not my girl-friend."

"It looked like she was bothering you." Pat sat down.

"It did not. It looked like she was interested in me, and that bothered you." Sarah hurried off without looking back. Ronnie was nearly to the exit when she caught up with her. "Ronnie, please wait."

Ronnie whipped around. "I don't mess with threesomes. They're too sticky." *And, they fuck up previous plans.*

"She was lying. Pat is the ex I told you about."

"Why are you on a date with her if she's your ex?"

"It's not a date. We had already reserved the tickets, and neither of us wanted to give up our seat. I didn't lie to you."

Ronnie was silent for a minute. She knew the time was right and decided to invite the woman home. "Okay. I'm sorry. I had no reason to be mad. I guess I just didn't like seeing you with someone else. I was hoping we could go out after the movie."

"I would love that."

"You know, I've already seen this one."

"Me, too." Sarah's heart was racing. For the first time, she noticed how nicely Ronnie was dressed. Her black pants, dark green shirt, and leather jacket looked even better than her company clothes. "Why is your jacket wet?"

"It's raining."

"Oh." Sarah smiled. Ronnie looked good wet. "So, what do you want to do?"

"We're right by my apartment." Ronnie looked Sarah in the eyes. "We could walk there, if you wanted."

"In the rain?"

"You won't melt, will you?" Ronnie asked as she held the theater door open.

"I guess not."

Ronnie took off her jacket and put it around Sarah's shoulders. It was a little large for her, but Sarah was thankful for any protection from the rain. As they walked, Ronnie took her hand.

"What are we going to do at your apartment?" Sarah asked. She was trying to play innocent.

"We can watch movies, if you like. We'll do whatever you want to do."

"Well, that leaves it wide open, doesn't it?" Sarah's innocence was gone. She knew what she wanted to do.

As they walked in the rain, Ronnie fought with her guilt. Sarah seemed so innocent. Ronnie couldn't believe she was taking advantage of her. She couldn't let herself think about how her actions would hurt Sarah. She couldn't let guilt get in the way.

They walked in silence until they were in front of Ronnie's apartment building. "May I kiss you?" Ronnie asked as she wrapped an arm around Sarah's waist.

"I've been waiting."

Ronnie kissed Sarah's lips, gently at first, then with more urgency as their tongues met. As they kissed deeper, Sarah put her arms around Ronnie's neck and ran her fingers through her hair. She felt Ronnie's hand slide down her back and to her rear, while the other hand firmly held the back of Sarah's head. Their lips broke and Ronnie madly kissed Sarah's neck. Like wildfire, the kisses spread to Sarah's collarbone and as far down as the v-neck blouse would allow. Neither noticed the rain coming down on them. They were both dripping wet, but not from the weather.

"We should go inside." Sarah's chest heaved as she took deep breaths. Her adventure was reaching its peak.

They hurried into Ronnie's apartment, anxious to touch each other again. Ronnie watched as Sarah took off the jacket. Her blouse was drenched and completely transparent, as was the bra she wore underneath. Urgency grasped Ronnie as she took Sarah's hand and led her to the bedroom.

The streetlight outside lit the room as Ronnie's eyes consumed Sarah. She ran her thumb across Sarah's dark pink nipples, which showed through the clothes. With both her hands, Ronnie cupped Sarah's round breasts and kissed her nipples through the wet shirt.

It was a new feeling for Sarah, and it was very enjoyable. The wet cloth against her skin mimicked the wetness of a mouth, but it was a tease. Ronnie gently tugged on one of Sarah's nipples with her teeth as she moved her hand under her skirt. Sarah let out a soft growl and she felt Ronnie's hand rubbing against her.

"How did the rain get you there?" Ronnie teased.

"Shut up and take my clothes off."

"Yes ma'am." Ronnie kissed Sarah hard as she tried to unbutton the blouse. Her hands fumbled with the small buttons, which refused to cooperate.

Sarah was nearly frantic with desire as she tried to help. She leaned close to Ronnie's ear and in a sultry voice whispered, "Just tear it off."

Sarah let out a soft cry as Ronnie grabbed the blouse between her breasts and ripped it open. She didn't expect the tearing to be so arousing, but it sent a wave of excitement through her. Ronnie grabbed the waist of Sarah's skirt and in one yank, sent it falling off her white hips. She pulled the torn blouse off Sarah and threw it on the floor.

They stood next to the king-sized bed and kissed each other as Sarah unbuttoned Ronnie's shirt and pulled it off her. Sarah softly suckled one nipple, then the other as she held both breasts in her hands. Ronnie smoothed Sarah's long hair as she enjoyed the sucking.

As Sarah returned to Ronnie's mouth, Ronnie worked her hands behind Sarah's back and removed her bra. Ronnie gently laid her on the bed to remove Sarah's last bit of clothing. Sarah was excruciatingly aware of Ronnie's fingers as she slid them under the waist of the panties.

Ronnie wanted to ravish the woman, to devour every sweet inch of her; instead, she took her time and enjoyed herself. She slowly pulled the damp satin panties off Sarah's hips, taking time to admire the new view. The soft mound of blond hairs was damp with Sarah's excitement. Ronnie smelled the soft scent of that excitement, and it aroused her even further. She teased herself by running her fingertips along the inside of Sarah's thighs, and stopping just before the wetness.

Ronnie pulled herself on top of Sarah and once again kissed her. Ronnie loved being on top of Sarah. The kitten-like purring gave Ronnie her pace as she moved back and forth, rubbing her hip against Sarah's exposed clit. She could feel Sarah's wetness through her pants and wanted to taste her.

"This is good." Sarah purred with enjoyment as Ronnie's movements became deeper.

"We won't let it get too good." Ronnie looked down and smiled. "I still have my pants on."

Ronnie shifted again to lie directly on top of Sarah. She brushed Sarah's hair away from her neck and nibbled on the pale flesh. She gently bit Sarah's neck and ears before moving down to kiss her breasts. She held the breasts together and took both nipples in her mouth, gently sucking and biting both at once.

Another wave of excitement flowed through Sarah as she felt Ronnie move her free hand down to caress the little mound of blond hairs. Sarah breathed heavily as Ronnie fondled her in all the right spots.

The wetness was warm, its scent sweet. Ronnie wanted to enter her, but she liked the anticipation. She let her fingers rub against Sarah's wet flesh, and tempted both of them as she purposely dragged them over Sarah.

Ronnie lived in each breath Sarah took. She took her cues from the gentle sounds coming from the woman and took her just to the edge of her excitement. She loved to tease before giving the final pleasure, and she was an expert at it.

Just as Sarah thought she would come, Ronnie took her hand away. Sarah's chest rose with each breath as Ronnie moved down her body and positioned herself between quivering legs.

Ronnie felt herself grow wet as she parted Sarah's legs. Sarah's lower lips glistened with wetness as they separated gently. It was the beautiful smile of sex, inviting Ronnie's tongue in.

The warmth of Ronnie's mouth surrounded Sarah's clitoris as she softly sucked on it. She used her tongue expertly, covering all of Sarah's sex. Sarah grasped Ronnie's hair as Ronnie's tongue darted in and out of her. Sarah's back lifted when Ronnie again sucked on her clit. She parted her legs further as another moan rose from her throat. Sarah's excitement grew as Ronnie's fingers toyed with her.

"I want you inside me."

"I know."

Ronnie ran her tongue over Sarah's warm skin to taste all of her sweetness. She spread Sarah's lips and gave her a deep kiss. Her nose rubbed against Sarah's clit as the tip of her tongue pushed inside her. Sarah was even sweeter inside. Ronnie pushed her tongue as far as it would go; she wanted to taste all of her. She felt the wetness on her chin as she devoured the feast.

Ronnie buried her face between Sarah's spread legs and moved her tongue in long strokes. She teased the entrance by softly push-

ing her tongue against it, tempting Sarah with the slightest penetration. Ronnie slid a finger deep into Sarah. She wanted as far
inside this woman as she could get.

Sarah pulled a pillow under her head and watched Ronnie. They
looked in each other's eyes as Ronnie slid another finger in her. She
felt her wetness grow as Ronnie fucked her.

"I want more," she whispered.

Sarah watched Ronnie lift her head and slide a third finger
inside. The women kept eye contact as Ronnie's fingers moved in
and out. *I knew those fingers would be good.*

Ronnie had complete control over Sarah as she moved her
fingers in and out. Sarah's clit swelled even more, and Ronnie knew
it was time to finish her off. She bore down on the woman and thoroughly fucked her. Sarah screamed with delight, and Ronnie felt the
contractions of the orgasm gripping her fingers as she grabbed
Sarah's hips and pushed herself deeper inside. Her tongue moved
harder and faster; she knew this one would come at least twice.

"E-Enough." She could barely get the word out, but it didn't
matter. Ronnie grabbed her hips, and buried her face deeper.
"Fuck . . ."

It was all she was able to get out as Ronnie's tongue raced over
her clit. Sarah couldn't tell if another finger had gone in, or if
Ronnie was just screwing her harder, but either way she liked it. She
liked strong fingers; they were better at moving the muscles inside.

Ronnie pushed a fourth finger inside while she sucked hard on
the swollen clit between her teeth. Her hand pounded against Sarah
as her fingers plunged in and out of her depths. Sarah felt her liquid
spilling out of her as another orgasm quickly built up deep inside
her.

"Harder . . . Now . . ." Sarah's arms seemed to fly around her as
she reached for something to grab.

Ronnie followed her directions and fucked her harder. Sarah
could feel Ronnie's hand beating against her each time Ronnie
pushed her fingers in, and the fingers went deeper with each stroke.

She felt Ronnie's tongue, lips, and teeth taking turns with her clit and could no longer hold back. In a fit of passion, Sarah tried to scream. Her voice came out loud and deep, like a crazed animal. She grabbed Ronnie's hair as the woman continued to fuck her.

As Sarah screamed with passion, Ronnie thought she might come with her. Wetness flooded over her and Ronnie let it run down her face. Ronnie drank up the sweet nectar, and only stopped when Sarah pulled her up.

It was the most intense orgasm Sarah had ever experienced.

"I'm soaked." Ronnie's hands and face were dripping with Sarah's juices as she moved up on the bed. She held Sarah close to her and lovingly kissed her forehead.

"I'm sorry." Sarah's body was still shaking from the intensity of the orgasm.

"Don't be sorry. I enjoyed it . . . Oh hell." Ronnie's pager, still attached to the pants she was wearing, was vibrating. "It's work. I'm on call tonight. I've got to go."

Sarah frowned. "Well, I don't want you to get fired. Can I wait here until you get back?"

"That would be wonderful."

Ronnie quickly washed up, put her shirt back on, and left the apartment. She felt guilty about leaving Sarah in her apartment, especially considering what she was about to do.

She could still taste Sarah on her lips, and though she was by herself in her truck, Sarah's scent still covered her.

That's when she felt it. Guilt slammed into Ronnie as forcefully as if she had hit a tree. She couldn't believe she was going to Sarah's shop. The hit was really just a practice; she and Matt knew they wouldn't get much. Still, a couple thousand dollars of easy spending money was fine, and the experience would help them when they hit bigger businesses.

She parked her truck a block away from Sarah's shop and hid herself in the shadows as she walked to the back entrance. She prayed that Sarah hadn't had the alarm fixed yet. The back door proved safe, and she was in and out of the store in less than five minutes, with all the money from the register and the broken safe. Without any problems, Ronnie was back to her truck and driving home.

Home to Sarah, who would have no idea that all the work she'd put into the store during the last couple of days was gone. Taken by the woman she would be sleeping with that night.

Guilt again filled Ronnie, and she actually thought about putting the money back. She blamed her guilt on the adrenaline flowing through her, which kept her from thinking rationally. Sarah would never suspect it was her who took the money, and wasn't that what Ronnie and Matt were counting on? *Besides, it's Sarah's fault for having no security on the building, and a broken safe.* Even as she thought it, she knew she didn't mean it.

Ronnie stashed the bag of money under the seat of her truck; she would have to get it after Sarah left. She quietly let herself into her apartment and walked into the bedroom.

Sarah was asleep on the bed as Ronnie undressed herself. When she lay down next to the naked woman, Sarah stirred from her slumber.

"How'd everything go?"

"Fine." Ronnie was feeling guilty again. She had done the wrong thing.

"That's good." Sarah put her hand on Ronnie's bare back. "I want my share tonight."

"What?"

"My money. I figure, it's my shop, so I should get my money tonight instead of waiting until Monday like Matt had said. My insurance money will take weeks, and it's going to be so little that it's hardly worth the trouble."

Ronnie's confusion showed in her face. "What are you talking about?"

"Look. I've been in on this since the beginning. I was in before you were. Matt and I have been friends forever. This whole thing started as a foolish plan one night when we were drinking together. Then we wanted to see if we could really pull it off. My share of the money is actually going to help the business. It's so little that it won't do much, but the insurance money will help. And, I'll get a new safe and alarm out of the deal. You were kind of an added bonus for me."

Ronnie couldn't believe it. She was the one who was used, not Sarah. Sarah knew all along what Ronnie was doing, and Ronnie didn't have a clue. Instead of being angry, Ronnie suddenly felt a lot more respect for the woman. She was good. There's nothing better than a smart femme.

"I think I'm falling for you," she told Sarah.

"Good. I think we work together nicely." Sarah smiled. She couldn't wait to work together in bed again. But, business first. "Now, how much did you get?"

"I got everything that was in the register and the safe." Ronnie knew things were going to work out very well for the women. They were well suited, and fantastic in bed. She might even be able to settle down with this one.

"Okay, you got it all except a little stash I put away a few days ago so I wouldn't be entirely screwed when I opened on Monday."

"How much was that?"

"Sixty-eight dollars. Remember, you do me and I owe you one?"

Ronnie smiled. *Things are going to work out just fine.*

Pool Games

MJ Williamz

The doorbell always seems to ring when I'm right in the middle of something. Last Friday was no exception. I was in the kitchen slicing and dicing, in the midst of preparing dinner for my date. I checked the clock—it was only five-fifteen. Shira wasn't supposed to be there until seven. So, who could it be?

Assuming it was a salesperson that I could get rid of quickly, I wiped my hands on a kitchen towel and went to the door.

It was Sandy. I wondered what would bring her by this early in the evening. Her shift at the hospital usually didn't end until eight on Fridays. My first thought was that something had happened to Jessica, her partner. Hoping everything was all right, I opened the door and invited her in.

"Thanks anyway, Brynn," she said, refusing my invitation. "I really gotta get going. I know this is short notice, but Jessica's grandma took a pretty bad spill today. Jessica's pretty upset about it and wants to drive down and stay with her for a few days."

I looked past Sandy and saw Jessica sitting in the car. I waved, trying to look sympathetic. Jessica looked even younger than her twenty-seven years as she sat there. Even at that distance, I could see how upset she was. I looked back at Sandy, still wondering what this had to do with me.

"I know this is short notice, Brynn," she repeated, holding out a set of keys, "but I didn't know who else to ask. Would you mind looking in on the kids for us? I don't know how long we'll be gone."

The reservation must have shown on my face. Although I manage my own life just fine, the idea of assuming responsibility for the well-being of their cats while they were gone made me uncomfortable. Who knew how long they'd be gone? And what if I forgot to go over there?

"Brynn. Relax. I'm sure we won't be gone that long. Just check on them once a day and make sure they have food and water."

I was still unsure.

"There is an upside to this." Sandy had a gleam in her eye, like she knew something I didn't.

"And what might that be?" I asked, ever doubtful.

"You get to use the pool whenever you want."

My one vice—I worship the sun. Ignoring the dire warnings about skin cancer, I lie out every chance I get. And they had a pool. So, I could stay cool and soak up rays. I couldn't resist. I put my hand out, palm up, and she dropped the keys into them.

"Thanks, Brynn. You're a love." She waved over her shoulder as she jogged out to the car. She waved again as she backed out and took off.

As I stood there, I realized that I had been so busy worrying about the imposition that watching two cats would be, I hadn't even told her to tell Jessica I was sorry about her grandma. Oh well. It certainly wouldn't have been the first time I'd been accused of being self-absorbed.

❧

Saturday morning started out with me in a fog. I was dreaming. I was lying on my back, naked, in the middle of a beach. It was warm and sunny and the sand felt good against my bare skin. I was surrounded by naked women. They were all around me. And they were all masturbating. I couldn't move. I was lying there and I could turn my head and see them, but I was unable to move the rest of me, so I couldn't touch them. I could smell the scent of their arousal and hear their wetness as they pleasured themselves. I could imagine feeling their satiny softness. I could almost taste them. I imagined how it would be to join them, to have my hand touching them, instead of their own. The desire was too much to bear. Again I tried to reach out, but couldn't move. I lay there helplessly writhing in the sand, watching.

As the dream faded, I was left feeling overwhelmingly frustrated. I stretched, rolled over, and reached out to touch the woman lying next to me. There was no one there.

Suddenly fully awake, I rolled over onto my back, stared up at the ceiling, and reflected on my date of the previous evening. Shira had definitely enjoyed dinner but had been unwilling to provide the dessert. No wonder I had had that dream.

Feeling incredibly cranky, I got out of bed and stumbled into the kitchen to make coffee. On the counter in the kitchen, next to the coffee pot, was a strange set of keys. I was confused for a minute. Then I remembered my promise to Sandy to check in on her cats.

"Shit!" I muttered to myself. "Today just keeps getting worse and worse. And I've only been awake for five minutes!"

The coffee and a hot shower made me feel a little better, as did the promise of some time poolside. I was actually in a pretty good space as I caught my reflection in the mirror while I toweled dry.

Not bad, I thought. Actually, pretty damned good. I am fairly tall at five-eight. The gray that is creeping into my hair now that I am on the wrong side of thirty-five only added character, I thought. It contrasted well with my short black hair. And it really brought out my blue eyes.

Finished assessing that part of myself, I looked at my body and thought that Shira had really missed out last night. I again thanked the goddess that I had such a high metabolism. I could eat anything and everything and stay trim and toned. My breasts were on the small side, but I never got any complaints. And I was firm everywhere, although I spun around and checked out the rear view in the mirror, just to be sure.

What to wear over to the house wasn't really a hard choice, because I'd decided to sunbathe nude. I just needed something to cover me for the short trip over. Blue nylon running shorts and blue sports bra would do the trick. Once more I checked my reflection and was pleased with how I looked. I started to feel down because there was no woman there to appreciate how good I looked, but I got over it. I wasn't going to let a less-than-perfect date get me down.

It was already sunny and warm as I left the house. Driving my convertible to Sandy's was tempting, but riding my motorcycle won out. I felt I deserved to have something stimulating between my legs that day.

It was about ten-thirty when I got to the house. I went straight to the kitchen, determined to get the chore of the cats out of the way so I could relax and revitalize in the sun with no worries. Once they were fed, I walked to the back of the house to go check out the pool. As I made my way through the house, I reflected on how grateful I was that the fence surrounding their pool was so high. Sandy and Jessica weren't much for swimsuits either, and they didn't think the neighbors deserved to see them in their birthday suits.

As I stepped out of the back door, I froze in my tracks. There was someone else there. I replayed my conversation with Sandy from the previous evening. No, I was sure she hadn't mentioned that anyone else would be there. And besides, if they had been expecting this other woman to be here, why couldn't she feed the damned cats?

The door closing behind me got her attention. She rolled over onto her back and sat up.

221

"Hi," she said, as if this were completely natural. "You must be Brynn."

So she had known I would be here. At least Sandy was considerate enough to tell one of us to expect company.

My lack of immediate response apparently gave away my surprise at seeing her. She put a hand over her eyes to shield them from the sun as she went on.

"Sandy said you'd probably be by. She said it would be okay if I laid out. You don't mind, do you?"

What could I say? It wasn't my pool to begin with. And if Sandy had invited her, I really didn't have the right to tell her to get lost. I thought it might be nice of me to walk over and talk to her, so she wasn't still blinded by the sun.

Once I was standing next to the chaise, I decided not only would it not be too bad having her there, it might be quite nice. As I looked down at her, I couldn't help but notice the ample cleavage displayed by her purple and black bikini top. I could have stared all day, but resisting the urge to do so, I forced myself to look at her face. She was a very attractive woman, with shoulder-length blonde hair, sparkling green eyes, and a great smile. She had the kind of looks that could have made her anywhere from Jessica's age to mine.

I stuck out my hand. "Hi. Yes, I'm Brynn."

"Mandy. I live next door," she said, taking my hand. Her hand was soft and her skin smooth. Today might turn out to be a good day after all, I told myself.

"Nice to meet you, Mandy," I said in my most neutral voice. I wanted to start the seduction routine right then, but because I didn't know if she would be into that, I tried to remain neutral. I racked my brain, trying to remember if Sandy or Jessica had said anything about having a lesbian hottie for a neighbor, and I was pretty sure they hadn't. I knew I would've remembered that.

"Are you sure you don't mind me being here?" She seemed to still be stuck on my earlier hesitation. "I mean, I can take off, if you'd rather."

You can take off your bikini, if I'd rather, I thought. But out loud I said, "Heck no. That's okay. It'll be nice to have some company."

"Great," she said, and apparently content to have my permission, she rolled back onto her stomach, as though dismissing me. I wasn't so quick to be dismissed, though. I stood there that extra minute and enjoyed the shapeliness that was now in my view. For the second time, I had to fight the urge to reach out and touch this woman.

She turned to look at me and, with a mischievous glint in her green eyes, asked, "Is everything all right?"

I wanted to tell her that not only was everything all right, everything was quite nice. Delicious looking, even. Was I imagining it? Or was she flirting? I reminded myself that in my current sexually frustrated state, I could easily misread things. And I didn't need to be coming on to a straight neighbor of Sandy's.

"Fine," was all I said as I walked over to a chaise lounge a few feet away and tried to get comfortable. Having expected to sunbathe nude, I had not brought a suit with me. And now it was not only uncomfortable to be wearing clothes while lying out, but the throbbing that had begun between my legs was adding significantly to my discomfort.

I opted to lie on my back first, thinking that facing the pool, which meant facing away from Mandy, might ease my overactive hormones. That worked for a while. Until Mandy decided to get in the water.

The scraping of the lounge as she stood up caught my attention. I slyly looked over and was just in time to see her running her fingers along the edges of her bikini bottom. Apparently, it had done some creeping while she lay there. I wished my fingers could have helped her, but since they couldn't, watching her was the next best thing.

She walked gracefully to the edge of the pool, apparently oblivious to the fact that I was drooling over her. When she dove in the water, she wasn't the only one who was wet.

I made myself lie back and close my eyes. I didn't need this. I was making myself a horny wreck and nothing was going to happen, so I needed to just behave, or so I told myself. I finally realized that a dip in the pool just might cool me off, so I stood up and walked over to the edge. I got there just as Mandy was pulling herself out. I had an even better view of her cleavage than I had earlier. Her breasts were so full. They just begged to be touched. Standing there, I realized that as she looked up at me, she had a perfect view up my shorts. I found this incredibly stimulating and didn't know if I imagined it or not that she smiled and blushed.

Once she was out of the water, she sat on the edge next to where I was standing. I felt a conversation was appropriate.

"How was it?" I asked.

"Huh?" She blushed bright red and I wondered again if she had been sneaking a peek. "Oh, you mean . . . I'm sorry . . . I thought . . . Um . . . The water's fine. It felt great." She looked away from me.

Not wanting to let her off the hook that easily, I asked, "What else would I have meant?"

She turned back toward me, still blushing. I know I had a mischievous grin on my face, but I couldn't help it. Her eyes started at my feet and slowly made their way up my legs, lingering just a bit where they came together. They continued their ascent upward, pausing again on my bra, then my lips, before they finally reached my eyes.

As cool as could be, she said, "I don't know what you thought you meant."

I nodded slowly. If she wanted to play innocent, she could accept that I believed her. If she was flirting, she could guess that I was just placating her. Then I added, "I'm glad you enjoyed it," and I dove in.

I swam a few laps for a couple of reasons. One was to make some muscles work besides the ones between my legs. The other was to show off. I have a great physique and have been told by more than one woman that watching my body work its way through water is a turn-on. I thought Mandy might enjoy it.

As I got out of the pool, I saw that Mandy was now lying on her back. She was lying flat, so I felt immediate disappointment that she'd missed my show. Oh well. Her loss. I stood by the side of the pool dripping water as I looked over at her. She had the most delightful body. Truth be told, I know a lot of women thinner than her who wouldn't be caught dead in a bikini, but Mandy wore it well. She had wonderful curves, yet wasn't flabby. As I looked at her, I wondered what it would be like to run my hand over her body and let it slip inside the bottom of her suit.

I shook the thought away and lay down again. At least the outside of me was dry by then.

We both lay quietly for a while before she decided to swim again. Tempting as it was to go enjoy wet cleavage again, and let her have another view of what she was missing, I decided my mental state would be better off if I just stayed on my chaise and pretended I didn't notice.

I could hear her splashing in the pool. It was difficult to remain on my stomach, facing the other way, but I knew it was necessary. Although, as I heard her get out, I did spread my legs just a little wider, in case she wanted another peek. My ego told me she enjoyed the view, because it took a few minutes from when I heard her get out to when she walked over to her lounge.

"Excuse me," she said once she was lying on her stomach again. "Brynn?"

I rolled over and faced her.

She held up her bottle of sunscreen. "Would you mind putting some of this on my back for me?"

The look she gave me seemed more of a dare than a request.

I shrugged. "Sure." I thought I was so cool.

I stood up, walked over, and took the bottle out of her hand. Was it my imagination or did our fingers linger just a little too long?

I knelt down and started to rub the lotion all over her back. I decided that it would be better to err on the side of caution, so I barely touched her as I applied it.

She looked over her shoulder at me. "Hey! I won't break, you know."

I had no problem rubbing with more feeling. That was fine by me. She had her face down and her arms stretched out over her head. I began to let my hands linger a little as I applied.

Teasingly, I deliberately let my hands drift around her ribs to the front of her, not touching anything I shouldn't, but making her wonder if I would.

When I felt she was appropriately protected, I stood on shaky legs and started to walk back to my lounge.

"Hey," she said, turning her head slightly to face me. "If I move at all, I'll get burned, you know."

"How do you figure?" I asked.

"You need to put some *under* my suit, as well."

"Excuse me?" I asked, wondering if the evidence of my response to her statement was running down my leg.

"My strap, silly. The strap across my back. You need to put some under that on my back, to make sure I'm all covered."

With that, she turned her face down and kept her arms outstretched, as if there was no doubt in her mind that I would comply.

And why not comply, I asked myself. I'd have to be a fool to pass up the chance to put my hands back on that body. I put some more lotion in my hands and started rubbing her back under the strap, as instructed. With no notice, and with her arms still over her head, she quickly rolled over onto her back, leaving my hands under her bikini top and square on her breasts. Reflex alone caused my hands to squeeze those full, firm mounds as I let out a tiny cry that indicated the exquisite pain I was feeling. The pain only intense desire can cause.

Taking my eyes off her breasts, I looked into her eyes. The impish, questioning look she was giving me didn't last long. The mischievous gleam in her eye was quickly replaced with a look of smoldering passion as she put her hands behind my head and pulled me to her. I feigned resistance, but she would have none of it. She pulled my lips to hers and kissed me hungrily. There was no pretense of shyness or insecurity. Her tongue parted my lips and entered my mouth immediately.

Somewhere, deep in the recesses of my mind was a voice reminding me that she was Sandy and Jessica's neighbor. However, in the forefront of my mind, and every other body part, was the pent-up desire and sexual frustration that had been taunting me since I woke up that morning. At that point, I didn't care whose neighbor Mandy was. All I knew was that she obviously wanted me, and I wanted and needed her as well.

Our tongues worked around each other, doing their dance of passion. She pulled me on top of her. I did not fight it. My right hand released her breast and pushed her bikini bra up so I could move my hands over her unimpeded. I pulled my mouth from hers and began kissing down her cheek and neck and chest, pausing to lightly lick the hollow at the base of her neck.

I continued until my lips finally found their way around an exposed nipple. It was her turn to cry out. My tongue flicked across her nipple, my mouth alternately teasing and sucking her. While I was focused on her breasts, I felt her hand on my inner thigh as it made its way up and slid inside the leg of my shorts. She playfully teased me, running fingers through my hair, without actually going inside of me. I scooted lower, hoping to at least make contact between my swollen clit and her hand, but she would not allow it. She moved her hand all over me, around all swollen areas without touching or entering.

I slid my hand down her stomach until it was just inside her waistband. Two could play at this game. I dragged my fingers back and forth horizontally across her, just inside her waistband. Then I slipped my hand inside until my fingertips stopped just shy of her clit. I ran my fingers through her soft triangle of hair, driving myself crazy with the need to touch and be touched by her.

She won the game. I could not be that close to heaven and not give it the attention it deserved. I slowly lowered her bikini bottom, and let my mouth relinquish its hold on her nipple. I started trailing kisses down her stomach, stopping to suck and nip as I went. As I worked my way down, I was surprised at how quickly and willingly she opened up for me. She was not shy at all and had her legs spread wide. I stopped my kisses for just a moment as I gazed hungrily at her womanhood before I lowered myself to take her in my mouth. My tongue entered her and she gasped again. Her sweetness was delicious. She gently placed her hands on the sides of my head as if afraid I would stop. I had no such intentions. As my tongue worked around her and in her, her hips began a rhythmic gyration that responded to my every move. As my tongue stroked her clit with a ferocity matched only by the desire I was feeling, I felt her tense up. Faster and faster she moved against me until she cried out again and again. She was so easy to please and obviously obtained such pleasure from my mouth that she was causing my own desires to reach a fever pitch.

I straddled her leg so I could also finally experience release as she had. She immediately changed positions so this wouldn't be possible.

I looked at her, wondering what she was doing. She slid away from me and positioned me so I was flat on my back. Straddling my legs one by one, she slowly peeled my shorts off, and every time she shifted positions, her wetness touched me. If I thought I couldn't get any more aroused, I was wrong.

Once my shorts were removed, she sat between my legs at my feet, placed her hands on my knees and then worked them up my inner thighs. Halfway up, she forced my legs wider.

"Open up," she said, her voice deep with passion.

I obliged. There was something unexpectedly stimulating about this. Maybe I'm a closet exhibitionist. My legs were spread as wide as they could be, each one hanging over the edge of the chaise. It was broad daylight, I was outside, and I was visible to anyone who might happen to look into the yard.

❧

She then leaned forward and rubbed her breasts against me. She pulled herself along, rubbing her stomach against me next, until she worked her face up to mine to kiss me. As our lips met, her curls were pressing against me and I didn't think I would be able to maintain any semblance of composure. Up and down, she ground against me as her mouth devoured mine. I wrapped my legs around her to establish better contact and she stopped. She looked down at me, swaying her breasts back and forth just above mine.

I pulled her to me. I wanted to feel her breasts on me and I wanted to feel her between my legs. Again, she pulled away.

Working backward, she rubbed her stomach between my legs again and then her breasts. Then she sat back and spread my legs wider again.

Again, she moved her hands up my thighs, stopping just shy of the promised land. The torment was unbelievable. If she didn't touch me soon, I would cry.

She slowly dragged the back of her hand over my wet, throbbing clit, until her fingernails dragged along it. She then moved her hand the other way, letting her fingernails tease me. She began to move one fingernail, ever so slightly over my clit. She was barely touching me. It was stimulating and torturous, but I needed more. I arched my back, trying to press myself against her harder. She simply pulled away slightly. But she never stopped. She just kept at it. Faster and faster, but barely touching me. I spread my legs wider still, hoping she'd go inside, but she didn't. She never took her eyes from mine as she kept lightly teasing my clit.

I found myself moving against that fingernail, matching her strokes, however distant they were. I couldn't believe the effect she was having on me. I lay back and closed my eyes, seeing myself edging closer to the cliff. I could feel the ball in the pit of my stomach. The tension moved to my outer limbs. And still she barely touched me. I was losing all conscious thought. I could feel the buildup, I could see the edge. I was getting close, so close. Just a little farther and I would slip over the edge of the cliff to sail into a world of ecstasy.

I was so close, I was almost there, and WHAM! Just as the ball inside of me exploded and sent wave after wave of orgasm through my body, I heard, as well as felt, her slide her other hand inside of me, to allow my orgasmic spasms to engulf her. Over and over I convulsed on her, until I lay back, completely spent.

She moved back up to kiss me and I held her in my arms. Completely relaxed, we fell asleep.

I don't know how long we slept, but we woke to the sound of someone clearing her throat. I looked over Mandy's shoulder to see Sandy standing there, one hand on her hip, the other hand out, with my shorts dangling from a fingertip.

Recovering from the shock of seeing her, I tried to cover as much of Mandy as I could to give her a little dignity. I wasn't too worried about myself. If Sandy saw anything, well, good for her.

"What are you doing home?" I managed to ask. Luckily for me, Sandy is a true friend. She played it off like it was nothing to find us out there nakedly entwined.

"Oh. Jessica's grandma is fine. It wasn't that bad of a fall. And of course, the whole family is there fawning all over her, so we decided we didn't need to stay. It was really too much."

"What about Joey?" I had to ask. Joey is Jessica's older brother. He hasn't accepted his sister's lifestyle at all.

Rolling her eyes, she did her best impression. " 'What the hell's she doin' here?' he asked Jessica, turning his back as soon as I walked into the room. Fucking prick. You need these?" She tossed the shorts my way.

I caught them but didn't put them on, still trying to afford Mandy a little dignity.

Sandy walked over then and put her hand out as if to shake Mandy's hand.

"I'm Sandy, by the way."

Completely confused, I looked from one woman to the other.

"Uh, nice to meet you," Mandy said as she jumped up and put her bottoms on. She leaned over, kissed me good-bye, and left through the back gate.

"Shy girl. Where'd you meet her?" Sandy inquired.

"Here."

"Huh?"

I put my shorts on and walked in the house with Sandy, explaining how Mandy had told me she was their neighbor. We found Jessica in the kitchen and asked her if she'd ever met Mandy.

Her denial led to a conversation about who Mandy was and how she could have known I was going to be there. They seemed more disturbed about it than I was; I suppose that was because it was their backyard she was in.

As I excused myself and said I had to get going, Sandy stopped me. "I almost forgot. We're gonna go see Grandma when things quiet down around there. I don't suppose you'd mind . . ."

I gave her a big ol' smile. "Are you kidding? Believe me, it would be my pleasure!"

Riding home, I realized I'd forgotten to tell Jessica that I was glad her grandmother was going to be okay. Oh well. It wouldn't be the first time I'd been accused of being self-absorbed.

Miss August

Nairne Holtz

On a summer night as hot as a flush, I had come to the bar wearing very little clothing and hoping to find a woman to remove what was left. I was wearing lingerie as outerwear, which can be done if you accessorize properly. I wore a black silk vest over a black lace bra, red silk boxer shorts a size too small and more like hot pants, and army boots. I guess some would call my look gender-bending, except that I was the sort of femme that when I put on any type of men's clothing, butches would ruffle my long brown hair and say, "Oh, you look cute."

The bar I was in was called Shag—a straight West End Toronto neighborhood bar that was more like an ongoing party in someone's basement. Tonight was dyke night. It was a tiny, dark place with patio lanterns strung along the walls. Different DJs played every week, and the music ran the gamut from crooners to metal to techno. At the back, you could sit on large, ugly, comfortable couches and make out or watch lesbo porno and B-movies flickering on a small screen.

"Excuse me, I know this sounds stupid, but don't I know you?"

I looked up and thought, this is my lucky night. A handsome woman I had admired before stood in front of me. I knew her name was Maria, and that she was Portuguese. A big woman with soulful brown eyes and pouty cheeks, she had dated my friend Olive. Olive was a very thin, hyper blonde who worked in the film industry. More an acquaintance than a friend, Olive was a self-avowed sex radical, a bottom, a dyke who fucked boys, but she had an essential niceness. Maybe it was the easy way she told me what she felt during the handful of late-night conversations we had at Shag or perhaps it was her little round glasses, I wasn't sure.

"I'm Mallory." I offered Maria my hand to shake. "I met you once with Olive, and I've seen you around with various women."

Maria sighed wearily and did not take my hand. "My problem is, I'm too good in bed." Maria ran a hand over her sleekly gelled, dark brush-cut. "I have sex with a girl and she falls for me."

I thought, oh shit, you're full of yourself. But she was hot and I was horny, so I decided to give her a chance. I told her, "If you're trying to impress me, it's not working. I'd be much more intrigued if you told me you were really bad in bed. In fact, I'd feel compelled to contradict you, and prove you wrong."

Maria started laughing, and I was relieved to see that she had a sense of humor. Then she looked me in the eye. "C'mon. Don't take me so seriously." She paused and briefly lowered her eyelashes. "You're supposed to see through my rough exterior to my insecurities."

It was another line but it was delivered with awkward irony, and I liked her for that. I smiled and raised my eyebrow at her.

"Would you like a drink?" Maria ran a finger down my bare arm, and although my skin was damp with sweat in a bar blocked with people and smoke, I shivered lightly.

"Sure. Jack Daniel's on the rocks."

"You're tough."

Maria moved away to the end of the bar where a white girl with dreadlocks and a huge hockey shirt was taking orders. The local arts weekly described Shag as an "edgy dyke bar." Piercings were popular, as were shaved heads and dykes in their versions of raver, skater and hip-hop aesthetics. The place certainly had style, but I was from Montreal and felt that it lacked a certain abandon. It was exhibitionist but not decadent.

I had moved from Sin City to the Big Smoke a year before to pay off my student loans and to get over the heartache of being dumped. Getting a good job had been easy, but getting laid was not. Toronto women all seemed to have an agenda. Woman-to-woman personal ads specified the type of professional they wanted to date, such as "someone in the entertainment industry" or "discreet lawyer seeks discreet lawyer." Lesbians I met introduced women they had been dating for a month as their partner. Casual sex was hard to come by, but maybe tonight would be different.

Maria returned with my drink, and we drifted over to one of the ratty plaid couches that had been recently vacated. Above us, a film projector played *Faster, Pussycat, Kill, Kill* with the sound off. Maria placed her hand flatly and deliberately between us. I moved ever so slightly so that the edge of her hand touched my thigh. She pretended not to notice and asked me the quintessential Toronto question, "So Mallory, where do you work?"

"Right downtown. I'm a securities law clerk at a law firm." I enjoyed my job, but I could see how a lot of people would find it boring.

"Securities. Law. Clerk." She said the words one at a time as if she was trying to remember them. "What do you do exactly?"

"I gather financial documents for lawyers, like say offerings of unsecured, subordinated debentures, and then I file them with the exchange commission."

"What the hell's that?" Maria scoffed.

"It's a way of selling debt. A bad idea, basically." I had wanted to make her smile, but instead she just handed me the chip on her shoulder.

"I bet you had to go to school a long time to do that." She looked impressed in spite of herself, and withdrew her hand from where it had lingered at my thigh.

"It depends. What do you do?" I realized that she was working class, and that I had intimidated her without meaning to. It was hard to tell where butch girls came from just by looking. They all wore jeans and T-shirts. Some of the ones with a Marlon Brando swagger turned out to be corporate trainers.

"I work in a factory, but I apprenticed to be a car mechanic. I'd like to open my own garage some day."

"That's cool." It didn't matter to me. I didn't care what job a potential lover had. Smart was what counted, and I had long since learned that intelligence did not necessarily go with a university education.

"Yeah." Maria looked bored and distant.

Maybe I had said the wrong thing. I worried about it while I played with the ice in my drink and she lit up a cigarette. She held her pack out, but I shook my head. She smoked and watched a woman with short blonde hair in a white vinyl mini-skirt move her hips to James Brown on the dance floor. I felt jealous. I did not want to marry her, but I needed her to at least find me the sexiest woman in the bar.

"Do you want to go home with me?" Maria blurted out.

"Very much."

She leaned over and pushed her tongue thickly into my mouth. She was not subtle, but what did I care? I was really in the mood. I was about to get my period and I had been masturbating all week. When I moaned into Maria's mouth, she stopped and said, "My truck's out back."

Outside it was late, but the air on my skin was like a pink, tender sunburn. The heat was breaking some kind of record set back in the

1930s, according to the news. Maria opened the door of her truck for me. When I got in, I rolled down the window and wished for a breeze.

"Let's go by Olive's place," Maria said. She spun her red truck around, and we headed south to the warehouse district where Olive lived.

"Why?"

Maria did not answer.

"Why are we driving past Olive's house?" I repeated. As far as I knew they had broken up six months ago and had not gone out for very long—a month or two. Olive had told me she thought Maria was too controlling.

"There's her place." Maria slowed down and pointed to an old factory that had been converted into lofts. "I bet she's sucking some guy's dick right now."

"What's that supposed to mean?"

"I'm seeing her, okay. She's cute, she's femme, she seems like she's part of the club. But then she goes and gives a blowjob to this guy she met on a shoot. It's not like we agreed to be serious or monogamous but still—I don't want to hear something like that." Maria made a face.

"Wouldn't it be just as bad if she went down on some chick?" Guys did not threaten me. If a woman was dumb enough to prefer one over me, I lost all respect for her. But then the kind of women who turned me on were rarely bisexual, so it hadn't exactly come up as an issue.

"No, it's different," Maria insisted. "I'm getting screwed over by some guy."

"Do we have to talk about Olive?"

"Oh. Sorry. Hey, are you hungry?"

"Not really."

"So you just want to go straight to my place?"

"Yes." I watched the handsome woman beside me expertly shift from third gear to first and her easy skill attracted me more than the obvious ways in which she was butch. "Are you nervous?"

"Yeah." She kept her eyes on the road ahead of her.

"We don't have to do anything if you don't want."

But when we got to her place, she immediately put on some Cuban jazz, dimmed the lights, and covered my body with hers on the futon couch. Her tongue fished around in my mouth and after thirty seconds, she grabbed my breasts and squeezed them like fruit being checked for bruises. It felt like the paint-by-numbers way teenage boys had tried to fuck me. It was as if they had all read the same manual that began, "*first you kiss the girl . . .*" I drew back from Maria, and was wondering how I could get her to slow down and relax when she stood up.

"Excuse me," she said in a deep voice and then walked down the hall to her bedroom. I heard her rustling around in her drawers, and I had a sinking feeling she was putting on a strap-on dildo.

"You can come in," she called to me. She had turned off the lights so the room was fairly shady, although some light seeped in from the hall. I found her sitting stiffly on the bed. I walked over to her, put my hands on her shoulders, and pushed her down onto the bed. Hard rubber jabbed my thigh. I had been right about the dildo.

"What are you doing?" She sounded shocked.

"Surely you don't think being femme means I get into the missionary position while you fuck me with your dick and I scream like a porn star?" I laughed.

Maria did not laugh.

I took a deep breath. "I don't really like penetration. It's always been physically uncomfortable. I don't even wear tampons." I didn't like to put it into words. I would have preferred for her to have just figured it out. It made me feel a little inadequate, like I could not provide everything on the menu.

"I guess we can't have sex," Maria muttered.

"What?" I shrieked. "Are you serious?" I suddenly realized that if I had been a lesbian in the 1960s, I would have joined all of the feminists who rebelled against the unreconstructed butch-femme lesbians.

"Well, what can we do?"

"Kiss? Fool around?"

Maria got up from the bed and removed the dildo and harness. She walked across the room to an old chest of drawers that were scraped as a tomboy's knee, opened the top drawer, and placed the dildo and harness inside. Then she came back and sat beside me. She leaned over and kissed me full and hard, but this time it didn't feel like she was trying to prove something. We slid our hands over each other's bodies and she peeled off most of my clothes and some of hers. Maria was too shy to tell me what she liked; she would just nod slightly when I asked or guessed. She watched me cautiously when I sucked her nipples, even though I could feel them getting erect and fuller in my mouth. I began to lose myself in her. I felt my bikini underwear slip into the slickness of my cunt. I could tell Maria was getting hot too, so after a few moments, I placed my fingers lightly on the waistband of her boxers to slide them down. She stopped me by putting her hand on top of mine.

"Why?" she asked me.

"Because I want to feel your naked body. And look at you."

"I've got kind of a beer gut happening."

"Maria, your body's fine. You're beautiful." She was chubby in a lush, well-proportioned way, and I liked it.

Maria pulled her boxers down, folded them and set them on a chair. She got back into bed and this time we crawled under the sheets. We kissed some more and when she stopped, I looked into her eyes. There was fear and pleasure in them.

"I feel so girly." She sighed. "I never do this. Take off all my clothes, I mean, maybe once or twice. My ex-girlfriend lived with me here for three years, and she never saw me naked unless she walked in on me in the shower."

I was shocked. I had heard about these lesbian untouchables, but I had never met one. Stone butch. This hard cool thing. It was supposed to be about wanting to be a man, but for Maria it sounded

depressingly like the same thing almost every woman I knew felt—
I don't like my body, I'm too fat, it's hard to trust.

"Ohh." Maria distracted me by crawling between my legs and
licking me. It felt good rocking against her but I could not turn that
corner and come. Like Maria, I used to find it hard to let go. Too
much sex with men when I was younger and didn't want to—I think
that was why. After coming out, it took a few years for my body to
trust, to dissolve into another woman's. But not this time. Maria was
not with me; she was just working hard to make the girl come. But
the girl couldn't.

Instead I motioned for her to come up and hold me. I reached
down, played with myself, and came in about thirty seconds. When
I opened my eyes, I realized I had made a mistake. She lay away
from me and looked at me like I was a freak. I felt like a freak. I
wanted to cry. I put my hand on her thigh, delicately, not wanting
to do anything, just feeling a tight hunger for reassurance I was too
humiliated to ask for. She flinched.

"What are you doing?"

"Nothing."

We lay like unhappy mollusks, each of us contained within her
shell. She broke the silence and surprised me again. "I like being
going down on, but not tonight. I have my period."

"I'll do whatever you want," I said. It didn't make any difference
to me whether I strapped it on or licked a woman or touched her.
As long as she had a good time.

"It's okay. I've kind of lost the mood."

I did not push it. I tended to pass out after I came, so women had
a rather short window of opportunity with me if they did not get
done first. I felt my thoughts blurring, so I rolled over to say one last
thing to Maria before I slept.

"Maria, you don't have to be insecure about your body."

"Thank you," she said softly.

≈≫≈

When I woke up, I found Maria sitting on the end of the bed, fully dressed.

"Did you sleep well?" she inquired.

"Fine."

"I didn't sleep at all."

I rubbed my eyes sleepily and patted the pillow next to me, but she ignored this. I spied a clock radio on a night table beside the bed and discerned that it was seven in the morning, which meant I had had four hours of sleep at the most. Above the clock, I saw a black-and-white framed photograph I had not noticed earlier. It was a picture of an extremely hard muscular ass and back rising above a sheet. A fringe of long hair framed the person's back. The face was invisible, and I wondered if it was a man or a woman.

"Do you like it?"

I thought it was tacky, but I said, "Great butt. Is it a guy or a girl?"

"What would I be doing with a picture of a man in my bedroom?" she demanded.

Of course. What was I thinking. "I don't know. Maybe you like gender ambiguity?" I suggested hesitantly.

"Do I look like someone who's into gender ambiguity?" Maria bellowed. "I don't feel close to you." She stalked out of the bedroom.

I got up and dressed as quickly as I could. I started to feel really weird. I followed her into the kitchen where my boots were and began to lace them up. I wondered if I should just leave. I really wanted some coffee, but I was afraid to ask her for some. She stared at me like I was a tile on the floor. "Are you mad at me?" I asked.

"No," she insisted. "It's just we're obviously totally sexually incompatible. Sex with you was terrible. I never want to have sex with you again."

Her rudeness was like a stun gun. I usually had something to say, but not this time. I had reached similar conclusions to Maria, but for somewhat different reasons. I had not felt this degraded since I was a straight teenager dealing with guys who could not respect girls who had sex with them.

Maria insisted on driving me home. I let her. I noticed that this time she did not open the door for me. When we got to my place, I turned around to face her. "Listen," I said, "sex for me is not about coming. It's not about one particular act. It's about having fun and taking care of each other's needs."

Maria thought about this for a moment, and then said, "You're probably right. I'm sorry."

"Do you want to have breakfast?" I did not know why I was asking her. She was basically a jerk, but I kept holding out for her to be sweet so that the crummy feeling inside of me would go away. It reminded me of this boyfriend I had when I was sixteen. We did not like each other very much, but I kept waiting for it to get better. He smoked pot every day and his mom had abused him. I knew I liked girls, but I was scared to be a dyke. I guess you could say, what he and I had in common was no self-esteem. Somewhere along the line, I'd acquired it, but Maria had taken me back to when I had none.

"I'll call you," Maria said, but I knew it was the last thing she would do.

Over the next few weeks, I thought a lot about Maria. I was relieved when she didn't call, because I sensed that she would do nothing but hurt me. But I also imagined her calling and telling me that she was sorry, that I had pulled out her feelings and vulnerabilities like soft taffy and it had scared her. In this fantasy, we would fuck again and it would be wild mutual erotic surrender.

Maria never spoke to me again. At Shag one night, she pointed me out once to a friend who then came over to ask for a light and I guess to get a closer look at me. I imagine Maria had said something like, "See that pretty femme. I fucked her once."

An Old-School Femme

Jennifer Collins

Marlena Belleveau looked around the bar in disgust, her finely manicured hands curled around the rim of her martini glass. The olive bumped the side of the glass and she fished it out, placed the dark green orb into her mouth with a flourish, and licked the salt off her fingers as only a proper femme could.

"Ugh, just look at them, Sally," Marlena sneered. Her martini was nearly gone and she liked to soak up the last little bit with olives. Leaning back against the bar, she tossed her long blonde hair out of her eyes and over her shoulder, and beckoned to the bartender with her dark eyelashes.

"Look at who?" Sally raised a perfectly plucked eyebrow at her friend.

"Whom, Sally," Marlena corrected. "At all of these so-called *butches*." She flashed a smile at the bartender, who had slid a shallow dish of olives over next to Marlena's elbow. The smile evaporated as quickly as it had appeared, making any accidental observers uncertain as to whether they'd actually seen it at all.

"Bunch of faggots, all of them," Marlena continued. "They only want to get with each other anymore. Where are the *real* butches? That's what I want to know." This last she heaved with a plaintive sigh. Sally snorted in agreement, just as an elbow brushed brusquely against Marlena's arm. Annoyed, Marlena whipped her head around, but the owner of the offending elbow spoke before Marlena could lay into her for intruding upon her personal space.

"A real butch you're looking for? Well, it looks like I showed up right on time." Tamar leaned up against the bar, pressing her lips against Marlena's cheek—greeting and apology all at the same time. Marlena rolled her eyes at Sally.

"Ugh, Tamar, you're no help at all. You're just a case in point."

"Yep, prime example," Sally chimed in, tossing dark braids away from her face and taking a swig of her beer in what Marlena felt was a decidedly unfeminine manner. Marlena had long ago quit giving femme pointers to Sally; they just seemed to confuse her, which Marlena found even more annoying.

Tamar acquired a neat scotch, paid the bartender, then turned to face the crowd with Marlena and Sally. Marlena silently ran her eyes over Tamar's firm form: Calvin Klein's that were loose in the leg and tight around her ass, tight white T-shirt exposed under an unbuttoned short-sleeve shirt. *Such a waste*, Marlena thought to herself.

"Example of what?" Tamar asked after a sip of her drink.

Marlena took a deep breath and explained, with an exaggerated exhale. "Example of a butch who's lost her way. Gone south. Turned her back on her true calling . . ."

"Marlena . . ." Tamar interrupted.

"Gone fag," Sally added, a tutorial tone to her voice. Tamar lifted her glass, emptied it, then ordered a double of the same.

"Nice language, you two," Tamar finally responded. "Who do you represent these days, Focus on the Family?"

"Tamar," Marlena said. "You can't deny that it's true."

"That what's true? That I'm attracted to other butches?"

"That *all* butches are attracted to other butches nowadays." Marlena took a long sip of her drink, her first finger held up in an indication that she wasn't finished speaking. Tamar waited; Marlena had used this gesture often while they were dating.

Marlena swallowed, then continued. "All the butches want to be just like men. They're all butch boys or transfags or some other bullshit now. All these 'boys'"—and yes, she did signal the quote marks around *boys* with a dainty motion of the first two fingers of each hand, careful not to spill her drink—"want other 'boys.' We girls are just supposed to go fuck ourselves, I guess."

"Or each other," Tamar mumbled under her breath.

Marlena ignored her. "It's misogynistic, Tamar."

"Misogynistic," Tamar repeated, a rising note of frustration in her voice.

"Absolutely. What's this fascination with wanting to be men, and wanting to *fuck* men, if not internalized misogyny?"

"*What?* You're one to talk." Tamar frowned. Sally sucked in her breath delightedly, which both Tamar and Marlena ignored. Tamar continued, "I'll tell you what's misogynist, Marlena. It's you and femme women like you, who are stuck in some glamorized version of Ozzie and fucking Harriet. You have these horrible strict roles for butches . . ."

"What's wrong with roles, Tamar?" Marlena interrupted. "They give you a framework, something to settle into."

"I'm not finished yet, Marlena."

"Well, sor-ry," Marlena drew out the word and rolled her eyes.

"Roles can also be stifling, Marlena. Some of the butches I've talked to are tired of feeling stuck. 'Butch' doesn't meant the same thing to everybody. Grow up." Tamar turned her head away from Marlena and sipped her drink, trying to swallow resentment along with the scotch.

Marlena gasped. "*I* should grow up?" she demanded. "Why don't *you* grow up and quit playing around. Don't you ever want to settle down, Tamar? Butch on butch never works, and you know it." Marlena folded her arms and cocked her head.

It was Tamar's turn to roll her eyes, subtly. Tamar could name, offhand, at least seven butch couples in their community who'd been together ten years or more. But she held her tongue. Marlena wouldn't pay attention to that kind of evidence right now anyway—she was lonely and loaded, and horny to boot. Tamar turned back to find Marlena staring out at the dance floor. She eyed Marlena's gorgeous face, now pulled into a pout. Marlena wore a loose green silk tank top, with no bra constraining the small, fine breasts underneath. Under a pleated micro-miniskirt, her legs were bare (no psychedelic print tights tonight) and her feet were shod in platform heels that must've been at least four inches high. Tamar smiled, remembering how Marlena always liked to keep her shoes on in bed. Sometimes she'd change them several times during a long session of fucking: Marlena liked to wear shoes to match her mood.

Tamar didn't want to continue an argument that never went anywhere, and knew Marlena wasn't going to be the one to back down. "Look, honey." She placed a hand on Marlena's shoulder, which Marlena immediately shrugged off. "I know it's frustrating trying to find somebody."

"Don't change the subject," Marlena said.

Tamar continued as though Marlena hadn't spoken. "Maybe you need a change of scenery—you know *everyone* here." *And have fucked about three-quarters of 'em*, Tamar thought, but did not say. "Let's get out of here. You and me."

"And Angel Ass," Marlena said, using her not-so-nice nickname for Tamar's new girlfriend.

"Well," Tamar hesitated. "She'll be there."

"No, thank you anyway. I don't need to be your third wheel. Right, Sally?" Marlena looked over to her friend for confirmation, but Sally had peeled herself off the bar and away from Marlena and Tamar's oft-repeated argument. Marlena looked out over the dance floor and found her *supposed* best friend doing the bump-and-grind with some baby butch so green it looked like there was grass growing behind her ears. Still, Sally was dancing and there Marlena stood, butt against the bar.

"How'd she do that?" Marlena sighed quietly to herself.

"Her standards aren't as high as yours," Tamar stated. Marlena suppressed a smile. Tamar always did know how to sweet-talk her. "Come on, Marlena. It's an old-school dyke bar—one of Angela's favorites."

At the mention of her perceived rival's name—no matter that Marlena and Tamar had been apart for months before Tamar even met Angela—Marlena wanted to growl. But Tamar had ducked her head down, puppy-like, raising her dark eyes up to meet Marlena's green ones. Marlena couldn't resist that look, and Tamar knew it.

Marlena brought her hand up the back of Tamar's closely shorn neck, razing her nails lightly until she came to the dark curls on top, the ones that drooped down over Tamar's forehead when she was dancing, or fucking. Marlena tightened her grip on the curls until Tamar winced.

"Okay. Let's go, you big tease," Marlena said with a grimace, releasing Tamar.

"*Me* a tease?" Tamar exclaimed, as Marlena settled up with the bartender. Although she was aggravated that Tamar didn't even offer to take care of the tab, she hooked her hand gently through the crook of Tamar's arm, and they set off.

"That business with the hair was the tease, Marlena," Tamar continued as she led them around the dance floor.

Marlena whispered directly into Tamar's ear. "That was a promise, and you know it. You just won't take me up on it." She felt the barest of shudders ran down Tamar's back.

As they exited the club, away from the noise and lights, the cool evening air acted as a bracer to Marlena's lust. She disengaged herself from Tamar's arm as they approached Tamar's little midnight blue BMW.

At least Tamar remembered to open the door for her. She opened her purse and pulled out her cigarette case while Tamar walked around to the driver's side.

"Mind if I smoke?" she asked as she lit one with her Betty Page Zippo.

Tamar lowered Marlena's window. "Nope," she said. Marlena stared out the window as the city moved past. Tamar reached down and pushed a button on the console, filling the car with Euro-pop. Marlena flicked the butt of her cigarette out into the night and let herself get lost in the infectious rhythm of the music and the chill breeze.

Tamar parked the BMW in front of a single-story brick building. Waiting for Tamar to open her door for her, Marlena used the vanity mirror to quickly check her makeup. She flipped up the visor as Tamar opened her door and held out a hand. As they crossed the sidewalk to the door of the club, Marlena strained to hear any signs of life from inside the place. Where had she let Tamar take her?

Tamar opened the heavy door and ushered Marlena inside. After a loud display of butch affection with the bouncer, Tamar made a beeline for the bar (and Angela). Forgotten and annoyed, Marlena raised a single, irritated eyebrow at the bouncer, who'd finally turned her attention to Marlena. The woman, about to ask for ID, closed her mouth and said nothing.

Marlena glanced over at the bar. A small clutch of butches tightened themselves around Tamar and Angela, loud and raucous. She couldn't tell what they were saying, and decided not to go find out, despite the fact that Tamar was waving her over. A handful of butches sat at the bar. Between her and the bar was a small dance floor, where four or five couples slow-danced while Janet sang about goin' deep. Most of the dancers, along with the few couples sitting at tables, were butch-femme couples, which at least somewhat mollified Marlena's rising concern that this was a butch-only bar.

This place is dead, she thought to herself as she pulled her purse off her shoulder. *Why do I listen to Tamar?* She fingered a cigarette out of the pack in her purse, and placed it between her lips. Before she could get out her lighter, a flame appeared before her.

Raising her gaze, but not her head, Marlena met the eyes of the person behind this bold offer. Glossy black they were, surrounded by long, thick lashes. Around the flame, before she lowered her eyes and inhaled deeply, Marlena caught a glimpse of high cheekbones and the curve of that half-grin butches are so famous for.

Once her cigarette was lit, Marlena took care to exhale to the side, away from her suitor's face. Then she took a good long look while the woman lit her own cigarette, cupping the flame with a well-manicured hand. The butch was well-dressed, all right: black button-down, gray-and-black silk tie, fine-tailored gray slacks, and Italian leather shoes. Her short black hair was slicked back. Probably late twenties, and been around the block a time or two. Or three.

Marlena folded one arm across her waist, rested the elbow of the hand that held her cigarette on that arm, and flicked her cigarette ash on the floor. "Where's your boyfriend?" She raised her eyebrows as she took a drag, then exhaled through pursed lips.

The butch squinted in wary confusion. "My *what?*"

Marlena smiled. "Good answer." She unfolded her arms, switched the cigarette from her right hand to her left, and extended the right hand out in front of her. "I'm Marlena."

"I know," said the butch, taking Marlena's hand. Her voice was rich and thick, like heavy cream. Marlena glanced over at Tamar and Angela, who watched this introduction with looks of extreme amusement. Marlena turned back to the butch—she would deal with those two later. This one still had potential, even if it was a set-up.

"Okay. So you know me. And you are?" The butch still held her hand, and she gently caressed Marlena's fingers with her own before releasing it. Marlena found this forwardness a little irritating, and yet couldn't deny the heat the butch's touch had ignited.

"I'm Carmen." She bent her elbow and offered it to Marlena, who slid her fingers under Carmen's (ooh—very hard) bicep and rested her fingertips there. Carmen led them to the bar. "May I buy you a drink, Marlena?"

Marlena liked how Carmen held her name in her mouth, let it roll out between her lips like it was something precious, luscious.

Liked the fact that Carmen's offer had not really been a question but simply a next step.

They reached the bar and Marlena slid onto one of the stools. Carmen stood next to her, one hand protectively resting on Marlena's barstool (and certainly not intentionally pressed against the bit of thigh just exposed when her skirt rode up).

Carmen looked into Marlena's eyes and said, "What do you want, Marlena?" She ended the question with a little smile, indicating that the innuendo was perfectly intentional.

When she opened her mouth to speak, Marlena found her mouth was dry. She swallowed, cleared her throat delicately, and looked into Carmen's deep eyes. "Martini, very dirty. With extra olives."

Carmen ordered and Marlena smoked, ignoring the noise from the end of the bar. After a few moments, Carmen presented Marlena with her glass. The martini held one olive, and Carmen indicated with a flick of her eyes to Marlena's left a double shot glass of olives. With much effort, Marlena suppressed a smile. She stubbed out her cigarette in the ashtray Carmen had found them, then took the martini.

Carmen raised her glass slightly. "To Marlena," she said, meeting Marlena's eyes just as she spoke her name. Marlena felt a flush rise up from her sex and spread over every inch of her body. She touched the rim of her glass to Carmen's and nodded in recognition of the toast.

"*Salut,*" she managed to say.

"*Salut,*" Carmen repeated. They both drank, eyes on each other.

"Thank you for this," Marlena said, meaning the drink. "It's not bad." Carmen nodded.

"What are you drinking?" Marlena asked.

"Bourbon."

Marlena was pleased, and the shadow of a grin passed over her lips. She believed anything drunk straight to be a good solid butch drink.

They sipped their drinks, watching the few dancers. Someone had loaded the jukebox up with quarters and punched up every slow jam the box contained. No one wanted to bounce around anymore. They all wanted to stay up between their partners' thighs, trying to find the moves that would get them invited home.

When her martini was nearly gone, Marlena fingered an olive out of the shot glass. She nuzzled it against its gin-soaked cousin, then lifted it out of the glass using her thumb and middle finger. Keeping her eyes down, she placed her fingers in her mouth and licked them as she released the olive. Then, just as she pulled her fingers from between her lips, Marlena raised her eyes to Carmen's.

Carmen was not standing there with her mouth hanging open like a dog's, the way butches often reacted to this display. Instead, her face smoldered with cloaked desire, and this show of butch restraint was almost more than Marlena could stand. She repeated her little show with the three other olives.

Carmen set down her empty glass and raised Marlena's hand to her own mouth. She placed Marlena's middle finger between her lips, and suckled it for the barest of moments before sliding Marlena off the bar stool. Holding the hand she'd just molested, Carmen said, "Come dance with me, Marlena."

Marlena could not speak, and could hardly walk. She leaned into Carmen, who led them out onto the dance floor. Carmen danced them into a niche in Lauren Hill's bass and groove. She pulled Marlena in close, holding Marlena's right hand in her left up against her chest. Marlena wanted to settle up against Carmen, rest her head on the butch's shoulder. But in her platform heels, she was too tall.

"Wait," Marlena managed to say. She moved off the dance floor before Carmen could complain, sat at an empty table, and rapidly unbuckled her shoes. It was not something she'd ever done before.

Unshod, Marlena was about half a head shorter than Carmen. She let Carmen fold her up against her chest, and she tilted her head up so she could press her hot cheek against Carmen's. She could feel Carmen's heart pounding.

Carmen moved them around a small bit of dance floor, shifting her hips against Marlena's every now and then. Marlena allowed her legs to be eased apart as Carmen pressed her thigh between them. Carmen took them down slow, until Marlena rested a good deal of her weight on that aforementioned thigh. They rode that way through the next several songs, and Marlena began to make little, somewhat unladylike noises.

Eventually, Marlena's thighs began to complain. She pushed slightly away from Carmen, though she didn't disentangle herself from Carmen's arms. Her thighs ached from overwork and her cunt was throbbing.

"Do you have a car?" Marlena whispered into Carmen's ear. Carmen nodded. "Well, then—can you take me home?" Again, Carmen simply nodded. Perhaps she was unable to speak. She simply moved them off the dance floor and through the throng toward the door. Before exiting, Marlena shot a look over her shoulder to the corner, where Tamar was waving good-bye. Marlena managed to mouth the words "Thank you," before Carmen led her out of the bar and into the night.

They'd been walking for a moment or two before Marlena came down enough to realize that the strange surface under her feet was concrete. "My shoes!" she yelped.

Carmen looked down, as if requiring confirmation that indeed Marlena's shoes had not magically reattached themselves to her feet when they'd walked out of the bar. She touched Marlena's cheek, which caused Marlena to flush all over again, and said, "Wait right here."

Carmen took off in a near jog back down the block to the bar. Marlena took the opportunity to take out her compact and check her face. She was just reapplying lipstick when the door to the bar opened and she could hear laughter following Carmen out into the night. Marlena's butch was smiling broadly, and giving someone (probably Tamar or Angela) the finger. Then she trotted back to where Marlena stood, carrying Marlena's shoes in her left hand and a cigarette in her right.

"Come over here." Carmen gently pushed Marlena back against the brick wall of an office building. Carmen placed her cigarette between her lips, then bent down with the shoes and said, barely touching Marlena's right ankle, "Lift your foot."

Marlena could hardly believe what was happening. She raised her right foot, and Carmen smoothly brushed her sole before replacing the platform heel. She fastened the buckle and lowered Marlena's foot with hardly an untoward touch. Marlena lifted her left foot, watched as Carmen squinted her eyes against her exhale of smoke, refastening Marlena's second shoe as smoothly as she had the first.

Marlena found this unabashed show of gallantry so exciting that, had she not been leaning against the wall, she would have found standing difficult. When Carmen stood, she quickly took the cigarette from her mouth with the first finger and thumb of her right hand and exhaled over her shoulder. Marlena stayed where she was.

Carmen took Marlena's hand in hers and said, "Okay—we ready now?" She squinted and gave Marlena that half grin.

"Oh, not yet," Marlena said. Holding Carmen's left hand, she reached out and took Carmen's cigarette from her. Marlena took a long, deep drag, then dropped the butt to the concrete and ground it out under her toe. Exhaling, she pulled Carmen to her and wrapped her right arm around Carmen's neck.

When their lips met, Marlena felt her knees go to liquid and her cunt do the same. Carmen tasted of smoke, sweet bourbon, and arousal. Marlena hoped Carmen didn't think less of her for making this first move, but she just couldn't help herself. Carmen didn't seem offended. She'd moved one of those strong hands to Marlena's hair and caressed her neck. Marlena razed her nails down the back of Carmen's neck and shoulders for a moment, before Carmen pulled away.

"Come on, woman," Carmen said. "Let me take you home while I'm still able to drive." She laughed a little, a laugh that said *I'm so turned on I could fuck you right here and I'm trying not to let it show.*

Marlena moved away from the wall and stumbled a bit, much to her embarrassment. "God—I don't even think I can walk."

Carmen slipped an arm around Marlena's waist. "It's all right. I've got you, girl."

Marlena's knees buckled. "Maybe you just better not talk to me again until we get to your car," she said with a self-deprecating laugh.

Carmen laughed as well, her pleasure in Marlena's state of arousal evident.

When they reached Carmen's car, she unlocked and opened Marlena's door. Marlena bent her head and slid into the passenger seat. Carmen firmly closed the door behind her, then strode around to the driver's side.

"Okay," Carmen said as she started the car and shifted into reverse, slowly easing the car back. "Where to?"

Marlena was watching Carmen's strong jaw and neck, imagining how it might feel under her lips. She said, rather dreamily, "What?"

Carmen shifted into first and looked at Marlena, her face breaking out into a full, strong grin. "That's what I love about you old-school femmes, Marlena. You're not afraid to show what you want."

Marlena pursed her lips into a pinched, wry grin, and said, "Go straight down this road about six blocks, to Maple, then turn left at the light."

Carmen held Marlena's eyes for a moment longer, then turned back to face the street. She turned the stereo on. Latin dance music throbbed loudly out of the speakers before Carmen had the chance to turn the volume down.

"I'm sorry, Marlena," Carmen said, mollifying. "I was in a different mood when I was driving to the bar—music cranked, windows down—you know."

The music washed over them, the beat working its way in between Marlena's thighs. She recognized the song, something she'd heard at the clubs a year or so ago.

"Mmmm." Marlena sighed and pressed back against her seat.

Languid, Marlena pointed to the right turn Carmen was to take up ahead.

Carmen made the turn and Marlena pointed up the street. "That one's mine, the six-story on the left. Two hundred thirteen. Just park anywhere."

Carmen pulled up past the building, made a U-turn, and pulled forward into a spot directly in front. Marlena gave Carmen a look of amused impatience, lest Carmen get too full of herself for this lucky bit of parking karma. Carmen recognized the look and smiled, shrugged just a bit, then got out to open Marlena's door.

They got up to Marlena's apartment with a minimum of unintended brushing against one another in the elevator. Carmen stayed an appropriate distance back while Marlena got her keys out of her purse and unlocked the door.

Marlena entered, walked through her tiny kitchen into the living room, and switched on a table lamp for a bit of somewhat forgiving illumination.

"Please come in," she said to Carmen, who'd waited outside until invited inside. Marlena turned on her radio to the R&B station, which was doing the Saturday-night-dance-mix thing. "Make yourself comfortable. Can I get you something to drink?"

"No, thank you, Marlena. I'm all set." Carmen appeared to be taking stock of the kitchen, where Marlena had a small table with four chairs set around it. Just beyond, the comfortable living room was set up with a couch against one wall, a small entertainment center, and a rocking chair near the window. Off the living room, where the lamplight didn't reach, appeared to be a hallway.

Marlena was momentarily derailed. *Now what?* It wouldn't be polite just to jump her beau right in the living room, but it wasn't ladylike to invite someone you'd just met directly back to your bedroom without even a bit of conversation, some segue.

Marlena walked over to Carmen, took her by the left hand, and led her into the living room. She settled down onto the overstuffed softness of her couch, and pulled Carmen down next to her. She ran her hands through Carmen's hair, over behind her ears and down her neck, until Carmen closed her eyes.

"Carmen?"

"Yes, Marlena?"

"What's your last name?" Marlena ran the pads of her fingertips over Carmen's face, over her lips as she answered.

"Ramirez. Why?"

"Carmen Ramirez," Marlena said, running her hands through Carmen's hair and loosening the bangs until they fell forward a bit. "I prefer to know the full names of my gentleman callers." Marlena had moved in close and her lips were just millimeters away from Carmen's ear. She exhaled slowly, warmly.

"Marlena," Carmen breathed, raising her hands from Marlena's thighs, to her cheeks. "May I—?" Before she could finish the sentence, Carmen kissed her. Their lips met with an explosion of groans and sighs.

While they kissed, their hands roamed. Marlena reached up to the collar of Carmen's shirt and began fussing with the tie. God, she loved butches who wore ties. She loosened the knot and unfurled the silk, leaving it loose and open around Carmen's neck. She fumbled for Carmen's buttons and reached under the shirt, running her hands over Carmen's white undershirt and the hot skin underneath. The small breasts were warm swells under the cotton.

Carmen placed her hand on Marlena's thigh. She stroked and pressed up until she had moved under the skirt. Marlena groaned into Carmen's mouth when Carmen's fingertips stroked a bit of upper thigh very near her panties.

Marlena moved away from Carmen and then stood rather unsteadily. "Come on. While I can still walk."

She moved from the couch and down the dark hall, clutching her undone butch, who stumbled after her into the dark. At the door to her bedroom, Marlena stopped suddenly, and Carmen nearly ran her over.

"What? Are you okay?" Carmen asked.

"Wait, just . . ." Marlena broke off and caught her breath. "Do you want this?"

Carmen raised her eyebrows. "Yes, I want this. I want *you*, Marlena. Please." She leaned in for a kiss, but Marlena stopped her with a hand on her chest.

"What did Tamar tell you about me?"

Carmen said, "Please, Marlena. If I don't touch you, I might die. I mean it."

Marlena exhaled. "Well, come on." She grabbed Carmen's shirt and roughly pulled the butch to her. They stumbled backward into her bedroom and fell upon the bed.

Carmen wrapped herself around Marlena's thin body, and stroked the silk covering her back. While she worried Marlena's lower lip with nibbles, Carmen gently eased up the green silk until her hot hands were under the tank top.

Marlena gasped when she felt that warmth, wanting it all over her body. She was busy removing Carmen's shirt and getting her hands under the butch's undershirt. But before she could pull that shirt off, Carmen moved down Marlena's body. She nuzzled along Marlena's neck, then glanced up at Marlena's face while she pushed up the green silk tank top. Marlena's eyes were closed tightly, her forehead a knot of worry and desire, and her mouth was wet and open.

Carmen lowered her mouth to one of Marlena's small breasts, gently biting the nipple until it was swollen and reddish. Marlena dug one hand into Carmen's neck, and clutched at her T-shirt with the other. Carmen moved to the other breast, leaving a hand on the first to soothe the aching nipple. When Marlena began to shift and undulate her hips, Carmen slid to kneel on the floor, and moved away from the femme's breasts and to her belly. She licked the warm flesh, rather like a cat, and placed her hands on Marlena's hips to steady them. Carmen had her face under Marlena's skirt then, gently removing her ivory silk panties with her teeth. Marlena gasped loudly, realizing what was to come next.

"I wanted you the second I saw you standing there in the bar," Carmen began, as she pulled Marlena's panties down her legs, taking care to work them over the platform shoes.

Carmen began to kiss and bite back up Marlena's legs, which made Marlena yelp and moan. "You were sure no one in that bar would know you. But I know you, girl."

And with that, Carmen stroked her tongue right up along the cleft of Marlena's cunt, and Marlena let out a cry. Carmen licked and suckled until Marlena was thrashing about on her bed, grabbing Carmen's hair and clenching as hard as she could. Carmen hissed, but didn't miss a beat.

Finally, Marlena reached over to the bedstand, where she managed to grab a small bottle of lube and a latex glove from the drawer. She slammed the drawer shut and threw the sex gear at Carmen's head.

Panting, Marlena said, "Please fuck me, Carmen—not too deep, I can't—but just please . . ." She fell back on the bed while Carmen stretched on the glove. Marlena jumped when she heard the snap of the glove against Carmen's wrist, and moaned when a lube-slicked finger worked its way into her.

"Oh, yes, Carmen—that's the way—oh, that's the way . . ." Carmen knelt between Marlena's legs, and Marlena opened her eyes to the shadow image of her butch, shirt and tie undone, thick black bangs loosed from their gelled slickness and falling over her forehead, eyes watching her femme, lips parted and full.

"Oh, God," Marlena moaned as she rocked with the rhythm of Carmen's thrusts. "Yes, that's it—that's it . . ." She reached up and grabbed Carmen by the back of the neck. "Don't stop what you're doing, baby. Just come up here."

Carmen followed Marlena's direction. She affixed her strong lips to the nipple closest to her, which made Marlena cry out. Carmen slid another finger into Marlena's cunt and, after a beat, a third. Marlena slid the hand that wasn't entangled in Carmen's hair up to her other nipple, squeezing hard.

"That's it, that's it,—oh yes oh yes oh yes oh . . ." Carmen followed the motion of Marlena's hips, thrusting faster, faster—not too deep but just enough. When she felt some muscles beginning to tighten, she bit down on Marlena's nipple, making her scream loud and hard.

But then she was crying. Carmen slipped out, ripped off the glove, and wrapped Marlena up in her arms.

"It's okay, baby," Carmen crooned. "I'm here. I'm here."

"You're here." Marlena exhaled slow and ragged, calming herself. "Oh Carmen, it's been so long since anyone was here."

Marlena wiped her eyes and rose up on one elbow. "Don't go anywhere," she sniffled. "I'm just gonna go blow my nose." She smiled a bit, then swung her legs over the edge of the bed, and walked on unsteady legs, still in those platforms, to the bathroom.

Carmen returned the lube to the bedside table—if Marlena wanted to fuck her, she wouldn't need any lube. She could hear Marlena pissing, letting out little yelps.

Carmen switched on the bedside lamp. She scooted up until she could lean back against the headboard and then took one of the pictures on the table into her hands. It showed three happy-looking people: two older adults with their arms around the teenage boy between them.

"This your family?" Carmen called out just as Marlena flushed the toilet. She waited a moment for Marlena, studying the photo.

Marlena appeared in the doorway. "What, honey?" She leaned regally against the doorjamb, clothing disheveled and hair mussed.

"This your family?"

"That's them," she said with a sad smile. "Haven't seen them in nearly ten years."

"So . . ." Carmen paused. "This is you?"

Marlena made a grim little smile. "Yeah. I burned all the other pictures of that boy."

She sighed, nodded at the frame Carmen held in her hands. "Nearly got rid of that one, too, before realizing I didn't have any other pictures of my folks."

Carmen placed the photo back on the bedstand and opened her arms wide, inviting Marlena back to her. "You always were beautiful, weren't you?"

"Of course." Smiling broadly, Marlena left her post at the door and returned to her butch's embrace.

Dance Fever

Jean Roberta

"One, two, feet together," chanted Lawrence, our dance instructor. He was married, so I assumed he was heterosexual, but the precision of his body language and his willingness to teach ballroom dancing to an all-lesbian class made me wonder about his particular kinks. Watching us seemed to amuse him.

We were officially matched up like the animals in Noah's ark: ten femmes and ten butches. Lawrence would never call us anything so retro for fear of offending us, but even he couldn't change the rules of the game, had he wanted to. In the first session, he told us we had to decide whether we were "leaders" or "followers."

I remembered the famous line about Ginger Rogers doing everything Fred Astaire did, only backwards and in high heels. Looking at the "leaders," most of whom seemed to have signed up to please their girlfriends, I almost laughed aloud. I had chosen to join the "followers" who were already twitching to the beat, eager to get started. One of the bossiest and most girlish-looking was the one who had told Lawrence she would find him twenty lesbian students if he would set up a class and offer us a discount.

We all retreated back to our lines like two rows of teenagers at a high school dance. Beside me stood a former model, two divorced mothers, a lawyer, a secretary, a hotshot writer for an advertising firm, and several other women I didn't know well. All were poised and swaying slightly with a subtle but distinct feminine flair: I Am Woman, Watch Me Move.

Across from us, ten dykes of varying heights and builds, from long-drink-of-water to jock to tubby-bear, stood shuffling and shifting their feet, looking irritated or confused. One looked across at her partner with an expression that said: *I'm doing this for you, babe. You'd better be grateful.*

I sighed. According to Lawrence's rules, I would have to dance with each butch in turn. I comforted myself with the knowledge that they were sweating more than we were.

Lawrence restarted the tape and turned up the volume. The melodramatic Latin beat of the tango filled the room as we each moved into the arms of our partner of the moment. Lynn, who towered over me, made a doomed effort to keep the beat, forcing me to choose between following her and following the music. The music won. Her flushed face showed that she knew when her fragile authority was being ignored.

We changed partners. Watty was closer to my height, which helped, but she was solid enough to push me around in a way that was likely to throw both of us out of synch. I counted just loudly enough for her to hear: "One-two-three-four." *You don't have to remember the steps*, I tried to beam into her brain, *as long as you keep the beat.*

Just when I noticed some improvement in Watty's moves, we had to change partners again. I looked at Dale, and she grinned at me like an old friend, although we had met for the first time in the first session, two weeks before.

She calmly grasped my waist and one shoulder. Her touch sent shivers all through me, so I distracted myself by looking at her pressed denim shirt. That was a mistake. I immediately switched my gaze so she wouldn't think I was watching her breasts bounce. The clean, slightly musky smell of her armpits wafted toward me as she guided me through the steps: one, two, feet together. Her short brown hair looked like polished wood, and the fluorescent light bounced off it in a way that suggested a wink. She was smooth, and her rhythm was impeccable.

I felt sweat stinging my hairline, but I couldn't brush the hair out of my face. I felt an uncomfortable loosening of the clip that held my shoulder-length red hair out of the way. I felt almost as if my clothes were slipping off by themselves. I told myself to concentrate.

I tried to go into a turn and found Dale's wiry body blocking my path. "Not yet, babe," she smiled. My face burned. She was putting me in my place, as Lawrence had given her the right to do.

Think of the devil and he appears at your side. Lawrence watched me, running his eyes down both our bodies as he tapped one foot. "Looks good," he told Dale, man-to-man. For a moment, I was aghast at the suggestion that Dale was being complimented on her ownership of a prime bitch. I told myself that Lawrence could only have been commenting on Dale's form, since any other meaning was unthinkable.

"Now you can swing her out like this," Lawrence went on, raising one arm to show Dale how she should guide me into a turn on her terms. Dale copied him, grinning, then reached for one of my hands. I couldn't resist showing both of them how well I could follow instructions.

Dale returned me to my former position. She and Lawrence looked like conspirators. "Time for the next dance," he told us. "Don't move." The sultry tango ended abruptly. After several false starts, Lawrence found the opening bar of a rocking cha cha: right-back, cha-cha-cha, left-back, cha-cha-cha. I thought of this dance as the *abuela* or forerunner of all the flashier Latin dances performed for audiences at dance contests. I knew these steps the way I knew my own heartbeat. I had partied with Latinas in high school, and I had felt more at home with them than with the white preppies who had freckles and blue eyes like mine. Dale and I slid back and forth, face to face, like synchronized swimmers. I relaxed, despite the energy the steps demanded. At least this dance wasn't an in-your-face sexual confrontation like the tango. I smiled at Dale and she smiled back.

Instead of telling us to change partners, Lawrence strolled back to us. He nodded approvingly, then launched into a topic that made me stare. "You watching the hockey game on TV Thursday?" he asked Dale.

"Wouldn't miss it," she responded, keeping a firm grip on me. They discussed teams and scores like two beer-drinking buddies while Dale and I kept pace: rock-step, quick-quick-quick.

I tried to go into a turn, but Dale stopped me with a steely grip on my raised hand. She continued her chat with Lawrence without missing a beat as the rest of the class struggled on, unsupervised. Hot shock rose from my uneasy guts to my lungs and into my head.

Was I really such a show-off that I deserved this lesson? Was that what Lawrence thought of me? Was that how I looked to Dale? Would they prefer me to have two left feet?

I was unreasonably concerned about what Dale thought of me. I really hoped she wasn't looking for a passive dishrag of a wife. *Give me a little slack*, I thought, *and I can surprise you with my loyalty.* But this train of thought seemed irrelevant. Dale wasn't really my date, and I probably wasn't her type.

After endless cha-chas, Lawrence clicked off the tape. "Does anyone remember the foxtrot from last week?" he asked us. "Leaders, watch me." Lawrence raised his arms and danced with an invisible partner to refresh our collective memory. His long legs moved gracefully through space in a pair of loose pants. I could hardly believe that crotch belonged to a straight man.

I reminded myself that his crotch was none of my business, despite my excessive awareness of every body in the room. I wanted to be touched, stroked, and squeezed. I wanted someone to want me.

Lawrence told us to change partners, and I was disappointed. "I want to talk to you later, babe," Dale told me in a low voice. Her simple request made me ridiculously happy.

The rest of the class rolled by in a blur of moving bodies, some in harmony with the music and some awkwardly ignorant of that language. I no longer cared whether anyone thought I was a prima donna type. Whatever I was, Dale wanted to talk to me privately.

The class ended, and Lawrence told us all with a smirk that he would see us next week. Dale approached me and grabbed my elbow as though she still wanted to lead me. "Rosie," she said, "I think we need to practice our tango. Do you have time to come to my place?"

"Now?" I asked. I must have turned pale at the implications of her invitation. She wanted to get me alone as soon as possible. I didn't need to ask why. Her deep brown eyes held mine. "Yes," I told her softly. *You know I will*, I thought.

Outside the dance studio, she unlocked her Toyota and I slid into the passenger's seat. "You're a good dancer," she told me, grinning, "but you need to learn to follow better. I want you to practice more, with me."

"Is that all you think I can do, Dale?" I asked her. "Follow your moves?"

"Pushy," she laughed approvingly. "Did you know I won the ball-room dance championship in Montreal with my girlfriend, Brenda, two years ago? Dancing is my life. I can't dance with her since we broke up, but I know I could win again with the right partner. I've been watching you, and I know you feel the rhythm. It's just in you."

I felt like a fool. Why hadn't I guessed that she was a dance champion looking for a partner, and not a clueless dyke with nothing better to do? "I didn't know," I stammered.

We arrived at her apartment building. "It's not much," she apologized. "I moved into a bachelor suite after our messy divorce."

She reached for my hand. "It takes talent to be the woman in dance," she told me, as if I didn't know. "I know you want to do your thing, and you can, Rosie. But you have to learn to follow before I let you strike out on your own. If you want to do this, we have to learn to move like one person."

I felt as if I could hardly breathe. "I'm sorry," I told her. "I underestimated you."

"It's okay," she assured me. "The rest of those 'leaders' are a pack of fucking idiots. I don't envy you."

Dale's apartment was up two flights of stairs, and I welcomed the need to keep focusing on movement, one foot after the other. Conversation could wait.

I shivered when Dale unlocked her door. I knew I was about to cross a threshold into something that could change my life.

Once inside her private space, Dale pulled me close. She looked at me, watching my reaction. Impulsively, I pressed my mouth to hers. Oh goddess, she was warm and full of life. It had been too long since I had been this close to another woman.

She rocked me to a song that I could almost hear. "Want me?" she crooned in my ear. "You a horny little bitch? You can tell me, honey. It's okay."

I moaned, holding her strong back. "Dale," I pleaded, feeling desperate. "Don't blame me. I want what I want. I don't want anyone who acts like a stupid man." She pulled the clip from my hair and ran her fingers through it, sending tingles all through my scalp. "How about a smart butch?" she laughed. She turned me around so she could pull my butt into her crotch while she cupped my breasts with both hands.

"That's . . . oh," I gasped as she rolled my nipples between her fingers.

"Is this too hard, babe?" she asked with concern. "I don't want to hurt you, just give you what you need."

I felt as hungry as a starving she-wolf with a den full of yipping puppies. "Don't worry, Dale," I laughed, gasping. "I'll tell you if it's too much."

To my secret delight, she unbuckled my belt and unzipped my

pants. "A skirt would make this easier," she hinted. "Looks good on the dance floor too."

"Next time," I managed to say as she pulled my pants down my legs.

"Right here," she grinned, turning me to face her and then pushing me against the wall. "Just to take the edge off before we take our time." She pushed my legs apart and entered me with two fingers.

"Oh!" I greeted her invasion. Lowering my volume seemed impossible.

"You're loud," she remarked as three of her fingers pushed steadily past my resistance, stroking my wet silk and exploring my core.

"Let me," I begged, breathing hard.

"Honey, I want to hear you," she urged me. "Hell, I want the neighbors to hear you." She was fucking me without restraint, pushing me against the wall to an obscene beat. Animal sounds were coming out of my throat. I couldn't pretend I hadn't asked for this.

She looked into my eyes with curiosity, amusement, and determination. The urgency of her strong right hand in me conveyed control, not impulsiveness. She wouldn't have pressured me if I had refused, and we both knew it. The pleasure she gave me was almost unbearable.

She tickled a spongy area deep in my pussy, near my cervix. At the same time, the heel of her hand ground against my excited clit. She managed to push and stroke and rub while keeping up a catchy syncopation. I was almost screaming.

My energy rose to a boil, crested and spilled over. Air moved in and out of my lungs with such velocity that each outgoing breath was like a tropical bird-cry. Dale slowed gradually as I spasmed and shook around her precious fingers. To my relief, she left them in my overflowing center as I fell back into myself and felt the sweat cooling on my skin.

"Ah," I exhaled.

"Better?" she teased.

"Much," I answered. The value of what she had given me was sinking into my mind as her determined fingers had sunk into my heat. "Oh, Dale," I sighed. "I'll give you what you want."

"I know, honey," she chuckled. "I knew from the day we met."

I realized how much my legs were trembling when she gently led me by the hand to her cool and slick leather sofa, where I sat, naked from the waist down. Dale unbuttoned her shirt with one hand and pulled it off in one smooth motion. She stepped out of her pants as I pulled off my sweater and unhooked my bra. Exposing myself after being fucked felt like an anticlimax.

Dale bent graciously to suck each of my nipples in turn, as though wanting to rescue them from feeling like wallflowers. I felt them turn rock-hard in her warm mouth and I squirmed to the rhythm of her tongue.

I forced myself to look at Dale's body: the modest breasts, the defined arm muscles, the hard flat stomach. The sight of her moved me beyond words.

"I was serious about practicing," she reminded me. "It'll be better with no clothes to get in the way. I have a CD of the tango that was used in the regional competition." She strode to her stereo and started up the music.

The languid notes of a sentimental old Argentine tango floated from the speakers. I remembered that the tango had once been a scandalous dance that sprang from the streets and whorehouses of Buenos Aires, where the straight and stuffy would never go or at least not use their real names. It seemed perfectly fitting.

We fit together, two low-rent tangeras, as Dale jokingly pulled me closer by my butt cheeks. I closed my eyes, the better to sense her movements and even anticipate them. I opened my eyes to watch her. "That's it," she encouraged me. She showed me how to twist in her arms as though the intensity of contact made me want to escape, and then she pulled me back. She showed me how our bare feet could carry on a dialogue full of in-jokes. I imagined us dancing for an audience, arousing the envy of everyone watching. I wanted to follow her so well that she would be proud to spin me out, offering me to the crowd in a solo riff that would never break the harmony between us.

Betting on my instincts, I slid to my knees and inhaled the warm musk of her cunt. I carefully spread her apart with both hands and stretched a pointed tongue between her inner lips. I licked and explored as she rocked against me. I found her clit and gave it every stroke I could improvise as I slid a finger into her as accompaniment. Too soon, she was moving uncontrollably, groaning her appreciation. I was proud.

She ruffled my hair. "Good moves, babe," she praised me.

"I bet you know some others," I suggested.

"Oh yeah," she guffawed. "You haven't seen my toys yet. Do you like it in the ass, honey?"

I felt unbearably ignorant. "None of my exes would go there," I muttered. "Thought it was too dirty in every way. I want you to take me that way—just please be patient."

She had pulled me up and was rocking me back and forth to the rhythm of the second tango on the CD. "My leetle rosebud," she cracked, "we wheel make byoo-tee-ful music together." I was already trying to decide what to wear in a public tango with Dale. An image of a tight, sapphire-blue velvet dress with a slit skirt presented itself for my imaginary inspection. I pictured the dress inches away from a pair of blue pants that showed off Dale's muscular thighs.

I found a trace of resentment lingering in my guts even after the cleansing explosions brought on by Dale's fingers and my tongue. "You have fun and games with Lawrence, don't you?" I sneered. "Did he know from the beginning that you were a dance champion?"

Dale sat comfortably and pulled me onto her lap. She thoughtfully wrapped a tight arm around my waist to hold me in place as she considered her answer. "I've known Lawrence for years, Rosie," she told me. "But I'm in his class because I don't want to get out of practice. I don't think I'm there on false pretenses, if that's what you think. Lawrence and his wife, Gail, are both bi, though they're discreet about it. They go to play parties when they're in other cities for dance contests." I was pleased to hear that our instructor was not as straight as an arrow, since this made him seem like less of a threat or more of a brother, and it also showed that my instincts were still sound. "At first I thought he was totally gay," I blurted without thinking.

"Because he's a dancer?" she demanded. "So you thought he had to be a queen?"

"Yeah," I confessed. "I guess I was stereotyping, but that's been my usual experience. With men," I added to prevent the conversation from flowing into more dangerous channels. I had no wish to challenge her psychic testosterone.

Dale rested her nose on the back of my neck and breathed deeply. I couldn't help thinking of the courtship of a stud dog and a bitch in heat. "He likes men but he's really into women too, you know," she pointed out. "Didn't you figure that out?"

The likelihood that Dale and Lawrence, the comic Step Brothers, had discussed me behind my back didn't make me happy. Dale seemed to catch my thought. "He helped me find a woman, anyway," she snickered into my hair. "He pointed you out to me after the first class, as if I hadn't noticed."

There are times when I can't stifle the words that want to come out of me. "Do you and Lawrence think I show off too much?" I felt stupid, but I really wanted to know.

Dale's hands came up to hold my breasts and tweak my nipples into pointed ornaments. "Nah," she crooned. "We just thought you needed attention because you weren't getting enough. That's changed now, though," she bragged. "You won't have to go hungry any more, babe," she promised.

Her kisses on my neck became more insistent until she turned me around to kiss me deeply on my waiting mouth. When she pulled away, my breathing told her all she needed to know. "Neither will you, honey," I answered recklessly. As her persistent hands continued to discover new areas of my body, I knew that our dance had only begun.

Pen and Willow

Nathalie Graham

The Past

It was just after midnight as the two lovers shared a cigarette in the king-sized bed within the luxurious bedroom. Their clothes were strewn throughout the room as evidence of their eager haste to touch each other. They'd made love for hours on end until spent, and now lazily held each other as they watched the smoke from the cigarette drift to the vaulted ceiling.

"You're sure this is safe?" one of them queried for what seemed like the hundredth time.

"Of course. I told you. She won't be home from London until her plane arrives at three o'clock this afternoon, after which she will whisk me away to Barbados where we will spend a week getting reacquainted and celebrate our fifth anniversary."

"I hate that I won't see you for at least a week."

"Don't worry, my pet, I'll bring you something special."

"Why don't you just divorce her and come live with me?"

"Don't be a bloody fool. I love you, darling, but you can't support me in the fashion to which I've become accustomed. Only she can do that."

"But you don't love her."

"I've never loved her."

"Then why stay? It can't be just the money?"

"But of course it's the money, and the sex. She is good in the sack. No, my darling, you will have to share me with her money. I will not leave those millions. Now come here and fuck me so hard that I will feel you for the next week."

As the two women melted together beneath the silk sheets, they did not notice the lone figure who stood outside the bedroom door. The figure turned to walk slowly down the hall. In one hand she held a dozen red roses and in the other a bottle of the finest, most expensive champagne. As if in a trance she walked down the grand staircase and then out the front door, leaving the roses and champagne on the front step before getting into her Jaguar and swiftly driving out of the estate.

The next morning in another part of town another woman sat tearfully on her couch as she watched her lover pack up her belongings in cardboard boxes.

"Come now, Wills, don't be like this," the other woman said.

"I'm sorry, how am I supposed to be?"

"Be happy that we had these years together. We've had some fun times."

"Then why are you leaving?"

"I've already told you. I'm suffocating. I need to get out of here and see the world. I need to experience something other than domestic bliss."

"And what's wrong with domestic bliss?"

"I'm far too young to be tied down. There is so much more out there to explore."

"You mean more women to fuck."

"Maybe. Look, I know you want to be married and live in a little house with a white picket fence, but that's not for me."

"It was once."

"I know. But not anymore. I need something else."

The woman finished her packing, and after she loaded the boxes into her car she drove away without even a backward glance. Left behind once again, Wills still sat on her couch as the tears streamed down her cheeks. Once again her dream was shattered. Once again she was alone.

The Present

The Tier was packed with people. Artists. Art critics. Art lovers. All coming to see the newest sensation to hit the waterfront galleries. This gallery was so named because its young director had taken an old warehouse and created tiered levels to showcase the pieces of art.

Willow Dyer stood on the uppermost tier watching the people below as they meandered about, champagne in hand, talking among themselves. She hoped they were saying good things. She prayed they were saying good things. She had invested too much in this evening for it not to go well.

Sharon Grant, the gallery's owner, walked up with two glasses of champagne. "Did anyone ever tell you that you worry too much?"

"I get paid to worry," Willow answered, tossing her long blonde hair over her shoulder and taking the proffered glass. "Remember? I worry. You enjoy."

"Well, I am certainly enjoying what I'm seeing down there." She indicated the throng below. "I had no idea this many people would actually show."

"Now let's see if they buy."

"They will. Congratulations, Willow. You did a fine job putting this together." She toasted Willow, who blushed slightly from the praise. "I'm going back down, and I suggest you do the same. You're being asked for." She began to walk away, then stopped to look back at Willow. "Do you know Pen St. Pierre?"

"The recluse?"

"She's here."

"You're kidding? Pen St. Pierre is here? I thought she never left her dark tower."

"Apparently she was curious about the idea for this place and wanted to see it firsthand."

"Where is she?" Willow began to scan the floors below, looking for the famous recluse. "What does she look like?"

Sharon scanned the floor then nodded toward a couple standing directly below them. "There she is."

"Where? All I see is that blond man talking with Mario."

Sharon laughed and started to walk toward the stairs again. "That's her. Haven't you heard? Pen St. Pierre is the butch's butch."

Willow looked down just as the woman looked up. Willow was startled at the brilliance of crystal green eyes that seemed to blaze with an energy all their own. Pen St. Pierre murmured something to Mario, a local artist, who smiled brightly at Willow and waved her down with his usual excitement. Willow waved back tentatively, then began to make her way down. They met her at the base of the stairs. Willow was unable to take her eyes off the bold woman at Mario's side, who scorched her with her eyes.

"Willow, where have you been hiding yourself?" the older man scolded playfully. "Ms. St. Pierre has been looking for you!"

"I'm sorry. I've been overseeing things. How do you do?" She reached out to shake Pen St. Pierre's hand, but the woman surprised her by taking her hand and kissing it lightly. Surprised at the gesture, Willow smiled, all the while feeling an unfamiliar but pleasant jolt pass through her. "Are you enjoying yourself?" she asked, feeling closely scrutinized by those incredible green eyes.

"I am, thank you. And you? Are you enjoying yourself?" The woman's voice was deep.

"I'm afraid I won't be enjoying myself until I start seeing some Sold signs on the paintings."

"Perhaps I should see to that then, so you'll enjoy yourself." Pen reached inside her double-breasted jacket and pulled out a checkbook.

"That's not necessary, Ms. St. Pierre. I was only joking," Willow said, laying her hand on Pen's arm, attempting to stop her. Her hand lingered on the high-quality silk that covered well-defined muscles rippling beneath.

"The name is Pen, and I'm not." She motioned for one of the waiters with the trays of champagne. Instantly he was at her side. "Please have Ms. Grant come speak with me." The young man nodded, but before he moved away Pen removed two glasses from the tray. She offered one to Willow.

"You really don't have to buy a painting," Willow protested.

"But of course she does, Willow," Sharon admonished, joining them. "Which painting would you like, Pen?"

Pen looked at Willow. "The most expensive of course," she said, putting her hand up to stop Willow from protesting any further. "It's pointless to argue with me. I never lose."

"She's right, Willow. She never loses," Sharon agreed, with a wink at Willow before she smiled at Pen. "I'll have the painting delivered the day after the show closes."

"Thank you." Pen bowed her head slightly as she handed Sharon a blank check.

"That wasn't necessary, but thank you," Willow said.

"Now, perhaps you can enjoy yourself." She looked at the expensive Rolex on her wrist and frowned slightly. "Unfortunately, I have an appointment. Good luck on the rest of your evening."

Willow couldn't help but admire Pen's physique as she moved through the crowd. She also couldn't help but realize she was very disappointed that the tall blonde was leaving. She looked at the hand Pen had kissed earlier. She could almost still feel her lips as they brushed her knuckles, and it sent a tingle of excitement through her.

Later, Willow found Sharon enjoying a glass of whiskey in her office, her feet propped up on Willow's desk. "*Salut.* You've made me a very rich woman."

"I've seen the receipts," Willow responded, removing her high heels and rubbing her feet. "I'll have to commission some more paintings tomorrow."

"Tomorrow, my dear, you are lunching with someone who wants us to sell some of her paintings."

"Really? Who?"

"Pen St. Pierre." Sharon obviously caught Willow's quick frown. "What's the matter with you, Willow? She's obviously taken an interest in you. Do you know how many women have tried to get that woman's attention? Including myself?"

"You can have it," Willow commented as she walked to the small refrigerator in the corner and pulled out a bottle of beer. She took a long swallow, then leaned against the wall. "Why do I have to go? Why don't you go?"

"Because she asked specifically for you. She wants to discuss the possibility of selling some of her own work. She thinks she has too much." Willow moped, which made Sharon sigh with exasperation. "Would you please tell me what is bothering you?"

"She's not my type."

"Darling Willow, Pen St. Pierre is *everybody's* type."

"She's not mine. She's too rich, too handsome . . ."

"Too butch?" Sharon asked knowingly.

"You know me, Sharon. I've never dated a butch."

"Don't knock it until you've tried it. Besides, if I know Pen, she usually doesn't stick around long enough for her demeanor to be a bother for long."

"Oh, so I'd just be a dalliance? Wham bam, thank you ma'am?"

"She's been known for just that."

"Well, she can count me out. I'll help sell her paintings if I must, but I will not be a conquest."

"Don't be so sure, Willow. You may surprise yourself."

Pen St. Pierre. The very name exuded power and wealth. From her black tower, she commanded an empire that encompassed the world. A nod of her head could bring empires down. The flash of her smile could melt the coldest heart. The touch of her hand . . .

Willow Dyer shook herself out of her reverie and attempted to concentrate on the receipts she was reconciling into the computer. Sharon had long since departed for the evening, and the gallery was empty. Still excited by the success of their opening night, Willow hadn't been ready to go home yet, electing instead to stay and get some work done. She was determined not to think about Pen St. Pierre, but it was a battle she was losing.

Finally, she pushed away from her desk and walked to the window. In the distance, across the bay, she could see that very black tower. A single dark monolith rising above the other buildings as if watching over the city.

Willow closed the blinds and went to the refrigerator for another beer. She couldn't figure out why she was having such a hard time getting the vision of Pen St. Pierre out of her head. Yes, she had found her attractive. Yes, she had felt something flash through her when Pen had kissed her hand. However, as she had explained to Sharon earlier, she didn't date butches. It wasn't as if she had decided early on not to date butches, she just had never been attracted to those types of lesbians. She liked women much like herself. Pretty, not handsome. Stylish in a feminine way, not masculine. She had once heard another woman say about butches, "If I wanted to sleep with a man, I'd be straight." At the time, and until earlier this evening, she had agreed, but now, she found herself thinking about the masculine Pen St. Pierre.

The woman had been magnificent standing in the crowd, her

blonde hair cut manly short but with long bangs that swept over her eyes. She was handsome by most standards; classically chiseled features that included a Roman profile with a sharp nose, strong chin, and smooth complexion. She had the broad shoulders of a swimmer with a tapered waist that gave way to slim boyish hips and strong muscular legs. She had the body of a god, and Willow knew Pen worked hard to keep it that way. It was her eyes however, those incredible green eyes that seemed to have an energy of their own, which drew everyone to her. Once you were captured by those eyes there was no going back. At least, there was no going back until she was finished with you. Pen St. Pierre was nothing if unavailable. She allowed no one to get close. She was known to use women's bodies to pleasure her own and then, with an expensive trinket, she sent them on their way.

Willow knew way too much about Pen St. Pierre to ever allow herself to become entangled in her web, even if she did date butches. But she didn't, so it was irrelevant.

She found herself drawn to the window again. She opened the blinds and gazed at the looming tower. She wondered if Pen was there now or prowling the night seeking yet another plaything to grace her bed. Sighing with annoyance, Willow tossed her beer bottle into the trash and began to close her office. She needed to go home and to bed. After a good night's sleep, she would be fine. She pulled on her wool coat, collected her purse and briefcase, and turned out the lights. She walked through the darkened gallery, her heels clicking loudly in the silence, and stepped into the brisk winter air, pulling her collar up against the cold as she walked to the ferry that would take her across the bay to her apartment. A dark sedan suddenly pulled in front of her as she crossed the street. She stepped back in alarm. The rear passenger door opened and Pen St. Pierre stepped out.

"What do you think you're doing?" Willow exclaimed in anger, her body trembling with fear. "You nearly scared me to death!"

"I'm sorry. That was not my intention," Pen quickly apologized.

"I've been waiting for you and we nearly missed you, so I told my driver to hurry before you disappeared into the night."

"What can I do for you, Ms. St. Pierre?" Willow asked shortly, wanting to get away from this strangely compelling woman.

"I wanted to see you again. I didn't like having to leave so abruptly earlier."

"I thought we were meeting for lunch tomorrow."

"We are," Pen answered with a disarming smile. "But I wanted to see you again tonight."

Willow felt a thrill shoot through her. "Well, it's rather late."

"Yes, I know, but I thought I'd take a chance. We could go for a coffee. I know a place nearby that is open."

Willow started to refuse, but Pen gave her such a fervent look that she found herself agreeing.

Fridays was a small intimate restaurant that catered to an exclusive crowd and was only open from midnight Thursday to midnight Friday; hence, its name. The waiting list was so long only people with connections actually had a chance to get in. But it was now after midnight, and the place was empty except for staff.

"You must be well acquainted with the owner to have it opened just for you," Willow commented as Pen pulled out her chair.

"Intimately." Pen grinned mischievously. Willow raised an eyebrow at the implication. "I own it," Pen whispered into her ear.

"Really? I'm impressed."

"Don't be. It is not my intention to impress you." Pen signaled for their server, who quickly brought over a pot of coffee. "You may leave it," Pen commented, pouring the coffee. The server disappeared into the darkness.

"And just what is your intention?" Willow asked as she stirred cream into her cup.

"I'm sorry?"

"You said that your intention was not to impress me. What is your intention?"

"Oh." Pen leaned forward, her arms on the table. "I simply want to get to know you better."

"Couldn't that have waited?" Though Willow was flattered at having the attention of such an attractive, charming woman, she remembered her promise to herself to not be drawn into Pen's web. "I mean, we are meeting for lunch."

"As I said earlier, I couldn't wait. I wanted to see you tonight."

"Are you always so impetuous?"

"When I see something I want, yes, I am."

"You realize I know all about you."

"Oh you do, do you?"

"Yes, I do. I know all about your conquests and I don't intend on being one of them."

Pen smiled her amusement. "I am not easily deterred."

"Neither am I." They grinned at each other for a moment. "So, Pen . . ." Willow intended to ask her if there were any other secret ownerships she should know about, but instead found her attention drawn to another question. "How ever did your parents come up with the name Pen?"

"It is not my given name. At a young age, I shortened my name and would only answer to Pen."

"Short for what?"

"Privileged information."

"I'm sorry, I didn't mean to pry."

"You didn't. Perhaps, if we become . . . closer, I will tell you." They looked at each other across the table, Pen's eyes drilling holes through Willow. "So how did you come to have your name?"

"I'm named after my great-grandmother. She was an artist. I get my eye for art from her, or so I'm told."

Pen's cell phone interrupted. She frowned as she answered it. When she turned away, Willow couldn't help but admire her strong profile. Willow had to admit she was surprised at how genuinely interested Pen seemed to be in her. She had always heard this powerful woman was self-centered and only interested in talking about herself and her money. So far, that was not the case. Pen asked about Willow's life while revealing very little about her own.

"I'm sorry," Pen said, returning her phone to her jacket pocket. "I've turned it off so we won't be interrupted again. Now, where were we?"

"You were going to tell me all about yourself."

"I was? I seem to remember we were talking about you."

"Well, I'm tired of that subject. Why don't you tell me about you?" Pen seemed to be uncomfortable with this and instead took her time refilling their coffee cups. "It won't kill you, you know."

"What is it you want to know?"

"How about telling me about your childhood? What were you like?"

"I never had a childhood. My parents saw to that."

"What did they do?"

"It's what they didn't do." Pen began to trace patterns in the linen table cloth with her spoon. "My great-grandfather built St. Pierre Industries from nothing. His whole life was devoted to making it the most successful enterprise in the world. He instilled this devotion into his own son, who made the business even greater." She paused for a moment. "My father, however, was a disappointment. He took after my grandmother, who was nothing more than arm candy for my grandfather. She loved the money and was a very lazy woman. My father inherited this trait from her and wanted nothing more than to play and spend money he didn't earn. He had no desire to go into the business. My grandfather was even more disappointed when he found that my father was not only lazy but incapable of fathering a son. I was an only child and a girl at that. One day when I was about seven years old I overheard my grandfather tell an associate that his greatest fear was that St. Pierre Industries was going to fall into my hands and I would sell it to buy trinkets." She stopped playing with her spoon and looked at Willow. "I don't know what happened, but hearing him say that did something to me. From that moment on I set out to prove him wrong. I wanted to become the son he had always wanted."

"Apparently you succeeded."

"Yes, I did, and I received his highest praise for it. He gave me the company instead of giving it to my father."

"I'll bet he was none too happy about that."

"Actually, I keep my parents on an allowance—a very generous one—and they live in the south of France. Their only requirement is to stay in Europe."

"Is your grandfather still alive?"

"Yes, he lives on the estate in upstate." She seemed to want to say more but stopped, a look of consternation coming across her face.

"What's the matter?" Willow asked.

Pen stared at her for a long moment before answering, "I have never told anyone that story. I don't know what made me tell you."

"My powers of persuasion, I imagine," Willow quipped with a good-natured smile before she looked at her watch. "Good lord, it's nearly three a.m. I've really got to get some sleep." Pen nodded but seemed disappointed.

The limo drive home was strangely quiet. Willow had begun to think that perhaps this infamous recluse was not the enigma everyone had made her out to be, but Pen's sudden, pensive silence made her rethink that judgment.

"Thanks for the coffee. I guess I'll see you at lunch," Willow said as they stood before her apartment. On an impulse, she took Pen's hand in her own. "Don't worry, I'll keep your secret."

Pen gave her a shy smile. "Thank you, and I look forward to seeing you again." She looked deeply into Willow's eyes, then ran her hand through Willow's hair before she kissed her gently on the lips. Her hand trailed down from Willow's hair to rest possessively on her hip. "Get inside now or I will not be responsible for my actions." Her voice was even deeper than usual.

"It will take more than that, Pen," Willow responded with false bravado. She quickly turned and rushed into her apartment.

Once inside, Willow leaned against the door, her knees weak. She had gotten away from Pen just in time. Their kiss still tingled on her lips, as if it had left a permanent impression, and her heart felt like it was slamming against her rib cage. If that kiss had lasted another second, she would have been helpless against any action Pen wished to take.

She had to stay away from Pen St. Pierre, that much was certain. After tomorrow, the woman would be out of her life.

The next day, Willow walked along the front hall in Pen's penthouse, admiring the incredible collection of paintings. Behind her a throat cleared and she turned to find Pen standing at the end of the hall. As the night before, she was dressed smartly in a beautifully tailored suit and silk tie with expensive Italian shoes.

"This is quite a collection," Willow remarked, trying not to meet those crystal-green eyes.

"Yes, it is. How are you this morning?" Pen asked, her hands clasped behind her back as she advanced toward Willow, who found herself admiring the woman openly. She caught herself and quickly became interested in an Italian masterpiece, but not before she saw Pen smiling with amusement.

"I'm fine, thank you."

"Did you sleep well?"

"Absolutely," Willow lied. She had, in fact, had trouble sleeping because of dreams of Pen torturing her with those lips.

Pen seemed to know what she was thinking as she smiled smugly. "I'm glad." She stood beside Willow, pretending with her to be only interested in examining the painting.

"Your collection seems to be quite eclectic. Who's your favorite artist?" Willow asked, acutely aware of Pen's tantalizing cologne. Its subtle woodsy essence made Willow's pulse quicken and so she moved away, trying to keep her mind on the task at hand.

"I don't have a favorite. I purchase what I like."

"I can't imagine you would want to give any of them up."

"It won't be easy, so I prefer you pick the three paintings."

"You can't be serious." Though the idea of selecting out the three paintings excited the art director in her, she did not like the idea of being accountable for perhaps choosing ones that Pen truly enjoyed.

"But I am."

"I don't think I like that responsibility."

"I'm sure you will choose wisely. Come, lunch is ready." Pen took her by the elbow and led her to a beautifully set table in a bright and airy solarium.

After seating her, Pen sat down across from her, and as if on cue an immaculate butler brought in a tray. He placed Caesar salads before them, poured an Italian white wine, and exited without a word.

"I was told you prefer salads for lunch."

"Actually, I prefer pizza, but this will do," Willow joked. She regretted it when she saw Pen's troubled expression. "I'm kidding. This is great. Really."

"You're sure?"

"Very. It looks absolutely delicious."

Pen smiled in relief and picked up her glass.

Throughout lunch they continued discussing art. Following a delicious dessert of fresh raspberries with a brandy cream sauce, Pen gave Willow a tour of the penthouse.

"Don't you ever get tired of living in a mausoleum?" Willow asked as they stood in the midst of the front room. Nothing was out of place. Nothing had a trace of dust on it. Nothing had any warmth. She looked at Pen, suddenly mortified. "I'm so sorry. That was uncalled for. You can live any way you choose."

"Have dinner with me," Pen said.

"Excuse me?"

"Have dinner with me."

"We just had lunch."

"Have dinner with me."

"You know, Pen, I really need to get back to work. Why don't you just send the paintings you want to sell down to the gallery?"

She walked to the penthouse elevator and found there were no buttons. "Please open the doors."

Pen folded her arms in front of her and smiled patiently. "Have dinner with me."

"Oh for Pete's sake!" This woman was absolutely exasperating!

"No, for my sake."

"Ha ha ha," Willow said humorlessly. "Quit smiling at me like that and please open the door." Still smiling, Pen reached down to the table and pushed a button. The butler appeared.

"Please show Ms. Dyer out, Sebastian." He bowed and used a remote control to open the doors. "I'll pick you up at eight," Pen stated and Willow's eyes grew wide. "I know, I know, you won't be one of my conquests. We can still have dinner."

Willow almost disputed this but realized Sharon was right. Pen St. Pierre never lost.

Later, at her apartment, Willow held up the black sheath dress that had just been delivered by special courier from St. Pierre Industries. "Oh my God," she murmured, feeling its luxurious silkiness as she held it against her. She picked up the card that had come with it.

Willow,

A token of my esteem. I would appreciate it if you wore this dress this evening.

Thank you,

Pen

The dress fit as if it had been made especially for her. It outlined her curves, its neckline low enough to give just a hint of cleavage. A slit up the side showed off her long legs to perfection. Despite its simple appearance, she knew the dress probably cost more than two months' salary. She looked at herself objectively in the mirror. The dress really did fit beautifully. Willow knew that she was an attractive woman with her full lips, ocean-blue eyes, long lashes, high cheekbones a model would die for, and a body that she didn't have to go to a gym to keep. Soberly she thought about the fact that she knew how to attract women; she just didn't know how to keep them.

Willow was surprised when, instead of Pen, she was picked up by Pen's driver. He informed her that Pen would meet her at the penthouse, where they would be having dinner. This annoyed Willow somewhat because it seemed Pen was trying to maintain the home field advantage.

Pen smiled in greeting when Willow entered, but the smile was quickly replaced with a raised eyebrow when Willow removed her coat and revealed a blue strapless sheath dress much like the one Pen had sent, but much less expensive. "You didn't like it?"

"I can't accept such an expensive gift. I don't know you well enough," Willow said, handing the box to Pen. "Thank you, though. It was stunning." Pen nodded and gave the box and Willow's coat to Sebastian. "So, you couldn't find a restaurant on such short notice?"

"No, I just thought we could have more privacy here. You don't min, do you?" Pen said, leading Willow to the formal dining room and holding out a chair for her.

"Not at all."

"I have an excellent chef. I think you will be pleased," Pen continued as she sat down.

"Well, lunch was excellent, so I'm sure I won't be disappointed." And disappointed she wasn't, as a veritable feast was put before them.

"What's the matter?" Pen asked at Willow's troubled expression.

"I don't believe I'm capable of eating quite this much."

"According to Sharon, you can put away a horse."

"She's just jealous I have a high metabolism."

"Don't worry. What you don't eat I'll send home with you in a doggy bag." They stared at each other for a moment, then Willow laughed, throwing her head back.

Throughout dinner Willow had to keep reminding herself that if she wanted to date a man, she would be straight. But the problem was, Pen wasn't like a man. She kept displaying the same sweet shyness Willow had glimpsed the night before, and the thought of her austere, mausoleum-like front room made Willow want to pull her into her arms and comfort her like a child.

But thoughts of the kiss they had shared the night before quickly reminded Willow that Pen was an attractive, full-grown woman. A cutthroat businesswoman, an assertive force who never lost, a classic type-A personality that went through women the way others went through hand soap. A woman—a butch—Willow had promised herself to be careful around.

But Pen's quick humor and undeniable charm, along with her devil-may-care smile, kept drawing Willow in, until they were slow dancing on the enclosed terrace to piped-in music.

"Is this part of your seduction?" Willow asked with a huskiness in her voice as Pen held her close.

"Is it working?" Pen asked with a devilish gleam in her eye and a grin on her face.

"I'm not going to sleep with you, Pen. This has been a wonderful evening, but I'm not going to become another one of your women."

Pen feigned shock. "You make it sound as if I have a harem."

"From what I understand you might as well. Is it true you have a long list of women at your beck and call?"

"You have been listening to too much gossip," she answered irritably as she pushed Willow away. "I am not what people like to make me out to be."

"Really?" Willow remarked doubtfully. She had heard of too many broken hearts for some of the stories not to be true. "Don't you get lonely up here in your mausoleum?" Willow felt herself blush when Pen gave her a hurt look. "I'm sorry. I didn't mean to ask that. I guess I'm just surprised you haven't found someone permanent to share your life with."

"I don't see a wedding ring on your finger," Pen pointed out sarcastically. Willow turned away and walked to the windows. It was snowing, giving an ethereal look to the city below.

Pen came up behind her and rested her hands lightly on her shoulders. "Forgive me. I have a nasty habit of going for the throat when I get defensive." Willow didn't respond but continued to silently gaze out of the window. "Willow, please," Pen implored as she gently turned Willow to face her, looking deep in her eyes and running a tender hand over her cheek.

Willow couldn't meet her gaze. Couldn't look into eyes she knew were now caring and understanding. With that one simple statement, Pen had touched on one of Willow's most sensitive fears—that she was destined to spend her life alone.

She had to get out of here.

"I should probably be going." Willow attempted to pull away, but Pen wouldn't let her go. Instead she pulled her into her arms, running her hand gently through Willow's hair. Willow laid her head on Pen's shoulder; the fine material of her suit felt so soft against Willow's cheek. It was as if all of Pen's power and strength were being given to her.

Willow looked into Pen's eyes.

Alarms went off in her head when their lips met, but she ignored them and pulled Pen closer, encircling Pen's neck with her arms. A warmth spread through her when she opened her mouth, allowing Pen to enter her with her tongue. She forgot all else as the heat coursed through her, as Pen pressed against her, pushing her against the window. The cold against her bare back reminded her of the snow falling outside, but she didn't care because it was warm inside. Warm inside the protection of Pen's strong arms.

After what seemed like forever, Pen raised her head and smiled down at Willow. "Stay with me tonight." Willow moved out of Pen's grasp to walk over to the bar. She picked up her glass of wine and finished it off. She was struggling to catch her breath and control the weakness in her knees. She knew the heat of their kiss was still flaming through her, making her want to throw caution to the wind. "It's getting late. I need to be going."

"No."

Willow looked at her with surprise. "What?"

"I said, no. I want you to stay with me tonight." Pen walked up to her. "I don't want you to leave."

She knew she should be angry, but she wasn't. "Pen, I can't stay." If she stayed now, she might never want to leave.

"Of course you can." Pen pulled her into her arms. Her arms were strong, but her hands were tender.

"No, I can't."

"You want to."

"No, I don't," Willow lied, trying halfheartedly to push her away. "Please summon your driver to take me home or I'll call for a cab." She was ready to cry from the confusion she felt. She wanted to stay but knew she had to go.

Still holding Willow in her arms, Pen looked down at her, then pushed a button beneath the bar. Sebastian instantly appeared.

"Have the car readied. Ms. Dyer will be leaving," she said, still not releasing Willow. Willow hoped she never would.

"Yes, Madam." He returned shortly thereafter with Willow's coat, which he helped her to put on. It was all so efficient, Willow wanted to scream.

"I had a wonderful evening, thank you." She smiled politely at Pen, then followed Sebastian through the suite, surprised that Pen remained in the terrace. Pen should've followed her. If she truly wanted her, she would have.

Willow rode alone in the elevator down to the underground garage, wondering what had happened upstairs. If Pen had asked her one more time to stay, she would have. Every glance and casual touch of Pen's had sent shivers up her spine and sent her heart rate rocketing. Even now, with the snow falling peacefully outside, she felt like she didn't need her coat to keep her warm. Pen's kiss, her touch, had been heat enough to ensure Willow didn't need a coat for the next three winters.

She sighed, leaning back against the elevator wall and watching the numbers as they quickly raced down to the sub-levels. Suddenly, the elevator stopped and began to ascend. Concerned, she began pushing numbers, but the elevator steadily rose back to the penthouse. When the elevator stopped and the doors opened she found Pen facing her, hands in pockets, staring at her.

"You can't leave. I control all of the elevators and all of the fire doors in the stairwells. I'll hold you prisoner."

The plea was so emphatic that Willow found herself moving into Pen's arms.

The color was rising in Pen's cheeks. "I want you in my bed tonight."

Their mouths met hungrily and Willow didn't even notice the elevator doors closing behind her.

Pen picked her up in her strong arms and carried her up a marble staircase to the magnificent bedroom at the very top, furthermost corner of the building. With one wall nothing but glass, Willow could see the entire city from here. It was almost frightening, giving the illusion of being completely open, as if you could fall with one false step. Pen must have felt her discomfort, for she moved to the center of the room and set her down gently at the foot of the only piece of furniture in the room, a platform bed.

"God, you are beautiful," Pen murmured as her eyes boldly caressed Willow's body. She pulled Willow's coat off her and stared before running her hands over Willow's curves. Willow tilted her head, exposing her throat to Pen's mouth. She felt and heard the zipper of her dress being slowly opened. Dressed only in bra, panties, garter belt, stockings, and high heels, she felt self-conscious at first as Pen stopped for a better view, but she smiled at Pen's sharp intake of breath.

Confident now, Willow reached behind and unclipped her bra, letting it drop it to the floor. She gasped as Pen's hands reached out to cup her breasts, her thumbs grazing over the hardening nipples. Willow grabbed Pen's jacket and pulled her closer, her hands quickly pushing the jacket off the broad shoulders. The material that had seemed so soft earlier now teased her nipples, but nonetheless, Willow began to work on the tie. Next came the shirt, and Willow smiled with pleasure as she revealed the sculpted body she knew was hidden beneath the expensive material. Pen was also braless and she allowed Willow's hands to slide over her arms, breasts, and then six-pack abs. Willow smiled mischievously as her hands rested on the belt. Quickly she undid the belt, then unzipped the zipper. Her hand slid easily into the now open fly, and she giggled in delight when she discovered that Pen was not wearing any underwear. Pen's breaths now came increasingly faster.

"What have we here?" she asked, sliding her hand further between Pen's legs. "Wow, are you wet."

She laughed, then squealed as Pen growled and pushed her onto her back on the bed. Her eyes held Willow's as she slowly removed Willow's silk panties, leaving her dressed only in the garter belt and stockings. She placed her hand between Willow's legs and lightly caressed her, smiling as she encountered Willow's wetness.

Willow gasped as Pen roughly pushed her legs apart. Pen's eyes held hers as the palm of her hand pressed against her, making gentle little circles. Every nerve was on fire and every touch threatened to send Willow over the edge.

"Please," Willow moaned, reaching out for Pen, but the woman withdrew and backed away. She removed the rest of her clothing and Willow, through her haze of need, marveled at the muscularly firm body. Pen grasped Willow's ankles and pulled her to the edge of bed, where she knelt between her legs and spread them wide. She opened Willow's lips and blew gently on the rising bud, making Willow go wild. She raised her hips as Pen's tongue licked her, sliding back and forth, lapping up the juices. Her fingers slid in one by one, and then Willow cried out as Pen's entire fist slid into her.

At this entirely new feeling, Willow felt a jolt of panic at first, but Pen was gentle with her, and soon all anxiety was swept away by the breathtaking sensations that were coursing through her body.

Tenderly, yet mercilessly, Pen pumped her hand within her as her mouth relentlessly sucked her. Willow's hips bucked, her hands grasping at the comforter beneath her as the orgasm built within her. She felt it start in her stomach, then spread down her legs. She held her breath as the pressure of Pen's fist increased within her, and then it hit as Willow's world climaxed into a world of shimmering colors. Pen allowed the convulsions to diminish, then crawled onto the bed and thrust her thigh between Willow's legs.

"Stay with me, darling," Pen murmured against Willow's lips as she began to move against her.

"I don't think I have anything left," Willow answered breathlessly.

"Oh yes you do, darling. You have plenty left." Pen continued to press her thigh against Willow's swollen flesh and then used her fingers. To Willow's surprise, she felt her body responding. Her hips rose to unbelievably meet the pace of Pen's fingers against her. She pulled Pen tight to her, raking her nails down the woman's back and she screamed into the night.

Afterward, Pen pulled the sheet over them, and then curled around Willow, who was still recovering from the most intense orgasm she had ever felt.

"Are you all right?" she asked, kissing Willow's ear. All Willow could muster was a sleepy mmmmmmmm. Pen chuckled, holding her close, then slowly slid her fingers back into her.

Before Willow knew what was happening, her seemingly exhausted body was responding to Pen's tender ministrations, beckoning for more attention, calling Pen to take her harder, faster, again and again and again, almost against her will. Pen was taking her further than she'd ever been before, controlling her and owning her as she'd never been taken. Pen only stopped when Willow was too exhausted and begging for sleep.

The sky was pale when Willow woke a few hours later. She opened her eyes to see Pen watching her, a tender smile on her face.

"Good morning," Pen said and then kissed her forehead. "How are you?"

"Strangely exhilarated," Willow answered as she rolled onto her side to look out the window. "What a view."

"You're telling me," Pen stated, lifting up the sheets. Willow laughed, turning back to face her. "I want to ask you something."

"What's that?"

"Well . . . I want to fuck you."

"Okay, but that's not a question," Willow said. "And isn't that what you did for practically the whole night?"

Pen grinned and ran her hand over Willow's naked breast, pushing the sheet away. "Not the way I want to fuck you now." She took Willow's hand and directed it under the sheet. Willow was surprised when she felt the dildo between Pen's legs.

"Oh my God." She pulled her hand away and looked at Pen doubtfully. "I don't know, Pen. I've never . . ."

"I promise to be gentle and if you don't like it, I'll stop."

Willow regarded her for a long moment, then finally acquiesced. "What do I do?"

"Just enjoy."

To Willow's relief, Pen just didn't mount her but instead began to awaken her body. She lay on top of her, kissing her long and slowly. She traced her lips and tongue down her throat, then tantalized each nipple until they rose to their full height. Willow felt the throbbing begin between her legs and the wetness flowed as if Pen had tapped a new wellspring within her.

Using her arms to brace herself, Pen entered Willow carefully. She didn't move at first, waiting for any signs of discomfort from Willow. She began to move her hips, sliding the dildo in and out. It didn't take much for Willow's body to respond and before long she was convulsing beneath Pen. Breathing heavily, Willow looked up at Pen, who was watching her, still keeping the dildo within her. Pen kissed her as once again her hips began to move. Willow didn't think it was possible, but her body responded and she began to match Pen's movements . . . or so it seemed. In fact, they seemed to be moving as one.

They stared into each other's eyes as the buildup began yet again, as Willow could feel her orgasm building. Pen kept a steady pace, bringing Willow slowly to the edge, only to stop when Willow was ready to go over. Pen was an expert, teasing Willow unceasingly. No matter how Willow squirmed, she knew Pen was in control.

Regardless of Willow's moans and cries, Pen would only begin again when she was ready to. Willow felt invaded, overcome, out of control, but then she'd look up into those green eyes and know she was in control, for Pen would stop at Willow's first word.

It was only when Willow begged, screamed for release, that Pen gave her what she so craved. Ruthlessly, Pen quickened her pace, pounding inside of Willow. Once again Willow's nails raked Pen's back as she climaxed with such force she felt she might black out.

After Willow recovered from the intense love making, they took a long shower together, where Pen once again made love to her.

"I am not going to be able to walk if you keep this up," Willow remarked as Pen tried to prevent her from getting dressed. "I need to get home to change for work."

"I'm sure you will be fine," Pen responded, sitting back on the bed, her robe invitingly open. She reached down and picked up Willow's panties. Willow held out her hand, but Pen grinned as she put them in her pocket.

Willow arched an eyebrow. "A trophy?"

"Souvenir."

"Well, make sure you do something with them before you shock Sebastian."

"There is nothing I could do that would shock Sebastian."

Willow gathered the rest of her things and they walked to the elevator. "Let me ask you something," she said as they stopped at the doors. "Is that how you get all of your women to stay? By holding them hostage?"

"No, I've never had anyone want to leave before." The doors opened and Pen enveloped her in her arms. "I'll have you picked up after work."

"How do you know I don't have plans?"

"You don't. I'll see you tonight." She gently pushed Willow into the elevator.

Thus began the whirlwind love affair of Pen and Willow, *whirl-wind* being the operative word. When they weren't making love, which wasn't often, Pen was squiring her about town to all of the chic clubs and restaurants. She took Willow skiing in St. Moritz, gambling in Monte Carlo, and beachcombing on the black sand beaches of Hawaii. Pen introduced her to the world of the elite, and Willow introduced Pen to flea markets and inline skating. They even spent a weekend at the St. Pierre family estate, where Willow was introduced to Pen's very charming grandfather, Patrick. She would later find out from Sharon that Pen had never taken anyone to meet her grandfather.

When they couldn't leave the city and Pen's attention was on her business, Willow was always showered with flowers and gifts. Every evening Pen's driver picked Willow up and took her back to the penthouse. Sometimes Pen would still be in meetings, leaving Willow to her own devices. Inevitably Willow would find Sebastian and keep him company with whatever chore he was undertaking. At first this seemed to disturb the older gentleman, but soon he became enchanted by Willow's kind gentleness, and she would find a cup of coffee waiting for her when she joined him.

When Pen would finally arrive from her office, she would gather Willow up and take her to the bedroom. They always made love first before sitting down to dinner, served by Sebastian, who didn't seem to be bothered by their dining in robes. After dinner, they would sometimes enjoy a long bath or Pen would just take her to bed.

Pen was insatiable and able to make love most of the night and still function on only a few hours' sleep. Willow, on the other hand, would be so exhausted she wouldn't make it to the gallery before noon. She endured Sharon, who seemed amused by the affair, ribbing her. But Sharon was also quick to remind her that, like all good things, this too would end. Willow would assure her boss and friend she was aware of this fact and that she was only having fun, but she wasn't so sure that her heart believed it. She wouldn't admit that Sharon's talk disturbed her. But from what she was hearing from others, Pen was treating her as she had not treated anyone else. Willow had been allowed into Pen's inner circle, a place no one had ever been before. That had to mean something.

"You really need to get rid of these sharp angles and corners," commented Willow one morning as they were having breakfast before going off to work.

"I like sharp angles and corners," Pen responded as she looked through *The Wall Street Journal.*

"You need to soften up," Willow continued. Pen put the paper down and looked around. They were in the breakfast nook, which was off the front room. "Don't you think you need some warmth in here?"

Smiling, Pen reached across the small table and covered Willow's hand. "You make me hot."

"Is that all I am to you?" Willow suddenly found herself moving into an area of their relationship she had been wondering about but too afraid to venture to question.

Pen removed her hand and sat back in her chair. "I don't understand."

"Am I just some sex toy to you?" Willow asked softly.

Pen stared at her for a moment. "I . . . no, of course not. What would make you ask such a question?" She opened the newspaper again.

Willow started to respond but saw the set line of Pen's mouth and knew she was withdrawing from the subject. "I guess I'll be going to work now." She got up from the table and gave Pen a kiss on the cheek before leaving the room.

Willow was waiting for the elevator when Pen suddenly wrapped her arms around her from behind.

"You are not a sex toy, Willow. You are very important to me," she whispered into her ear. "You will always be important to me."

Willow turned to smile up at her. "You always know what to do, don't you?"

Pen looked at her seriously before framing her face with her hands. She kissed her tenderly, then looked into her eyes. "No, I don't always know what to do. I'll miss you."

"I'll miss you too. See you tonight." The doors opened and Willow backed into the elevator, looking at Pen, who suddenly seemed troubled. Willow stopped the doors from closing. "Are you okay?"

Pen reached out to caress her cheek. "Go." She gently moved Willow's hands and the doors closed.

That afternoon, Willow was going over some paperwork, when Sharon appeared at her office door with a stricken look.

"Sharon? What's happened?"

Sharon handed her a jewelry case. "It's from Pen."

"Oh? What did she send this time?" She opened the case to reveal a diamond necklace. "My God, it's beautiful." She looked at Sharon. "What's the matter? She's sent me gifts before." Sharon quietly handed her an envelope. Willow pulled the slip from the envelope.

Willow,

I've truly enjoyed the time we've spent together. I want you to accept this token of my affection. I wish you nothing but the best for the future.

Pen

Sharon pulled Willow into her arms. "Oh baby, I'm sorry."

"How did you know?" Willow asked, sobbing.

Sharon stroked her hair. "You must have left some things at her place. She had those delivered as well."

Willow turned back to her desk and forced a smile. She sniffled a couple of times, wiping her eyes with a tissue. "We both knew it wasn't going to be forever."

"You're okay? Really?"

"Yeah, I'm just pissed that she couldn't tell me herself. I think she tried this morning. She told me she was going to miss me. I just thought she meant for today." Willow took a deep breath, then with determination picked up the necklace and reached for her purse, "She's not going to get away with it this time."

"Willow, you can't."

"Like hell I can't."

Willow knew Pen spent her early afternoons dictating letters in her office and was surprised when security let her into the building. Apparently they hadn't been notified yet about the breakup. They were used to seeing Willow taking the private elevator, so no one stopped her there either. When she reached Pen's floor, she walked briskly through the office and before the secretaries could stop her, burst into Pen's inner sanctum.

Pen stood before the window while she talked into her tape recorder. For a moment, Willow hesitated, but then Pen turned and saw her. She raised a hand to stop her secretary, who had come in behind Willow, and motioned for her to leave.

"Who the fuck do you think you are?!" Willow demanded, throwing the jewel case at her. Pen deftly caught it.

"You don't like it, I take it. Fine, I'll send for a replacement."

"What is it with you? Didn't you have the balls to tell me yourself that we were finished?"

Pen grinned, looking down at herself. "I don't have any balls at all. Something you can attest to, I believe."

"Don't try to be funny, Pen. This isn't funny." Willow's voice cracked, and despite her best intentions, she felt tears welling up in her eyes. "Damn you." She sat down in one of the leather visitor's chairs and put her hands over her face. Pen knelt beside her and handed her a handkerchief. Willow refused it at first but then accepted it begrudgingly.

"I thought you understood," Pen said quietly, as she put her hand on Willow's bowed head. "I thought you, of all people, would understand."

Willow looked at her. She sniffled, trying to take hold of her emotions but finding it a daunting task. "I'm afraid I've disappointed us both."

"Oh Willow, please," Pen murmured sorrowfully.

"Oh Willow, please what? Dammit Pen, do you think I want this to happen? Do you think I want to be like this? I have not one iota of pride left." Willow stood up and Pen followed suit. "Look, I'm sorry. I have no idea why I did this. I was just so angry at that gift."

"I'll get you something else."

"No, don't get me anything else. Don't you understand? I don't want some consolation prize from you. I don't need any more reminders." She took a deep breath to get her emotions under control, then gave Pen a sorrowful smile. "You are the bravest woman I have ever met. What you've done in the business world is just incredible. You've gone into a man's world and made it your own." She put her hand over Pen's heart. "Maybe one day you'll be brave enough to let someone in here." She moved toward the door but stopped before exiting. "You know, we would have been good together."

Later that evening, Pen stood at the front windows in her penthouse suite overlooking the city. The beauty of the city lights did nothing for her that night. Sebastian suddenly appeared beside her with a Scotch straight up. Silently she took the drink, then returned to her vigil. He moved away but Pen called out. "Sebastian?"

"Madam?"

"You liked her, didn't you?"

"Madam?"

"Don't be coy, Sebastian. You know what I mean."

"Yes, Madam, I did indeed like her." He waited. "And you, Madam? Did you like her?"

❧

The weather was cool, with the wind whipping around her as Willow walked along the sand near Sharon's beach house on the Cape. The heat of the summer had passed and faded, like the heat of her affair with Pen. Willow had thrown herself into her work, but her heart wasn't in it, and so Sharon had insisted she take some time off and spend it at the beach house where she could enjoy the solitude. Unfortunately, solitude left her too much time to think.

She had known what she was getting into when she had begun her affair with Pen. It seemed so long ago now. She had known it wasn't going to last a lifetime. She knew one day Pen would end it. Everyone had told her that from the beginning of the relationship. She knew Pen's reputation. What was bothering her was that during those few incredible months, she had seen what could have been. She knew Pen had come to love her, though she might never have said the words. She had seen Pen come as dangerously close to a commitment as she had ever come. Then, she pulled away. Pen just didn't have the courage to take that final step and take a chance on them, and Willow had no control over it. And though she loved Pen with all her being, it wasn't enough to keep her.

She brushed her tears impatiently away, then turned to walk back to the house. She stopped short when she saw a figure standing on the deck of the house. They stared at each other from across the sand, and then Willow began to slowly approach Pen as she came down the steps. They stopped a few feet from each other.

"How did you get Sharon to tell you?"

"I'm irresistible." Pen grinned disarmingly, then grew serious as Willow gave her a doubtful look. "Actually, I threatened to put a gallery right next to hers."

"Why are you here?"

Pen stared at her for a long moment. "If I let you in, what guarantees do I have?"

Willow felt her heart leap into her throat. "There are no guarantees," she said as Pen sighed impatiently, looking past her at the ocean. "Surely, you've made business decisions that were risky and you had no guarantees."

"Business is one thing. I can always recoup any losses on another endeavor. There is no emotion in business." She looked back at Willow. "This is different."

Willow stepped closer to her and put her hand on her cheek. "I love you, Pen. I've loved you since the first time I laid eyes on you. I will always love you. That is the only guarantee I can give you."

Pen suddenly pulled her into her arms and kissed her passionately, leaving them both breathless. Pen looked deeply into her eyes. Willow looked back at her questioningly and was surprised to see the hint of a tear, which was quickly blinked away.

"I was named Penelope Margaret St. Pierre."

requiem

Elizabeth Dunn

She fell out of love with me in the spring. The most unlikely time, don't you think? Just when New York is starting to thaw out from its icy winter, and a girl can wear open-toed shoes without her feet feeling numb by nine o'clock. Just when the pretentious cafés of the East Village claim their sidewalk space and serve *mojitos* to the Prada-bagged and Gucci-shoed set, my butch found another femme.

Cream and I had been together three years. Our flirtation began on Valencia Street and wound up that night in room number three of the Broadway Manor motel in Oakland. It was summer, oddly warm for the Bay Area, and when she held my hand while talking to the front desk clerk, it was sweaty.

"One bed, two girls, one night," she demanded with a certain authority that made me romance-novel swoon. The fellow barely glanced at us, and we paid our twenty dollars quickly. I stumbled over the cracked asphalt in my favorite pair of 1950s heels into our den of iniquity/paradise . . . a perfect punk rock Mae West boudoir, with cloudy mirrors on the ceiling, a brown velour chair wide enough for me to straddle her in, a shower whose grimy tiles I knew I would press my palms against while she fucked me from behind (which she did, the hot water and Tres Flores pomade from her hair dripping down my back and onto my ass). One night became a week, days spent stealing Cheez-Its from the 7-Eleven on the corner, counting out quarters to buy the biggest bottle possible of Seagram's gin from the late-night liquor store, and drunken visits to the nearby cemetery.

That spring, when she fell out of love with me, I looked at the Polaroids we had taken at the time. Here's me with a bloody "C" carved on my back, switchblade resting on the rumpled sheet around me. There's her, black T-shirt with the sleeves rolled and serious skull belt buckle, smoking a cigarette, leaning against a tombstone. Me again, naked, propped up on an off-white pillow, red lipstick smeared, hickeys galore, smiling. The look in our eyes is the same in all these photographs, the same words we said to each other and thought to our ourselves at this time: More. Take it, bitch. Don't stop. Get rid of my dress. I want you so bad. Suck my cock. More. I love you.

Three thousand miles and three years away from these images, I fondled them like holy relics that spring; it made sense to me that our early backdrop was something we rented—a cheap motel room—and not something permanent at all.

Cream and I were that cutesy phrase that appears in women's magazines to describe ideal partnerships: "not just lovers, but best friends, too." In the New York apartment we shared, the mundanities of living seemed a delight, our individual tasks natural and comfortable. I did the grocery shopping, she cooked the meals. I washed the dishes, she carried the heavy bag of laundry down the street and sat with it till it was done. While she was at work, I hand-washed her vintage gabardine shirts in the small bathroom sink, smiling over the cold water and cologne that rinsed over my hands, missing her. I straightened the house in the late afternoons while listening to NPR, my heart beating fast and my g-strings getting wet when I heard those loud boots clunk up the stairs of our apartment building. At the sound of her keys sliding into the lock, I would race around, deciding where best to arrange myself: Lounging on the red couch? Idly filing my nails next to the window? Leaning invitingly over the stove? I cared desperately that she would find me more desirable than when she'd left me that morning in our wide, warm bed.

But, dear reader, you know what happens as the months roll by when a couple, no matter how perfect, lives together, don't you? The ice cube trays are not always refilled, the dishes start piling up in the sink, it seems more logical to go out with friends than stay home and fuck from dusk to dawn while listening to Hank Williams. Instead of my thighs aching, her sly smile saying "you're too wet to go sleep" (those perfect fingers crawling into me once more), we began to watch bad late-night TV, read our respective books, or take turns using the Wahl. More and more I fell asleep holding my stuffed bunny, and she a pillow, not even realizing how I missed being held as I began to dream.

There were other girls, of course; we were both too big of sluts to cut out that part of our personalities. Some we shared, sarcastically, in our bed, and some we made out with alone, in stairways of dance clubs and at dirty D.I.Y. play parties. But none of them, not even the youngest and most luscious, were able to enter into our own private opera of a world.

Cream started "working late" that spring, first a night or two, then almost daily. At first an hour or two, then till 4 a.m., when the sharp, self-confident thud of her boots became mismatched from too much whiskey.

"Sugar, darlin', it's the new job. I have to be there longer, spend time with the boss, shoot the shit, you know . . ."

She'd be sloppy, throwing off her boots in the middle of the room, not asking about what writing I had done that day, or how the discussion in my Deconstructing Barbie class had gone. She developed a fondness for frying eggs at this time (a smell I vehemently despise), and would push at her crooked tie while she prepared them. Instead of the Marcel Proust-like nostalgic enjoyment I had formerly had from gathering up her things in the morning, I began to resent them. They stared at me while I ate breakfast alone, and I knew that the carefully picked outfit had nothing to do with me now. Something, someone, was giving her the novel thrill she'd had with me at the Broadway Manor.

There is sorrow in knowing you are no longer loved the way you used to be. Big sorrow, like the roll around on the floor in anguish kind, and small sorrow . . . the kind you might feel on a cold twilight evening walking alone past a lingerie shop and noticing the sales bras have slipped, unnoticed, off their hangers and into a dusty corner of the store's floor. But there is nothing but anger in being the femme that is no longer desired.

It doesn't matter how I finally found out: A letter, a phone message, some recorded evidence of passion I'd had no part in. My own reconstruction of the doings of Them, dear reader, is what I will always recall, memories of things I never saw. In the bars I imagined they had been to, I ran my hand along the cold bathroom sinks, thinking of how the stranger's fingers had clutched at them while she raised herself on my girl's cock. I spent hours considering what the stranger's pussy looked like: Thick and tangled? Bald and obvious?

Outside, New York was sliding into summer. Thick, hot days that smelled of dog piss on the pavement and long, breathy nights that my neighbors enjoyed loudly with their windows open. Cream and I moved out of the studio, box by box of our former life together carried down the steep stairs, and into new apartments with new roommates. I wept as I cleaned out the refrigerator for the last time, unpacked my dolls, bought a new bed. I prayed for cold weather, something that would bring the sharp clarity of crisp afternoons and perhaps a reawakening of my desire. Summer seemed the most tedious season; even Coney Island was pointless. I lay awake in my new strange bed every night, feeling very much alone, and stared at the shining lights of the big buildings downtown. Their sharp angles comforted me; it was reassuring to gaze down at a part of New York that had always been there, but never in my view.

The weeks went on, as they do. I attempted dates, papers, museum outings, pills—anything that would ease the separation and make my life more than wondering why she wasn't calling. I saw the stranger around town, and it neither pleased nor angered me that their affair had not worked out.

"I think the thrill of it was in you not knowing," she confided in me at a party one night.

I smiled bitterly, as they say in novels, and thought how distasteful it was that my role for a few months had been to serve as a foil to a relationship I knew nothing about.

I went on lots of walks. I started waking up early in the morning and forgot about myself while listening to children play in a neighboring rooftop playground. I began cooking again, and was satisfied with the results. I carried my own bag of laundry, and mustered up the courage to kill a cockroach.

One Tuesday morning I was slowly awakened by the incessant wailing of sirens down Houston Street. In my half-conscious state, I couldn't tell if they had been going for two minutes or ten, but since I had to set my hair for work later that day, I thought I might as well get up. The sirens didn't stop, of course—it was September 11, and those perpetually lit monoliths that had been my bedtime view were now unbelievably crumbling. My roommate and I hurried up to the roof, sat on the silver floor of it with our neighbors, and stared at the destruction. It is difficult to know the impact of an event on the world at large when it is happening a quarter mile away from your kitchen. I sat on the roof for more than an hour, transfixed by the horrible billowing smoke that was streaming low over the very bottom of the island. Because I knew no one who worked in the World Trade Center, the loss of life was not the first thing that came to my mind, believe it or not. (I somehow thought that, of course, everyone had gotten out of the destroyed buildings, magically.)

Returning to the apartment downstairs, I listened to the many calls I had missed—most of which were from Cream. The phone only worked to receive calls, not place them, so I adjusted the radio and expected her to call back with a certainty I had not felt for more than half a year.

"Baby, are you okay? I have to see you, I've been so worried. Can I come over?"

And she did, bringing cookies and bagels and cigarettes and coffee. And, like the Broadway Manor era, a few hours turned into days.

Dear reader, as awful as it sounds, those days of hell for so many were, in many ways, beautiful to me. I again heard those boots walking up the stairs for me, and when she came in and grabbed me and held me close, I knew it wouldn't be too long before we were in my new bed.

I didn't worry about positioning myself to look the most delectable, or that I wasn't wearing the sexiest underwear I own. I didn't think of the coiffure of the stranger's pussy or the Lower East Side bars in which they had furtively enjoyed themselves. I was amazed and delighted in the small changes that had occurred without my even noticing it; she was not the first thing I had thought of when disaster struck, but I had been for her.

When my roommate went to her ex-boyfriend's apartment down the street, Cream spread me out on the couch in the living room, placing a pillow beneath my head, carefully unbuttoning my blouse. The feel of her soft lips on the tops of my breasts was so wonderfully familiar and safe, but also incredibly new and different. She smoothed my hair over the pillow and gently closed my eyelids with her fingers. I wriggled eagerly out of my pants and let her begin sucking on my toes with their red nail polish, pushing apart my knees, moving her head to and fro to open my thighs wider. The first lick on my clit was cool and promising, like the air of the spring I had lost. Her pompadour pressed against me, and I was pleased to discover she remembered the exact moment to stick her fingers in. As I came, smearing myself across her nose and mouth and hand, I remembered the things I loved about my girl, things that had nothing to do with our recent crumbling.

That night we went to the nightclub where I worked, walking past young men in camouflage uniforms and cops with piles of "I ❤ New York" paper coffee cups at their feet. She wore a dark blue suit with a satin 1940s tie, and I put on a black ball gown from the early 1950s. We had both decided that if we were going to die at any moment, we wanted it to be together, and in gorgeous threads.

The streets below 14th Street were deserted. In the evenings to come, we did the same, walking through empty avenues past screaming sirens and under huge American flags. Cream applauded each ambulance that rushed by, teared up at the missing-person flyers taped to any surface, paused solemnly at the discarded dust masks that littered Second Avenue. I had forgotten this part of her, her caring and compassion.

Though I had felt as though I was living outside of time in the warm months, now all of New York was, as well. Each of us was in a strange and horrible Alice in Wonderland world, and I felt again that I finally belonged in this eastern brick city.

At the bars, which had run out of much of their booze and more of their customers, Cream pulled me onto the rough wool of her lap. Through the layers of my dress I felt her thick cock and strong arms that held my hips firmly down upon it. In the early morning we went back to my apartment, and I finally got my anger out by demanding to be fucked hard, harder, while the crematorium smell wafted in through the cracks in the window. We kissed and she pulled my hair as I heard the reports on the radio of the count of people missing, presumed dead. Down the block, candles in shrines for valiant firefighters and police officers flickered in the new cold wind. There was no mail, no newspapers, no milk across the street at the deli, but I didn't care.

The way my baby held me made me feel lucky to be alive.

About the Authors

L. Elise Bland currently resides in the great Lonestar State of Texas, where she writes and plays in taboo territories. As a southern Femme Domme, she relishes old-fashioned butches who are into newfangled fun. She has published in *Scarlet Letters, Faster Pussycats* (Alyson), *Shameless: An Intimate Erotica* (Seal), and *Up All Night: Real-Life Lesbian Sex Adventures* (Alyson, forthcoming). The story in this publication, "Leather and Laces," was inspired by Wen, a chivalrous butch submissive with a fetish for leather boots. In October 2003, Wen died tragically in a car crash. May her memory and fantasies live on in this anthology.

M. Christian's work has appeared in such celebrated anthologies as *Best American Erotica, Best Gay Erotica, Best Lesbian Erotica, Best Transgendered Erotica, Best Fetish Erotica, Best Bondage Erotica*, and over 150 other books and magazines. He's the editor of over fourteen anthologies, including *Guilty Pleasures, Best S/M Erotica*, and

The Burning Pen. He's also the author of three collections: *Dirty Words* (gay erotica), *Speaking Parts* (lesbian erotica), and *The Bachelor Machine* (science fiction erotica). For more info, check out his website at www.mchristian.com.

Jen Collins is a butch/genderqueer freelance writer whose work can be found in *Set In Stone: Butch on Butch Erotica, Young Wives' Tales: New Adventures in Love and Partnership, Best Bi Women's Erotica, Tough Girls, Best Fetish Erotica,* and *Bare Your Soul: The Thinking Girl's Guide to Enlightenment.* She recently relocated to San Francisco with her partner, Anna, and dog, Tor, and can usually be found writing smut at any of a hundred cafes in the city.

Elizabeth Dunn currently lives in California.

Amie M. Evans is a confirmed femme-bottom, postmodern slut who lives life like a spontaneous, choreographed piece of performance art. She is the founder and a member of The Princesses of Porn with The Dukes of Dykedom, a lesbian burlesque troupe that problematizes gender and explores sexuality with lesbian camp and traditional burlesque performance elements. Her erotic stories have appeared in *Best Lesbian Erotica 2002* (Cleis, 2001), *Best S/M Erotica* (Black Books, 2002), *Venus in the Mirror* (Words Like Kudaz, 2002), *Harrington Lesbian Fiction Quarterly, Set in Stone* (Alyson, 2001), *Lip Service* (Alyson, 1999), *On Our Backs, Scarlet Letters, Bad Attitude, Three Rivers Literary Review,* and *Fifth Column.*

"Pen and Willow" is **Nathalie Graham's** first foray into the literary world. She currently resides in Colorado.

Peggy J. Herring lives in south Texas on seven acres of mesquite. She has a cockatiel, two wooden cats, seven hermit crabs and enjoys camping and fishing. Peggy is the author of six books from Naiad Press: *Once More with Feeling, Love's Harvest, Hot Check, A Moment's Indiscretion, Those Who Wait,* and *To Have and To Hold.* She is also the author of four lesbian romance novels published by Bella Books: *Calm Before the Storm, The Comfort of Strangers, Beyond All Reason* and *Distant Thunder*. She is currently working on her next romance, *White Lace and Promises*, to be published by Bella Books in 2004. In addition, Peggy has contributed short stories to several Naiad anthologies, *The First Time Ever, Dancing in the Dark, The Touch of Your Hand, The Very Thought of You*, and *Lady Be Good*.

Nairne Holtz is a lesbian writer living in Montreal. Since 2001, her short fiction has been published in several Canadian and American literary journals and anthologies. She has also created an annotated bibliography of Canadian lesbian fiction, available on the web at http://www.uwo.ca/pridelib/manifesto.html.

Barbara Johnson came out in the 1970s, an era when butch and femme were considered dirty words. She came out again in the late 1980s as a true femme, and makes no bones about her preference for butch women, especially ones who make her laugh. Naiad Press published her four novels, *Stonehurst, The Beach Affair, Bad Moon Rising*, and *Strangers in the Night*, as well as several of her short stories in the anthologies *Lady Be Good, The Touch of Your Hand, The Very Thought of You, The Mysterious Naiad, Dancing in the Dark*, and *The First Time Ever*. Barbara's adaptation of Cinderella will appear in Bella Books' *Once Upon a Dyke: New Exploits of Fairy-Tale Lesbians*.

Karin Kallmaker is best known for more than a dozen lesbian romance novels, from *In Every Port* to *Maybe Next Time*. In addition, she has a half-dozen science fiction, fantasy, and supernatural lesbian novels under the pen name Laura Adams, including the critically acclaimed Tunnel of Light trilogy. Karin and her partner will celebrate their twenty-seventh anniversary in 2004, and are Mom and Moogie to two children.

In addition to novels, she has written numerous short stories for anthologies, and a collection of short stories inspired by her romance novels, *Frosting on the Cake*. Her essay "When I Grow Up I Want to Be a Lesbian" appears in *Multicultural America: A Resource Book for Teachers of Humanities and American Studies*.

Lesléa Newman has published forty books for adults and children. She is the author of *The Femme Mystique*, *The Little Butch Book*, *Girls Will Be Girls*, *She Loves Me, She Loves Me Not* and *The Best Short Stories of Lesléa Newman*. She is the editor of *Pillow Talk: Stories of Lesbians Between the Sheets* (Volumes I and II), *Bedroom Eyes: Stories of Lesbians in the Boudoir*, and *My Lover Is a Woman: Contemporary Lesbian Love Poems*. Visit www.lesleanewman.com to learn more about her work.

Jesi O'Connell has published short nonfiction in *Awakening the Virgin: True Tales of Seduction* and *My Lover, My Friend*. She lives and plays in the red rock country of southern Utah, where she has ample time to hike, explore, dream, and write stories about adventurous sexy women. She shares space with five cats, two dogs, and one horse, who all keep her busy when she is not plotting the delicious moves of the characters in her novel.

Joy Parks is proud of "coming out femme" at the tender age of sixteen. Her articles, book reviews, and poetry have appeared in many lesbian publications, and her monthly book review column ran in the now defunct *The Body Politic* for six years. Joy now writes for *Girlfriends*, *The Lambda Book Report*, *Velvet Park*, and *The San Francisco Chronicle* and has revived her book review column under the new name "Sacred Ground."

Jean Roberta is a kind of nonstandard femme Crone who shovels snow, teaches English at a Canadian prairie university, and likes to dance. She embarrasses her friends and relatives with her erotic writing and opinionated editorials. Her lesbian novel, *Prairie Gothic*, is in the catalogue of Amatory Ink (www.amatory-ink.co.uk).

Carol Rosenfeld is a New York City–based writer, poet, event organizer, rogue promoter, incurable romantic, and counsellor-at-law. Her work also appears in *Best Lesbian Erotica 1999* (Cleis), Lambda Literary Award winner *Best Lesbian Erotica 2003* (Cleis), *Shadows of the Night: Queer Tales of the Uncanny and Unusual* (Haworth), and *Poetry Nation: The North American Anthology of Fusion*

Poetry (Vehicule). Carol is currently working on a novel, *Fool's Mushroom*. Please visit her website at www.carolrosenfeld.com.

Jean Stewart: I was a crazy little tomboy. Until I was eight, I wanted to grow up to be Willie Mays and hit a homer in the World Series. Then, my older brother and his buddies informed me that I couldn't "be" Willie Mays and that girls couldn't play in the majors. This was life's first cruel blow. It didn't keep me from continuing to beat up boys who tried to exclude me from the neighborhood sandlot games. At age eleven, my Mom realized I was a little too sought after for tackle football games (I was the only girl the guys allowed to play) and so she told me I couldn't go hairing off with my brothers anymore. I thought my life was over. No amount of begging changed my fate. End result, I had a lot of time on my hands and I was bored. I started hanging out at the library, getting tips on good books from the bluestocking revolutionaries masquerading as librarians. By age twelve, I wanted to be Emily Brontë. This was an ambition, I made sure, no stupid rules could keep me from attaining. Whatever you do, do it with passion.

krysia lycette villón is a mixed-race Latina stonefemme lesbian poet and writer born to a white American woman and Peruvian man. The eldest of five children, she was born and raised in the Boston area. She has a self-published chapbook entitled *it just kinda happened*, and other writings of varying genres can be found in publications such as *Fireweed: A Feminist Quarterly of Writing, Politics, Art & Culture*, and *ISSUES!*, a lesbian of color magazine. She received her B.A. from Mount Holyoke College, had a brief stint living in and loving the Bay Area of California, and currently resides in western Massachusetts with her very own handsome butch FTM partner, her two precious princess kitties, and her two spoiled-rotten pooches.

Julia Watts's novel *Finding H.F.* won the 2002 Lambda Literary Award for best young adult novel. She identifies as femme even though she prefers comfortable, low-heeled shoes.

D. L. White (aka Dee) realizes that twenty-five is that delightful middle ground where everything finally starts to congeal and gain clarity in her formerly naïve mind. She's still in awe of how age can positively transform character. Dee is a reader, a writer, a thinker— a freaking idea waiting to pop up. She thirsts to know and produce more, and at the end of her day she enjoys immersing herself in a cocktail of creativity and acid jazz. She burns music and time in her free moments and freely admits her addiction to watching people in those rare, unguarded situations when the moment is still and the world is somewhere near perfect. Tortured and artistic, broken and witty . . . she furiously pens the lines that will one day convert into novel-length reality.

Sabrina Wilcox is a professional writer from central California. In addition to being a full-time mother, she is a women's rights activist and vigorous community volunteer. She is working toward publication of her first novel and a nonfiction series. The self-proclaimed femme can also be found painting her nails, meticulously applying eyeliner, shooting pool, or camping in the mountains.

MJ Williamz: Portland, Oregon, is the city my partner, son, and I call home. We are relatively new to the area, having left Chico, California, less than three years ago. This is my first experience with city life and I'm finding the sights and sounds to be just what an imagination like mine needs to get the creative juices flowing. But flowing they are and I'm finally pursuing my dream—writing. Life in the Great Northwest is good.

Laura DeHart Young is a native Pennsylvanian. She has written six romance novels: *There Will Be No Goodbyes, Family Secrets, Love on the Line, Private Passions, Intimate Stranger* and *Forever and the Night.* Her seventh book, *Love Speaks Her Name*, will be published by Bella Books in 2004. When not writing for publication, Laura works as Director of Human Resources for an information technology company. Her career took her to beautiful Atlanta, Georgia, where she now lives with her beloved pug, Dudley.

About the Editor

Therese Szymanski believes in erotic freedom, and maximizing the erotic content of life. An award-winning playwright, she is the author of the Brett Higgins Mysteries/Motor City Thrillers. *When the Dancing Stops, When the Dead Speak, When Some Body Disappears* and *When Evil Changes Face*, a 2000 Lambda Literary Award Finalist, are available from Bella Books, as well as the upcoming *When the Corpse Lies* (due out in 2004). Also due out in 2004 from Bella Books' Bella After Dark Imprint is *Once Upon a Dyke: New Exploits of Fairy-Tale Lesbians*, which contains novellas by Szymanski, Karin Kallmaker, Barbara Johnson and Julia Watts.

Szymanski's short stories can be found in the Naiad anthologies *The Touch of Your Hand* and *The Very Thought of You*, as well as in the Alyson anthology *Up All Night* and Haworth Press's *Shadows of the Night: Queer Tales of the Uncanny and Unusual*. (She also has stories in Alyson Press's *Roughed Up* and *Sex Buddies*, but those only came about as a dare.)

Oh, and yeah, she is a butch.

Publications from
BELLA BOOKS, INC.
The best in contemporary lesbian fiction

P.O. Box 10543, Tallahassee, FL 32302
Phone: 800-729-4992
www.bellabooks.com

BACK TO BASICS: A BUTCH/FEMME ANTHOLOGY
edited by Therese Szymanski—from Bella After Dark. 314 pp.
ISBN 1-931513-35-X $12.95

SURVIVAL OF LOVE by Frankie J. Jones. 236 pp. What will Jody do
when she falls in love with her best friend's daughter?
ISBN 1-931513-55-4 $12.95

DEATH BY DEATH by Claire McNab. 167 pp. 5th Denise
Cleever Thriller.   ISBN 1-931513-34-1 $12.95

CAUGHT IN THE NET by Jessica Thomas. 188 pp. A wickedly
observant story of mystery, danger, and love in Provincetown.
ISBN 1-931513-54-6 $12.95

DREAMS FOUND by Lyn Denison. 201 pp. Australian Riley embarks
on a journey to meet her birth mother . . . and gains not just a family but
the love of her life.   ISBN 1-931513-58-9 $12.95

A MOMENT'S INDISCRETION by Peggy J. Herring. 154 pp.
Jackie is torn between her better judgment and the overwhelming
attraction she feels for Valerie.   ISBN 1-931513-59-7 $12.95

IN EVERY PORT by Karin Kallmaker. 224 pp. Jessica's sexy,
adventuresome travels.   ISBN 1-931513-36-8 $12.95

TOUCHWOOD by Karin Kallmaker. 240 pp. Loving
May/December romance.   ISBN 1-931513-37-6 $12.95

WATERMARK by Karin Kallmaker. 248 pp. One burning
question . . . how to lead her back to love? ISBN 1-931513-38-4 $12.95

EMBRACE IN MOTION by Karin Kallmaker. 240 pp. A
whirlwind love affair.   ISBN 1-931513-39-2 $12.95

ONE DEGREE OF SEPARATION by Karin Kallmaker. 232 pp. Can an Iowa City librarian find love and passion when a California girl surfs into the close-knit dyke capital of the Midwest?
ISBN 1-931513-30-9 $12.95

CRY HAVOC A Detective Franco Mystery by Baxter Clare. 240 pp. A dead hustler with a headless rooster in his lap sends Lt. L.A. Franco headfirst against Mother Love.   ISBN 1-931513931-7 $12.95

DISTANT THUNDER by Peggy J. Herring. 294 pp. Bankrobbing drifter Cordy awakens strange new feelings in Leo in this romantic tale set in the Old West.   ISBN 1-931513-28-7 $12.95

COP OUT by Claire McNab. 216 pp. 4th Detective Inspector Carol Ashton Mystery.   ISBN 1-931513-29-5 $12.95

BLOOD LINK by Claire McNab. 159 pp. 15th Detective Inspector Carol Ashton Mystery. Is Carol unwittingly playing into a deadly plan?   ISBN 1-931513-27-9 $12.95

TALK OF THE TOWN by Saxon Bennett. 239 pp. With enough beer, barbecue, and B.S., anything is possible!   ISBN 1-931513-18-X $12.95

MAYBE NEXT TIME by Karin Kallmaker. 256 pp. Sabrina Starling has it all: fame, money, women—and pain. Nothing hurts like the one that got away.   ISBN 1-931513-26-0 $12.95

WHEN GOOD GIRLS GO BAD: A Motor City Thriller by Therese Szymanski. 230 pp. Brett, Randi, and Allie join forces to stop a serial killer.   ISBN 1-931513-11-2   12.95

A DAY TOO LONG: A Helen Black Mystery by Pat Welch. 328 pp. This time Helen's fate is in her own hands.
ISBN 1-931513-22-8 $12.95

THE RED LINE OF YARMALD by Diana Rivers. 256 pp. The Hadra's only hope lies in a magical red line . . . climactic sequel to *Clouds of War*.   ISBN 1-931513-23-6 $12.95

OUTSIDE THE FLOCK by Jackie Calhoun. 224 pp. Jo embraces her new love and life.   ISBN 1-931513-13-9 $12.95

LEGACY OF LOVE by Marianne K. Martin. 224 pp. Read the whole Sage Bristo story.   ISBN 1-931513-15-5 $12.95

STREET RULES: A Detective Franco Mystery by Baxter Clare. 304 pp. Gritty, fast-paced mystery with compelling Detective L.A. Franco   ISBN 1-931513-14-7 $12.95

RECOGNITION FACTOR: 4th Denise Cleever Thriller by Claire McNab. 176 pp. Denise Cleever tracks a notorious terrorist to America. ISBN 1-931513-24-4 $12.95

NORA AND LIZ by Nancy Garden. 296 pp. Lesbian romance by the author of *Annie on My Mind*. ISBN 1931513-20-1 $12.95

MIDAS TOUCH by Frankie J. Jones. 208 pp. Sandra had everything but love. ISBN 1-931513-21-X $12.95

BEYOND ALL REASON by Peggy J. Herring. 240 pp. A romance hotter than Texas. ISBN 1-9513-25-2 $12.95

ACCIDENTAL MURDER: 14th Detective Inspector Carol Ashton Mystery by Claire McNab. 208 pp. Carol Ashton tracks an elusive killer. ISBN 1-931513-16-3 $12.95

SEEDS OF FIRE: Tunnel of Light Trilogy, Book 2 by Karin Kallmaker writing as Laura Adams. 274 pp. Intriguing sequel to *Sleight of Hand*. ISBN 1-931513-19-8 $12.95

DRIFTING AT THE BOTTOM OF THE WORLD by Auden Bailey. 288 pp. Beautifully written first novel set in Antarctica. ISBN 1-931513-17-1 $12.95

CLOUDS OF WAR by Diana Rivers. 288 pp. Women unite to defend Zelindar! ISBN 1-931513-12-0 $12.95

DEATHS OF JOCASTA: 2nd Micky Knight Mystery by J.M. Redmann. 408 pp. Sexy and intriguing Lambda Literary Award-nominated mystery. ISBN 1-931513-10-4 $12.95

LOVE IN THE BALANCE by Marianne K. Martin. 256 pp. The classic lesbian love story, back in print! ISBN 1-931513-08-2 $12.95

THE COMFORT OF STRANGERS by Peggy J. Herring. 272 pp. Lela's work was her passion . . . until now. ISBN 1-931513-09-0 $12.95

CHICKEN by Paula Martinac. 208 pp. Lynn finds that the only thing harder than being in a lesbian relationship is ending one. ISBN 1-931513-07-4 $11.95

TAMARACK CREEK by Jackie Calhoun. 208 pp. An intriguing story of love and danger. ISBN 1-931513-06-6 $11.95

DEATH BY THE RIVERSIDE: 1st Micky Knight Mystery by J.M. Redmann. 320 pp. Finally back in print, the book that launched the Lambda Literary Award–winning Micky Knight mystery series. ISBN 1-931513-05-8 $11.95

EIGHTH DAY: A Cassidy James Mystery by Kate Calloway. 272 pp. In the eighth installment of the Cassidy James mystery series, Cassidy goes undercover at a camp for troubled teens.   ISBN 1-931513-04-X $11.95

MIRRORS by Marianne K. Martin. 208 pp. Jean Carson and Shayna Bradley fight for a future together.   ISBN 1-931513-02-3 $11.95

THE ULTIMATE EXIT STRATEGY: A Virginia Kelly Mystery by Nikki Baker. 240 pp. The long-awaited return of the wickedly observant Virginia Kelly.   ISBN 1-931513-03-1 $11.95

FOREVER AND THE NIGHT by Laura DeHart Young. 224 pp. Desire and passion ignite the frozen Arctic in this exciting sequel to the classic romantic adventure *Love on the Line*.
                                            ISBN 0-931513-00-7 $11.95

WINGED ISIS by Jean Stewart. 240 pp. The long-awaited sequel to *Warriors of Isis* and the fourth in the exciting Isis series.   ISBN 1-931513-01-5 $11.95

ROOM FOR LOVE by Frankie J. Jones. 192 pp. Jo and Beth must overcome the past in order to have a future together.
                                            ISBN 0-9677753-9-6 $11.95

THE QUESTION OF SABOTAGE by Bonnie J. Morris. 144 pp. A charming, sexy tale of romance, intrigue, and coming of age.   ISBN 0-9677753-8-8 $11.95

SLEIGHT OF HAND by Karin Kallmaker writing as Laura Adams. 256 pp. A journey of passion, heartbreak, and triumph that reunites two women for a final chance at their destiny.   ISBN 0-9677753-7-X $11.95

MOVING TARGETS: A Helen Black Mystery by Pat Welch. 240 pp. Helen must decide if getting to the bottom of a mystery is worth hitting bottom.   ISBN 0-9677753-6-1 $11.95

CALM BEFORE THE STORM by Peggy J. Herring. 208 pp. Colonel Robicheaux retires from the military and comes out of the closet.   ISBN 0-9677753-1-0 $11.95

OFF SEASON by Jackie Calhoun. 208 pp. Pam threatens Jenny and Rita's fledgling relationship.   ISBN 0-9677753-0-2 $11.95

WHEN EVIL CHANGES FACE: A Motor City Thriller by Therese Szymanski. 240 pp. Brett Higgins is back in another heart-pounding thriller.   ISBN 0-9677753-3-7 $11.95

BOLD COAST LOVE by Diana Tremain Braund. 208 pp.
Jackie Claymont fights for her reputation and the right to love
the woman she chooses.   ISBN 0-9677753-2-9 $11.95

THE WILD ONE by Lyn Denison. 176 pp. Rachel never
expected that Quinn's wild yearnings would change her life
forever.   ISBN 0-9677753-4-5 $11.95

SWEET FIRE by Saxon Bennett. 224 pp. Welcome to
Heroy—the town with the more lesbians per capita than any
other place on the planet!   ISBN 0-9677753-5-3 $11.95